Matilde Serao, Henry Harland, Paul Sylvester

Fantasy

A Novel

Matilde Serao, Henry Harland, Paul Sylvester

Fantasy
A Novel

ISBN/EAN: 9783337349264

Printed in Europe, USA, Canada, Australia, Japan

Cover: Foto ©Andreas Hilbeck / pixelio.de

More available books at **www.hansebooks.com**

BY

MATILDE ˏSERAO

TRANSLATED FROM THE ITALIAN

BY

HENRY HARLAND & PAUL SYLVESTER

Fourth  Edition

LONDON
WILLIAM HEINEMANN
1891

INTRODUCTION.

—•◦•—

THE most prominent imaginative writer of the latest generation in Italy is a woman. What little is known of the private life of Matilde Serao adds, as forcibly as what may be divined from the tenour and material of her books, to the impression that every student of literary history must have formed of the difficulties which hem in the intellectual development of an ambitious girl. Without unusual neglect, unusual misfortune, it seems impossible for a woman to arrive at that experience which is essential to the production of work which shall be able to compete with the work of the best men. It is known that the elements of hardship and enforced adventure have not been absent from the career of the distinguished Italian novelist. Madame Serao has learned in the fierce school of privation what she teaches to us with so much beauty and passion in her stories.

Matilde Serao was born on the 17th of March 1856, in the little town of Patras, on the western coast of Greece. Her father was a Neapolitan political exile, her mother a Greek princess, the last survivor of an ancient noble family. I know not under what circumstances she came to the Italian home of her father, but it was probably in 1861 or soon afterwards that the unification of Italy permitted his return. At an early age, however, she seems to have been left without resources. She received a rough education at the Scuola Normale in Naples, and she obtained a small clerkship in the telegraph office at Rome. Literature, however, was the profession she designed to excel in, and she showed herself a realist at once. Her earliest story, if I do not mistake, was that minute picture of the vicissitudes of a post-office which is named _Telegraphi dello Stato_ ("State Telegraphs"). She worked with extreme energy, she taught herself shorthand, and she presently quitted the post-office to become a reporter and a journalist. To give herself full scope in this new employment, she, as I have been assured, cut short her curly crop of hair, and adopted on occasion male costume. She soon gained a great proficiency in reporting, and advanced to the writing of short sketches and stories for the newspapers. The power and originality of these attempts were acknowledged, and the name of Matilde Serao gradually became one of those which irresistibly attracted public attention. The writer of these lines may be permitted to record the impression which more than ten years ago was made upon him by reading a Neapolitan sketch, signed by that then wholly obscure name, in a chance number of the Roman _Fanfulla_.

The short stories were first collected in a little volume in

1879. In 1880 Matilde Serao became suddenly famous by the publication of the charming story *Fantasia* ("Fantasy"), which is now first presented to an English public. It was followed by a much weaker study of Neapolitan life, *Cuore Infermo* (" A Heart Diseased "). In 1881 she published " The Life and Adventures of Riccardo Joanna," to which she added a continuation in 1885. It is not possible to enumerate all Madame Serao's successive publications, but the powerful romance *La Conquista di Roma* (" The Conquest of Rome "), 1882, must not be omitted. This is a very careful and highly finished study of bureaucratic ambition, admirably characterised. Since then she has written in rapid succession several volumes of collected short stories, dealing with the oddities of Neapolitan life, and a curious novel, "The Virtue of Cecchina," 1884. Her latest romances, most of them short, have been *Terno Secco* (" A Dry Third "), a very charming episode of Italian life, illustrating the frenzied interest taken in the public lotteries, 1887; *Addio Amore* (" Good-bye, Love "), 1887; *La Granda Fiamma*, 1889; and *Sogno di una notte d' estate* (" A Summer Night's Dream "), 1890.

The naturalism of Matilde Serao deserves to be distinguished from that of the French contemporaries with whom she is commonly classed. She has a finer passion, more of the true ardour of the South, than Zola or Maupassant, but her temperament is distinctly related to that of Daudet. She is an idealist working in the school of realism; she climbs, on scaffolding of minute prosaic observation, to heights which are emotional and often lyrical. But her most obvious merit is the acuteness with which she has learned to collect and arrange in artistic form the elements of the town life of Southern Italy. She still retains in her nature something of the newspaper reporter's quicksilver, but it is sublimated by the genius of a poet.

EDMUND GOSSE.

FANTASY.

PART I.

I.

"The discipline for to-morrow is this . . . ." said the preacher, reading from a small card. "You will sacrifice to the Virgin Mary all the sentiments of rancour that you cherish in your hearts, and you will kiss the schoolfellow, the teacher, or the servant whom you think you hate."

In the twilight of the chapel there was a slight stir among the grown-up girls and teachers; the little ones remained quiet; some of them were asleep, others yawned behind tiny hands, and their small round faces twitched with weariness. The sermon had lasted an hour; and the poor children had not understood a word of it. They were longing for supper and bed. The preacher had now descended from the pulpit, and Cherubina Friscia, the teacher who acted as sacristan, was lighting the candles with a taper. By degrees the chapel became flooded with light. The cheeks of the dazed, sleepy little girls flushed pink under it; their elders stood immovable, with blinking startled eyes, and weary indifferent faces. Some prayed, with bowed heads, while the candle-light played with the thick plaits of their hair, coiled close to the neck, and with certain blonde curls that no comb could restrain. Then, when the whole chapel was lighted for the recital of the Rosary, the group of girl scholars in white muslin frocks, with black aprons

A

and the various coloured ribbons by which the classes were distinguished, assumed a gay aspect, despite the general weariness. A deep sigh escaped Lucia Altimare.

"What ails thee?" queried Caterina Spaccapietra, under her breath.

"I suffer, I suffer," murmured the other dreamily. "This preacher saddens me. He does not understand, he does not feel, Our Lady." And the black pupils of her eyes, set in bluish white, dilated as in a vision. Caterina did not reply. The Directress intoned the Rosary in a solemn voice, with a strong Tuscan accent. She read the Mystery alone. Then all the voices in chorus, shrill and low, accompanied her in the *Gloria Patri*, and in the *Pater*.

She repeated the *Ave Maria* as far as the *Frutto del tuo ventre;* the teachers and pupils taking up the words in unison. The chapel filled with music, the elder pupils singing with a fulness of voice that sounded like the outpouring of their souls : but the little ones made a game of it. While the Directress, standing alone, repeated the verses, they counted the time, so that they might all break in at the end with a burst, and nudging each other, tittered under their breath. Some of them would lean over the backs of the chairs, assuming a devout collectedness, but in reality pulling out the hair of the playfellows in front of them. Some played with their rosaries under their pinafores, with an audible click of the beads. The vigilant eye of the Directress watched over the apparently exemplary elder girls; she saw that Carolina Pentasuglia wore a carnation at the button-hole of her bodice, though no carnations grew in the College gardens; that a little square of paper was perceptible in the bosom of Ginevra Avigliana, beneath the muslin of her gown; that Artemisia Minichini, with the short hair and firm chin, had as usual crossed one leg over the other, in contempt of religion; she saw and noted it all. Lucia Altimare sat leaning forward, with wide open eyes fixed upon a candle, her mouth drawn slightly on one side; from time to time a nervous shock thrilled her.

Close to her, Caterina Spaccapietra said her prayers in all tranquillity, her eyes void of sight, as was her face of motion and expression. The Directress said the words of the *Ave Maria* without thinking of their meaning, absent, preoccupied, getting through her prayers as rapidly as possible.

The restlessness of the little ones increased. They twisted about, and lightly raised themselves on their chairs, whispering to each other, and fidgeting with their rosaries. Virginia Friozzi had a live cricket in her pocket, with a fine silken thread tied round its claw; at first she had covered it with her hand to prevent its moving, then she had allowed it to peep out of the opening of her pocket, then she had taken it out and hidden it under her apron; at last she could not resist showing it to the neighbours on her right and on her left. The news spread, the children became agitated, restraining their laughter with difficulty, and no longer giving the responses in time. Suddenly the cricket dragged at the thread, and hopped off, limping, into the midst of the passage which divided the two rows of chairs. There was a burst of laughter.

" Friozzi will not appear in the parlour to-morrow," said the Directress severely.

The child turned pale at the harshness of a punishment which would prevent her from seeing her mother.

Cherubina Friscia, the sacristan-teacher, of cadaverous complexion, and worn anæmic face, descended the altar steps, and confiscated the cricket. There was a moment of silence, and then they heard the gasping voice of Lucia Altimare murmuring, " Mary . . . . Mary . . . . divine Mary ! "

" Pray silently, Altimare," gently suggested the Directress.

The Rosary began again, this time without interruption. Al. knelt down, with a great noise of moving chairs, and the Latin words were recited, almost chanted, in chorus. Caterina Spaccapietra rested her head against the back of the chair in front of her. Lucia Altimare had thrown herself down, shuddering, with her head on the straw seat, and arms hanging slack at her side.

"The blood will go to your head, Lucia," whispered her friend.

"Leave me alone," said Lucia.

The pupils rose from their knees. One of them, accompanied by a teacher, had mounted the steps leading to the little organ. The teacher played a simple devotional prelude for the Litany to the Virgin. A pure fresh voice, of brilliant quality, rang out, and permeated the chapel, waking its sleeping echoes ; a young yearning voice, crying with the ardour of an invocation, "*Sancta Maria . . . . !*" And from below, all the pupils responded in the minor key, "*Ora pro nobis !*" The singer stood in the light on the platform of the organ, her face turned towards the altar. She was Giovanna Casacalenda, a tall girl whose white raiment did not conceal her fine proportions ; a girl with a massive head, upon which her dark hair was piled heavily, and with eyes so black that they appeared as if painted. She stood there alone, isolated, infusing all the passion of her youth into her full mellow voice, delighting in the pleasure of singing as if she had freed herself, and lived in her song. The pupils turned to look at her, with the joy in music which is inherent in childhood. When the voice of Giovanna came down to them, the chorus rising from below answered, "*Ora pro nobis !*" She felt her triumph. With head erect, her wondrous black eyes swimming in a humid light, her right hand resting lightly on the wooden balustrade, her white throat throbbing as if for love, she intoned the medium notes, ran up to the highest ones, and came down gently to the lower, giving full expression to her song : "*Regina angelorum . . . . !*" One moment of silence, in which to enjoy the last notes ; then from below, in enthusiastic answer, came childish and youthful voices : "*Ora pro nobis !*" The singer looked fixedly at the altar, but she seemed to see or hear something beyond it—a vision, or music inaudible to the others. Every now and then a breath passed through her song, lending it warmth, making it passionate ; every now and then the voice thinned itself to a golden thread, that sounded like the sweet trill of a bird, while occasionally it sank to a murmur, with a delicious hesitation.

"Giovanna sees heaven," said Ginevra Avigliana to Artemisia Minichini.

"Or the stage," rejoined the other, sceptically.

Still, when Giovanna came to the poetic images by which the Virgin is designated—Gate of Heaven, Vase of Election, Tower of David—the girls' faces flushed in the ecstasy of that wondrous music: only Caterina Spaccapietra, who was absorbed, did not join in, and Lucia Altimare, who wept silently. The tears coursed down her thin cheeks. They rained upon her bosom and her hands; they melted away on her apron; and she did not dry them. Caterina quietly passed her handkerchief to her. But she took no notice of it. The preacher, Father Capece, went up the altar steps for the benediction. The Litany ended with the *Agnus Dei.* The voice of the singer seemed overpowered by sheer fatigue. Once more all the pupils knelt, and the priest prayed. Giovanna, kneeling at the organ, breathed heavily. After five minutes of silent prayer, the organ pealed out again slowly over the bowed heads, and a thrilling resonant voice seemed to rise from mid-air towards heaven, lending its splendour to the Sacrament in the *Tantum Ergo.* Giovanna was no longer tired; indeed her song grew in power, triumphant and full of life, with an ebb and flow that were almost voluptuous. The throb of its passion passed over the youthful heads below, and a mystic sensation caused their hearts to flutter. In the intensity of their prayer, in the approach of the benediction, they realised the solemnity of the moment. It dominated and terrified them, until it was followed by a painful and exquisite prostration. Then all was silent. A bell rang three peals; for an instant Artemisia Minichini dared to raise her eyes; she alone; looking at the inert forms upon the chairs, looking boldly at the altar; after which, overcome by childish fear, she dropped them again.

The holy Sacrament, in its sphere of burnished gold, raised

high in the priest's hands, shed its blessing on those assembled in the church.

" I am dying," gasped Lucia Altimare.

At the door of the chapel, in the long gas-lighted corridor, the teachers were waiting to muster the classes, and lead them to the refectory. The faces were still agitated, but the little ones hopped and skipped about, and prattled together, and pinched each other, in all the joyous exuberance of childhood released from durance vile. As their limbs unstiffened, they jostled each other, laughing the while. The teachers, running after some of them, scolding others, half threatening, half coaxing, tried to range them in a file of two and two. They began with the little ones, then came the elder children, and after them the grown-up girls. The corridor rang with voices, calling :

" The Blues, where are the Blues ? " " Here they are, all of them." " Friozzi is missing." " Where is Friozzi of the Blues ? " " Here ! " " In line, and to the left, if you please." " The Greens, in line the Greens, or no fruit for dinner to-morrow." " Quick, the refectory bell has rung twice already." " Federici of the Reds, walk straight ! " " Young ladies of the White-and-Greens, the bell is ringing for the third time." " Are the Tricolors all here ? " " All." " Casacalenda is missing." " She is coming ; she is still at the organ." " Altimare is missing." " Where is Altimare ? "

" She was here just now, she must have disappeared in the bustle ; shall I look for her ? "

" Look ; and come to the refectory with her."

Then the corridor emptied, and the refectory filled with light and merriment. With measured, almost rhythmic step, Caterina went to and fro in the deserted passages, seeking her friend Altimare. She descended to the ground-floor, called her twice from the garden ; no answer. Then she mounted the stairs again, and entered the dormitory. The white beds formed a line under the crude gaslight ; Lucia was not there.

A shade of anxiety began to dawn on Caterina's rosy face. She passed by the chapel twice, without going in. But the third time, finding the door ajar, she made up her mind to enter. It was dark inside. A lamp burning before the Madonna, scarcely relieved the gloom. She passed on, half intimidated, despite her well-balanced nerves, for she was alone in the darkness, in church.

Along one of the altar steps, stretched out on the crimson velvet carpet, a white form was lying, with open arms and pallid face, a spectral figure. It was Lucia Altimare, who had fainted.

II.

The fan of Artemisia Minichini, made of a large sheet of manuscript, waved noisily to and fro.

"Minichini, you disturb the Professor," said Friscia, the assistant teacher, without raising her eyes from her crochet work.

"Friscia, you don't feel the heat?" returned Minichini, insolently.

"No."

"You are lucky to be so insensible."

In the class room, where the Tricolor young ladies were taking their lesson in Italian history, it was very hot. There were two windows opening upon the garden, a door leading to the corridor, three rows of benches, and twenty-four pupils. On a high raised step stood the table and armchair of the Professor. The fans waved hither and thither, some vivaciously, some languidly. Here and there a head bent over its book as if weighted with drowsiness. Ginevra Avigliana stared at the Professor, nodding as if in approval, though her face expressed entire absence of mind. Minichini had put down her fan, opened her *pince-nez*, and fixed it impudently upon the Professor's face. With her nose tip-tilted, and a truant lock of hair curling on her forehead, she laughed her silent laugh that so irritated the teachers. The Professor explained the lesson in a low voice. He was small, spare, and pitiable. He might have been about two-and-thirty, but his emaciated face, whose dark colouring had yellowed with the pallor of some long illness, proclaimed him a convalescent. A big scholarly head surmounting the body of a dwarf, a wild thick mane in which some white hairs were already visible, proud yet shy eyes, a small dirty black beard, thinly planted towards the thin cheeks, completed his sad and pensive ugliness.

He spoke without gesture, his eyes downcast; occasionally his right hand moved never so slightly. Its shadow on the wall seemed to belong to a skeleton, it was so thin and crooked. He proceeded slowly, picking his words. These girls intimidated him, some because of their intelligence, others because of their impertinence, others simply because of their sex. His scholastic austerity was perturbed by their shining eyes, by their graceful and youthful forms; their white garments formed a kind of mirage before his eyes. A pungent scent diffused itself throughout the class, although perfumes were prohibited; whence came it? And, at the end of the third bench, Giovanna Casacalenda, who paid not the slightest attention, sat, with half-closed eyes, furiously nibbling a rose. Here in front, Lucia Altimare, with hair falling loose about her neck, one arm hanging carelessly over the bench, resting her brow against her hand and hiding her eyes, looked at the Professor through her fingers; every now and then she pressed her handkerchief to her too crimson lips, as if to mitigate their feverishness. The Professor felt upon him the gaze that filtered through her fingers; while, without looking at her, he could see Giovanna Casacalenda tearing the rose to pieces with her little teeth. He remained apparently imperturbable, still discoursing of Carmagnola and the conspiracy of Fiesco, addressing himself to the tranquil face of Caterina Spaccapietra, who pencilled rapid notes in her copy-book.

"What are you writing, Pentasuglia?" asked the teacher Friscia, who had been observing the latter for some time.

"Nothing," replied Pentasuglia, reddening.

"Give me that scrap of paper."

"What for? There is nothing on it."

"Give me that scrap of paper."

"It is not a scrap of paper," said Minichini, audaciously, taking hold of it as if to hand it to her. "It is one, two, three, four, five, twelve useless fragments . . . ."

To save her schoolfellow, she had torn it to shreds. There was silence in the class: they trembled for Minichini. The teacher bent her head, tightened her thin lips, and picked up her crochet again as if nothing had happened. The Professor appeared to take no notice of the incident, as he looked through his papers, but his mind must have been inwardly disturbed. A flush of youthful curiosity made him wonder what those girls were thinking of—what they scribbled in their little notes—for whom their smiles were meant, as they looked at the plaster bust of the King—what they thought when they drew the tricolor scarves round their waists. But the ghastly face and false grey eyes of Cherubina Friscia, the governess, frightened him.

"Avigliana, say the lesson."

The girl rose and began rapidly to speak of the Viscontis, like a well-trained parrot. When asked to give a few historical comments, she made no reply; she had not understood her own words.

"Minichini, say the lesson."

"Professor, I don't know it."

"And why?"

"Yesterday was Sunday, and we went out, so I could not study."

The Professor made a note in the register; the young lady shrugged her shoulders.

"Casacalenda?"

This one made no answer. She was gazing with intense earnestness at her white hands, hands that looked as if they were modelled in wax.

"Casacalenda, will you say the lesson ?"

Opening her great eyes as if she were dazed, she began, stumbling at every word, puzzled, making one mistake upon another: the Professor prompted, and she repeated, with the winning air of a strong, beautiful, young animal : she neither knew nor understood, nor was ashamed, maintaining her sculpturesque placidity, moistening her savage Diana-like lips, contemplating her pink nails. The Professor bent his head in displeasure, not daring to scold that splendid stupid creature, whose voice had such enchanting modulations.

He made two or three other attempts, but the class, owing to the preceding holiday, had not studied. This was the explanation of the flowers, the perfumes, and the little notes : the twelve hours' liberty had upset the girls. Their eyes were full of visions, they had seen the world, yesterday. He drew himself together, perplexed; a sense of mingled shame and respect kept every mouth closed. How he loved that science of history ! His critical acumen measured its widest horizons ; his was a vast ideal, and he suffered in having to offer crumbs of it to those pretty, aristocratic, indolent girls, who would have none of it. Still young, he had grown old and grey in arduous study; and now, behold—gay and careless youth, choosing rather to live than to know, rose in defiance against him. Bitterness welled up to his lips and went out towards those creatures, thrilling with life, and contemptuous of his ideal : bitterness, in that he could not, like them, be beautiful and vigorous, and revel in heedlessness, and be beloved. Anguish rushed through his veins, from his heart, and poisoned his brain, that he should have to humiliate his knowledge before those frivolous, scarcely human girls. But the gathering storm was held back ; and nothing of it was perceptible save a slight flush on his meagre cheekbones.

"Since none of you have studied," he said slowly, in a low voice, "none of you can have done the composition."

"Altimare and I have done it," answered Caterina Spaccapietr... "We did not go home," she added apologetically, to avoid offending her friends.

"Then you read, Spaccapietra; the subject is, I think, Beatrice di Tenda."

"Yes; Beatrice di Tenda."

Spaccapietra stood up and read, in her pure, slow voice :—

"Ambition had ever been the ruling passion of the Viscontis of Milan, who shrank from naught that could minister to the maintenance of their sovereign power. Filippo Maria, son of Gian Galeazzo, who had succeeded his brother, Gian Galeazzo, differed in no way from his predecessors. For the love of gain, this Prince espoused Beatrice di Tenda, the widow of a Condottiere, a soldier of fortune, a virtuous and accomplished woman of mature age. She brought her husband in dowry the dominions of Tortona, Novara, Vercelli and Alessandria; but he tired of her as soon as he had satisfied his thirst for wealth. He caused her to be accused of unfaithfulness to her wifely duty, with a certain Michele Orombello, a simple squire. Whether the accusation was false, or made in good faith, whether the witnesses were to be relied upon or not, Beatrice di Tenda was declared guilty, and, with Michele Orombello, mounted the scaffold in the year 1418, which was the forty-eighth of her life, she having been born in 1370."

Caterina had folded up her paper, and the Professor was still waiting; two minutes elapsed.

"Is there no more?"

"No."

"Really, is that all?"

"All."

"It is a very meagre composition, Spaccapietra. It is but the bare narrative of the historical fact, as it stands in the text-book. Does not the hapless fate of Beatrice inspire you with any sympathy?"

"I don't know . . . ." murmured the young scholar, pale with emotion.

"Yet you are a woman . . . . It so happens that I had chosen a theme which suggests the manifestation of a noble impulse; say of pity, or contempt for the false accusation. But like this, the story turns to mere chronology. The composition is too meagre. You have no imagination, Spacca-pietra."

"Yes, Professor," replied the young girl, submissively, as she took her seat again, while tears welled to her eyes.

"Let us hear Altimare."

Lucia appeared to start out of a lethargy. She sought for some time among her papers, with an ever increasing expression of weariness. Then, in a weak inaudible voice, she began to read, slowly, dragging the syllables, as if overpowered by an invincible lassitude . . . .

"Louder, Altimare."

"I cannot, Professor."

And she looked at him with such melancholy eyes that he repented of having made the remark. Again, she touched her parched lips with her handkerchief and continued:—

" . . . . through the evil lust of power. He was Filippo Maria Visconti, of a noble presence, with the eye of a hawk, of powerful build, and ever foremost in the saddle. The maidens who watched him pass, clad in armour under the velvet coat, on the breastpiece of which was broidered the wily, fascinating serpent, the crest of the Lords of Visconti, sighed as they exclaimed: ' How handsome he is !' But under this attractive exterior, as is ever the case in this melancholy world, where appearance is but part of the *mise-en-scène* of life, he hid a depraved soul. Oh! gentle, loving women, trust not him who flutters round you with courteous manner, and words that charm, and protestations of exquisite sentiment; he deceives you. All is vanity, all is corruption, all is ashes ! None learnt this lesson better than the hapless Beatrice di Tenda, whose tale I am about to tell you. This youthful widow was of unblemished character and matchless beauty; fair was her hair of spun gold, soft were her eyes of a blue worthy to reflect

the firmament ; her skin was as dazzling white as the petals of
a lily. Her first marriage with Facino Cane could not have
been a happy one. He, a soldier of fortune, fierce, blood-
thirsty, trained to the arms, the wine, and the rough speech of
martial camps, could scarcely have been a man after Beatrice's
heart. Woe to those marriages, in which one consort neither
understands nor appreciates the mind of the other. Woe to
those marriages in which the man ignores the mystic poetry,
the mysterious sentiments of the feminine heart ! These be the
unblessed unions, with which alas ! our corrupt and suffering
modern society teems. Facino Cane died. His widow shed
bitter tears over him, but her virgin heart beat quicker when
she first met the valorous yet malefic Filippo Maria Visconti.
Her face turned as pale as Luna's when she drags her weary
way along the starred empyrean. And she loved him with all
the ardour of her stored-up youth, with the chastity of a pious
soul loving the Creator in the created, blending divine with
human love. Beatrice, pure and beautiful, wedded Filippo
Maria for love : Filippo Maria, black soul that he was, wedded
Beatrice for greed of money. For a short time the august pair
were happy on their ducal throne. But the hymeneal roses
were worm-eaten : in the dewy grass lay hidden the perfidious
serpent, perfidious emblem of the most perfidious Visconti.
No sooner had he obtained possession of the riches of
Beatrice, than Filippo Maria wearied of her, as might be
expected of a man of so hard a heart and of such depraved
manners. He had, besides, formed an infamous connection
with a certain Agnese del Maino, one of the most vicious of
women ; and more than ever he was possessed of the desire to
rid himself of his wife. There lived at the Court of the
Visconti, a simple squire named Michele Orombello, a young
troubadour, a poet, who had dared to raise his eyes to his
august mistress. But the noble woman did not reciprocate
his passion, although the faithlessness and treachery of Filippo
Maria caused her the greatest unhappiness, and almost jus-
tified reprisals ; she was simply courteous to her unfortunate

adorer. When Filippo Maria saw how matters stood, he at once threw Michele Orombello and his chaste consort into prison, accusing them of treason. Torture was applied to Beatrice, who bore it bravely and maintained her innocence. Michele Orombello, being younger and perchance weaker to combat pain, or because he was treacherously advised that he might thereby save Beatrice, made a false confession. The judges, vile slaves of Filippo Maria, and tremblingly submissive to his will, condemned that most ill-starred of women and her miserable lover to die on the scaffold. The saintly woman ascended it with resignation; embracing the crucifix whereon the Redeemer agonised and died for our sins. Then, perceiving the young squire, who, weeping desperately, went with her to death, she cried: 'I forgive thee, Michele Orombello;' and he made answer: 'I proclaim thee the purest of wives!' But it availed not; the Prince's will must needs be carried out; the axe struck off the squire's dark head. Beatrice cried: 'Gesù Maria;' and the axe felled the blonde head too. A pitiable spectacle and full of horror for those assembled! Yet none dared to proclaim the infamy of the mighty Filippo Maria Visconti. Thus it ever is in life, virtue is oppressed, and vice triumphs. Only before the Eternal Judge is justice, only before that God of mercy who has said: 'I am the resurrection and the life.'"

A profound silence ensued. The pupils were embarrassed, and looked furtively at each other. Caterina gazed at Lucia with frightened astonished eyes. Lucia remained standing, pale, panting, contemptuous, with twitching lips. The Professor, deep in thought, held his peace.

"The composition is very long, Altimare," he said at last. "You have too much imagination."

Then silence once more—and the dry malicious hissing voice of Cherubina Friscia, "Give me that composition, Altimare."

All trembled, seized by an unknown terror.

III.

They, the Tricolors, the tallest, the handsomest, the proudest girls, had the privilege of sitting together in groups, during the hours set aside for needlework, in a corner of the long work-room. The other pupils sat on benches, behind frames, in rows, separated from each other, in enforced silence. The Tricolors, whose deft fingers produced the prettiest and most costly work, for the annual exhibition, enjoyed a certain freedom. So, in a narrow circle, with their backs turned to the others, they chatted in whispers. Whenever the work-mistress approached them, they turned the conversation, and asking for her advice, would hold up their work for her approval. It was their best hour, almost free of surveillance, delivered from the tyranny of Cherubina Friscia's boiled fish eyes, with liberty to talk of whatever they chose. The work dragged on ; but word and thought flew.

Giovanna Casacalenda—who was embroidering an altar-cover on finest cambric, a cloudy, diaphanous piece of work, a very marvel—had a way of rounding her arms, with certain graceful and studied movements of the fingers, as they drew the thread. Ginevra Avigliana was absorbed in a piece of lace made with bobbins, like Venetian point, to be presented to the Directress at the end of the term ; every *palma* (a measure of six inches) cost five francs in silk. Carolina Pentasuglia was working a red velvet cushion in gold. Giulia Pezzali was making a portfolio-cover in chenille. But little thought they of their work, while the needles clicked and the bobbins flew ; especially little on that morning, when they could talk of nothing but the Altimare scandal.

"So they have ordered her to appear before the Directress's Committee?" inquired Vitali, who was working with beads on perforated cardboard.

"No, not yet. Do you think they will?" asked Spacca-pietra, timidly. She did not dare to raise her eyes from the shirt she was sewing.

"*Diamine!*" exclaimed Avigliana. "Didn't you hear what ambiguous things there were in the composition! A girl has no right to know anything about them."

"Altimare is innocent as a new-born babe," replied Spaccapietra, gravely. No one answered, but all looked towards Altimare. Separated from the rest, far away from them, she sat with bowed head, making lint. It was her latest fancy; to make lint for the hospitals. She had voluntarily withdrawn herself, but appeared to be calm.

"Nonsense, girls, nonsense," observed Minichini, passing her hand through her hair with a masculine gesture. "Every one knows these things, but no one can speak of them."

"But to write about a wife's deceiving her husband, Minichini, what do you think of that?"

"Oh, dear, that's how it is in society; Signora Ferrari deceives her husband with my cousin," added Minichini, "I saw them . . . . behind a door . . . ."

"How, what, what did you see?" asked two or three in concert, while the others opened their eyes.

"The *maestra* is coming," said Spaccapietra.

"As usual, Minichini, you are not working," observed the teacher.

"You know it hurts my eyes."

"Are these your glasses? You are not so very short-sighted; I think you might work."

"And why, what for?"

"For your own house, when you return to it . . . ."

"You are perhaps unaware that my mother has three maids," said the other, turning on her like a viper.

The teacher bent over the work of Avigliana, muttering something about "pride . . . . insolence," and then presently withdrew. Minichini shrugged her shoulders. After a moment:

"I say, Minichini, what were the Signora Ferrari and your cousin doing behind the door?"

"Do you really want to know?"

"Yes, yes, yes."

"Well . . . . they were kissing."

"Ah!" exclaimed the chorus, alternately blushing and turning pale.

"On the lips, of course?" asked Casacalenda, biting her own to make them redder.

"Yes."

The girls were silent, absorbed in thought. Minichini always unsettled the work-class with her tales : she would tell the simplest thing with a certain malicious reticence and brusque frankness, that wrought upon their imagination. " I shall work myself a wrapper like this altar-cloth, when I leave this house," said Casacalenda, "it is so becoming to the skin."

And she tried it over her hand, a pink and exquis'te transparency.

"*Dio*, when shall I get out of this house!" exclaimed Avigliana.

"Three more months, eight days, and seven hours," said Pentasuglia.

"Doesn't Altimare wish she were out of it?" murmured Vitali.

" Goodness knows how they will punish her," said Spacca-pietra.

"If I were she, I should give the Directress a piece of my mind."

Then all at once they heard : " Hush-sh." The Vice-Directress had entered the room; quite an event. Altimare raised her eyes, but only for an instant, and her lids quivered. She went on making lint. To avoid a sensation, the Vice-Directress bent over two or three frames, and made a few remarks. At last :

" Altimare, the Directress wishes to see you."

Altimare stood up, erect and rigid, and passed straight down through two rows of pupils without looking either to right or left. The girls kept silence and worked industriously.

"Holy Mother, do thou help her," said Caterina Spacca-pietra under her breath.

"My married sister told me that Zola's books are not fit to be read," said Giovanna Casacalenda.

"That means that they may be read, but that it wouldn't do to say before gentlemen that one had read them."

"Oh! what a number of books I have read that no one knows anything about," exclaimed Avigliana.

"I know of a marriage that never came off," said Minichini, "because the *fiancée* let out that she read the *Dame aux Camélias*."

"*La Dame aux Camélias!* how interesting it must be! Who has read it, girls?"

"Not I, nor I, nor I," in chorus, accompanied by gentle sighs.

"I have read it," confessed Minichini.

"The *maestra* is coming," whispered Vitali, the sentinel.

"What is the matter, that you don't sew, Spaccapietra?" asked the teacher.

"Nothing," replied Caterina, casting down her eyes, while her hands trembled.

"Do you feel ill? Would you like to go out into the air?"

"No, thank you, I am well; I prefer to stay here."

"Are you in trouble about Altimare?" asked Avigliana.

"No, no," murmured the other, shyly.

"After all, what can they do to her?" said Casacalenda.

"*Diamine*, they won't eat her," said Minichini. "If they do anything to her, we will avenge her."

"The Directress is cruel," said Avigliana.

"And the Vice-Directress is a wretch," added Vitali.

"And as far as malignity goes, Cherubina Friscia is no joke," observed Pentasuglia.

"*Dio mio*, may I soon leave this house!" exclaimed Casacalenda.

All heads bent in acquiesence to this prayer. There was a spell of silence. Caterina Spaccapietra, overcome by a great lassitude, dragged slowly at her needle.

"Minichini, darling, tell us about the *Dame aux Camélias*," entreated Giovanna Casacalenda, her sweet voice thrilling with the passion of the unknown.

"I cannot, my heart."

"Why not? is it so dreadful? Tell it, Minichini. Artemisia, sweetest, tell us about that book." The others did not speak, but curiosity burned in their eyes; desire dried the words on their parched lips. Giovanna pleaded for them, her great eyes brimming over with entreaty, while a languid smile played about her full lips.

"Well, I'll tell it you. But you will never tell any one, Giovanna?"

"No, dear love."

"It is too late to finish the tale to-day . . . ."

"Never mind, never mind, go on."

"Well then, work hard, without looking at me; as if you were not listening to me. I shall turn towards Giovanna, as if I were chatting with her: she must nod approval from time to time, and say a word or two. But, for goodness' sake, don't show that you are listening to me:

"Once upon a time, there lived in Paris, a poor little dressmaker, whose name was Marguerite Duplessis . . . ."

"Violetta Valery," interrupted Pezzali; "I have seen the *Traviata.*"

"Don't interrupt; in making the opera, they changed the name . . . . She was a radiant beauty at fourteen, delicate, *svelte*, with long blonde chestnut hair, large blue eyes, and an ethereal form. She was very poor; she wore a faded cotton frock, a little black shawl, transparent from age, and shabby shoes, down at heel. Every day she went to the man who sold fried potatoes, and bought herself two *sous* worth of them. She was known as the Blonde of the fried potatoes. But she was born for beautiful things, for luxury and elegance: she could not bear poverty and misery; she held out for a time, but not for long. One fine day, the pretty dove had a perfumed nest . . . ."

"What had she done?" asked Avigliana, bewildered.

"She had become . . . . one of those . . . ."

"Here is Altimare," said Spaccapietra, half rising from her chair.

Every one turned round. Lucia advanced slowly, with uncertain gait, stumbling here and there against the chairs, as if she did not see them. Her hands hung down against her dress as if they did not belong to her. Her face was not pale, it was livid, with wild eyes. She sat down, but did not take up her work. Her companions looked at her aghast. The emaciated figure of the ardent ascetic had always intimidated them : now it terrified them. Something very serious must have passed between herself and the Directress. Without saying a word, Caterina Spaccapietra laid down her work, left the charmed circle of the Tricolors, and went and seated herself by Lucia. Altimare took no notice of her, but sat as still as one petrified, with an expression of pain on her face.

"What is the matter, Lucia ? "

"Nothing."

"Tell me, Lucia, have they made you suffer much ; do you still suffer ? "

Not even a sign that she breathed ; not a line moved in her face.

"Lucia, *sai*, I don't know what to say to comfort you, I don't know how to say it, I don't . . . . " Then she was silent. She took one of Lucia's hands in hers ; it was icy cold. The hand lay there, inert and lifeless. Caterina caressed it as if to put warmth into it ; indeed, she was trying to think of something to say, but she found nothing. She sat by her side, leaning slightly towards her, endeavouring to make Lucia look at her. The Tricolors watched from a distance. The whole College was watching.

"Why do you not cry, Lucia ? " suggested Caterina, timidly.

Nothing, no impression. Caterina felt her own embarrassment and confusion increase. "Tell me, Lucia, tell me what ails you ? Be comforted ; see, I cannot console you ; but speak, cry, give it vent, it will choke you."

Nothing. All at once Lucia's hand contracted nervously ; she stood up, still petrified, then thrust her hand into her hair

and tore it, gave one long, heartrending, horrible cry, and
rushed like a whirlwind down the room. The confusion was
indescribable. Caterina Spaccapietra was stunned for a
moment.

"To the terrace!" cried Minichini, "that's where the danger
is. To the terrace!"

Lucia Altimare fled along the hall with bowed head, the
dark plaits of her hair hanging loose over her shoulders, her
white gown clinging to her limbs. She fled along the room,
and down the corridor, feeling the hot breath of her pursuers
close upon her. In the long corridor, she doubled her speed;
at the steps leading to the refectory, she cast aside her tricolor
scarf.

"Altimare, Altimare, Altimare!" said her panting school-
fellows. She did not turn; she bounded up the steps, stumbled,
instantly rose to her feet again, drew a long breath and gained
the corridor on the upper story that ran parallel with the
dormitory. She rushed to the door; but uttered a cry of rage
and anguish when she found it closed.

"Altimare, for pity's sake, Altimare!" called the voices of
her pursuers, in a tumult. She ran to another door, pushed it
open and entered the dormitory. She made a wild gesture of
salutation to the Christ over her bed. At the further end of
the long room was a large bay window, which overlooked the
terrace. Wherever she went, the whole College pressed within
a dozen yards of her footsteps; but she did not hear them.
With one supreme bound she reached the window, opened it,
and rushed out upon the black asphalt, burning under the
July sun. Blinded by the brilliant outdoor light, mad with
despair, she dashed forward, wishing, almost believing, that
the stone parapet would give way at her desire. But when
she got there, and hurriedly made the sign of the cross, two
iron arms caught her round the waist.

"Let me go, Caterina, let me throw myself down."

"No."

"Loose me, I will die!"

" No."

And for an instant there was a struggle on the broad, deserted terrace, close to the outer wall, beyond which was the precipice. Caterina held her close, panting, yet never loosening her hold. Lucia struggled with serpentine flexibility ; striking, scratching, and biting. Then she gave a scream, and fell down insensible on the asphalt. When the others arrived, when the whole College assembled on that wide terrace, Caterina was fanning Lucia's face with her handkerchief, and sucking away the blood from the scratches on her own hands.

"But for thee, she would have died," said Minichini, kissing her. " How did you manage ? "

" I came up by the chapel stair," said Caterina, simply. " Directress, I beg your pardon, but would you mind sending for some vinegar ? "

IV.

The little ones were doing their gymnastics in the garden, laughing and screaming. Attenuated by the distance, their voices floated up to the terrace, where the big girls were taking their recreation. In the serene violet sunset, the young ladies walked slowly to and fro, in groups of twos, and threes, and fours ; white figures, on which the black aprons stood out clearly defined, as they lingered near the terrace wall. Three or four teachers moved about with crochet or tatting in their hands. Their eyes bent on their work, and their faces expressionless, none the less they heard and took heed of everything. That hour of recess was the most longed for and yet the most melancholy of the whole day. The fresh, calm air—the vast horizon opening out before and around the line of houses that appeared to flow like a stream into the sea, from Capo-di-monte, where the College stood—the atmosphere of liberty— all lent a saddening influence to temperaments that were either oppressed by exuberance or impoverished by anæmia. The mystic melancholy, the yearning tenderness, the effusion of anguish, the vague aspirations, all those impulses of tears and sighs, which the dawn of womanhood brings in its train, breathed in that hour.

The fair collegians mounted the terrace steps, longing for the open air, and uttering little cries of joy at their deliverance. Merry words ran from one to the other, and rippling laughter. They chased each other as if they were but ten years old, those great girls of fifteen and eighteen; they all but played at hide-and-seek. Here they could forget the unedifying subjects upon which their precocious minds were prone to dwell. They did not even think of murmuring against the Directress or the teachers, an eternal theme on which to embroider the most malicious variations. Up here they once more became frank, light-hearted children. One day, Artemisia Minichini had in a fit of gaiety forced Cherubina Friscia to waltz round the terrace with her; and it had seemed to every one, natural and amusing.

But after the first quarter of an hour, the excitement abated, until it gradually died out. The laughter was silenced; the voices lowered, as if in fear; the race abandoned for a slow solemn walk; separate groups of twos and threes formed where there had been a compact crowd. And the words came languidly and far between to their lips. All the suppressed sadness of the full young life with which their pulses throbbed, made their heads hang listlessly in that summer sunset. Lucia Altimare, drawn to her full height, stood gazing across at Naples, as if she did not see it. Her slight figure stood out clearly against the paling sky, and in that light the fine lines of her profile acquired the purity and refinement of an antique statue. Indeed, that dark hair coiled up high, looked not unlike a classic helmet. Next to her stood Caterina Spacca-pietra, her clear grey eyes bent upon Naples. She seemed absent and dreamy; but the moment Lucia looked down the precipice, she started forward as if to hold her back.

"Don't be afraid, I won't throw myself over," said Lucia Altimare, in her low, weak voice, her face breaking into the

shadow of a smile. "Last week, I was mad, but you have
made me sane. That is to say, not you, but God. Through
your lips, by your hands, has the Lord saved me from eternal
perdition."

She drew her blue rosary from her pocket, and kissed the
silver crucifix and the medal of the Madonna. "Yes, Caterina,
it was madness. But here"—she bent down to whisper—"no
one understands me, no one but you! You are good, and you
understand me; oh! if I could but tell you all! They
cannot understand me here. That day, the Directress was so
cold and cruel to me. She said that I had written things that
were unworthy of a gentleman's daughter, that I appeared to
know of things which it is unmaidenly even to think of; that
the Professor, the teacher, and my companions were scandalised; that she should be obliged to send the composition to
my father, with a severe letter. I held my tongue, Caterina;
what could I say? I held my tongue, I did not weep;
neither did I entreat her. I returned to the hall in an agony
of grief and shame. You spoke to me, but I did not hear
you. Death passed like lightning through my soul, and my
soul fell in love with it. God . . . . disappeared."

She left off speaking, tired in voice and body. Caterina,
who had listened spell-bound by her sentimental talk, replied:
"Cheer up, Lucia; September will soon be here. We shall
leave then."

"What does that matter?" said the other, shrugging her
shoulders. "I shall but exchange one sorrow for another.
Do you see a little tower yonder, under the Vomero hill? I
was christened in that church. In that little church there
is a Madonna, all robed in black; her gown is embroidered
with gold. She holds a little white handkerchief in her hand;
she can turn her eyes in anguish, and in her divine heart of
woman and mother, are seven swords of pain. Caterina, they
christened me in the church of Our Lady of Seven Sorrows.
The Madonna Addolorata is my patron saint; I shall suffer
for ever."

Caterina listened to her with a pained expression on her face.

"You exaggerate; what do you know of life?"

"I know it," said the other, shaking her head. "I feel as if I had lived enough, suffered enough—I feel as I had grown so old. I feel as if I had found dust and ashes everywhere. I am sick at heart. We are only born to sorrow."

"That's Leopardi again, Lucia; you promised me not to read Leopardi again."

"I will not read him again. But listen; we are blind, miserable beings, destined to pain and death. Do you see beautiful Naples, smiling, voluptuous, nestling between her fruitful hills and her divine sea, in the magic of her radiant colouring? Do you really love Naples?"

"Yes, for I was born there," said the other in a low voice.

"I hate her, with her odour of flowers, of humanity, of sparkling wines; her starred and seductive nights. I hate her; for she is the embodiment of sin and sorrow. There, where the tall lightning conductors shoot into the air, is the aristocratic quarter; the home of corruption and sorrow. Here below us, where the houses are closer together and look darker, are the people's dwellings; but here, too, are corruption and sorrow. She is a sinner, like the city of Sodom, like the city of Gomorrah; she is a sinful woman, like the Magdalen. But she writhes in her sin, she inundates her bed with her tears, she weeps in the fatal night of Gethsemane. Oh! triumphant city, accursed and agonising!"

Her gesture cut the air like an anathema; but immediately her excitement calmed down, and the flush died out of her cheeks.

"It is bad for you to stand here, Lucia; shall we walk?"

"No, let me speak; I think too much, and thought ploughs too deep a furrow, when I cannot put it into words. Have I saddened you, Caterina?"

"A little; I fear for your health."

"I beg your pardon. I ought not to talk to you of these things. You don't like to hear them."

"I assure you . . . ."

"You are right, dear. But really, without exaggeration, life is not beautiful. Have you ever thought of the future; of the vague, dread future, that is so close upon us?"

"Sometimes."

"And you have not feared?"

"I don't know."

"The future is all fear, Caterina . . . . Do you know what you will do with your life?"

"I know."

"Who has told it you, thoughtless child? Who has read the riddle of the future?"

"My aunt intends me to marry Andrea Lieti."

"Shall you obey?"

"Yes."

"Without regret?"

"Without regret."

"Oh! poor child, poor child! Does this Andrea love you?"

"I think so."

"Do you love him?"

"I think I do."

"Love is sorrow; marriage is an abomination, Caterina."

"I hope not," replied the other, with clasped hands and bowed head.

"I shall never marry, no, never," added Lucia, drawing herself up and raising her eyes to heaven, in the pride of her mysticism.

The violet twilight deepened. The collegians stood still in the grounds, near the parapet, looking at some of the windows that reflected the sun's last rays, at the distant sea that was turning to iron grey, at the swallows that shot like arrows across the roofs with the shrill cry that is their evensong.

Giovanna Casacalenda confessed to Maria Vitali that the hour of twilight made her long to die a sudden death, so that they might embalm her, dress her in a white satin gown, and loosen her long hair under a wreath of roses . . . . and after a

hundred years a poet might fall in love with her. Artemisia
Minichini assumed her most lugubrious air, her fists were
doubled up in her apron pockets, there was a deep furrow
across her forehead, and her lips were pursed up. Carolina
Pentasuglia, the blonde, romantic, little sentimentalist, told
Ginevra Avigliana that she wished herself far away in Denmark, on the shore of the Northern Sea, on a deserted strand,
where the north wind howls through the fir-trees. Even
Cherubina Friscia forgot her part of eavesdropper, and with
vague eyes and listless hands meditated upon a whole life to
be passed within College walls, without friends or relations, a
poor old maid, hated by the girls.

"I think," said Lucia to Caterina, "that my father intends
marrying again. He has not dared to before, but human
patience is so fragile a thing ! My father is worldly, he does
not understand me. My presence saddens him. He would
like to have a merry, thoughtless girl in the house, who would
enliven it. I am not the one for that."

"But what will you do ? Something will have to be done,
Lucia."

"Yes, something I will do, not for myself, but for others.
Great undertakings call for great sacrifices. If I were a man,
I would go to Africa and explore unknown regions. If I were
a man, I would be a monk, a missionary to China or Japan,
far, far away. But I am a woman, a weak, useless woman."

"You could stay with your father, meanwhile."

"No, his is a tardy youth, and mine a precocious old age.
My presence in his house would be a continual reproach. Well,
listen, I shall try to come upon a good, noble, holy idea, to
which I can consecrate my mind and my energy. I will seek
for a plague to lessen, an injustice to remove, a wrong to right,
everywhere I will search for the ideal of humanity, to which I
may sacrifice my life. I know not what I shall do, as yet I
know not. But either as a Sister of the Red Cross on the
battlefield, or as a Sister of Charity in the hospitals, or as a
visitor in prisons, or as founder and teacher in some orphan

asylum, I shall dedicate the strength and the courage of a wasted existence to the alleviation of human suffering."

Caterina did not answer. Lucia contemplated her friend with the faintest shade of disdain on her lips.

" Will it not be a beautiful life, Caterina ? "

"Very beautiful. Will your people give their consent ? "

"I should like to know how they could prevent it. It would be cruel tyranny."

" And your health ? "

"I shall struggle against it . . . . or if I die, death will be the more welcome to me, worn with toil, with the consciousness of accomplished duty."

"I am not capable of such great things," murmured Caterina, after a short silence. " Mine is not a great soul."

"Never mind, dear," said the other, stroking her hair as if she were a child, " the ideal of humanity is not for every one."

Evening had closed in, recreation was over, the collegians re-entered the dormitory, passed thence to the corridor, and descending the stair, approached the chapel, for evening prayer. On they went, without looking at each other, in silence, prey to a melancholy so intense that it isolated them. They walked two and two, but not arm in arm. Two of them took each other by the hand, but with so languid a pressure that they scarcely held together. Behind them, the lights of Naples glimmered like evening stars; they entered into the garnered peace of the College, and did not turn to look back. The oppression of that long hour of twilight weighed upon their spirits, and there was something funereal in the long, unsmiling march to the chapel. The window, hastily closed by the last comer, Cherubina Friscia, grated on its rusty hinge with a noise like a laugh of irony.

V.

It was the last lesson. August was dying; the lessons were all coming to an end. After the September and October holidays, the children were to return to school for the Feast of San Carlo. But the Tricolors, maidens of seventeen or eighteen, having finished their education, left in September, to return no more. On that day, at two o'clock, they attended the history lesson the last of all. After that lesson, their course of study was absolutely finished.

That was why there was something so abnormal in the girls themselves, and in the very atmosphere about them. That was why the curly, blonde hair of Carolina Pentasuglia was dressed more like a poodle's than it had ever been before; a roguish cherub's head, one mass of curls. Giovanna Casacalenda, divested of her apron, was in pure white, a resplendent whiteness, broken only at the waist by her tricolor scarf. Artemisia Minichini wore a big gold locket on the velvet ribbon round her throat. Ginevra Avigliana had three roses in her waistband, right under her heart. But all of them sat demure and composed in the class-room, that already seemed so deserted: there was not a book on the desks, nor a scrap of paper, nor a pen. The inkstands were closed. A few drawers stood open. In a corner, on the ground, behind the blackboard, was a heap of tattered paper, torn into shreds or rolled up in balls. On a black panel destined to the exhibition of caligraphic achievements, there was chalked a tabulated list which set forth in finest imitation of printed letters, combined with copy-book and old English characters, embellished by countless flourishes, the fact that: " In the scholastic year —— the Signorine .... had completed the studies of the fifth gymnasial course...." And first on the list was Lucia Altimare. It was the *clôture*, the end of the volume, the word *finis* .... The young ladies never turned towards that tablet. The eyes of some of them were rather red. Oh ! on that day the lesson was a serious and arduous one. They had all studied that period of 1815, with which the historical programme ended. From time to time the Professor made a critical remark, to which the pupils listened attentively. Caterina Spaccapietra, that diligent scribe, took notes on a scrap of paper. On that day the Professor was paler and uglier than ever: he seemed thinner, a pitiable figure in the clothes that set so awkwardly upon him. The most ludicrous item of his attire was a large cameo pin, stuck in a dark red cravat of the worst possible taste. On that day he was more careful than ever to avoid the glances of his pupils. He listened to them with profound attention, his eyes half closed, nodding his approval, murmuring an occasional *bene* under his breath. Now and again he would make an absent comment, as if he were talking to himself. Then the half-hour struck. As the minutes passed, the voice of the girl who repeated the lesson grew more and more tremulous: then at last the Professor added certain historical anecdotes concerning Napoleon. He spoke slowly, carefully picking his words. When he had ended the third quarter struck. The Professor and his pupils, impressed by a sudden and painful embarrassment, looked at each other. The history lesson was over.

"The class asks permission to read its farewell letter," said Cherubina Friscia, whose placid face was undisturbed by emotion.

He hesitated, a painful look of indecision passed over his face.

"I should prefer to read it at home. I could give more attention to it . . . ." he stammered, for want of something better.

"No, no; listen to it here, Professor," cried two or three eager voices.

"It is customary, Professor," said Friscia, dryly.

There was a moment's silence. All the girls' faces turned pale from emotion. His head was bent in thought; at last: "Read," he said, and appeared ready to listen in earnest from behind the hand with which he hid his eyes.

Altimare rose, took the letter from an envelope and read it, halting at every word, dividing every syllable, her voice suffused with tenderness:

"Honoured and beloved Professor, fate has indeed been both blind and cruel in choosing me to offer you, most

respected Professor, the last farewell of a departing class. I
am assuredly too much affected by our common sorrow; so
conscious of the solitude in which this separation will leave
us, that a nameless pang at the heart will prevent the anguish of
our minds from passing into words, in parting from him who
has been our master and our guide. Oh, judge not the depth
of our feeling for you from what I write . . . . Words are so
pale, so weak and inadequate, and our emotion is so heartfelt.
Professor, we are leaving . . . ."

Ginevra Avigliana wept aloud, her face buried in her
hands.

". . . . this college where we have lived the sweetest
years of our life, where our childhood and youth have been
passed in the companionship of beloved friends and in the
salutary occupation of our studies. We are leaving the house
where we have laughed and learned, the roof that has overlooked our sports, our strivings for knowledge, our dreams.
God is our witness that we feel that the past is slipping from
us . . . ."

Silently and with a pressure at her heart, Carolina Pentasuglia wept until she felt faint.

". . . . that a whirlwind is snatching it from us, that our
joyous youth has vanished, and that the weight of the future,
heavy with responsibility, is hanging over us. We cannot face
the future undaunted, we would fain prolong this last day at
school, we would fain cry aloud to our Directress and our
teachers—' Why turn us away? we were so happy! oh! keep
us, keep us with you . . . ..!'"

The reader broke down, her voice was hoarse, sobs checked
her utterance, tears blinded her. She dried her eyes and
cheeks, and continued :

". . . . but this is a hard law which governs human beings.
They must meet, love and part—part for ever from those with
whom one would gladly pass one's life. Well, on this day, we
gather our memories together, we recall the life we have lived
and all the benefits we owe to your knowledge, your teaching,

and your patient, indulgent affection. For all you have done for us, take our blessing and our thanks. Yours is the tenderest memory that will abide with us, in the battle of life, a guiding star in the darkness that perchance awaits us. If we have failed in aught, forgive us. We entreat you, by this hour of sorrow upon which we enter, prepared for it, and yet shrinking from it, we entreat you, think of us without bitterness . . . ."

The reader fell back on her bench exhausted, sobbing violently. The letter had fallen from her hand. Cherubina Friscia rose, crossed the class, picked up the letter, put it into its envelope and placed it on the Professor's desk. Nearly all of them wept in the despair of childish sorrow, at the many farewells, at the details of their departure, and in doubt and dread of the world they were about to enter. Artemisia Minichini, in the vain attempt to keep up her reputation of a strong-minded woman, bit her lips and blinked with her eyelids, but the flush on her cheek betrayed the effort it cost her. Little Giulia Pezzali, with her head hanging over her arms, which she had crossed on the back of the bench in front of her, like the child she was, moaned as if some one were hurting her. Even the plump white beauty of Giovanna Casacalenda was dimmed, her surprised black eyes were swollen with tears. Caterina's were dry and burning, but from time to time a sigh escaped her lips. The Professor did not weep, but he appeared to be more than usually unhappy in the heavy atmosphere that bowed those youthful heads and forced from them such noisy tears.

"Listen," he said, "do not weep . . . ." Some faces looked up through their tears. "Do not weep. There should be no tears at your age. The time will come for them later—very late, I trust . . . . To-day you feel unbearable sorrow in departing from this educational institution, where you must needs leave behind you so much of yourselves. To-morrow will bring a joy that will blot out all this sorrow. Life is made up of these alternations. They are not hard to bear, if you have within you faith and courage. I have taught you all I know, hoping that in the history of man's deeds you might find guidance for your own actions. Why do you thank me? I have done so little. But if you will perforce thank me, I pray you let it be in this wise only: be good, be so in a humane, womanly spirit. Remember one who says these words to you, remember . . . ."

By this time his voice was very faint, and his hands were trembling. The girls had abandoned themselves to a fresh fit of weeping. Motionless he stood for a second on the little platform, looking down at the bowed heads, at the faces buried in pocket-handkerchiefs, at the convulsed forms on the benches; then he noiselessly descended, scribbled a single word in chalk on the blackboard and slipped away, bowing to Friscia as he passed.

On the dingy slate, in big uncertain characters, stood the word "Addio."

VI.

There was only one flickering jet of gas burning at the entrance to the dormitory that contained the little white beds in which the Tricolors passed the last night of their school-days. There had been short dialogues, interrupted by sighs, melancholy reflections and regrets, until a late hour. They would have liked to sit up all night, to indulge in their grief. But fatigue had melted their project away. When they could hold out no longer, sleep mastered those restless beings, weary with weeping. A languid "Good-night" was audible here and there, gradually the irregular breathing had subsided, and the sobs had died out. Complete repose reigned in the dormitory of the Tricolors.

When the great clock struck two after midnight, Lucia Altimare opened her eyes. She had not slept; devoured by impatience, she had watched. Without rising she gently and noiselessly took her clothes from the chair near her bed, and put them on, thrust her bare feet into her slippers, and then

c

crept out of bed. She moved liked a shadow, with infinite precaution, casting, in passing, an oblique glance at the beds where her companions slept. Now and again she looked towards the end of the hall where Cherubina Friscia lay. There was no danger. Lucia passed like a tall white phantom, with burning eyes, through the heavy gloom, to Caterina's bedside.

Her friend slept quietly, composedly, breathing like a child. She bent down and whispered close to her ear:

"Caterina, Caterina!"

She opened her eyes in alarm; a sign from Lucia froze the cry that rose to her lips. The surprise on her face spoke for her, and questioned her friend.

"If you love me, Caterina, dress and follow me."

"Where are we going?" the other ventured to ask, hesitating.

"If you love me . . . ."

Caterina no longer questioned her. She dressed herself in silence, looking now and then at Lucia, who stood there like a statue, waiting. When Caterina was ready she took her by the hand to lead her.

"Fear nothing," breathed Lucia, who could feel the coldness of her hand. They glided down the passage that divided the beds from the rest of the room. Artemisia Minichini was the only one who turned in her bed, and appeared for a moment to have opened her eyes. They closed again, but perhaps she saw through her lids. No other sign of waking. They shrank closer together when they passed the last bed, Friscia's, and stooped to make themselves smaller. That moment seemed to them like a century. When they got into the corridor, Caterina squeezed Lucia's hand as if they had passed through a great danger.

"Come, come, come!" murmured the siren voice of Lucia, and suddenly they stopped before a door. Lucia dropped Caterina's hand and inserted a key into the keyhole; the door creaked as it flew open. A gust of chill air struck the two young girls; a faint diffuse light broke in upon them. A lamp was burning before the image of the Virgin. They were in the chapel. Calmly Lucia knelt before the altar and lighted two candelabra. Then she turned to Caterina, who, dazed by the light, was catching her breath, and once more said, "Come."

They advanced towards the altar. In the little whitewashed church, with two high windows open on the country, a pleasant dampness tempered the heat of the August night. The faintest perfume of incense still clung to the air. The church was so placid and restful, the candelabra in their places, the tapers extinguished, the Sacrament shut away in its pix, the altar-cloth turned up to cover it. But a quaintly fashioned silver arabesque, behind which Lucia had lighted a taper, projected on the wall the profile of a strange monstrous beast. Caterina stood there in a dream, with her hand still clasped in Lucia's, whose fever it had caught . . . . Even at that unusual hour, in the dead of night, she no longer asked herself what strange rite was to be solemnised in that chapel illuminated only for them. She was conscious of a vague tremor, of a weight in the head, and a longing for sleep; she would fain have been back in the dormitory, with her cheek on her pillow . . . . But like one who dreams of having the well-defined will to do a thing, and yet while the dream lasts has neither the speech to express nor the energy to accomplish it, she was conscious, between sleeping and waking, of the torpor of her own mind. She looked around her as one in a stupor, neither understanding nor caring to understand. From time to time her mouth twitched with an imperceptible yawn. Lucia's hands were crossed over her bosom, and her eyes fixed on the Madonna. No sound escaped her half-open lips. Caterina leant forward to observe her; in the vague turn of thought that went round and round in her sleepy brain, she asked herself if she were dreaming, and Lucia a phantom. . . . . She passed one hand across her brow either to awake herself or to dispel the hallucination.

" Listen, Caterina, and try and comprehend me better than I know how to express myself. Do you give your whole attention?"

" Yes," said the other with an effort.

" You alone know how we have loved each other here. After God, the Madonna Addolorata, and my father, I have loved you, Caterina. You have saved my life, I can never forget it. But for you, I should have gone to burn in hell, where suicides must eternally suffer. I thank you, dear heart. You believe in my gratitude?"

" Yes," said Caterina, opening wide her eyes the better to understand her.

" Now we who so love each other must part. You go to the left, I to the right. You are to be married. I know not what will happen to me. Shall we meet again? I know not. Shall we again come together in the future? Who knows? Do you know?"

" No," replied Caterina, starting.

" Well, then, I propose to you to conquer time and space, men and circumstances, should they stand in the way of our affection. From afar, howsoever we may be separated, let us love each other as we do to-day, as we did yesterday. Do you promise?" .

" I promise."

" The Madonna hears us, Caterina. Do you promise with a vow, with an oath?"

" With a vow, with an oath," repeated Caterina, monotonously, like an echo.

" And I too promise, that no one shall ever by word or deed lessen this our steadfast friendship. Do you promise?"

" I promise."

" And I too promise, that neither shall ever seek to do ill to the other, or willingly cause her sorrow, or ever, ever betray her. Promise—the Madonna hears us."

" I promise."

" I swear it—that always, whatever befalls, one shall try to help the other. Say, do you promise?"

" I promise."

"And I too. Besides, that either will be ever ready to sacrifice her own happiness to that of the other. Swear it, swear ! "

Caterina thought for an instant. Was she dreaming a strange dream, or was she binding herself for life? " I swear," she said, firmly.

" I swear," reiterated Lucia. " The Madonna has heard. Woe to her who breaks her vow ! God will punish her."

Caterina bowed her assent. Lucia took her rosary from her pocket. It was a string of lapis-lazuli bound together by little silver links. From it depended a small silver crucifix, and a little gold medal on which was engraved the image of the Madonna della Saletta. She kissed it.

" We will break this rosary in two equal parts, Caterina. Half of it you shall take with you, the other half I will keep. It will be our keepsake, to remind us of our vow. When I pray at night, I shall remember. You too will remember me in your prayers. The missing half will remind you of your absent friend."

And taking up the rosary between them, they pulled hard at it from either side . . . . Lucia kept the half with the crucifix, Caterina the half with the medal. The two girls embraced. Then they heard the clock strike three. When silence reigned once more in the College and in the empty chapel, both knelt down on the steps of the altar, crossed their hands on their bosoms, and with closed eyes repeated in unison—

" Our Father . . . . "

PART II.

I.

THE green hue of the country disappeared under the heavy November rain. Caserta, down below, shrouded by the falling water as by a veil of mist, seemed but a large grey blot on a background of paler grey. The Tifata hills, that are tinged with so deep a violet during the long autumn twilights, had vanished behind the thick, opaque downpour. The small and aristocratic village of Centurano, entirely composed of lordly villas, separated from each other by narrow lanes and flowering hedges, held its peace.

At the corner of the high road that leads to Caserta, the fountain which Ferdinand of Bourbon had bestowed on Michelangiolo Viglia, his favourite barber, overflowed with rain-water. The long, melancholy, watery day was slowly dying, in a rainy twilight that seemed already evening. No sound was heard. The last lingerers among the *villeganti* kept within their houses, yawning, dozing, or gazing through closed windows at the drenched, denuded gardens, where the monthly roses hung their dishevelled heads, and the water trickled in little muddy rivulets among wasted flower-beds; while here and there the stalks of stocks and wallflowers showed like the bare bones of so many skeletons. Behind one window were visible the cadaverous old face and red velvet smoking-cap of Cavalier Scardamaglia, judge at the Court of Santa Maria; behind another, the aquiline nose and the long thin cheeks of Signora Magaloni, wife of the architect who was directing the repairs of the royal palace. The children of lawyer Farini

were running after and shouting at each other on the covered
terrace of their villa. Francesca, their nurse, sat in the arch of
the window, knitting, without dreaming of scolding them. The
water poured along the gutters and filled the pipes to bursting;
the butts for the family washing overflowed; the walls were
stained as with rust.

From behind her balcony windows, Caterina looked out
upon the fountain that overflowed the road. She tried to see
farther away, down the highway to Caserta, but in this the
rain thwarted her. She looked back again at the fountain,
and re-read the two first lines of its fatuous inscription :

DIEMMI DELL'ACQUA GIULIA
UN RIVOLETTO IL RE.

But she soon wearied of this contemplation, and again applied
herself to her sewing. She was seated on the broad window-
sill : before her stood her work-table, covered with reels of
cotton, a needle-case, a pincushion, scissors of all sizes, and
bundles of tapes ; near to her was a large basket of new ready-
basted household linen, at which she was sewing. Just now
she was hemming a fine Flanders tablecloth ; four that she
had finished were lying folded on the little table. She sewed
deliberately, with a harmonious precision of movement.
Whenever she cut her thread with her scissors, she turned to
the road for a moment to see if any one was coming. Then
she resumed her hem again, patiently and mechanically, passing
her pink nail across it to make it even. Once a noise in the
street caused her to start : she stopped to listen. It was the
little covered cart in which the Avvocata Farini was returning
from Nola, whither he had gone on some legal errand. The
lawyer, as he alighted, made her a low bow.

Despite her disappointment, she responded with a pretty,
gracious smile, and followed him with her eyes, to where his
children welcomed him with shouts and outstretched arms.
Once more the regular profile bent over the Flanders cloth,

and the needle flew under her agile fingers. Caterina appeared
to have grown bigger, although she still retained a certain
girlish delicacy and a pretty minuteness of feature. The look
in her grey eyes was more decided, the contour of her cheek
was firmer, the chin had assumed a more energetic character.
On the low brow, the bright chestnut hair was slightly waved;
its thick plaits were gathered up at the nape by a light
tortoiseshell comb. She wore a short indoor dress of ivory-
white cashmere—a soft thick material that clung closely to her,
especially at the waist—a relic of the coquetry of her school-
days. Round her throat was a broad creamy lace tie, with a
large bow, wherein the chin seemed to bury itself. It gave
value to the delicate pink colouring of her face. There were
full lace ruffles around her wrists; no jewels, except a plain
gold ring on one finger. Her whole person breathed a serene
simplicity, a delightful happy calm.

"Shall I bring the lights?" asked Cecchina, the maid,
entering the room."

" What time is it ? "

" Nearly six o'clock."

" Wait a little longer."

" And master not yet back ! "

" He will come in good time."

" The Lord knows how soaked he'll be."

" I hope not. Is his room quite ready ? "

"Everything, Signora."

" Then you needn't wait."

Cecchina left the room. Caterina did not return to her
sewing, for it was nearly dark, and she wanted to believe that
it was still early. Meanwhile, the lamplighter of Centurano
was proceeding under cover of his waterproof and his umbrella
to light the few petroleum lamps of the tiny village. Caterina
folded and refolded her linen in the twilight. Cecchina, who
was getting impatient, brought in two lamps.

" The cook says, ' What is he to do ? ' "

" He's to wait."

" Till what hour ? "

" Till seven—like yesterday."

But all at once a faint bark was audible down the lane.

" That is Fox," said Caterina quietly. " Your master is coming."

Immediately there was the noise of a great opening and shutting of doors; a rush of sound and movement. After that a lusty voice resounded in the courtyard.

" Here, Fox ! Here, poor beast ! Here, Diana ! She's as wet as a newly hatched chicken ! Caterina, Caterina ! Matteo, take care of the gun, it's full of water ! Caterina !"

" Here I am," she said, leaning over the balustrade.

A big curly head and a green felt hat, then a herculean body, clothed in a velveteen jacket, leather breeches, and top-boots, appeared on the lower steps. With a great sound of clanking spur, and cracking whip, soaked from head to foot, but laughing heartily, Andrea seized his wife by the waist, and raised her like a child in his strong arms, while he kissed her eyes, lips, and throat, roughly and eagerly.

" Nini, Nini !" he cried, between each sounding kiss.

" You're come . . . . you're come !" she murmured, smiling ; her hair loosened from its comb, and on her fair skin sundry red imprints left by his caresses.

" Oh ! Nini, Nini !" he repeated, burying his big nose in the soft folds of her tie. Then he placed his wife on her feet again, drew a deep breath like a bellows, and stretched himself.

" How wet you are, Andrea !"

" From head to foot. Beastly weather ! Yesterday capital sport, but to-day, *perdio !* this rascally rain ! I'm soaked to the bone."

Leaning out of the landing window, he called in to the court-yard : " Take care of the dogs, Matteo. Rub them down with warm straw."

" And yourself, Andrea ?"

" I will go and change my clothes. But I am not cold. I

have walked so fast that I am quite warm. Is everything ready for me?"

"Everything."

"And dinner? I'm dying of hunger."

"Dinner is ready, Andrea."

"Macaroni, eh?"

"Macaroni patties."

"Hurrah!" he shouted, tossing his cap up to the ceiling. "Thou art a golden Nini."

And he took her once more in his arms, like a small bundle.

"You are drenching me," she murmured, without looking at all vexed.

"I'm a brute; right you are. Thy pretty white frock! what a lout I am!"

And he delicately shook out its folds. He took his handkerchief, and went down on his knees to dry her gown, while she said: "No, it was nothing, she would not let him tire himself."

"Let me; do, do let me, I am a brute .... I am a brute!" he persisted. When he had finished, he turned her round and round like a child.

"Now you're dry, Nini. What a sweet smell you have about you. Is it your lace tie or your skin? I'll go and dress. Go and see if the macaroni patties will be done in time."

She went away, but returned immediately to listen at his door, in case he should call her. She could hear him moving to and fro in his dressing-room, puffing and blowing and in the highest spirits. He was throwing his wet boots against the wall, tramping about like a horse, or halting to look at his clothes; singing the while to an air of his own composition:

"Where are the socks .... the socks .... the socks .... Here you are. Now I want a scarf to bind up my inexpressibles. Here's the scarf .... Now where's my necktie?"

Then there was silence.

" Have you found the necktie, Andrea ?   May I come in ? "
she asked shyly.

"Oh ! you are there !   And here is the necktie . . . . I'm
ready.   Call Cecchina to take away these wet things while we
are at dinner."

He opened the door and came out with a face red from much
rubbing.   He looked taller and broader in indoor dress.   His
curly leonine head, with its low forehead, blue eyes, and bushy
auburn moustache, was firmly set on a full, massive, and very
white throat.   Round it he wore a white silk tie and no collar.
His broad shoulders expanded under the dark blue cloth of his
jacket, his mighty chest swelled under the fine linen of his
shirt.   The whole figure, ponderous in its strength, was re-
deemed from awkwardness by a certain high-bred ease and by
the minute care of his person, visible in the cut of his hair
and the polish of his well-tended nails.

" H'm, Caterina, are we going to dine to-day ? "

" Dinner is on the table."

The dining-room was bright with lighted candles, spotless
linen, and shining silver.   The centre-piece of fruit—grapes,
apples, and pears—shone golden with autumn tints.   Through
the closed shutters the faintest patter of rain was perceptible.
The light fell upon two huge oaken cupboards, whose glass
doors revealed within various services of porcelain and crystal,
and on the panels of which were carved birds, fish, and fruit.
Two high-backed armchairs faced each other.   The whole
room was pervaded by a sense of peace and order.   The
macaroni pasty, copper-coloured within its paler crust, was
smoking on the table.   Andrea ate heartily and in silence; he
had helped himself three times.   Caterina, who had taken her
share with the appetite of a healthy young woman, watched
while he ate, with her chin in the air and a little smile on her
face.

" *Perdio !* how good this pie is !   Tell the cook, Caterina, to
repeat it as often as he likes."

"I will make a note of it in the household book. Will you have some more?"

"No, *basta.* Ring, please. Has it rained all day here?"

"Since last night."

"At Santa Maria, too. Would you believe it? I went as far as Mazzoni, to the Torone, our farm over there."

"Did you sleep there last night?"

"Yes; a good bed. Coarse but sweet-smelling sheets. But I was furious with the weather. Have some beef, Nini. There is no sport to be had now. Who has been here?"

"Pepe Guardini, one of the Nola tenants. He wants a reduction."

"I've given him three reductions. He is a drunkard and too ready with his knife. He must pay."

"He says he can't."

"He can't, he can't!" he roared; "then I'll turn him out."

She looked at him fixedly, but smiling. Andrea lowered his voice.

"I don't know why I lose my temper," he muttered. "I beg your pardon, Nini, but it annoys me when they come and bother you. What did you say to him?"

"That I would speak to you about it; that we should see. . . . . Have your own way. Give me some wine. By-the-by, Giovanni has been here; the vats are opened; he says the wine promises well."

"I will look in to-morrow. When that's over, in a week we'll leave for Naples. Are you impatient? No fowl! I assure you, it is excellent."

"Tell the truth, 'tis you who want more."

"I blush, but I say yes. So you pine for Naples?"

"And you?"

"I, too. Here there's no sport, and dull neighbours. We are expected there. By-the-by, send for Cecchina and tell her that in the pocket of my shooting-jacket there is a letter for you. I found it at the post-office at Caserta."

"Whose handwriting?" she queried, with a start.

"The writing of one who sends thee long letters in a scratchy hand, on transparent paper. Of one on whose seal is graven a death's-head, with the motto, 'Nihil'. Of one whose paper is so heavily scented with musk, that my pocket reeks intolerably of it. Here's a pear peeled for you, Nini. 'Tis thy lover who writes to thee."

"It's Lucia Altimare, is it not?"

"Yes" .... stretching himself with a sigh of satisfaction, as one who has dined well; "the Signorina Lucia Altimare, a skinny, ethereal creature, with pointed elbows, *poseuse par excellence.*"

"Andrea!"

"Do you mean to say that she is not a *poseuse?* Indulgent Nini! What is this under the table? Your foot, Nini! I hope I haven't crushed it. But your friend is repugnant to me, at least she was so the only time I ever saw her."

"I am so sorry, Andrea. I hope that when you see her again, you will alter your mind."

"If you're sorry, I hope I shall alter my mind. But why does she scent her letters so heavily? I recommend you this coffee, Caterina; it ought to be good."

"Lucia is sickly and unhappy. One is so sorry for her. Do you think five teaspoonfuls of coffee will be sufficient?"

"Put six.... I see;.... to please you I will pity her. But don't read her letter yet; for, to judge by the weight of it, it must be a very long one. Make the coffee first. If you don't, I shall say that you care for Lucia more than for me," murmured Andrea, with the vague tenderness induced by digestion.

"I will read it later."

He leant back in his chair, breathing slowly and contentedly, with his necktie unfastened and his hands resting on the table-cloth, while he watched her making the coffee—to which she gave all her attention, intent on listening for the hiss of the machine. A calm lithe figure that neither fidgeted nor moved too often, absorbed by her occupation, she bent her whole mind to it.

"It's ready," she said, after a time.

"Let's discuss it in the drawing-room," he replied. "As a reward I will let you read my rival's letter."

A bright wood fire burned on the drawing-room hearth. With another sigh of satisfaction, Andrea sank into a broad, low, leathern armchair that was drawn up before it.

"If it were not for the shooting, I should get too fat. Now don't begin to sew again, Caterina; sit down here and talk to me. Did you use to dance when you were at school?"

"The dancing-master came twice a week."

"Did you like dancing?"

"Pretty well; do you?"

"Now, when we are at Naples we can dance as much as we like. We've got three invitations already."

"Giovanna Casacalenda . . . . that's one."

"And my relations the Valgheras . . . . two."

"And Passalancias . . . . three."

"We'll dance, Nini. If I didn't dance I should get too fat. It will be capital exercise for me. Does your melancholy skeleton of a friend dance?"

"Lucia?"

"Yes."

"She didn't dance much. She liked the lancers and the mazurka, I remember. The waltz tried her strength too much."

"A woman who is always ill! who faints away in your arms at any moment! What a bore!"

"Oh, Andrea!"

"At least you are always well, Nini."

"Always."

"So much the better, come here and give me a kiss! Has the *Pungolo* arrived?"

"Here it is."

"Caterina, I am going to bury myself in the newspaper. Read your letter. I won't tease you any more."

But while he lost himself in the political diatribes that filled the *Pungolo*, Caterina, notwithstanding the permission granted to her, did not begin to read. She kept the letter in her hand, looking at it and inhaling its scent. It was charged with the violent, luscious perfume of ambergris. Then she glanced shyly at her husband; he was falling gradually asleep, his head sinking towards his shoulder. In five minutes the paper fell from his hands. Caterina picked it up, and gently replaced it on the table. She turned down the lamp, to make a twilight in the room. Then she crept back to her chair, and knelt to read her letter by the light of the fire. For a long time, the only sound within the quiet room was the calm, regular breathing of Andrea, accompanied by the faint rustle of foreign letter-paper as Caterina turned the pages. She read carefully and attentively, as if weighing every word. From time to time an expression of trouble passed across her firelit face. When she had finished reading she looked at her husband; he slept on, like a great child, beautiful and gentle in his strength, an almost infantile sweetness and tenderness on his countenance. He lay there calm and still in the assurance of their mutual love, his tired muscles relaxed and at ease in the peace of his honest soul. She bent her head again towards the flame, and once more read the letter from beginning to end, with the same minute attention. When she had read it through for the second time, Caterina slipped it into her pocket, and leaving her hand half hidden in its depths, rested her head on the back of her low chair. Time passed, the quarter struck, then the half-hour, and another quarter, at the clock in the tower of Centurano: by degrees the fire burned out on the hearth. Andrea awoke with a start.

"Caterina, wake up."

"I am not asleep, Andrea," she replied placidly, with wide-open eyes.

"It's late, Nini, very late; time for by-bye," said the Colossus, as in loving jest he gathered her up in his arms like a child.

II.

The circular drawing-room had been transformed into a
garden of camellias, on whose close, dense, dark-green background of foliage the flowers displayed their insolent waxen
beauty, white or red, perfumeless, icily voluptuous, their full
buds swelling as if to burst their green chalices. A luxuriant
vegetation covered the walls and the very roof, lending them a
silent enchantment. In the midst of the shrubbery a *Musa
paradisiaca* reared its lofty head, spreading out its vivid green
leaves like an umbrella. Round the *Musa* ran a rustic divan
roughly wrought in wood. Here and there were low rustic
stools. Massive branches of camellia nearly hid the two doors
leading to this room. A faint diffuse light shone through its
opaque rose-coloured shades.

Three or four times during the evening, in the intervals of
the dances, this room had filled with guests. Ladies, young
and old, uttered little cries of delight in the rustic effect, in the
coolness and the repose of it, as compared with the hard white
glare of the ball-room, its oppressive atmosphere and noisy
orchestra. They assumed attitudes of graceful languor. The
men looked round with an air of suppressed satisfaction, as if
they too were far from insensible to the beauties of Nature. A
few timidly culled buds were offered as gifts . . . . A young
lady in pale yellow, with a shower of lilies of the valley in her
dark hair, recited some verses in a low murmur. Quiet women
fanned themselves gently with noiseless, winged fans of soft
grey feathers; but hardly had the triumphant appeal of
the first notes of a waltz or the plaintive melting strains of the
mazurka reached their retreat, when one and all flung themselves into the whirl of the ball and every couple vanished.
Once more the shrubbery was silent and deserted, the red
camellias again opened their lips. What were they waiting for?

Giovanna Casacalenda, the daughter of the house, entered
the shrubbery on the arm of a young man. Taller than her

partner, she seemed to look down upon him from the height
of her regal beauty. She was draped in the clinging folds of a
long dress of ivory crape, that ended in a soft floating train.
Wondrous to behold was the low bodice of crimson satin,
fitting without a crease; her arms were bare to the shoulder.
One row of pearls round the firm white throat. A wreath
of damask roses, worn low on the forehead, crowned her dark
hair, drawn up close from the nape of her neck. This audaciously simple costume was worn with the repose of conscious
beauty, proof against any weakness on its own account. A
smile just parted her curved lips while she listened to her
companion, a meagre undersized youth, with a bilious complexion; there were lines about his eyes and the hair was
scanty on the temples. He was correct, refined, and
finnikin.

"But, Giovanna, I have your promise," he protested, "*thy*
promise."

"You need not 'thou' and 'thee' me," she observed.

"Forgive . . . . I beg your pardon, I am always betraying
my feelings," he murmured; "it's very clear that you are
casting me off, Giovanna . . . ."

"If it is so clear, why trouble to talk about it?"

"Why do I . . . .? That you may contradict me. What
have I done to thee?"

"Nothing; treat me to *you*, if you please. Now go on, I
am in a hurry."

"Then it has been a dream?"

"Dream, caprice, folly; call it what you will. You must
make up your mind to the fact that we cannot marry. You
have an income of eight thousand lire; I shall have six
thousand. What can one do with fourteen thousand lire a
year?"

Smiling, she said these things, without changing her
easy attitude; the arm that plied the fan was carefully
rounded, and she looked at him with a little air of
superiority.

D

"But if my uncle dies . . . ." whined her victim.

"Your uncle is not going to die just yet. I have observed him carefully; he's solid."

"You are positively malevolent, Giovanna . . . . remember . . . ."

"What would you have me remember? Do try to be sensible. Let us go back."

They went away, and those superb camellias that Giovanna so closely resembled told no tales, neither did they murmur among themselves.

"Very fine indeed!" said Andrea Lieti, admiring the general effect, while the divan creaked under his weight. "But give me Centurano."

"Real country must always surpass in beauty its counterfeit presentment," mumbled timid Galimberti, Professor of History. "But these Casacalendas have a fine, luxurious taste."

"Bah! respected Professor, they want to marry their daughter, and they are sure to succeed."

"Do you really think . . . .?"

"I don't blame them. So magnificent a creature is not meant to be kept at home. Was she so beautiful when she was at school?"

"Beautiful . . . . dangerously beautiful, even at school . . . . I remember . . . ." passing his hand across his forehead, as if he were talking to himself.

Andrea Lieti opened his big blue eyes in amazement. The Professor remained standing in an awkward attitude, stooping slightly, and ill at ease in his easy attire. His trousers were too long, and bagged at the knees. The collar of his old-fashioned dress-coat was too high. Instead of the regulation shirt, shining like a wall of marble, he wore an embroidered one, with large Roman mosaic studs, a view of the Colosseum, the Column of Trajan, the Piazza di San Pietro. There he stood, with hanging arms, with his hideous, pensive head. The brow appeared to have grown higher and yellower. His eyes had the old oblique look, at once absent and embarrassed.

"These balls must bore you fearfully, Professor," cried Andrea, as he rose and walked to and fro, conspicuous for his fine proportions and well-bred ease.

"Well . . . . rather . . . . I feel somewhat isolated in a crowd like this," said Galimberti, confusedly.

"And yet you don't dislike it?"

"A . . . . Two or three of my pupils are so good as to invite me . . . . I go out for recreation . . . . I read too hard."

Again that weary gesture, as if to ease his brow of its weight of thought, and the wandering glance seeming to seek something that was lost.

"You must come to us, too, Professor," said Andrea, full of compassion for the wretched little dwarf. "Caterina often speaks of you."

"She was a good creature . . . . such a good creature. So good and gentle and sensible. Yours was an excellent choice."

"I believe you," said Andrea, laughing heartily. "Is it true that you always reproached her with a lack of imagination?"

"Did she tell you that too? Yes—sometimes . . . . a certain dryness . . . ."

"Well, Caterina isn't troubled with sentimental vagaries. But I like her best as she is. Have you seen her to-night? She's lovely. If she were not my wife, I should be dancing with her."

"She is . . . . or was with her friend . . . ."

"With Lucia Altimare, to be sure."

"With the Signorina Altimare," repeated the Professor, gulping down something with difficulty.

"There's another of your pupils! She must have plagued you, no end, with her compositions, to judge from the tiresome fantastic letters she writes to my wife."

"The Signorina Altimare wrote divinely," said the Professor, dryly.

"Eh! maybe," muttered Andrea, choosing a cigarette. "Have one? No? I assure you they are not bad. I was saying"—he resumed his seat on the couch, and blew the smoke upwards—"that she must have bored you to tears."

"The Signorina Altimare is a suffering, interesting being. She is so very unhappy," persisted the Professor, with his cravat all awry, in the heat of his defence.

Andrea gazed at him with curiosity; then a faint smile parted his lips.

"She goes to balls, however," he replied, quietly enjoying the study of the Professor.

"She does. She is obliged to, and it changes the current of her thoughts. You see she never dances."

"Bah! because nobody insists on her doing so. What do you bet that, if I go and ask her, she won't dance the waltz with me?"

"Nothing would induce her to dance, she is subject to palpitations. It might make her faint."

"*Che!* If I give her a turn, you'll see how she'll trot! No woman has ever fainted in my arms . . . ." He stopped short from sheer pity. Galimberti, who had turned from yellow to red, and stood nervously clutching at his hat, looked at Andrea with so marked an expression of pain and anger, that he felt ashamed of tormenting him.

"But she is too thin, too angular; we'll leave her alone. Or you try it, Professor; you dance with her." With a friendly gesture he took him by the arm, to lead him away.

"I don't dance," mumbled Galimberti, and his big head sank on his breast. "I don't know how to dance."

Enter once more Giovanna Casacalenda, leaning this time with a certain *abandon* on the arm of a cavalry officer. Her arm nestled against his coat, her face was raised to his. He, strutting like a peacock in his new uniform, was smiling through his blonde moustache; an ornamental soldier, who had left his sword in the ante-room.

"Well, Giovanna, has the old boy made up his mind?"

"There is something brewing, but nothing settled," she replied, wearily. "Indeed, it's a sorry business."

"All's well that ends well. Courage, Giovanna; you are enchanting to-night."

"Am I?" she murmured, looking in his face.

"More than ever . . . . when I think that old . . . ."

"Don't think about it, Roberto . . . . It must be," she added seriously.

"I know that it must be; as if I hadn't advised it! Of course your father would not give you to me: it's no good thinking of it. Besides, he is a very presentable old fellow."

"Oh! presentable . . . ."

"Well, with the collar of his order under his coat, his bald head, and his white whiskers, he looks dignified enough for a husband, and . . . ."

"It's all so far off, Roberto," she said, looking at him languidly but fixedly, with parted lips and sad eyes.

"Well, get it over; it rests with you . . . ."

"You will never forget me, Roberto, my own Roberto?"

"Forget you, Giovanna, transcendent, fascinating as you are? Do you realise the extent of my sacrifice? I leave you to Gabrielli. Do you realise what I lose?"

"You do not lose all," murmured Giovanna, with a catch in her breath. He bent down and imprinted a long kiss on her wrist. Her eyelids drooped, but she did not withdraw it; she was ready to fall into his arms, notwithstanding the nearness of the ball-room. The young officer, whose prudence was more than equal to his love, raised his head.

"It would be rash to loiter here," he said; "the old boy might get jealous."

"*Dio mio*, what a bore! *Basta*, for your sake."

"Why do you not sing to-night?"

"Mamma won't let me . . . ." And they passed on.

The two friends were approaching the rustic seat: after carefully arranging their trains, they sat down together. Lucia Altimare sank as if from sheer fatigue. Her dress was of strange pale sea-green, almost neutral in tint ; the skirt hung in plain ample folds, like a peplum. The bodice closely defined her small waist; her arms and shoulders were swathed in a pale veil, like a cloud in colour and texture. Some of her dark tresses were loosened on her shoulders, and, half buried in their waves, was a wreath of natural white flowers, fresh, but just beginning to fade. A bunch of the same flowers was dying in the folds of tulle that covered her bosom. The general effect was that of the fragile body of an Undine, surmounted by the head of a Sappho.

Next to her sat Caterina Lieti, radiantly serene and fresh, in her pretty pink ball-dress, wearing round her throat a dazzling *rivière* of diamonds, and in her hair a diamond aigrette that trembled as she leant over her friend, talking to her the while with animation. Lucia appeared to be lost in thought, or in the absence of it. She said, in her dragging tones, as if her very words weighed too heavily for her, "I knew I should meet you here. Besides, my father is so very youngish—it amuses him, he likes dancing. Why did you not answer my last letter?"

"I was on the eve of returning to Naples . . . . and so you see . . . . "

"I hope," said the other, with a somewhat contemptuous pout, "that you do not permit your husband to read my letters."

Caterina, blushing, denied the impeachment.

"He is a good young man," admitted Lucia, in an indulgent tone. "I think your husband suits you. You are pretty to-night: too many diamonds, though."

"They were a present from Andrea," proudly.

"I hate jewels ; I shall never wear them."

"If you were to marry, Lucia . . . ."

"I marry? You know what I wrote you."

"But listen ; there is that Galimberti, who follows you everywhere; who admires you from a distance; who loves you without daring to tell his love. I am sorry for him."

" Alas! 'tis no fault of mine, Caterina, *sai.*"

"You know; perhaps he is poor; perhaps his feelings are hurt in all these rich houses, where he follows you. You are good. Spare him. He looks so unhappy."

"What can I do? He is, like myself, a victim of fate, of fatality."

" Of what fatality?"

" He is ill-starred, he deserves to be wealthy and handsome, and that is just what he is not. I ought to have come into the world either as an ignorant peasant or as queen of a people to whose happiness I could have ministered. We console ourselves by a correspondence which gives vent to our souls."

" But he will fall over head and ears in love."

" I cannot love any one : it is not given to me to love ;" and Lucia fell into a rigid, all but statuesque attitude, like a Greek heroine caught in the act of posing. Caterina neither asked her why nor wherefore. In Lucia's presence she was under the spell that fantastic divagations sometimes exercise over calm reasonable beings.

" Caterina, I have begun to visit the poor in their homes. It is an interesting humanitarian occupation. It is the source of the sweetest emotion. Will you come with me? "

" I will ask Andrea."

" Must you needs ask his permission for everything? Have you bartered your liberty so far as that? "

" *Sai*, a wife!"

" Tell me, Caterina, what is the happiness, the charm of married life? "

" I can't explain it."

" Tell me why is marriage the death of love."

" I don't know, Lucia."

" Then marriage is to be the eternal mystery of life? "

" Who tells you these things, Lucia? "

" My own heart, Caterina," replied the other, rising.

Then, assuming a solemn tone and raising her hand to swing it swordwise through the air—" One thing only exists for certain."

" What ? "

" Passion, it's the only reality."

" The favoured mortal is always a young man," remarked the Commendatore Gabrielli, his mouth twitching with a nervous tic to which he was subject.

" But that is not my ideal," replied the enchanting voice of Giovanna . . . . ". I have always felt a tacit contempt for those idlers, deficient alike in character and talent, who waste their youth and their fortune on gambling and horses and other less worthy pursuits . . . ." She pretended to blush behind her fan.

" Well, Signora Giovanna, you are perhaps right. But a reformed rake makes a good husband."

" I do not think so, Commendatore ; with all due deference, I am not of your opinion. Think of Angela Toraldo's husband ; what a pearl ! I hear that if she weeps or complains he boxes her ears. A horror ! These young husbands are brutes. Look at Andrea Lieti ! how roughly he must treat that poor little Caterina ! . . . . While with a man of mature age . . . ."

" Has this often occurred to you, Signora Giovanna ? "

" Always . . . . A grave man who takes life seriously ; who lives up to a political idea . . . ."

" You would know how to grace a political salon," he murmured, gazing at her.

She shut her fan and shrugged her beautiful shoulders, as if they were about to take leave of their crimson cuirasse. The Commendatore's catlike eyes blazed behind his gold spectacles. Giovanna again plied her fan ; it fluttered caressingly, humbly.

" Oh ! I am not worthy such honour . . . . He would shine ; and I should modestly reflect his light. We women love to be the secret inspirers of great men. Could you read our hearts . . . ."

And she leant on his arm, against his shoulder, smiling perpetually, smiling to the verge of weariness, while the bald head of the Commendatore shone with a crimson glow.

" What madness," whispered Lucia Altimare, sinking on the divan. " Perfect madness, for which you are responsible. I ought not to have waltzed . . . ."

" Pray forgive me," said Andrea, apparently embarrassed, but really bored. He was standing before her in a deferential attitude.

" It is your fault," she said, looking up at him through her lashes. " You are strong and robust, and an odd fancy came into your head. I ought to have refused . . . . At first it was all right, a delicious waltz . . . . You bore me along like a feather, then my head began to whirl . . . . The room swam round, the lights danced in my brain . . . . I lost my breath . . . ."

" May I get you something to drink ? "

" No," she answered curtly at his interruption of her eloquence.

" A glass of punch ? Punch is a capital remedy," he continued hurriedly ; " it warms, and it's the best possible restorative. I am going to have some. Pray drink something, unless you mean to overwhelm me with remorse. All our ills come from the stomach. Shall I call Caterina to insist on your taking it ? "

" Caterina did not see us come in here ? "

" I think not, she was dancing with my brother-in-law, Federigo Passalancia. Caterina is looking her loveliest to-night, isn't she ? "

But Lucia Altimare made no answer ; she turned extremely pale, breathed heavily, and then slipped off the divan on to the floor, in a dead faint.

Andrea swore inwardly, with more energy than politeness,

against all women who waltz, and at the folly of men who waltz with them.

III.

Every morning, Lucia Altimare, draped in the folds of a red, yellow, and blue striped dressing-gown, fastened round her waist and kilted up on one side with gold cord, her sleeves tucked up over bare wrists, an immense white pocket-handkerchief in her hand as a duster, proceeded, after dismissing her maid, to dust her little apartment, a bedroom and a small sitting-room, within whose walls her father allowed her complete liberty. The dainty office, accomplished methodically and always at the same hour, after she had dressed and prayed, was a source of infinite delight to her. It appeared to her that the act of bending her great pride and her little strength to manual labour, was both pious and meritorious. When the moment for dusting the furniture came round, she would tell her maid, with a sense of condescension :

"You may go, Giulietta, I will do it myself."

"But, Signorina . . . ."

"No, no, let me do it myself."

And she felt that she was kind and humane to Giulietta, sparing her the trouble of dusting, and at the same time proving that she did not disdain to share her humble labour.

"In God's sight we are all equal. If my strength permitted, I would make my own bed, but I am so delicate ! If I stoop too much, I get palpitations," she thought, as she tied on her black apron and tucked up the train of her Turkish dressing-gown.

But the greatest pleasure, the pleasure that thrilled her every nerve, to which she owed her most exquisite sensations, was derived from dawdling over each separate object that had become part of her existence. A charm, wherewith to recall the past, to measure the future, to pass from one dream to another, whereon to weave a fantastic web.

The cold frigid aspect of Lucia's bedroom reminded her of her old dream of becoming a nun, of falling sick of mysticism, of dying in the ecstasy of the Cross. The room was uncarpeted, and the bare floor, with its red tiles, had an icy polish. The bed, whose wrought-iron supports Lucia rubbed so indefatigably, had no curtains. Under its plain cover, with its single, meagre little pillow, it was the typical bed of ascetic maidenhood. Next to the bed, in a frame draped in black crape, hung a Byzantine Madonna and Child, painted on a background of gilded wood. She wore an indigo dress, a red mantle, and her eyes were strangely dilated, while one hand clutched the Infant Jesus : a picture expressive of the first stammerings of the alphabet of art. Lucia always kissed it before she dusted it ; the lugubrious drapery made her dream of the mother she had hardly known, and from whom the Madonna came to her. Her lips would seek the traces of maternal kisses on the narrow, diaphanous, waxen-hued hand of the Virgin.

By the side of the bed, under the Madonna, stood a wooden prie-dieu of mediæval workmanship, which Lucia had bought of a second-hand dealer. The family arms were effaced from its wooden escutcheon. Lucia, instead of replacing them by the *alte onde in tempesta,* the polar star and the azure field of Casa Altimare, had had it graven with a death's-head and the motto "Nihil," which she had adopted for her own seal. She had to kneel down on its red velvet cushion to polish it, and then mechanically she would say another prayer. She could hardly tear herself away from it. When she did so, it was to pass the handkerchief over the tiny chest of drawers that she had taken with her to school. That brought back some of her past life to her, the books hidden in the folds of the linen, the little images from Lourdes mixed up with the ribbons, the sweets that she did not eat. On the top of this chest of drawers were a red silk pincushion, covered with finest lace—which had been given to her by Ginevra Avigliana, the most patient needlewoman of them all—and

Thomas à Kempis's "Imitation," its margin finely annotated in ink red as blood. When she passed the handkerchief over the book, she read a few words in it.

Her mind would run in another channel when she found herself in front of the large mirror in her wardrobe, where she could see herself from head to foot. She looked at herself, perceiving that her gown wrinkled about the bodice, and reflecting that she must have become much thinner lately. She joined her fingers round her narrow waist, remarking inwardly that had she chosen she might have made it as slender as a reed . . . . Then she posed in profile, with her train pushed on one side, and her head a little inclined towards the right shoulder. She had once seen the fantastic portrait of a thin unknown woman in white, in this attitude . . . . Lucia liked to imagine that the unknown lady had suffered much, then died; and that afterwards the unknown atom had joined the Great Unknown. The same fancies followed her to the oval mirror on her dressing-table. A thin white covering hung over it from the night before, put there because it is unlucky to look into an uncovered mirror the last thing at night. She threw the large white handkerchief, now no longer white, into a corner and supplied herself with another, with which she slowly rubbed the glass. She was tired, and sat gazing at her image—her forehead, her eyes, and her lips—intently, as if seeking to discover something in them. Every now and then she took up a bottle of musk from the table and sniffed it, looking at herself to mark the intense pallor and the tears induced by the pungent odour. In the drawer there was a little box of rouge and a hare's foot to lay it on with; but she did not use it. One morning she had slightly tinted one cheek, it had disgusted her. She preferred her pallor, the warm pallor of ivory, that "white heat of passion," as a rapturous poet, of unrecognised merit, had described it. A butterfly was pinned to the frame of the looking-glass. His wings were expanded, for he was a cotillon butterfly of blue and silver gauze, a memento of the first ball her father had taken

her to last year. Every morning a puff of her breath caused
his wings to flutter, while his little body stuck fast to the
mirror. That motionless, artificial butterfly reminded her of
certain artificial lives, full of noble aspirations, but lacking the
energy, the power to rise. Then she wondered if she were very
interesting or very ugly, when she looked sad ; and she pos-
tured before the mirror in her most melancholy manner,
calculating the effect of the white brow, half hidden beneath
the wealth of wavy hair, the depth of sadness in her eyes, the
dark colouring of the underlid which accentuated their expression, the straight line of the profile, the angle drawn by the
bitter smile that sharpened the curves of her lips. A sigh of
satisfaction escaped her. In her sad mood, she might inspire
interest, if not love. Love she did not want. What would
be the good of it ? The capacity for loving was denied her.

Then came the turn of the bottles on the toilet-table.
They contained, for the most part, those fantastic remedies
which a quasi-romantic science has voted sovereign against
the most modern of maladies, mock nevrose. In one bottle,
chloral for insomnia, chloral to produce a sleep full of exquisite
and painful hallucinations, the very disease of fantasy. In
another, digitalis, wherewith to calm palpitations of the heart.
In another, a beautiful one, enamelled, with a golden stopper,
"English" salts wherewith to recall the fainting spirit. And
at last, in one, a white limpid fluid—morphine. "For sleep
. . . . sleep," murmured Lucia, while she reviewed her little
pharmacy.

After the toilet-table, she passed her handkerchief over the
second wardrobe, the one containing her linen, and dusted the
three chairs. Then having finished, she cast a look round, to
assure herself that her cell, as she called it, had assumed the
cold, spotless appearance she desired to give it. Her fantasy ˙
was assuaged; she addressed herself aloud to her room:
"Peace, peace, sleep on, inert and inanimate, until to-night,
when my tortured spirit will return to fill thy space with
anguish."

She passed into the sitting-room, her favourite resort, the room where her life was passed. The dark rosewood cabinet, containing five wide deep drawers, was her first stage. Her fancy transformed it into a bier. She delicately dusted the oxidised silver inkstand, representing a tiny boat, sinking in a lake of ink. Then the handkerchief was passed over the portrait frames with their hermetically sealed doors, so that no one might ever steal a glimpse of the portraits hidden within. In reality, they were empty, but the white cardboard backs, the void only known to herself, suggested an unknown lover, a mystic knight, that fair-haired Knight of the Holy Grail whom Elsa had not known how to love; whom *she* would have known how to keep by her side. Gently she brushed the dust off a small Egyptian idol with a tiny necklace of blue fragments : it was an upright copy of a mummy of the Cheops dynasty. It served as a talisman, for these Egyptian idols avert the evil of one's destiny. Lucia touched the Bible, bound in black morocco, on whose fly-page she had inscribed certain memorable dates in her existence, with mysterious signs to denote the events to which they referred. With reverence she took up the diamond edition of Leopardi, on whose crimson binding was inscribed "Lucia," in letters of silver. She read in both books, every day, kissing the Bible and Leopardi with equal fervour. The ivory penholder, with its gold pen ; the sandal-wood paper-knife, on which was inscribed the Spanish word *Nada ;* the agate seal, that bore the same motto as the prie-dieu ; the letter-weight, upon which stood a porcelain child in its shift ; the half-mourning penwiper of black cloth, embroidered in white ; all the fantastic playthings she had accumulated on her writing-table, were objects of equal interest to her. She always spent half an hour at the writing-table, with fingers that dallied over their pastime, shoulders bent in contemplation, and an imagination that sped on wings to unknown heights.

Then, after the writing-table, came a photograph in a red frame, suspended against the wall, a portrait of Caterina.

Underneath it hung a *bénitier* containing fresh flowers, which were changed every morning. Caterina contemplated her friend with kind serene eyes; the portrait had her own air of composure. Every morning, in passing the linen over the glass, Lucia greeted Caterina: "Blessed art thou, that dreamest not, blessed . . . . that will never dream." Next came a small group in terra-cotta of Mephistopheles and Margaret. The guilty, enamoured girl was kneeling in a convulsed attitude, with rigid limbs. Her hands clasped the prayer-book that she could not open, her bosom heaved, her throat had sunk into her crouching shoulders, her face was contorted, her lips convulsed with the cry of horror that appeared to escape them. Mephistopheles, tall, meagre, diabolic, with a subtle, jeering smile, his hand in the act of making magnetic passes over her head, stood behind her; a great, splendid, crushing Mephistopheles. Whenever she looked at Margaret she felt herself blush with desire; whenever she looked at Mephistopheles, Lucia paled with fear: with vague indefinite desire of sin ; with vague fear of punishment ; a mysterious struggle that took place in the very depths of her being. It was Lucia's hand that had carved in crooked, shaky characters, on the wooden pedestal, *Et ne nos inducas in tentationem.* When she came to the low table on which the albums stood, she sat down, for her fatigue grew upon her. She turned their leaves ; there were a few portraits—girl friends, relations, three or four young men. Among the latter, by way of eccentricity, was a faded photograph of Petröfi Sandor, the Hungarian poet who fell in love with a dead maiden. Lucia never saw that portrait but through a haze of tears, when she pondered over a love so sad, so strange, and so funereal. Then she opened her book of "Confessions." Its pages were scribbled over by Lucia herself, by the lady who taught her German, by the Professor of History, by Caterina, Giovanna Casacalenda, and others. There were in response to the wildest questions, the most irrelevant, silly, or eccentric answers. Giovanna's was stupid, Lucia's mad and fantastic,

Caterina's honest and collected, the Professor's insane, the German teacher's sentimental, Alberto Sanna's fluctuating and uncertain. Lucia lingered here and there to read one of them. Then she put that album aside and opened another, her favourite, the dearest, the handsomest, the best beloved; a faded rose was gummed on the first page, underneath it was a line from Byron. On the next, a little wreath of violets; in their centre, a date and a line of notes of interrogation; farther on, the shadowy profile of a woman, barely sketched in, signed "Clara." And pell-mell, dried flowers, verses, thoughts, landscapes, sketches, an American postage-stamp, a scarabæus crushed into the paper, two words written with gold ink.

She smiled, revelling in melancholy, as she turned these pages. Then she left the albums, and stroked the head of a bronze lizard that lay beside them on the table. She had a great fondness for lizards, snakes, and toads, thinking them beautiful and unfortunate.

The grand piano, littered with music, was a long business. When she passed the duster over the shining wood, she half closed her eyelids, as if she felt the caressing contact of satin; then she passed it over the keys, drawing from them a sort of formless, discordant music, in whose endless variations she revelled. Lucia neither played well, nor much; but when she met with a philharmonic friend, she would instal her at the piano, and herself in a Viennese rocking-chair, where she would close her eyes, beat time with her head and listen. Voiceless and spell-bound, she was one of the best and most ecstatic of listeners. Most of the music lying on the table was German; she specially affected the sacred harmonies of Bach and Haydn. But *Aïda* was always open on the reading-desk. Then there was the embroidery-frame, a stole for the church of the Madonna, her Madonna of the Bleeding Heart. Next to it stood a microscopic work-table, on which lay the beginning of a useless, spidery fabric. The chairs, the *pouffs*, the little armchairs, were all in different styles and colours, for she loathed uniformity. Her first prize for literature, a gold medal set in white satin, hung on the wall; underneath it was her first childish essay in writing. A bookshelf contained a few worn school-books, some novels, and the Lives of the Saints. And last of all came a large tea-rose with red marks, like blood-stains, on its petals, gummed into a velvet frame, the *Rosa mystica.* When she had finished, Lucia cast aside her duster, washed her hands, swallowed a few drops of syrup diluted with water to clear her throat of dust, returned to the sitting-room, threw herself down on her sofa, and let her fancies have free play.

IV.

Caterina Lieti entered, looking tiny in her furs; with her pink face peeping from under her fur cap.

"Make haste, dear; it's late."

"No, dear; it's no good going to my poor people before four; it's hardly two o'clock."

"We are going elsewhere."

"Where?"

"Somewhere where we shall amuse ourselves."

"I'm not going, I don't want to amuse myself; I am more inclined to cry."

"Why?"

"I don't know . . . . I feel miserable."

"Oh! poor, poor thing. Now listen to me, you'd better come with me and try to amuse yourself. You will injure your health by always staying in this dark room, in this perfumed atmosphere."

"My health is gone, Caterina," said the other in a comfortless tone; "every day I get thinner."

"Because you do not eat, dear; you ought to eat; Andrea says so too."

"What does Andrea say," said Lucia, in a tone of indifference, which annoyed Caterina.

"That you should eat nutritious food, drink plenty of wine and eat underdone meat."

"I am not a cannibal. That kind of diet does very well for muscular organisms, but not for fragile nerve-tissues like mine."

"But Andrea says that nerves are cured by beefsteaks."

"It's no good trying; I couldn't digest them; I can't digest anything now."

"Well, do dress, and come with me. The cold is quite reviving."

"Where to?"

"I won't tell you. Trust me!"

"I will trust you . . . . I am tempted by the unknown. I will drag this weary existence about wheresoever you please. Will you wait for me?"

She returned in half an hour, dressed in a short black dress, softened by lace accessories. A black hat, with a broad velvet brim, shaded her brow and eyes.

"Shall we walk?" asked Caterina.

"We will walk; if I get tired we can call a cab."

They walked, entering the Toledo from Montesanto. The tramontana was blowing hard, but the sun flooded the streets with light. Men, with red noses and hands in their pockets, were walking quickly. Behind their short black veils the ladies' eyes were full of tears and their lips were chapped by the wind. Caterina drew her furs closer to her.

"Are you cold, Lucia?"

"Strange to say, I am not cold."

People turned to gaze at the two attractive-looking women, one small and rosy, with clear eyes and an expression of perfect composure, attired like a dainty Russian; the other, tall and slight, with marvellous eyes set in a waxen pallor.

A gentleman who passed them in a hired carriage, bowed profoundly to both.

"Galimberti . . . ." murmured Lucia, in a weary voice.

"Where can he be going at this hour?"

"I don't know . . . . to his lesson . . . . I suppose."

"Do you know what Cherubina Friscia told me, a few days ago?"

"Have you seen her again?"

"Yes, I went there, because I heard that the Directress was ill. Friscia told me that they were very dissatisfied with Galimberti. He is always late for his lesson now; he either leaves before the hour is up, or misses it altogether."

"Does he . . . . ?" indifferently.

"Besides, he is not so good a teacher as he used to be. He takes no interest in his class, is careless in correcting the compositions, and has become prolix and hazy as an exponent . . . . In short, a mere ruin."

"Poor Galimberti ! . . . . I told you that he was an unlucky creature. He'll end badly."

"Forgive me if I ask you . . . . not from curiosity, but for friendship's sake . . . . does he still write to you?"

"Yes, every day; he writes me all his troubles."

"And you to him?"

"I write him a long letter, every day."

"And is it true that he comes to your house every day, to give you a lesson in history?"

"Yes, every day."

"And does he stay long?"

"Yes, naturally. We don't talk only of history, but of sentiment . . . . of the human affections . . . . of religion . . . ."

"Of love?"

"Of love too."

"Forgive me for importuning you. Galimberti is very much in love. Perhaps it is for the sake of going to you that he gets there so late; perhaps when he misses his lessons there altogether, it is because he stays so long with you. You who are so good, think what it means for him."

"It's nothing to do with me; if it is his destiny, it is fatal."

"But does your father approve of these long interviews?"

"My father! He doesn't care a pin for me, he is a heartless man."

"Don't say that, Lucia."

"A heartless man! If my health is bad, he doesn't care. He laughs at my piety . . . . Do you know how he describes me, when he speaks of me at all? 'That interesting *poseuse*, my daughter.' You can't get over that; it sums up my father." Caterina made no reply. "That Galimberti will end by becoming a nuisance. Were he not so unhappy, I would send him about his business."

"*Sai*, Lucia, a girl ought not to receive young men alone . . . . it is not nice . . . . it is playing with fire."

"*Nè fiamma d'esto incendio non m'assale*," she quoted.

They had arrived at the Café de l'Europe, where the wind was blowing furiously. Caterina, turning to protect herself against it, saw the cab in which Galimberti sat with the hood drawn up to hide him, following them step by step.

"*Dio mio!* now he is following us . . . . Galimberti . . . . What will people think? . . . . Lucia, what shall we do?"

"Nothing, dear. I can't prevent it; it is magnetism, you see."

"Now he is missing his lesson for the sake of following us."

"It is no good struggling against fate, Caterina."

Caterina was silent, for she knew not what to say.

It was three o'clock when they entered the Samazzaro Theatre, all lit up by gas, as if for an evening entertainment. Nearly all the boxes were occupied, and a hum of suppressed chitchat arose towards the gilded ceiling. From time to time there was a peal of irrepressible laughter. People who, in groups of threes and fours, invaded the parterre were dazed by the artificial light. The gas was gruesome after the brilliant light of the streets. The ladies were all in dark morning costumes; most of them wore large hats, some were wrapped in furs. There was the click of cups in one box where the Duchess of Castrogiovanni and the Countess Filomarina were drinking tea, to warm themselves. Little Countess Vanderhoot hid her snub nose in her muff, trying to warm it by blowing as hard as she could. Smart Neapolitans, with their fur coats thrown back to show the gardenia in their button-hole, with dark gloves and light cravats, moved about the parterre and the stalls and began to pay a few visits in the boxes.

"What is going on here?" asked Lucia, as she took her seat in Box 1, first tier.

"You'll see, you'll see."

"But what is that boarding for, which enlarges the stage, and entirely covers the place for the orchestra?"

"There's a fencing tournament to-day."

"Ah!" exclaimed Lucia, without much show of interest.

"Andrea is to have three assaults."

"Ah!" repeated the other, in the same tone.

The *maître d'armes* seated himself at the end of the stage, next to a table, laden with foils and jackets. Every one in the parterre immediately resumed his seat, in profound silence. The theatre was crowded.

The *maître d'armes* was a Count Alberti, tall, powerfully built, bald, with bushy grey whiskers and serious mien. He was dressed in black, and wore his overcoat buttoned to the chin. His hand was resting on a foil.

"Look! what a fine type," said Lucia; "a fine imposing figure."

The first couple advanced to the front of the stage. They were the fencing-master, Giovanelli, and a Baron Mattei. The latter was tall and finely proportioned. His beard was trimmed to a short point, his cropped hair formed another point in the middle of his forehead; he wore a tight-fitting costume of maroon cloth, with a black scarf. He at once captured the ladies' favour; there was a slight stir in the boxes.

"A Huguenot cavalier, that's what he looks like," murmured Lucia, who was becoming excited.

The fencers, after saluting the ladies and the general company, bowed to each other. Then the match began promptly and brilliantly. The fencing-master was short and stout, but uncommonly agile; the Baron, slight, cool, and admirable for ease and precision. They did not open their lips. After each thrust, Mattei fell into a sculpturesque attitude, which thrilled the company with admiration. He was touched twice. He touched his adversary four times. Then they shook hands, and laid down their foils. A burst of applause rang throughout the house.

" Do you like it ? " whispered Caterina to Lucia.

" Oh, so much ! " she answered, quite absorbed by the pleasure of it.

" There is Giovanna Casacalenda."

" Where ?

" On the second tier, No. 3."

" Ah ! of course. Behind her is the Commendatore Gabrielli. Poor Giovanna."

" The marriage is officially announced. But she does not look unhappy."

" She dissembles."

The second couple—Lieti, amateur, and Galeota, professional—appeared and placed themselves in position. Andrea was dressed in black cloth, with a yellow scarf and shoes, and chamois-leather gloves. His athletic figure showed to its utmost advantage in perfect vigour and harmony of form and line. He smiled up at the box, a second. Caterina had shrunk back a little out of sight, with eyes all but overflowing.

" Your husband is handsome to-day," said Lucia, gravely. " He looks like a gladiator."

Caterina nodded her thanks. Galeota, dark, slight and meagre, attacked slowly.

Andrea defended himself phlegmatically ; motionless they gazed into each other's eyes ; now and again a cunning thrust, cunningly parried. The audience was absorbed in profound attention.

" *Su, su,* on, on," Lucia cried, under her breath, trembling in her eagerness, and crushing her cambric handkerchief with nervous fingers.

The assault went on as calmly and scientifically as a game of chess, ending in two or three master-thrusts, miraculously parried. The two fencers, as they shook hands, smiled at each other. They were worthy antagonists. The applause which ·followed was wrung from the audience by the perfection of their method.

"Applaud your husband! Are you not proud of him?"

"Yes," replied Caterina, blushing.

A visitor entered the box, it was Alberto Sanna, a cousin of Lucia's.

"Good-morning, Signora Lieti. What a triumph for your lord and master!"

Caterina bowed and smiled. Lucia held out two fingers to her cousin, who kept them in his. He was a rather stunted little creature, slightly bent in his tight overcoat; his temples were hollow, his cheekbones high, and his moustache thin and scanty; yet he had the air of a gentleman. His appearance was sickly and his smile uncertain. He spoke slowly, hissing out his syllables as if his breath were short. He informed the ladies that cold was bad for him; that he could not get warm, even in his fur coat; that he had only looked in, just by a mere accident, to avoid the cold outside. He was fortunate in having met them. He entreated them, for charity's sweet 'sake, not to send him away. He added:

"I met your Professor of History, Lucia. He was walking up and down, smoking. Why don't he come in?"

"I don't know. Probably because he doesn't care to see the fencing."

"Or because he hasn't the money to pay for a ticket," persisted Sanna, with the triumphant malevolence of morbid natures.

Lucia struck him with the lightning of her glance, but made no answer. Caterina was too embarrassed to say anything. She looked at the stage; the fencers were two professionals; they had coarse voices, and arms that mowed the air like the poles of the semaphore telegraph. The audience paid small heed. Giovanna Casacalenda talked to her Commendatore, who was standing behind her, while she cast oblique glances at Roberto Gentile, the young officer in the brand-new uniform, who occupied a fauteuil underneath her box.

"Do you not fence, Signor Sanna?" asked Caterina by way of conversation.

"Fence!" said Lucia, vivaciously, giving her cousin tit-for-tat. "Fence, indeed, when he hasn't breath to say more than four words at a time!"

The Signora Lieti reddened and trembled, out of sheer pity for Sanna's pallor.

The silence in the box was more embarrassing than ever; then as if it were the most natural thing in the world, Lucia separated a gardenia from the bunch in her waistband, and gave it to Alberto. A little colour suffused his thin cheeks, he coughed weakly.

"Are you not well, Alberto? . . . ." laying her hand upon his arm.

"Not quite, it's the cold," said he, with the whine of a sickly child.

"Have a glass of punch, to warm you?"

"It's bad for my chest."

Caterina, pretending not to hear, gave her whole attention to the spectacle. Count Alberti had passed two foils: to Galeota, junior, the young fencing-master, and to Lieti. The interest of the audience was once more awakened. The younger Galeota was a beautiful, graceful youth, with fair, curly hair, shining blue eyes, a short wavy beard, and the complexion of a fair woman; a well-proportioned figure, habited in ultramarine, with a white scarf. Opposite him, stood Andrea Lieti, like a calm Colossus.

"*Dio mio!*" cried Lucia, "Galeota is like a picture of Our Lord! How sweet and gentle he looks! If only Andrea does not hurt him." But Andrea did not hurt him. It was a furious attack, in which the foils bent and squeaked; at last

Galeota's foil broke off at the hilt. Alberti stayed both hands. The fencers raised their masks to breathe.

"How like Galeota is to Corradino of Alcardi!" exclaimed Lucia. "But your husband is a glorious Charles of Anjou."

The assault began again; hotter and fiercer than ever. From time to time the deep sonorous voice of Andrea cried, *Toccato!* and above the din, the clear resonant tones of Galeota rang out, *Toccato!* The ladies became enthusiastic; they seized their opera-glasses and leant over the parapet of their boxes, while a thrill of delight moved the whole assembly. In Lucia's excitement she closed her teeth over her handkerchief, and dug her nails into the red velvet upholstery. Caterina had again withdrawn into her shady corner.

"Bravo! bravo!" cried the audience with one voice, when the assault was over. Lucia leant out of the box and applauded; for the matter of that, many other ladies applauded. After all, it was a tournament. Lucia's eyes dilated, her lips trembled; a nervous shiver shook her from time to time.

"Are you amusing yourself, Lucia?" said Caterina again.

"Immensely! . . . ." closing her eyes in the flush of her enjoyment.

"*Senti*, Alberto; if it is not too cold, go down and send us up something from the *buffet*."

"I don't want anything," protested Caterina.

"Yes, yes, you do; you shall drink a glass of Marsala, with a biscuit."

"I will have anything to please you," assented Caterina, to avoid discussion.

"Send an ice for me, Alberto."

"In this cold weather? I shiver to think of it."

"I am burning; feel my hand." And she put the poor creature's finger in the opening of her glove. "Now, go and send me an ice at once. Take care of draughts . . . . That poor Alberto is not long for this life," she added, addressing Caterina, when he was gone.

"Why not?"

"He is threatened with consumption. His mother and two sisters died of it. Don't you see how thin he is?"

"Then don't be cruel to him."

"I? Why, I'm devotedly attached to him. I sympathise with suffering of every kind. All the people about me are sickly creatures." -

"Andrea would say that such an atmosphere cannot but be injurious to your health."

"Oh! how strong your Andrea is! That is what I call strength. You saw to-day that he was the strongest of them all. But he never comes to see me."

"*Sai*, he never has a moment to spare. And he is afraid of talking too loudly—of making your head ache."

"He is not fond of musk, I fancy?" And she smiled a strange smile.

"Perfumes send the blood to his head. I will tell him to call on you."

"*Senti*, Caterina, strength like his is almost overwhelming. Does it not almost frighten you? Are you never afraid of him?"

Caterina looked astonished, as she replied: "Afraid! . . . . I do not understand you . . . . Why should I be afraid?"

"I don't know," said the other, shrugging her shoulders crossly. "I must eat this ice, for here comes Alberto again."

During this conversation the performance continued—alternately interesting and tiresome. Connoisseurs opined that the tournament was a great success, and the Neapolitan school had been worthily represented. The Filomarina averred, with the audacity of a Titianesque beauty, that Galeota was an Antinous. The Marchesa Leale, a great friend of Baron Mattei's, was enraptured. She was seated quietly by her husband's side; she wore a badge—a brooch representing two crossed foils—that the Baron had presented to her. On the latter's scarf was embroidered a red rose, the Marchesa's emblem.

In the excitement incidental to the clashing of swords and the triumph of physical strength, Giovanna Casacalenda, with flushed cheeks and moist lips, began to neglect her Commendatore, and to cast enthusiastic and incendiary glances at Roberto Gentile. Many ladies regretted having exchanged their fans for muffs in the increasingly heated atmosphere. By degrees a vapour ascended towards the roof, and excited fancy conjured up visions of duels, gleaming foils, shining swords, secret thrusts, and applauding beauty. A warlike ardour reigned in boxes and parterre.

"Has the ice refreshed you, Lucia?" inquired her cousin.

"No, I burn more than ever; there was fire in it."

"Perhaps you would feel better outside."

"It will be over in a few minutes," observed Caterina. "There is to be a set-to between my husband and Mattei."

The set-to proved to be the most interesting part of the performance. Lieti and Mattei, the two most powerful champions, stood facing each other. The audience held its breath. During five minutes the two fencers stood facing each other; they toyed with their foils, indulging in a flourish of salutes, *feintes*, thrusts, parries, and plastic attitudes—a perfect symphony, whose theme was the chivalric salutation. Applause without end; then again silence, for the assault-at-arms was about to begin. Not a word or sound was uttered by either fencer. They were equally agile, ready, scientific, and full of fire—parrying with unflagging audacity, and liberating their foils as in the turn of a ring. They were well matched. Lieti touched Mattei five times; Mattei touched Lieti four times. They divided the honours. In applauding the two champions the public broke through the cordon. A handkerchief fell at Andrea's feet. He hesitated a moment; then, without raising his eyes, stuck it in the scarf round his waist. The ladies' gloves were torn to shreds in the storm of applause.

When he joined them in the box, Andrea found the ladies standing up, waiting for him.

"Good evening, Signorina Altimare; good evening, Caterina,

Shall we go?" He spoke curtly and crossly while he helped
his wife, who looked confused, to put on her furs. Then he
burst out:

"Caterina, why did you behave so ridiculously? It is so
unlike you to be eccentric—to make a laughing-stock of yourself?"

She kept her hands in her muff and her eyes cast down, and
made no reply.

"You, a sensible little woman? Are we living in the
Middle Ages? *Perdio*, to expose oneself to ridicule!"

Caterina turned pale and bit her lip; she would not cry, and
had no voice left to answer with. Lucia leant against the door-
post, listening.

"You are talking about the handkerchief, Signor Andrea?"
she put in, slowly.

"Just so .... The handkerchief. A pretty conjugal
amenity!"

"It was I who threw the handkerchief, Signor Andrea, in
my enthusiasm. You were wonderful to-day—the first cham-
pion of the tournament."

Andrea had not a word to say. He calmed down at once,
with a vague smile. Caterina breathed freely once more.

Alberto Sanna returned and offered his arm to Caterina;
Andrea assisted Lucia in putting on her cloak. She, with face
uplifted towards his, her eyes, through their long lashes, fixed
on his, and a slight quiver in her nostrils, leant on him imperceptibly, just sufficiently to graze his shoulder, as she drew on
her coat-sleeves.

V.

"Is it you, Galimberti? Pray come in."

"Am I not disturbing you?" and, as usual, he stumbled
over the rug, and then sat down, hat in hand, one glove off
and the other on, but unbuttoned.

"You never disturb me." Her tone was the cold, mono-
tonous one of ill-humour.

"You were thinking?" ventured the dwarf, after a short silence.

"Yes, I was thinking . . . . but I don't remember about what."

"Have you been out to-day? It is a lovely morning."

"And I'm so cold. I am always cold when the weather is warm, and *vice versâ.*"

"Strange creature!"

"Eh?"

"I beg your pardon."

"And about yourself, Galimberti. Have you been to the College to-day to give your lesson?"

"Yes, I went there, although I felt so sad, and so disinclined to teach."

"Very sad—and why?" But the tone was indifferent.

He stroked his forehead with his ungloved hand. She sat with her back to the window, but the light shone straight on his face, which looked yellow and faded. Occasionally there appeared to be a squint in his eyes.

"Yesterday . . . ." he began, "yesterday, you did not deign to write to me."

"Yesterday . . . . What did I do yesterday . . . .? Oh! I remember. Alberto Sanna came to see me."

"He . . . . comes . . . . often . . . . to see you . . . . does he not?"

"He is my cousin," she replied, coldly.

Another halt in the conversation. He went on, mechanically fingering the gloves he had not put on. Lucia unwound a cord of the silken fringe of the low chair in which, with face upturned, she was lying.

"Shall I give you your history lesson to-day?"

"No. History is useless, like everything else."

"Are you too sad?"

"I'm not even sad—I'm indifferent. I do not care to think."

"So that—forgive me for mentioning it—I must not hope for a letter from you to-morrow?"

"I don't know . . . . I don't think I shall be able to write."

"But those letters were my only consolation," lamented the dwarf.

"A fleeting consolation."

"I am unhappy, so unhappy."

"We're all unhappy"—sententiously, and without looking at him.

"I fear that they no longer like me at the College," he went on, as if talking to himself. "I always find myself confronted by such icy faces. That Cherubina Friscia hates me. She is a canting hypocrite, who weighs every word I speak. She makes a note in her handbook when I'm only a little late. I don't know how it is, but sometimes I forget the hour. My memory is getting so weak."

"So much the better for you. I can never forget."

"And besides, the Tricolors of this year are lazy and insolent. They contradict me, refuse to write on the subjects I give them, and interrupt me with the most impertinent questions. Every now and then I lose the thread of my discourse, and then they giggle so that I can never find it again . . . . I'm done for, Signorina Lucia, I'm done for. I no longer enjoy teaching. I think . . . . I think there is intrigue at work against me at the College, a frightful, terrible, mysterious conspiracy that will end in my destruction." He rolled his fierce, scared eyes, injected with blood and bile, as if he were taking stock of the enemies against whom he had to defend himself.

"The remedy, my dear Galimberti, is a simple one," said Lucia with childlike candour.

"Speak, oh speak, you're my good angel . . . . I will obey you in everything."

"Shake the dust from off your sandals, and leave. Give them due warning."

Galimberti was so much surprised that he hesitated.

"Is not liberty dear to you?" she continued. "Are you

not nauseated by the stifling atmosphere you live in ? There is a means of reasserting your independence."

" True," he murmured. He did not dare to confess to her that leaving the aristocratic College would mean ruin and starvation to him. Thence he derived the chief part of his income—through *them* he obtained a few private lessons at the houses of his old pupils, by means of which he augmented the mite on which he lived, he in Naples, and his mother and sister in his native province. Without this, there would only remain to him an evening class for labouring people, by which he gained sixty francs a month : not enough to keep three people from dying of hunger. He was already too much ashamed of appearing to her, ugly, old, and unfortunate, without owning to being poverty-stricken besides.

" True," he repeated despairingly.

"Why don't you write to the Directress? If there be a conspiracy, she ought to be informed of it."

" There is a conspiracy . . . . I feel it in the air about me . . . . I will write . . . . yes . . . . in a day or two."

Then there was silence. Lucia stroked the folds of her Turkish wrapper. She took up her favourite album and in it wrote these lines of Boïto :

> L' ebete vita
> Vita che c' innamora
> Lunga che pare un secolo
> Breve che pare un ora.

She replaced the album on the table, and the gold pencil-case in her pocket.

" Will you believe in one thing, Signora Lucia ? "

" Scarcely . . . ."

" Oh ! believe in this sacred truth ; the only happy part of my life is the time I pass here."

" Oh ! indeed," she said, without looking at him.

" I swear it. Before I arrive here, I am overwhelmed with

anxiety, I seem to have so many important things to tell you. When I get to the door, I forget them all. I am afraid my brain is getting weak. Then time flies; you speak to me; I hear your voice; I am here with you, in the room in which you live. I am afraid I stay too long;' why don't you send me away? When I leave you, the first puff of wind on the threshold of the street-door takes all my ideas away with it, and empties my brain, without leaving me the power to hold on to my own thoughts."

"Here is Signor Sanna, Signorina," announced the maid Giulietta.

"I am going," said the perturbed Professor, rising to take his leave.

"As you please." She shrugged her shoulders.

But he did not go, not knowing how to do so, while Alberto Sanna entered. The latter, buttoned up to his chin in his overcoat, with a red silk handkerchief to protect his throat, held a bunch of violets in his hand. Lucia, rising from her seat, placed both her hands in his, and dragged him to the window, that she might see how he looked.

"How are you, Alberto; do you feel well to-day?"

"Always the same," he said; "an unspeakable weakness in my limbs."

"Did you sleep, last night?"

"Pretty well."

"Without any fever?"

"I think so; at least I hadn't those cold shivers or that horrid suffocation."

"Let me feel your pulse. It is weak, but regular, *sai.*"

"I ate a light breakfast."

"Then you ought to feel well."

"*Che !* my stomach can't digest anything."

"Like mine, Alberto. What lovely violets!"

"I bought them for you. I think you are fond of them?"

"I hope you didn't buy them of a flower-girl?"

"If I had, then I should not have offered them to you."

This dialogue took place in the window, while Galimberti sat alone and forgotten in his armchair. He sat there without raising his eyes, holding an album of photographs in his awkwardly gloved hands. He took a long time turning pages which held the portraits of persons in whom he could not have felt any interest. At last Lucia returned to her rocking-chair, and Alberto dragged a stool close up to her.

"Alberto, you know the Professor?"

"I think I have the honour . . . ."

"We have met before . . . ." the two men said in unison; the Professor in an undertone, the cousin curtly.

They sat staring at each other, bored by each other's presence, conscious of being in love with the same woman; Galimberti not less conscious of the necessity of taking his leave. Only he did not know how to get up, or what the occasion demanded that he should say and do. Lucia appeared quite unconscious of what was passing in their minds. She sniffed at her violets, and sometimes vouchsafed a word or two, especially to her cousin. However, conversation did not flow easily. The Professor, when Lucia addressed him, replied in monosyllables, starting with the air of a person who answers by courtesy, without understanding what is said to him. Sanna never addressed Galimberti, so that by degrees the trio once more collapsed into a duet.

"I looked in at your father's rooms before coming to you. He was going out. He wanted to persuade me to go with him."

"He is always going out . . . . And why didn't you go with him?"

"It rained this morning; and I feel a shrinking in my very bones from the damp. It's so cosy here, I preferred staying with you."

"Have you no fireplaces at home?"

"*Sai;* those Neapolitan fireplaces that are not meant for fire, a cardboard sort of affair. Besides, my servant never manages to make me comfortable. I shiver in my own room, although it is so thickly carpeted."

F

"Do you light fires at home, Galimberti?"

"No, Signorina; indeed, I have no fireplace."

"How can you study in the cold?"

"I don't feel the cold when I study."

"You, Alberto, when you have anything to do, bring it here. I will embroider, and you can work."

"I never have any writing to do, Lucia. You know your father manages all my business. And writing is bad for my chest."

"You could read."

"Reading bores me; there's nothing but rubbish in books."

"Then we could chat."

"That we could! You might tell me all your beautiful thoughts, which excite the unbounded admiration of every one who listens to you. Where do you get your strange thoughts from, Lucia?"

"From the land of dreams," she said, with a smile.

"The land of dreams! A land of your own invention, surely! You ought to write these things, Lucia. You have the making of an authoress."

"What would be the good of it; I have no vanity, have I, Professor? I never had any."

"Never! An excessive modesty, united to rare talent . . . ."

"*Basta*, I was not begging for compliments. I was thinking of how much I suffered from my usual sleeplessness, last night . : . ."

"I hope you took no chloral?"

"I refrained from it to please you. I bore with insomnia for your sake."

"Thank you, my angel."

Galimberti sat listening to them, while they exchanged lover-like glances, gazing at the red frame which held Caterina's portrait.

"I ought to go . . . . I must go . . . ." he kept thinking. He felt as if he were nailed to his chair; as if he had no strength to rise from it. He was miserable, for he had just

discovered that there was mud on one of his boots. It appeared
to him that Lucia was always looking at that boot. It was his
martyrdom, yet he dared not withdraw from it.

"And so the thought came to me amid so many others,
that you, Alberto, need a woman about you."

"What sort of a woman—a housekeeper? They are
selfish and odious, I can't abide them."

"Why, no, I mean a wife."

"Do you think so? . . . . How strange! I should never
have thought of it."

"But the woman whom you need is not like any other. You
need an exceptional woman."

"True, how true! I want an exceptional wife," said Alberto,
willing to be persuaded.

"An exceptional woman. Don't you agree with me,
Professor?"

He started in the greatest perturbation. What could she
be wanting of him, now?

Without awaiting his reply, she continued :

"You are, dear Alberto, in a somewhat precarious state of
health; or rather, your age is itself a pitfall, surrounded as,
you are with all the temptations of youth. What with balls,
theatres, supper-parties . . . ."

"I never go anywhere," he mumbled; "I am too afraid of
making myself ill."

"You do well to be prudent. After all, they are but empty
pleasures. But at home, in your cold, lonely house, you do
indeed need a sweet affectionate companion, who would never
weary of tending you, who would never be bored, never grudge
you the most tender care. Think of it! what a flood of light,
and love, and sweet friendship, within your own walls!
Think of the whole life of such a woman, consecrated to
you!"

"And where is such an angel to be met with, Lucia?" he
said, in an enthusiasm caught from her words, in despair that
no such paragon was within reach.

"Alas! Alberto, we are all straining after an impossible ideal. You, too, are among the multitude of dreamers."

"I wish I could but meet my ideal," he persisted, with the obstinacy of his weak, capricious nature.

"Seek," said Lucia, raising her eyes to the ceiling.

"Lucia, do me a favour."

"Tell me what it is? . . . . I beg your pardon, Galimberti, would you pass me that peacock fan?"

"Do you feel the heat, Signorina Lucia?"

"It oppresses me; I think I am feverish. Do you know that peacock feathers are unlucky?"

"I never heard it before."

"Yes, they are *iettatrici*, just as branches of heather are lucky. Could you get me some?"

"To-morrow . . . ."

"I was about to say, Lucia," persisted Alberto, holding on to his idea, "that there is a favour you could do me. Why not write me the beautiful thing you have just said down on paper? I listen to you with delight; you talk admirably. If you would but write these things on a scrap of paper, I would put it in this fold of my pocket book, and every time I opened it I should remember that I have to find my ideal—that's a wife."

"You are a dear, silly fellow," said Lucia, in her good-natured manner. "I will give you something better than this fleeting idea; all these things, and more besides, that are quite unknown to you, I will write you in a letter."

"When, when?"

"To-day, to-night, or to-morrow morning."

"No, this evening."

"Well, this evening; but don't answer me."

"I shall answer you."

"No, Alberto, your chest is too weak; it's bad for you to stoop. Positively I won't allow it."

And so the Professor was quite excluded from the intimacy of the little duet; he was evidently in the way.

"What am I doing here, what *am* I doing here, what am I here for?" he kept repeating to himself. By this time he had succeeded in awkwardly concealing his muddy boot; but he was tormented by a cruel suspicion that his cravat was on one side. He dared not raise his finger to it; and his mind was torn by two conflicting griefs: the letter Lucia was going to write to her cousin, and the possible crookedness of his cravat. The others continued to gaze at each other in silence. On Alberto's contemptuous face there appeared to be a note of interrogation. He was inquiring tacitly of his cousin: "Is this bore going to stay for ever?" And her eyes made answer: "Patience, he will go some time; he bores me too."

The strangest part of it all was that Galimberti had a vague consciousness of what was passing in their minds, and wanted to go, but had not the strength to rise. His spine felt as if it were bound to the back of the chair, and there was an unbearable weight in his head.

"Signorina, here is Signor Andrea Lieti," said Giulietta.

"This is a miracle."

"If you reproach me," said Andrea, laughing, "I won't even sit down. Good-morning, Alberto; good-morning, Galimberti!"

The room seemed to be filled with the strong man's presence, by his hearty laugh, and his magnificent strength. Beside him, Galimberti, crooked, undersized and yellow; Sanna, meagre, worn, pale, consumptive-looking; Lucia, fragile, thin, and languishing, made up a picture of pitiable humanity. Galimberti shrank in his chair, bowing his head. Alberto Sanna contemplated Andrea from his feet upwards, with profound admiration, making himself as small as possible, like a weak being who craves the protection of a strong one. Lucia, on the contrary, threw herself back in her rocking-chair, attitudinising like a serpent in the folds of rich Turkish stuff, just showing the point of a golden embroidered slipper. The glance that filtered through her lids seemed to emit a spark at the corner of her eyes. All three were visibly impressed by this fine physical type; so admirable in the perfection of its development. The room appeared to have narrowed, and even its furniture to have dwindled to humbler proportions, since he entered it; all the minute bric-à-brac and curios with which Lucia had surrounded herself had become invisible, as if they had been absorbed. Andrea sat down against the piano, and it seemed to disappear behind him. He shook his curly head, and a healthy current leavened the morbid atmosphere of the room; his laugh was almost too hearty for it, it disturbed the melancholy silence, which until his arrival had only been broken by undertones.

"I come here as an ambassador, Signora Lucia. Shall I present my credentials to the reigning powers?"

"Here are your credentials," she said, pointing to the portrait of Caterina.

"Yes, there's Nini. My government told me to go and prosper, and be received with the honours due to the representative of a reigning power."

"Did Caterina say all that?"

"Not all. It's in honour of your imagination, Signora Lucia, that I embellish my wife's few words with flowers of rhetoric."

"So you reproach me with my imagination," said the girl, in an aggrieved tone, casting a circular glance at her friends, as if in appeal against such injustice.

"By no means; mayn't one venture a joke? In short, Caterina said to me, 'At three you are to go . . . .'"

"Is it already three?" broke in Galimberti, inopportunely.

"Past three, as your watch will tell you, my dear Professor."

"Mine has stopped," he replied mendaciously, not caring to exhibit a huge silver family relic. "I must take my departure."

"To your lesson, Galimberti?" inquired Lucia, indifferently.

"Indeed, I find the time for it has slipped by. I had no idea that it was so late. After all it's no great loss to my pupils. Will you have your lesson to-morrow, Signorina?"

" To-morrow! I don't think I can ; I feel too fatigued. Not to-morrow."

" Wednesday, then ? "

" I will let you know," she replied, bored.

When, with a brick-coloured flush on his yellow cheeks, Galimberti had left them, all three were conscious of a sense of discomfort.

" Poor devil ! " exclaimed Andrea, at last.

" Yes, but he is a bore," added Alberto.

" What's to be done ? These ladies, in their exquisite good-nature, forget that he is only a teacher ; and he gets bewildered and forgets it too. He must suffer a good deal when he comes to his senses."

" Oh ! he is an unhappy creature ; but when I am sick or sad, the poor thing becomes an incubus : I don't know how to shake him off."

" Is he learned in history ? " inquired Alberto, with the childish curiosity of ignorance.

" So, so ; don't let us talk about him any more. This morning he has spoilt my day for me. What were you saying when he left, Signor Lieti ? "

" What was I saying? I don't remember . . . . "

" You were saying that your wife had sent you here at three," suggested Alberto, as if he were repeating a lesson.

" *Ecco!* Ah, to be sure . . . . And after breakfast I went to a shooting-gallery, then I had a talk with the Member for Caserta about the local Exhibition in September, and then I came on here, with weighty communications, Signora Lucia."

" I'm off," said Alberto.

" What, because of me ? As for what I have to say, you may hear every word of it."

" The reason is that now that the sun has come out, I want to take a turn in the *Villa* before it sets," said Alberto, pensively. " It will do me good, I want to get an appetite for dinner."

" Go, dear Alberto, go and take your walk. I wish I could come too ! The sun must be glorious outside ; salute it for me."

"Remember your promise."

"I remember, and will keep it."

When he was gone, they looked at each other in silence. Andrea Lieti had an awkward feeling that it would have been right and proper for him to leave with her cousin. Lucia, on the contrary, settled herself more comfortably in her rocking-chair; she had hidden her slippered foot under the Turkish gown, whose heavy folds completely enveloped her person.

"Will you give me that Bible, on the table, Signor Lieti?"

"Has the hour struck for prayer, Signorina?" he asked in a jesting tone.

"No," replied Lucia; "for I am always praying. But when something unusual, something very unusual happens to me, then I open the Bible haphazard, and I read the first verse that meets my eye. There is always counsel, guidance, a presentiment or a fatality in the words."

She did as she said. She read a verse several times over, under her breath, as if to herself and in amazement . . . . Then she read aloud: "I love them that love me, and those that seek me early shall find me."

He listened, surprised. This singular mysticism inspired him with a sort of anger. He held his tongue, with the good breeding of a man who would not willingly hurt a young lady's feelings, but the episode struck him as a very ridiculous one.

"Did you hear, Signor Lieti?" she added, as if in defiance.

"I heard. It was very fine . . . . Love is always an interesting topic, whether in the Old or the New Testament, or elsewhere . . . . "

"Signor Lieti!"

"I beg your pardon, I am talking nonsense. I am a rough fellow, Signorina Altimare. We who are in rude health are apt to regard these matters from a different standpoint. You must make allowances."

"You are indeed the incarnation of health," she said,

sighing. "I shall never, never forget that waltz you made me dance. I shall never do it again."

"*Ma che!* winter will come round again ; there will be other balls, and we will dance like fun."

"I have no streugth for dancing."

"If you are ill, it is your own fault. Why do you always keep your windows closed? The weather is mild and the heat of your room is suffocating ; I'll open them."

"No," she exclaimed, placing her hand upon his arm : at its light pressure he desisted : she smiled.

"Do you never dream, Signor Lieti?"

"Never. I sleep soundly, for eight hours, with closed fists, like a child."

"But with open eyes?"

"Never."

"Just like Caterina, then?"

"Oh! exactly like her."

"You are two happy people." Her accent was bitter.

He felt the pain in it. He looked at her, and was troubled. Perhaps, he had after all been hard upon the poor girl. What had she done to him? She was sickly and full of fancies. The more reason for pitying her. She was an ill-cared-for, unloved creature who was losing her way in life.

"Why don't you marry?" he said, suddenly.

"Why?" . . . . in astonishment.

"Why? . . . . yes. Girls ought to marry, it cures them of their vagaries."

"Oh!" exclaimed Lucia, and she hid her face in her hands.

"Now I suppose I have said something stupid again? I will give you Caterina's message and be gone, before you turn me out."

"No, Signor Lieti. Who knows but what your *bourgeois* common sense is right."

He understood the hidden meaning of her phrase, and felt hurt by it. That skinny creature, with her ethereal airs and graces, knew how to sting, after all! She suddenly appeared to him under a new aspect. A slight fear of the woman, whose weakness was her only strength, overcame him. He began to feel ill at ease in the perfumed atmosphere; the room was so small that he could not stretch out his arms without coming to fisticuffs with the wall, the air so perfumed that it compressed his lungs; ill at ease with that long, lithe figure draped in a piece of Eastern stuff; a woman who had a mouth like a red rose, and eyes that shone as if they sometimes saw marvellous visions, and at others looked as if they were dying in an ecstasy of unknown longing. He felt a weight in his head like the beginning of a headache. He would like to have let in air by putting his fists through the window-panes, to have knocked down the walls by a push from his shoulders, to have taken up the piano and thrown it into the street; anything to shake off the torpor that was creeping over him. If he could only grasp that lithe figure in his arms, to hurt her, to hear her bones creak, to strangle her ! The blood rushed to his head and it was getting heavier every minute. She was looking at him, examining him, while she waved the peacock-feather fan to and fro. Perhaps she divined it all, for without saying a word she rose and went to open the window, standing there a few minutes to watch the passers-by. When she returned, there was a faint flush on her face.

"Well," she said, as if she were awaiting the end of a discourse.

"Well; your perfumes have given me a headache. It's a wonder I did not faint; a thing that never yet happened to me, and that I should not like to happen. May I go? May I give you Caterina's message ?"

"I am listening to you. But are you better now? "

"I am quite well. I am not Alberto Sanna."

"No, you are not Alberto Sanna," she repeated, softly. "He is ill, I pity him. How do you feel now ?"

"Why, very well indeed. It was a passing ailment, walking will set me up again. Caterina . . . ."

"Do you love your wife as much as I love her?"

"Eh! what a question!"

"Don't take any notice of it; it escaped me. I don't believe in married love."

"The worse for you!"

"You are irritated, Signor Lieti?" she said, smiling.

"No! I assure you I am not. Mine was a purely physical discomfort, I am not troubled by any moral qualms. I don't believe in their existence. My wife . . . ."

"Are you a materialist?"

"Signora Lucia, you will make me lose my temper," he exclaimed, half in anger, half in jest. "You won't let me speak."

"I am listening to you."

"Caterina wishes you to dine with us next Sunday. Her little cousin Giuditta is coming from school for the day. You two could drive her back in the evening."

"I don't know . . . ." she said, hesitatingly; "I don't know whether I can . . . ."

"I entreat you to, in Caterina's name. She sent me here on purpose. Come, we have a capital cook. You won't get a bad dinner."

She shrugged her shoulders, and sat pondering as if she were gazing into futurity.

"You look like a sybil, Signora Lucia. *Via*, make up your mind. A dinner is no very serious matter. I will order a *crème méringue* to please you, because it is light and snowy."

"I will write to Caterina."

"No, don't write. Why write so much? She desired me to take no denial."

"Well, I will come."

And she placed her hand in his. He bent down chivalrously and imprinted a light kiss on it. She left her hand there and raised her eyes to his. By a singular optical illusion, she appeared to have grown taller than himself.

When he returned home, after a two hours' walk about Naples, Andrea Lieti told his wife that Lucia Altimare was a false, rhetorical, antipathetic creature; that her house was

suffocating enough to give one apoplexy; that she had a
ccurt of consumptives and rachitics—Galimberti, Sanna, and
the Lord knows whom besides; that he would never
put his foot into it again. He had done it to please her, but
it had been a great sacrifice; he detested that *poseuse,* who
received men's visits as if she were a widow; he couldn't
imagine what men and women found to fall in love with, in
that packet of bones in the shape of a cross. Of all this and
more besides, he unburdened himself. He only stopped when
he saw the pain on his wife's face, who answered not a word
and with difficulty restrained her tears. This strong antipathy
between two persons she loved was her martyrdom.

"At least," she stammered, "at least, she said she would
dine with us on Sunday?"

"Just fancy, for your sake I had to entreat her as if I were
praying to a saint. She wouldn't, the stupid thing. At last,
she accepted. But I give you due warning that on Sunday I
shall not dine at home. I shall dine out and not return till
midnight. Keep her to yourself, your *poseuse.*"

This time Caterina did burst into tears.

VI.

During the whole of the dinner in the Lietis' apartment in
Via Constantinopoli, a certain all-pervading embarrassment was
perceptible, despite the care with which it was disguised.
Caterina had not dared, for several days, to breathe Lucia's
name. But on Saturday, when she saw that Andrea had
quite regained his good temper, she begged him not to go out
on the morrow. He at first shrugged his shoulders, as if he
did not care one way or the other, and then said, simply:

"I will stay at home: it would be too rude to go out."

Yet Andrea's manner was cold when he came in from his
walk that day, and Lucia was very nervous, but beautiful,
thought Caterina, in her clinging, cashmere gown, with a large
bunch of violets under her chin. The talk was frigid.

Caterina, who had been driving Giuditta all over the town, was troubled. She feared that Lucia would notice Andrea's coldness, and was sorry she had invited her. She talked more than usual, addressing herself to Lucia, to Andrea, and to Giuditta, to keep the ball going, making strenuous efforts to put her beloved ones in good humour. For a moment she hoped that dinner would create a diversion, and breathed a sigh of relief when the servant announced, " The Signora is served."

But even the bright warmth of the room was of no avail. Andrea, at whose side Lucia was seated, attended absently to her wants. He ate and drank a good deal, devouring his food in a silence unusual to him. Lucia hardly ate at all, but drank whole glasses of water just coloured with wine, a liquid of pale amethyst colour. When Andrea addressed her, she listened to him with intent eyes, which never lowered their gaze; his fell before it, and again he applied himself to his dinner. Caterina, who saw that their aversion was increasing, was terrified. She tried to draw Giuditta into the general conversation, but the child was possessed by the taciturn hunger of a school-girl, to whom good food is a delightful anomaly. Towards the end of dinner, there were slight signs of a thaw. Andrea began to chatter as fast as he could and with surprising volubility; talking to the two ladies, to the child, even to himself. Lucia deigned to smile assent two or three times. There was a passage of civilities when the *crême méringue* made its appearance. Lucia compared it to a flake of immaculate snow; Andrea pronounced the comparison to be as just as it was poetic. Caterina turned from pale to pink in the dawn of so good an understanding. She felt, however, that this was a bad evening for Lucia, one of those evenings that used to end so disastrously at school, in convulsions or a deluge of tears. She saw that her dark eyes were dilated, that her whole face quivered from time to time, and that the violets she wore rose and fell with the beating of her heart. Once or twice she asked her, as in their school-days, " What ails thee ? "

"Nothing," replied the other as curtly as she used to reply at school.

"Don't you see that there is nothing the matter with her?" questioned Andrea. "Indeed, she looks better than usual. Signora Lucia, you are another person to-night, you have a colour."

"I wish it were so."

"Are you courageous?"

"Why do you ask?"

"To know."

"Well, then, yes."

"Then swallow a glass of cognac, at once."

"No, Andrea, I won't let her drink it. It would do her harm."

"What fun! don't you feel tempted, Signora Lucia?"

" I do . . . . rather . . . ." after a little hesitation.

"*Brava, brava !* You too, Caterina, it doesn't hurt you. And even Giuditta . . . ."

"No; it would intoxicate the child."

"*Ma che !* Just a drop in the bottom of the glass."

Lucia drank off hers without the slightest sign of perturbation, then she turned pale. Giuditta, after swallowing hers, blushed crimson, coughing and sneezing until her eyes filled with tears. Every one laughed, while Caterina beat her gently on the back.

"I think you are drinking too much to-night, Andrea," she whispered in his ear.

"Right you are ; I won't drink any more."

When they rose from table, Andrea offered his arm to Lucia, a courtesy he had omitted when they entered the room. Caterina said nothing. When she had installed them in the yellow drawing-room, one on the sofa and the other in a comfortable chair, she left them and went into an adjoining room to prepare the child for her return.

"Have you left off using musk, Signora Lucia?"

"Yes, Signor Lieti."

"Why?"

"I don't know."

"Allow me to congratulate you."

"Thank you."

"Those flowers become you better. Who gave them to you?"

"You are curious, Signor Lieti."

He smiled at her with approving eyes. To him she appeared like one transformed, thanks, perhaps, to the soft folds of her white gown. In his good-natured after-dinner mood, the beatitude of repletion infused a certain tenderness into his voice.

"My name is Andrea," he murmured.

"I know that," was the curt reply.

"Call me Andrea. You call Caterina by her name. Caterina and I are one."

"Not to me."

"I see. But as Caterina is so very much your friend, you might admit me into the bond. Do you forbid me to become your friend?"

"Perhaps there is no such thing as friendship."

"Yes, there is such a thing. Don't be so pessimistic. *Senta, cara Signorina,* let me whisper a word in your ear . . . ."

She bent forward until her cheek almost touched his lips. Then he said :

"There are in this house two people who care for you. Pray believe . . . ."

Lucia fell back against her cushion and half closed her eyes.

"Surely," thought Andrea, "it's another woman, with that round white throat set in its frame of lace."

"Andrea, Andrea," cried Caterina, from the bedroom.

He started, and shrugged his shoulders, as if to shake off a weight, glanced at Lucia, who seemed to be dreaming with closed eyes, and went away. There was a short whispered discussion between husband and wife in the adjoining room. It was suddenly interrupted by Andrea, who was stifling his laughter, pouncing upon his wife and kissing her behind her ear. Caterina defended herself by pointing to Giuditta, who was putting on her hat before the glass.

" It all depends on her," he said, in an undertone, as he re-entered the drawing-room.

" Signora Lucia, are you asleep ? "

" No, I never sleep."

" Caterina wants you a moment, in there."

" What does she want ? "

" I know, but have been ordered not to tell."

" I will go to her."

She went, followed by the serpentine folds of her white train. Andrea sat down, unconsciously rested his head where she had rested hers, and inhaled the lingering perfume of her hair. He rose and walked about the room to rid himself of the mists that seemed to be clouding his brain.

Caterina, in the other room, knew not how to break it to Lucia. The words refused to come, for the tall white-robed maiden, standing erect, without a quiver of her eyelid, intimidated her.

" I think . . . . I think it would bore you to have to come with me to the College."

" What for ? "

" To take Giuditta back."

" I won't go. You go alone. That College depresses me."

" I would go, if it were not for leaving you alone. But I shall not be long ; just the time to drive Giuditta there, and come back."

" Go ; I like being alone."

" It's . . . . that I should like to . . . ."

" Take Andrea with you, of course."

" No, no, on the contrary."

" Leave him with me ? . . . . He will be bored."

" What are you saying ? "

" He will bore himself, Caterina."

" 'Tis he who doesn't want to stay, for fear of boring you. If you don't mind . . . ."

" Really, was that all? I will stay alone, or with your husband, whatever you like. But don't be away long."

" Oh I no fear, dear." And in her delight at having settled the important question, she raised herself on tiptoe to kiss her.

" Dress and go."

When Caterina and Giuditta passed through the drawing-room they found Andrea and Lucia seated, as before, in silence.

"Go, Caterina. I will read a book, and your husband the *Piccolo*. Have you a Leopardi ? "

" No. I am so sorry . . . ."

" Well, I will amuse myself with my own thoughts. Go, dear, go."

Andrea listened, without saying a word.

" You may go to sleep," whispered his wife, as she bade him good-bye. They did not kiss each other in the presence of their visitors. She went away contented with having provided for everything. They followed her with their eyes. Then, without a word, Lucia offered the newspaper to Andrea, who unfolded it. While he pretended to read, he watched Lucia out of the corner of his eye. She was looking at him with so bewitching a smile, that again she appeared to him like a woman transformed—so placid and youthful in her white gown.

" Are you not bored, Signorina ? "

" No ; I am thinking."

" Tell me what you are thinking of."

" What can it matter to you? I am thinking of far-off things."

" It is morbid to think too much. Sometimes, but not often, it happens to me, too, to think."

"Are you thinking now, Signor Andrea?"

Her hand hung slack at her side. In jest he knitted his little finger for a moment in hers. There was a long silence.

"What were you thinking of just now?" asked Lucia, in her low tender tones.

"I do not wish to tell you. How white your hand is, and long and narrow! Look, what an enormous hand mine is!"

"That day at the tournament your hand did wonders."

"Really! . . . ." He reddened from pleasure.

Again they were silent. She drew her hand away and played with her violets. He half closed his eyes, but never took them off the pure pale face, with its delicate colouring, its superb magnetic eyes with pencilled brows, and the half-opened mouth that was as red as a pomegranate flower. He sank into a state of vague contemplation, in which a fascinating feminine figure was the only thing visible on a cloudy background.

"Say something to me, Signora Lucia?"

"Why?"

"I want to hear you speak; you have an enchanting voice."

"Caterina said the same thing to me this evening."

At that name he suddenly sprang to his feet, and took two or three turns about the room, like an unquiet lion. She pulled a chair in front of her, placed her feet upon it, and half closed her eyes.

"Are you going to sleep?" asked Andrea, standing still before Lucia.

"No, I am dreaming," she replied, so gently that Andrea resumed his seat beside her.

"Tell me what you were thinking of just now?" she pleaded.

"I was thinking of something dreadful, but true."

"About me?"

"About you, Lucia."

"Say it."

"No, it would displease you."

"Not from you . . . ."

"Permit me not to tell it you . . . ."

"As you please."

Lucia's countenance became overclouded; every now and then she drew a long breath.

"What is the matter?"

"Nothing; I am very comfortable. And you, Signor Andrea?"

Was he? He did not answer. Now and again the delicious languor that was stealing over him cooled the current in his veins. He scarcely ventured to breathe. Lucia's white gown appeared to him like a snowy precipice; a mad desire was on him to cast himself at this woman's feet, to rest his head on her knees, and to close his eyes like a child . . . . Was he? when every now and then a savage longing came upon him to throw his arm around that slender waist, and press it so that he might feel it writhe and vibrate with tigerish flexibility? He strove not to think; that was all.

"What stuff is this, Signora Lucia?"

"It is wool."

"A soft wool."

"Cashmere."

"It is so becoming to you. Why don't you always wear it?"

"Do you like it?"

"Yes, I do." He continued, unconsciously, to stroke her arm.

She leant over, quite close to him, and said:

"Have one made like it for Caterina."

This time Andrea did not rise, but shuddered perceptibly. He passed his hand through his hair, to push it back.

"I was thinking just now," he said, "that the man who fell in love with you would be a most unhappy fellow."

Lucia sank back in frigid silence, her face hardened with anger.

"Now," he said in a low tone of deprecation, "you are angry."

"No," in a whisper.

"Yes, you are angry; I am a brute." As he said this, he tried to force open her clenched hand. But he was afraid of hurting her, and so he failed. He begged her not to drive her nails into the palm of her hand. The pain of doing so accentuated the angles at the corners of her lips; her head was turned away from him, resting against the cushioned back of the sofa.

"Lucia, Lucia . . . ." he murmured, "be good to one who is unworthy." At last, with a sigh of triumph, he opened the hand which he held: four red marks disfigured its palm. Andrea looked at it, wishing but not daring to kiss it; he blew over it childishly.

. "*Bobo*, gone !"

She vouchsafed a smile, but no reply. Andrea tried to pacify her, whispering nonsense to her. He mimicked the tone of a child, begging its mother's pardon, promising "never to do so again," if only it may not be sent to the dark room, where it is frightened. And the strong man's voice assumed so infantile an expression, he imitated the whine, the grimaces, the feline movements of certain children to such perfection, that she could not restrain the fit of nervous laughter which overcame her, and throbbed in her white throat as she fell back in her cushions.

"Little mother, forgive?" he wound up with.

"*Si, si,*" and, still laughing, she gave him a little pat on the shoulder.

Again he fought down his desire to kiss her hand.

"Do you know that you are not so thin as usual to-night?"

"Do you think so?" she replied, as if weary with laughter.

"Certainly."

"I suppose it's the white dress."

"Or yourself; you can work miracles, you can assume what appearance you choose."

"What am I like to-night?" asked Lucia, languidly.

"You are like a sorceress," replied Andrea, with an accent of profound conviction.

Her eyes questioned him, eager to know more.

"A witch . . . . a sorceress . . . ." he repeated, as if in reply to an inner voice. The clock struck nine times, but neither of them paid heed to it. Stillness filled the room, which was lighted by a shaded lamp. No sound reached it. Nothing. Two people alone, looking at each other. The long pauses seemed to them full of a sweet significance; they could not resume their talk without an effort. They spoke in lowered tones and very slowly. He drew no nearer, neither did she withdraw her hand.

"What perfume do you use in your hair?"

"None."

"Oh! but it is perfumed. I could smell it just now . . . ."

"But I use no perfume."

"Just now I smelt it, when I leant my head where yours had been."

"None; smell!" she said, with unconscionable audacity, as she raised her head to his, that he might inhale the perfume of her hair.

Then he lost his head, seized Lucia by the waist, and kissed her throat madly and roughly. She freed herself like a viper, starting to her feet in a fury, scorching him with the flashing of her eyes. Not a word passed between them. Stunned and confused, he watched her moving about the room in search of her cloak, her gloves, her bonnet, and in such a tremor of rage that she could not find them for a long while. At last she slipped on her cloak, but her quivering hands could not tie the strings of her black bonnet. The white dress had disappeared; she was all in black now, lividly pale, with dark rings under her eyes.

"Where are you going now?"

"I am going away."

"Alone?"

" Alone."

"No, rather than let you do that, I will go myself." He
made her a low bow and disappeared within the bedroom,
shutting the door between them.

When Caterina returned, panting with haste, she found
Lucia calmly stretched out on the sofa.

" Have I been too long ? . . . . And Andrea ?"

" I don't know. He is in there, I think."

"What have you been doing with yourself all alone ?"

" *Sai*, I have been praying with the lapis-lazuli rosary."

Caterina entered the bedroom. A black form was lying
prone across the bed with open arms, like one crucified.

" Andrea !" she called, tentatively.

" What is it ?" was the curt reply.

" Are you sleeping ?"

" I was bored, and I came in here. Let me sleep."

" Lucia ? Who is to take her back ?"

" Thou. Leave me alone."

VII.

One morning, before going out, Andrea kissed his wife, and
said : " Have our boxes packed for to-night ; we are going to
Rome."

"For how many days ? " she asked, without surprise. She
was accustomed to these sudden orders.

"A fortnight at least : plenty of linen and smart gowns.
Leave the jewels at home."

They left for Rome without announcing their departure to
any one. It was like a second honeymoon. During their
eighteen months of married life, neither had travelled farther
than from Naples to Centurano. Caterina had all the artless-
ness and *naïveté* of a newly fledged bride ; but she at once
adapted herself to the change, like the well-balanced creature
that she was. Andrea teased her delightedly, when he saw her
head peeping out of the window at every station. He told

her fabulous stories of every place they passed through; laughing heartily at her incredulity, offering her things to eat and drink, inviting her to take a turn up and down; and she parried his attacks like a child. He walked about the carriage, put his big head out of the window, bumped it against the roof, conversed with the railway officials, indulged in discussions with newsvendors, and impressed his fellow-travellers with his herculean stature. In a word, he was exuberant with health, noise, and jollity.

Caterina did not ever remember seeing him in such high spirits, especially since that inauspicious dinner. Oh! there had been a period of dreadful and furious ill-temper; the house had trembled from slamming of doors, pushing of chairs, and thumping of fists on writing-tables; to say nothing of the bursts of vociferation which had echoed throughout it,—a three days' storm that she had succeeded in lulling by dint of silence, placidity, and submission. Then Andrea had calmed down, except for a certain nervous irritability and occasional bursts of anger, that became ever fewer and farther between. Still, he had not quite gone back to the old Andrea—the childlike, noisy, laughter-loving Andrea, overflowing with mirth and good temper—until they started on this journey. Caterina said nothing about it; but she felt as if her very heart were expanding, dilated with the pleasure of it.

In Rome, Andrea displayed a phenomenal activity. He woke early, with a smile for the rosy face that watched his awakening, and proceeded to call out his orders to all the waiters of the Hôtel de Rome; they drank their coffee in haste and went on a round of sight-seeing. Andrea was not devoted to antiquities and Caterina did not understand them; but it was a duty to see them all, if only by way of gaining an appetite for luncheon. So they continued to inspect every-thing, conscientiously, without neglecting a stone or sparing themselves a corner; exclaiming, with moderate enthusiasm: "Beautiful, beautiful, how beautiful!"

They amused themselves, all the same, because Caterina
had never seen anything before, and because Andrea had a
knack of imitating the guide's nasal voice, pouring forth, the
while, a jumble of rambling, explanatory description, in which
Caterina corrected the erroneous Roman history. They returned to the hotel in a state of collapse, and dawdled through
their luncheon. Then Andrea went out on important business. To-day, he had an appointment with the Under-Secre-
tary of State; to-morrow, with a Cabinet Minister; the other
day he had had matters to settle with the Director-General of
the Agricultural Department. Sometimes he had two appointments on the same day; with the huge, muscular Member for
Santa Maria, with the aristocratic Member for Capua, or with
the hirsute Member for Teano. The conferences with the
journalistic Member for Caserta—influential both as the
editor of a Neapolitan paper of large circulation and as the
intimate friend of the Prime Minister—were of infinite length.
Then he would accompany his wife in her drive to the Villa
Borghese or the Pincio, and leave her there; or to San Pietro,
where there was always something to look at; and two or
three times to the Ladies' Gallery in the House of Parliament,
where Caterina, who understood little or nothing of the subject
under discussion, bored herself immensely, and suffered
agonies of heat and thirst. She waited patiently for him
to come and fetch her, with the resignation of a woman who
would have waited for centuries, had she been bidden to wait.
Andrea returned to her, red, hasty and flurried; blowing and
puffing like a young bull, apologising for having kept her waiting so
long, recounting to her all his experiences; the useless journeys
to and fro, the inert functionaries, the diffident Secretary, the
enthusiastic Cabinet Minister, the Members' zeal for the honour
of their constituencies. To all these details, Caterina listened
with the attentiveness that delights a narrator, without a sign
of weariness. And indeed the local Agricultural Exhibition
was of supreme interest to them both. Andrea was President
of the Committee of Promoters: he was to exhibit wheat,

barley, wine, a special breed of fowls, and a new species of
gourd, a modification of the pumpkin. The schools' functions,
of which Caterina was Lady Patroness, were fixed for the
same epoch. There was to be a flower show for the delectation of the upper ten. The statue of Vanzitelli was to be
unveiled, on the chief Piazza of Caserta, which means, in
short, a universal fillip, the awakening of the entire province,
splendid fêtes, special trains, &c. &c.: the tenth of September, in the height of the fine weather; already cool, you
know, and still genial. It all hung upon whether or no
permission to hold the fête in the Royal Palace could be
obtained, that historic palace, beloved of the Bourbons.
Caterina supported her husband in demanding the *Reggia*, in
insisting on having the *Reggia*: what was the use of that
empty, solemn Royal Palace? It would be splendid for the
Exhibition. They must have the *Reggia*, at whatever the
cost. When they had said and many times repeated these
things, Andrea and Caterina would go here and there and everywhere to dine. They took a long time about it, and seriously
studied the *ménu* for the day; each of them ordering different
dishes and tasting what the other had ordered; Andrea
making friends with the waiter, and both of them relishing
whatever they did with the capacity of young and healthy
people for enjoyment. No one interfered with or otherwise
vexed them. Rome is humane and maternal, ever smiling on
those bridal couples who, under the shadow of her noble
walls, under her canopy of heavenly blue, lead their loves
through the maze of her uneven streets.

After a short halt at the Café du Parlement or the Café de
Rome, then a short walk, and home to sleep. Andrea was tired,
and had to rise early next morning. But often in those hours
between luncheon and dinner, Caterina would beg him to leave
her at home. She preferred staying there, in a tiny sitting-
room that was next to her bedroom. Andrea would ask on
his return what she had been doing. And she replied: " I
have been helping my maid to arrange my grey dress. She

didn't know how to do it, so I showed her. I walked a little, as far as Pontecorvo, to choose presents for Naples . . . ."

Sometimes she lowered her eyes and said, " I have been writing."

" Who to, Nini ? "

" To my aunt ; to Giuditta, at school ; to Giulietta, the maid at home ; to Matteo, the caretaker at Centurano . . . ."

" And to others ? "

" To others besides."

Without naming her, they instantly understood each other. They had lately avoided mentioning her. Caterina *felt* the profound antipathy of Andrea, but neither ventured to combat or complain of it. She had been to call on Lucia, alone. The latter had received her most warmly, smothering her with kisses, asking her loving questions, confusing her with those she read in her eyes : not a word of Andrea, to Caterina's infinite relief. Inwardly, she suffered from the species of hatred which existed between the two persons she loved best. At last, one day when Andrea returned to the hotel, he found Caterina more preoccupied than usual. She heard the news that the Prime Minister would honour the Agricultural Exhibition with his presence, without excessive transport ; she murmured a gentle but absent " Yes " to her husband's suggestion that they should spend three days in Florence, returning thence to Naples.

" *Ohè !* Nini, what is the matter ? "

" Nothing."

" Don't tell stories, little Nini. They are visible on your nose. There is one crawling, his legs are no longer than a spider's, but he is black and ugly ! What is it, Nini ? "

" Nothing, nothing . . . ." she said, in self-defence.

" Say it, Caterina."

" I entreat you . . . ."

" Bah, innocent witch, I know what it is."

" What is it you know ? . . . ." blushing.

" I know why you are so preoccupied; it's the Naples letter that upset you."

Her timid eyes entreated his forgiveness for both of them.

" I am not vexed with you," said he, slowly. " If I don't like the girl, I respect your affection for her: she is the friend of your childhood. You don't love her better than me, I hope?"

" No," she said, simply.

" Well, that is all I care for. Don't plague yourself about anything else. And . . . . is the letter interesting?"

" Very."

" ' *Urgente*' was written outside it. Is it really urgent, or is it only fancy?"

" Really urgent."

He took a turn in the room and glanced at the clock.

" Shall we go to dinner? It is rather early, I think."

" True, it is early."

" And what does she write you? . . . ." without infusing much interest into his voice.

" It's too long to tell."

" I understand you, Nini; I understand you. You would like to read the letter to me."

" No, no . . . ."

" Yes, you are dying to read it to me. You have not the courage to say so; but I guess it. I'm a bear, I suppose. Do you wish it noised abroad that I am a tyrant?"

" Andrea!"

" *Su !* small victim of a barbarous husband: as we have an hour to spare before dinner, and because the success of our enterprise inclines us to clemency, you may even read us your letter. Unto us shall be brought *vermouth* and cigars, to help us to endure this new torment with befitting patience. Oh! Lord, consider the sufferings of your unhappy Andrea ! . . . ."

" Andrea, one more word, and I won't read it."

" *Ma che!* you are dying to read it! *Su !* up, intriguer; up, witch. We accord you our august attention."

Caterina drew the hand that held the letter out of her pocket and read as follows:

"CATERINA MIA!

"This letter, which I am about to write to thee, will not be, like the others, laden with what my father calls vagaries. This is a serious letter. Caterina, collect all the sense, all the reason of which you can dispose; add to it all your experience, call to your help the whole height and depth of your friendship, and be helpful to me in counsel and support. Caterina, I have reached the most solemn moment of my life. A pilgrim and a wanderer, without a guide, I have come to the crossing of the roads. I must decide. I must reply to the dark question of the future, the mystic riddle will have its answer ; it calls for a ' Yes,' or a ' No'. Oh ! Caterina, how have I dreaded this decisive moment! how have I halted and stumbled, as with waning strength I neared it ! Behold, it has caught me up, it is upon me like an incubus. Listen to me patiently; I will try not to weary you. But I want to put my position clearly before you. Do you remember when we spoke of our future, on the College terrace? I told you then, that I should never marry; that I should seek to fulfil a lowly but noble mission, one to which I might consecrate my poor strength, the fervour of my soul, the impulses of a heart enamoured of sacrifice. I sought, and I had found—what human egoism has debarred me from : my father, my unloving father, has prevented me from becoming a Sister of Charity. He would not have them say, ' See, he had but one daughter, and he made her so unhappy that she has taken the veil ! ' If this was my destiny, may God forgive him for not having permitted me to follow it. Other missions are either too arduous for my state of health, or too meagre to satisfy my passionate yearning . . . . My time was passed in prayer, almsgiving, in seeking to console the afflicted, but without any definite occupation or vocation. At last, one day, as it befell Saint Paul on the road to Damascus, a great light struck my eyes, and I fell down before the voice of the Lord.

He has spoken to me: I have understood His words, and, lowliest among those lowly ones who dare to raise their eyes to the Virgin's throne, I have to say in her words: 'Lord, behold thy servant, thy will be done!'

"Near to me, my own Caterina, was a mission to be accomplished, a sacrifice to be offered up. Near to me was a suffering being, condemned by the fatal atavism which has poisoned his blood, to an agonising death. The doctors do not, among themselves, disguise the fact that his will not be a long life. Carderelli has said, with brutal frankness: 'He may live some time, if every precaution is taken.' But it is written that he will die the death. He has the germs of phthisis; he will die of consumption. You guess of whom I speak: my cousin, Alberto Sanna. He does not know the sad truth about himself, but we others do: he is condemned.

"Now picture to yourself the kind of life led by poor Alberto. He is very rich, but quite alone in the world, at the mercy of mercenary beings, in the hands of servants who neglect him, and have no love for him. Pleasure is always tempting him, but he may not, he dares not . . . . His friends are bad counsellors: for when he listens to them he loses the fruit of a month's care. When he falls ill, he is alone, uncared for, utterly miserable; it is piteous, my sweet Caterina. As soon as he begins to recover, he leaves his bed, wraps himself up and comes to me for comfort and consolation. He is saddened because of his illness, because he has no one to love him, because he will never have a family of his own, because all happiness is denied to him, because at the banquet of life he may only appear for a moment, to disappear, like the patient of *Gilbert.* He needs a soul, a love of his own: one who will care for him, love him, who, if she cannot make the remaining years of his life happy ones, is at least content to pour out all her tenderness in them. He looks around and sees that he is alone in the crowd, of no interest to any one. Living, none to love him; dead, none to mourn him. Well, this creature, this soul, this woman, will I be to him . . . . Yes, Caterina, I shall marry Alberto Sanna. It will be a boundless sacrifice of my youth, my whole life, and every dream of joy and splendour. It will be a silent holocaust that I shall offer up to God. For the happiness of a suffering fellow-creature, I will give my whole happiness. I will cast my life away for the life of an afflicted being, whose smile will be my only reward. I am not in love with Alberto Sanna. You know that this earthly and carnal sentiment has never existed in me, nor will it ever exist. I am overwhelmed with pity, compassion, for an unhappy fellow-creature, and out of sheer compassion I wed him. He loves me with a blind, passionate, and childlike affection— and believes that mine for him is love—and I wish him to believe it. In some cases, deception is true piety. I will be to him a faithful wife, a compassionate sister, a watchful mother, an untiring nurse: he shall never read signs of weariness nor fatigue on my countenance. I will cut myself off from the society that he may not frequent. I will say good-bye to all worldly avocations; they shall not disturb our quiet household. I will forget my own sufferings, in alleviating his. If one of us must needs be unhappy, I will be that one. Mute, calm, smiling, I will bury deep in my heart whatever might pain poor Alberto. I will be his smile . . . . The future is a melancholy one. I know not how I shall bear it. May God give me strength where strength will be needed. For the sake of my poor dear, for my poor afflicted one, I must live. I hope I shall not fall ill. God would not lay upon me the burden of having to die before Alberto. God does not recall those who have a mission upon earth until it is accomplished. This thought so supports me that I feel as if triple strength had been given to me. On the other hand, Caterina, it is necessary that I should leave my home. My father cannot bear me near him. He would willingly have left me at the College, had it not been for regard to public opinion. I have already told you as much. He is an egotist, and indifferent to all human suffering. From morning till night he finds something to complain of in my attire, the furniture of my poor rooms, my friends, the time they stay with me, and what he is pleased to call my 'fatal' attitude. Every day he wounds me cruelly. He says the most dreadful things to me : that his friends consider me eccentric; that my behaviour is mad ; that I am the worst coquette of his acquaintance. How have I wept; how have I writhed; poor victim that I am, eternally held up to martyrdom by the Philistine! I bend my head without attempting to reply to him. I am an obstruction in my own house, Caterina. I have had to make a painful effort in asking Galimberti to discontinue his frequent visits ; they were the subject of vulgar, scandalous gossip among the servants, who made a laughing-stock of him. Poor, beloved friend, I have been forced to sacrifice thee to the world; at the very moment when thou hadst need of the consolation of my friendship, just at the moment when the College authorities had, with barbarous injustice, turned thee away! I write to him from time to time, if only not to break off too suddenly. I fear that he is very miserable. I try, in my letters to him, to write the sweetest words that sympathy has ever inspired. Now you see what my father has done for me ! The truth is that my presence casts a gloom over his house, where he would fain have mirth and laughter. The truth is that he is younger at forty-two than I am at twenty; that he wishes I were married, so that he may be free of me. The horrible truth is that he, who has been a widower for fifteen years, is waiting for the hour of deliverance, the hour of my marriage, to marry again himself.

"So that all and everything combines to draw me closer to Alberto. In marrying I please my father, I give happiness to my affianced husband, and peace to my conscience. I need not say to you, who know me, that no idea of self-interest influences me. Alberto is much better off than I am; but what are his riches to me? We shall not receive, we shall only keep two horses in our stable, for the invalid's drives; I shall dress simply in black ; mourning for a blighted existence. . . . . We shall have but few servants, having so few wants.

. . . . Neither pomp, nor luxury, nor fêtes, nor balls; the state of Alberto's health does not admit of them. I shall be content if he will give me something for my poor. I shall have to administer our fortune, for he cannot do so. I will bend my neck under this hard, dry, ungrateful yoke; I will drink the last drop in the bitter chalice I have prepared for myself . . . .

"But tell me, Caterina, is not this beautiful? Tell me, my placid critic, if my self-imposed task is not a holy one? Is not my mission sublime? Is not the act I am about to perform all but a divine one? Do I not set the crown on my life, with this motto, which henceforward shall be mine: 'All for others, naught for self?' Am I not giving to others a fine example of altruism? I will have no praise; I will accomplish it in all humility, as one unworthy, but chosen. Give me your opinion, clearly, sincerely, loyally, as you have ever given it me, in all vital moments of my life. To you I can repeat that none have been more vital than is this one. Write me on a scrap of paper: 'Right, Lucia;' or only 'Lucia, wrong.' And return, Caterina, return, to one who loves thee as surely no other friend was ever loved.

"LUCIA."

The pure sonorous voice of the reader began to give way towards the last, and grew hoarse as if from fatigue. She folded up the transparent sheets, put them back in their envelope, and waited for her husband to speak. Andrea had sipped two glasses of *verm. uth,* and left half of a third one; his cigar had gone out once or twice.

"What do you think of it, Nini?" he said at last, as if he were waking out of a trance.

"I? I don't know; I have no ideas of my own. I never had any."

' "And what are you going to write her?"

"What you tell me."

"I would have you observe," he said, coldly, "that the Altimare did not tell you to read her letter to me, or to ask for my advice. She does not mention me."

"But, you see . . . ." she began, deprecatingly.

"Yes, I see, and I don't see. Anyhow, it appears to me to be an unfortunate marriage."

"To me, too."

"You are always of my opinion. That Alberto is such a wretched creature, he does not deserve a woman like Lucia."

"True, I will write her . . . . that she is doing wrong."

"Yes. Write to her. She won't listen to you, but you will have warned her in time. Or rather . . . . wait until to-morrow to write."

They said no more about it, but all that evening they were absent and preoccupied. They hardly spoke to each other. They went to the play, but did not stay for the last act. Andrea passed a disturbed night; between sleeping and waking, Caterina could hear him turn from side to side, drawing long breaths and tossing his coverings about. She called out sleepily to ask what was the matter with him.

"It's the coffee! it was too strong," he muttered.

Next morning, he took her aside out of her maid's hearing, and made her the following short discourse:

"Listen, Nini. Don't let us get entangled in other people's affairs. We are not infallible, we mustn't assume responsibilities that are too serious for us. Let the Altimare marry whom she will. She may be happy with Alberto. We have no charge of souls. We might give her bad advice. After all, no one can tell how a marriage may turn out. Write that it's all right."

She obeyed, for her whole business in life was to believe in the worth and wisdom of her husband.

PART III.

I.

As the trains arrived from Rome and Naples, a sea of human beings poured out of the dirty, wretched, little Caserta station, flooding the wide, dusty road that is bordered by two fields, where the garrison horses graze. The scorching sun shone down on black evening coats, framing expensive white shirt-fronts, as well as on dittos of light summer cloth, and blue-and-white striped linen costumes, by which the gilded youth of Naples—with metropolitan irreverence for matters provincial—implied their intention of ignoring the Hall of the Inauguration. It shone, too, on overcoats that represented tentative provincial elegance. Under the domes of their large white sunshades came ladies of every degree, in every shade of light, fresh, aërial dresses. They came from Naples, from Santa Maria, from Capua, from Maddaloni; chattering together, and gesticulating with their fans, and sniffing at their huge posies: the provincials quieter than the others, whom they watched and strove to imitate. The sun shone with all its might on that bright September day, and the ladies stepped out bravely, in their polished leather shoes with bright buckles.

In front of them towered the Palace, the poetic dream to which Vanvitelli has given architectural reality. It maintained its imposing air of majesty, due to purity of line, exquisite sobriety of ornament, and the severe harmony of its pale, unfaded colouring, with which time had dealt so gently. The windows of the first story were wide open, and so were the three huge doorways which traversed the whole body of the edifice. And all along the road waved the standard of the province, the Campania Felice, with the Horn of Plenty pouring out the riches of the Earth: and the national banners waved in unison.

Onward went the crowd, as if agriculture were the end and aim of its existence. This September function was in truth a rural feast, a pretext for journeys by road or rail, and for enjoying the coolness of the vast regal saloons . . . . Besides, the Prime Minister was coming to prove the love of a northern statesman for a southern province. To many he was unknown, and they were glad of a chance of seeing him in the pride and pomp of his ministerial uniform. The more sentimental among them, those who knew him to be eloquent, came to hear him speak. The ladies were there for the mysterious, unfathomable reason for which they go everywhere, especially where they are most likely to be bored. At the middle entrance, the chief porter, in the royal livery, with a plume waving in his carabineer's hat, and a gold-headed wand in his hand, impassively faced the crowd. People passing out of the dazzling light and dry heat into the grey twilight and moist freshness of the Hall, felt a sense of relief on entering it. The majesty of the Palazzo Reale lent composure to their countenances and subdued their voices; constraining admiration for its solidity of construction, the elegance of its arched ceiling, the strength of the quadruple pillars, and the eurythmy of the four triangular courts that grew out of its centre.

" It resembles a construction of the Romans," remarked the Mayor of Arpino—a fat personage with his badge of office slung across his portly figure, and gold spectacles, behind which he perpetually blinked—to the Mayor of Aversa, a lawyer of fox-like cunning and squat, sturdy appearance.

There was a murmur of argument and protestation at the foot of the grand staircase; the ushers were politely inflexible. Unless you wore evening dress, you might not enter the Hall of Inauguration. Many of the uninitiated appeared in their overcoats. A tall, fair, burly exhibitor, brick-red in the face, with a diamond flashing on his little finger, had come in a cut-away jacket.

"I exhibit a bull, two cows, two sheep, and twelve fowls : I shall pass in," he repeated; "besides, I've got my wife with me, I must escort her."

"No one can enter here without evening dress," replied the ushers.

"I don't mind being alone, Mimi," murmured his wife, a buxom provincial, dressed in mourning, with an enormous train, a hat and feathers, and superb brilliants in her ears.

"Well, go up then, Rosalia. I'll go and have a look at the fowls. You'll find me in the park after the speechifying in evening dress is over."

And thus did the overcoats disappear in the courtyards or the park, while men in evening attire and ladies slowly ascended the broad, low, milk-white marble steps of the majestic stair. The ladies heaved sighs of content, they revelled in the gradual ascent to regal magnificence and the charmed silence stirred by a luxurious silken rustle. Triumphant gentlemen in their black coats crowded upon them, hiding behind their opera-hats the self-satisfied ecstasy of their smile. The old Palace, which had witnessed the splendour of Carlo III., the folly of Maria Carolina, the military fêtes of Murat, the popular ones of Ferdinand I., was awakening for an hour to the luxury of modern dress, the perfume of youth and beauty, the cold lustre of precious stones and all the lavish pomp of a court. That feast of the people, of the peasants—that feast of the soil, of its fruits, and cereals, and animals, that should have been so humbly prosaic and commonplace—was like a refined and courtly function, the birth of an hereditary prince or an official New Year's reception.

"What victory for democracy, to have enthroned itself within the tyrant's halls, there to celebrate a rural feast," quoth the tun-bellied, squint-eyed lawyer Galante, from Cassino—he was bald, and the only Socialist the province boasted—to the monarchical chancellor, who was duly scandalised.

The inauguration was to take place in the vast Farnese Hall
with its four windows on the façade; between the windows was
the ministerial platform, covered with green velvet adorned
with gold cord, and furnished with a bell, an inkstand, three
glasses, a water-bottle, and a sugar-basin, all pregnant with
meaning. Around them were grouped five red velvet armchairs. A step lower, between the ministerial platform and
the body of the Hall, was the presidential platform, furnished
with a grey carpet and five antique leather chairs. To the
right, to the left, and in front, rows of chairs for those who
had received invitations, three rows of armchairs for the ladies,
and rush-bottomed ones for the men.

When Lucia Altimare-Sanna and Caterina Lieti appeared
at the entrance, escorted by a single squire, Alberto Sanna, of
the worn and gruesome countenance, Andrea Lieti hastily
stepped down from the presidential eminence, darted through
the crowd, and offered his arm to Lucia.

"Follow me with Caterina, Alberto; I'll find you a good
place."

A murmur followed Andrea and Lucia as they passed
through the crowd. Lucia in her long white satin robe, that
clung to her and gleamed like steel in the sun, where it was
not swathed with antique lace, was truly lovely and captivating.
On the loose plaits of dark hair which waved on her forehead
was draped a priceless veil of finest Venetian point, in lieu of
a bonnet; it wound round her neck and was fastened under
one ear by three white roses, fresh and dewy, with shell-pink
hearts. No jewels. The same tint flushed her cheek, which
was fuller than of yore; the red lips, now no longer parched,
were fuller too. She smiled on her tall, strong knight, who
bent his handsome person protectingly towards her.

"Who is she?" "The wife of Lieti?" "No, a relation of
his wife's." "She is beautiful!" "Too thin, but pleasing!"
"Too much dressed!" "*Che!* it's an official function."
"She is beautiful!" "Beautiful!" "Beautiful!"

The couple that followed in their wake passed unheeded

through the murmur, which, however, was not lost on either of them. Caterina was simply dressed in lilac. She wore a feather of the same pale colour on her tiny bonnet, and in her ears enormous diamond solitaires, "to please Andrea." But she was small, modest, and obscured by her friend's lustre, as if she had tried to hide herself behind it, and her escort was undersized and undistinguished by either badge or decoration. He and she heard the "*Bella, bella, bella !*" that hovered in whispers on people's lips.

"They admire Lucia," whispered Alberto, in the pride of his heart.

"Of course, she is, and always has been, very beautiful," said Caterina, in placid and persistent admiration of her friend.

"Oh! not as she used to be. She was not nearly so attractive before her marriage. Now she is another woman. Happiness . . . ."

"Lucia is an angel," declared Alberto, gravely. "I am not worthy of her.

By this time they reached their places in the front row, opposite the platform.

There were two armchairs for the ladies, who took their seats, while the men remained standing; Andrea by the side of Lucia, Alberto by Caterina. Lucia's train fell at her feet in a fluffy heap of silk and lace, just allowing a glimpse of a tiny foot shod in white, silver-worked leather; she fanned herself, for it was very hot. From time to time Andrea bent down to speak to her, and she raised her eyes as if to answer him in low tones, while a smile raised the corners of her lips and showed her teeth. Alberto, who was at a loss for a seat, was soon bored and wearied; he had a presentiment of a lengthy ceremony. Caterina, who had been elected a member of the jury for needlework, in the Didactic section, was somewhat preoccupied. The office appeared to her to be an onerous and important one; what would they expect of her, and what if she proved inadequate?

"Who is that immensely tall man, rather bald, with the long black whiskers, who has just entered? How tall he is? Who is he, Signor Andrea?"

"He is the Member for Santa Maria."

"*Dio mio!* he is taller than you. I did not think that was possible. Will he speak?"

"I think not."

"How sorry I am that you are not going to speak, Lieti. If I were your wife, I should have insisted on your speaking."

Caterina started. "I did not think of it," she murmured, her mind running absently on the meeting of the ladies of the jury.

"Alberto *mio*, are you too warm? How do you feel? Will you have my fan?"

"I don't feel the heat; I wish I could sit down. Thanks, dear."

"Lieti, will you find a chair for Alberto; he gets so soon tired. I could not stay here, if he had to stand."

Andrea sought, until he at last succeeded in finding a seat for Alberto in the next row, between two old ladies who sat behind Caterina.

Alberto, with visible satisfaction, tucked himself between their skirts.

"Are you comfortable now?"

"Very, dearest."

"Will you have a lozenge?"

"No, by-and-by. Don't think of me: look about you, chatter, amuse yourself, Lucia."

"My poor Alberto," said Lucia—speaking so that only Andrea could hear her—"is a continual source of torment to me. I would give my blood to enrich his."

"You are good," said Andrea.

Meanwhile the people were arriving in crowds, and filling every nook and corner, even to the recesses in the window, and the steps of the platform. In one corner sat a group of young men chatting without lowering their voices; one of them was scribbling notes in a pocket-book, another making telegraphic signs to the secretary of the committee, another yawning. Among them was a young woman, simply dressed in mourning; her face, under her black-brimmed hat, was pale and sickly.

" Those are the journalists," said Andrea to Lucia. " There are the correspondents of the *Liberta*, the *Popolo Romano*, the *Fanfulla*, for Rome; of the *Pungolo* and the *Piccolo*, for Naples."

" And is she a journalist? "

" I think so, but I don't know her name."

" I envy her, if she is intelligent; she at least has an aim."

" Bah ! you would rather be a woman."

" Glory is worth having."

" But love is better," he continued, in a serious tone.

" . . . . Love? "

Caterina did not hear. She was thinking of home, where she fancied she had left the jewel-safe open. With these fashionable gowns it was impossible to put your keys in your pocket. Despite her confidence in her servants at Centurano, she could not help feeling a little anxious.

" Do you remember, Lucia, if I locked the jewel-safe? "

" No, dear, I do not remember. It will be quite safe, even if you have not locked it."

" Do you, Signor Sanna? "

" Yes ; you locked it, and put the key under the clock."

" Thanks, thank you ; you take a load off my mind."

" Signora Lucia, Caterina, I must go and speak to the Prime Minister."

" Are you going to leave us? "

" I shall be here opposite to you. Caterina, don't yawn, child, remember that you are the wife of the vice-president of a committee."

She smiled absently, and nodded to him.

A treble hedge of ladies, and then a multitude of black coats, on which the light dresses stood out like splashes of colour: a vivid, undulating crowd, disported itself under the gildings of the regal ceiling.

"Oh! it's lovely, Caterina," said Lucia, flushed with excitement. At that moment there came from the staircase a suppressed sound of applause. A flutter stirred the whole assembly as it turned to face the Prime Minister, who entered, leaning on the arm of his friend, the Member for Caserta. He was lame on the one leg that had been wounded in battle ; he stooped slightly. His massive head was covered with thick iron-grey locks, well planted on a square brow : the head of a faithful watch-dog, with bold, honest eyes, wide nostrils and a firm jaw. The grey moustache covered a mouth of almost infantile sweetness, to which the *impériale* lent a certain meditative seriousness. He bowed, taking evident pleasure in the prolonged applause, one of the few pleasures of official life ; then ascended the platform, and after once more responding to the ovation, seated himself in its centre.

"He is a brave man : he has fought in every battle ; he comes of a family of heroes," explained Lucia to Caterina.

Then came the chorus of coughing, throat-scraping, and clearing of voices which precedes all speeches. Next to the Premier was seated the Member for Sora, a white-haired veteran whose chin was fringed with a white beard, a financier of somewhat furtive expression of countenance. On the left sat the Member for Capua, cool, composed, and distinguished-looking as ever. Two empty places. The Member for Caserta mingled with the crowd. The Prime Minister raised his voice to speak, amid breathless silence.

To tell the truth, the collar of his uniform came up too high at the back of his neck and gave him an appearance of awkwardness. He leant forward while he spoke, gazing fixedly at one point in the Hall, losing himself and his words from sheer absence of mind, and occasionally indulging in long pauses that passed for oratorical effects, but were probably due to the same cause. He pointed one hand on the table, while the right described a vague circular gesture, as if he were setting a clock.

" He is unwinding the thread of his eloquence," quoth Lucia, with much emotion.

He expressed himself poetically, here and there falling into the rhetorical, ready-made phrases which strike so pleasantly on the ear of an attentive crowd. " Yes, he was indeed happy to put aside for a moment the cares of State and the burden of politics, to be present at this festival of labour—of labour that, despite its humility, is so ennobling to the horny hand of the peasant . . . ."

No effect. The Hall was filled with well-dressed land-owners, who did not appreciate this sentimentalism.

" Besides," he continued, " this festival assumes an historic character. The Romans, ladies and gentlemen, our great ancestors, who were gifted with the very poetry of diction, named this province the *Campania Felice* . . . ."

Here the assembly, moved by the music of his words, broke into thunders of applause. The journalists scribbled in their note-books, supporting them with an air of infinite importance either on their knees or against the wall.

" We have named it *Terra di Lavoro*, a yet more poetic name, indicating as it does the daily call of man on his mother earth, on that earth—that earth—that Alma Demeter to whom of yore the labourers' hymns were raised. We also salute her, the beneficent mother, inexhaustible fount of social well-being, blessed bosom that nourishes us without stint or weariness."

Here, being tired, he sipped. A thrill of satisfaction ran through the assembly, well pleased with its statesman. He began again, shrugging his shoulders imperceptibly as if re-signed to their burden, and resumed. The moral atmosphere was cold, it needed warming. Then rang out the sonorous words and broad phrases of little meaning that floated like a vision before the mind's eye of the somewhat bewildered company. He spoke confusedly of enterprise, the new machinery we owe to England, the *contadino*, the vast future of agriculture; on Bentham, on universal suffrage, primary instruction, the Horn of Plenty, and decentralisation. He slipped for a moment on "Regionalism," but caught himself up; then lost his way and became absorbed in thought, with one hand suspended in mid-air, arrested midway while describing a circle. Slowly he came to himself again, referring to *la patria* and the fight for independence. The Hall rang with applause.

"This magnificent Exhibition, which unites to the sheaf of corn of the poor *contadino*, the domestic animal trained by the aged dame, the flower cultivated by the fine lady, the school exercise written by the labourer's child, is a happy manifestation of every energy, of every—yes, of every force . . . ."

And transported and intoxicated by his own words, his hand described so rapid a circle that the face of the invisible clock appeared to be in imminent danger; he had knocked down the bell and an empty glass. He referred to the Government, to efface the impression produced by this disaster.

"The Government, ladies and gentlemen—and especially the Minister for Agriculture, whom a slight indisposition has debarred from being here to-day—says to you by my lips that this festival, a living proof of fecund prosperity and of useful activity, is a national festival. The affluence of every single *commune* is the affluence of the State; this is the ideal the Government has in view. It will do its utmost within the limits of the means at its disposal, and the power it wields, to help this brave and laborious country where Garibaldi has fought and . . . ."

"*Viva* Garibaldi!" cried the company.

"And where landed proprietors work together with their tenants for the good of the community. The Government is imbued with good intentions that in the course of time will become facts. But what appears to me to be the feature the most touching in its beauty is the holding of this domestic

feast in the Palace of the banished Bourbons—is this triumph
of the people, where the people have so suffered . . . ."

"*Beneece!*"

"Only under a constitutional country like ours, only under
the beneficent rule of the House of Savoy, a race of knightly
soldiers, could this miracle be accomplished. I call upon you
to join with me in the cry, *Viva il Re! Viva la Regina!*"

He fell back tired, his eye dull under its flaccid lid, while
his under-lip hung slack. Mechanically he wiped his brow,
while the crowd continued to applaud; the Deputies closed up
around him, and there was some congratulatory hand-shaking.
He thanked them with studied courtesy, bestowing Ministerial hand-shakes and endeavouring to ensure his jeopardised
majority.

In the bustle which ensued Andrea hastened to join the ladies.

"You liked it, didn't you? Splendid voice!"

"He said some stupendous things that the stupid people did
not understand," pronounced Lucia, disdainfully.

And she opened her fan, so that she succeeded in attracting
the notice of the group of journalists; perhaps they would
mention her in their reports.

"Are you bored, Caterina?" queried Andrea.

"No, it's like the Chamber of Deputies," she replied, with
placid resignation.

"Are you hungry?" asked Andrea of Alberto, whose yawns
were savagely distending the pallid lips of his wide mouth.

"Hungry indeed! I wish I were!"

Then all resumed their seats, for the Member for Capua had
advanced to the front of the platform, so that his entire person
was visible; he waited for silence, to read his paper. The
Prime Minister had seated himself opposite to him, in that
attitude of mock attention whose assumption is so notable a
faculty in a statesman.

The clear light eyes of the tall, distinguished-looking Deputy
looked out at the crowd. He wore the riband of the order of
SS. Maurizio and Lazzero round his neck, and many foreign

decorations at his button-hole. With his powerful torso, erect carriage, and a countenance so impassive that it neither expressed sound nor hearing, he was a perfect type of the ex-soldier. There was no denying that his appearance was more correct than that of the Prime Minister, his features more refined, and his gestures more artistic. There was something British in the grave composure and sobriety of his diction. He read slowly, giving out every word with a high-bred voice that was almost acid in its sharpness. And, strange to say, his speech, which had been written beforehand, was a flat contradiction of the Prime Minister's rhetorical improvisation. He made short work of the poetry of the Horn of Plenty and the Sweat of the Brow. He said that the Exhibition was a step in the right direction, but it was not everything; that the economic and financial movement had not yet begun to work among the labouring classes; that its impetus must necessarily be deadened as long as the present harsh fiscal system continued to prevail; that certain experiments in English cultivation and model-farming had been unsuccessful. He said that it was of no avail to demand of the land more than it could yield : that only meant exhaustion. He added that the agricultural question was a far more serious one than it appeared to be, but that the splendour of southern skies and a mild climate softened the hardships of meridional provinces. This was the only concession to poetry made by this poet—for he was, above all, a poet. But the unbiassed conscience of a wealthy and experienced landowner spoke higher in him than sentiment. The Minister listened, nodding his approval, as if all these ideas had been his own, instead of a frank and decided contradiction to everything he had said. The Member added, after a telling pause, and with a smile—his first—that he did not wish to preach pessimism on a day of rejoicing, and that this insight into genuine agricultural life was in itself of some moment. The province tendered its thanks to His Majesty's Government, in the person of its Premier, for promises on which it built hopes of sure fulfilment, for he who made them was a hero, a patriot, and a brave soldier. Ever sensitive to praise, the Prime Minister flushed like a boy with the pleasure of it; then the Member calmly and quietly brought his speech to a close, without having sipped a drop of water or shown any signs of fatigue. The applause was prolonged, steady, and enthusiastic. The speech had been cold and lacking in sonorous rumble; but the audience had felt the truth of it. The Prime Minister all but embraced his beloved Deputy, who in the last division had voted against him. He accepted the demonstration quietly. The spectators could decipher no meaning on his high-bred sphinx-like face. In profile he was more soldier-like than ever, and the only trace of nervousness about him was a slight involuntary movement of one shoulder. The public rose to salute the departing Prime Minister; leaning on the Prefect's arm, he passed through the applause of the front rows, dragging the leg that had been wounded at Palermo, one of the personal glories that helped him to govern. Behind him came the Mayors and other functionaries, and all the journalists, in a bustle of importance. On the stairs there was a second, weak, scant attempt at applause.

"The Member for Capua was fine, but cold, Caterina," said Lucia, who was standing to see the people pass.

"Do you think so?" said Caterina, who held no opinion on the subject, with indifference.

"Oh! cold," added Alberto, who always adopted the opinion of his wife.

"Shall we go?"

"I," said Caterina, timidly, "have to go to the Didactic Exhibition; their first meeting is for to-day."

"Then Alberto and I will take a turn in the Exhibition, until you and your husband have shaken off these onerous duties."

"*Sai*, Lucia, I am tired, and I shan't take a turn in the Exhibition."

"Then we will go to the park."

"Worse than ever, because of the sun," he persisted,

beginning to sulk. Lucia smiled as if in resignation. Caterina
was embarrassed, for until the meeting was over and the Prime
Minister took his departure, she and her husband were not at
liberty.

"Well, Alberto *mio*, what will you do?"

" Drink an iced lemonade and go home. I shall sleep until
dinner-time."

" *Bene*, I will go home with you ; " she suppressed a sigh.

" Oh ! my poor heart, what a continual sacrifice," whispered
Caterina, as she embraced her friend.

A little later, Alberto passed alone through the Didactic
section, and calling Caterina aside, said to her :

" When you have finished, Signora Lieti, you will find Lucia
in the park, quite alone, near the lake ; she is there thinking,
dear soul. She pined for air, so I took her there and left her.
I'm not a selfish man, and I'm going away to sleep. Can you
go soon?"

"As soon as I can."

Alberto went off on those weak legs of his, of which the
trousers were always baggy, turning up the collar of his coat
because he was perspiring. He came upon Andrea in the
Hemp section, in the midst of a group of exhibitors who were
accompanying the Prime Minister.

" When you've done here, go into the park, where you'll find
your Signora with mine, awaiting you in the little shrubbery by
the lake. But make haste. I'm going home to sleep. Is
there a bar here ? "

" Yes, on the ground-floor."

" I want a glass of Marsala. Shall you be home in time for
dinner?"

" To be sure; pleasant dreams to you."

He watched him depart with pity for an existence so poor
in health and strength, useless alike to himself and others.
But this Minister was insatiable. As if he knew anything
about madder, or dried beans, or yellow gourds ! Now it's

the turn of the cocoons! Andrea was beginning to weary:
while the Prime Minister was engaged in conversation with the
Prefect and the Member for Nola with that cadaverous face
and ambiguous blond hair, he wouldn't be likely to speak to
him. Andrea would have liked to leave; he was getting bored
with the official circle and the stupid march of inspection
throughout the building. Besides, he suffered from the heat,
and how cool it must be out there in the park! Yet he
lingered, a victim of his ambition, in the hope that the
Minister would speak to him at last.

"In the Grain section, I shall bolt, unless he sends for me
before we get there," said he to himself. They passed not
only the grain, but the fodder. Andrea felt his anger rising as
they passed through the Hall of the Oils, upon which the sun
cast yellow rays. "I shall leave him at the Wines," he thought;
he was incensed and quite red in the face. But in the Wine
section, in front of a pyramid of bottles, the Minister called
out:

"Signor Lieti!"

"Your Excellency!"

"You are a brave worker in the common cause: here is
some of your wine. Fine Italian wines should be cultivated, if
only out of patriotism. We drink too much Bordeaux and
Champagne; France intoxicates us."

"Your Excellency . . . ."

"The congratulations of the Government are due to you, as
an influential citizen, who utilises his activity in this public
service . . . . to which I add my personal compliments."

Andrea bowed low, in mingled pride and shyness. He had
had his share: the Minister was now flattering the Member
for Cassino also on his wines. Besides, they had been all
over the Exhibition; now they were about to inspect the cattle
and poultry in the park.

"Now he has spoken to me he won't say anything to me
about my fowls; I shall take to my heels." Contented, with the
blood once more running freely through his veins, fanning himself

with his *gibus*, his gloves stuck in his waistcoat, he slipped away by a back staircase which shortened the distance.

"He will say nothing to me . . . . nothing to me . . . . nothing to me . . . . nothing about the fowls," he hummed, as he crossed the courtyard.

Once in the park, he walked rapidly, but was dissappointed in not meeting with any one at the lake of the Castelluccia.

"Where can they have got to?" he murmured, with flagging spirits. He went the round of the wide, oval shrubbery that fringes the little lake. In one corner, in a thin streak of light under the dome of her white, red-lined sunshade, sat Lucia, on a rustic bench. She was alone, and sat with her face turned away from him. Andrea thought he would turn back; yet Caterina could not be far off. So he approached rather shyly, intimidated by the white figure, crowned with blonde rays, their radiance playing on her cheeks and on the rustic background. Lucia did not hear his steps, despite the rustle in the dry leaves. She uttered a cry when he appeared before her.

"Oh! how easily you are frightened!" he said, with an assumed ease of manner.

She held out a trembling hand to him. Andrea, feeling rather awkward, remained standing before her.

"Won't you sit down?"

"No; I'm not tired."

"Has it been a long affair?"

"Have you been long waiting?"

"I think so; at least, it seemed long to me;" she smiled a melancholy smile. "How beautiful it is here, Lieti!"

"Oh! beautiful. What a fool I must look in evening clothes in the midst of this green country!"

"No; for this country is artificial, it savours of powder and patches. The branches of these trees look as if they had been trimmed with scissors. Oh! who will give me Nature—real great, omnipotent Nature?"

"When your voice falls in longing, it is enchanting," said Andrea, with admiration in his eyes.

I

"Do not you long for real country?"

"Eh! it is not always poetic. Sometimes it is barren, at others it smells too much of lime. But I know where to find your ideal; the dark wood, the narrow paths, the lake hidden in the thicket . . . ."

"*Dio!* . . . . You know where all that is, Andrea!" And she crossed her hands on her bosom, her voice trembling from desire.

"Here, in the English Garden."

"Far, far, far?"

"No; near, three-quarters of an hour's walk."

They looked fixedly at each other as if they were debating something. She cast a glance around her, and then bowed her head and sighed in resignation. Andrea felt inclined to sigh too, there was a weight upon his chest. With a gesture familiar to him, he threw down his hat and passed his hand through his curly hair. She stretched out a little foot whose jewelled buckle shone in the sun.

"You are too beautiful to-day. It is quite insufferable," said Andrea, with a forced laugh.

"To please Alberto . . . . I am not fond of dressing extravagantly; I cannot see the pleasure of it. I am, as you know, inaccessible to vanity."

"I know . . . . but I think Alberto is a fool."

"Don't say so, Signor Andrea; poor Alberto, he is but unhappy."

"You don't understand me. Why does he make you dress like that? Every one looks at you. Isn't he jealous?"

"No; I think not."

"If I were your husband I should be madly jealous," he cried.

For the space of a second, Lucia was startled and shrank back. Then she broke into her habitual smile, a smile of voluptuous and seductive melancholy.

"I am always frightening you," said Andrea, troubled, in a lamentable voice.

" No ; I know it's only your way."

" It's my temperament; sometimes the blood goes to my head, and mad ideas get into it. Listen, let me say all. If I were your husband, I should be madly jealous, jealous to insanity. I feel that I should beat you, strangle you . . . ."

Lucia closed her eyes, inebriated.

" And listen, listen," he gasped ; " I want to tell you what I have never dared to say to you until now . . . . to ask your pardon for that evening . . . . when I behaved like a brute . . . . Have you forgiven me?" Thrilling with the mere thought of the scene he had evoked, his entreaty was as passionate as the emotion caused by memory.

" Yes," she replied, a barely audible " yes," that came after some hesitation.

" You do really forgive me?"

" I forgive you. Do not let us talk about it."

" One word more. Did you say anything to . . . ."

" To whom?"

" . . . . to Alberto?"

" No, nothing."

" Thank you."

He drew himself up as if he were both relieved and satisfied : there was a secret between them about which they could talk without being understood by any one else—about which neither could think without knowing that the other shared the thought. Lucia started imperceptibly, and then turned and asked him :

" And you?"

" What?"

" Have you spoken of it?"

" To whom?"

" To Caterina, to your Nini?"

" No, no . . . . !" in evident agitation.

" You might have told her," she replied slowly, " you who love her so much."

" It would have pained her . . . . and . . . ."

" Pained her for whom? For your sake, perhaps."

" For yours.   She loves you."

" True.   Caterina is an excellent creature, Signor Andrea :
her good qualities are remarkable, although they make no
show.   Love her ever, for she deserves it ; love her with all
your might.   Before my marriage, I used to fear that my
Caterina, my sweet friend, was unhappy.   She loves you above
all ; make her happy . . . ."

Caterina was coming towards them, smiling, and a little out
of breath.

" Have I kept you waiting very long?   Have you been
here long, Andrea ? "

" No ; not very long."

" Did the Prime Minister speak to you ? "

" Yes ; he was very complimentary."

" About the wheat ? "

" No, about the wine made on the new system."

" And the fowls ? "

" Nothing, I didn't go there.   And what have you done,
Nini ? "

" Talkee, talkee, nothing settled.   The worst of it is that I
shall have to go there every morning."

" For how many days ? "

" I don't know ; eight or ten, perhaps."

" A bore, Nini ; but you are kind and patient."

" That is what we were saying," observed Lucia ; " that you
are an angel and worthy of adoration."

" An angel and worthy of adoration," repeated Andrea,
mechanically.

II.

The Princess Caracciolo, the great benefactress of the
poor, the aged, and the children, presided.   She reigned in
the Hall of Maria Carolina, where the ladies of the jury
were assembled, with the mingled air of regal hauteur and
amiable piety peculiar to her.   An ascetic pallor had left her
cheeks colourless and her lips faded ; while her person

retained the seductive grace of the woman who had loved, and
loved to be beautiful. She had left her own poor and her
children, for the sake of these other children. The thirty
ladies had, with one voice, elected her as their president.
There was only one man, the secretary, among them—a
professor, a pedagogue, saturated with the principles of Froebel
and of Pick ; a bald, ambiguous-looking, and perfectly innocuous being. The ladies of the jury sat in a circle, on brocaded couches, where the most opposite types were brought
into juxtaposition. Three German teachers had come from
Naples : one, tall, thin and brick-coloured, with her hair in a
green net ; another, older, stout, florid, and dressed in black ;
the third was a deal plank, with a waxen head stuck on the
end of it ; all three had gold spectacles and guide-books.
They were talking, with animation, to each other, in their own
language, the deal plank ejaculating rapid *ja's* by fits and
starts. Then there were the Directresses of the Institutes of
Caserta, Santa Maria, and Maddaloni; all frills and cheap
trinkets, black silk dresses, starched collars and light gloves.
A couple of professors' wives, of the genus that teaches, brings
children into the world, and does the cooking. They had pale,
emaciated faces, were flat where they should have been round, and
protuberant where they should have been flat. Then eight or
ten wealthy ladies from the neighbourhood, provincial aristocracy or plutocracy, wives of landed proprietors or communal
councillors ; with bored, inexpressive faces, and toilets that had
come from Naples, some being worn awkwardly and others with
supreme elegance. Among the notabilities were the Contessa
Brambilla, a fresh-looking young woman, with perfectly white
hair and very bright eyes ; the illustrious poetess Nina, small,
fragile and vivacious as a grain of pepper ; the wife of the
Member for Santa Maria, a calm austere woman, with full
pensive eyes. All these ladies inspected each other with a
curiosity they endeavoured to dissemble, while they discussed
the relative merits of hand-made stockings, hand-stitched
shirts, and darns in felt. Some of them carried special

communications to and fro from the presidential platform.

Caterina was the most silent of them all; she was reading,
or pretending to read, in her little note-book. It was a present
of the day before from her husband; on its morocco binding
was the name *Nini*. Andrea had become more tenderly
affectionate of late, and in this tenderness she sunned herself
with devout collectedness and the absence of demonstration
that characterised her. When they were alone, Andrea would
take her on his knee or carry her round their room in his arms,
murmuring "Nini, Nini," ever "Nini," while he kissed her. And
it sometimes happened that on these occasions his voice trembled
from emotion; he no longer laughed his noisy laugh that used to
make the house ring with its mirth. Perhaps it was because
of the guests who had been with them for the last fortnight.
Caterina had long known that Andrea's character had all the
delicacy of a woman's. In the presence of those two sickly
beings, Alberto, a martyr to his cough, and Lucia, a prey to
latent or pronounced *nevrose*, Andrea restrained the exuberance of his perfect health. When he went out he abstained,
from delicacy, from kissing Caterina in their presence; for
Alberto never kissed Lucia in public. Perhaps that was why
Andrea made such enthusiastic love to her when they were
alone, to make up for all the time they passed in a friendly
partie carrée.

Caterina was not less bored than the other eight or ten
ladies of her set. She could not appreciate the needlework
exhibits: stockings in coarse, yellowish thread, knitted with
rusty needles; shirts covered with the fly-marks accumulated
during the six months they had been in hand, sewn with big,
inexpert stitches, ill-cut and folded in coarse material; interminable productions in every kind of crochet, darns done with
hair, miracles of patience, that made her sick. The exhibits
had been sent in in heaps, badly arranged and catalogued,
from rural schools, in which the teachers laboured, almost
in vain, to teach the use of the needle to poor fingers

hardened by the use of the spade—rural schools that can neither provide needles, thread, irons, nor material wherewith to work. Caterina with her instinctive love of pure, fine, sweet-smelling linen, felt a sort of physical disgust in inspecting these objects of dubious whiteness. Besides, what did she know about it? These humble accomplishments had not been taught her. She felt her own ignorance, and offered up inward thanks that it had saved her from the vice-presidency of a district.

Meanwhile the meeting continued in academic form, in discussion that was at once official and colloquial. The vice-presidents read lengthy accounts of their own districts, and insisted on prizes being distributed to everybody : the poetess suggested buying materials for those pupils who were too poor to do so for themselves : the professor read letters of sympathy and adhesion from pedagoguish clubs and committees; but Caterina heard not a word of it all. There was the cook, who did just as he chose lately. Since Lucia and Alberto had come to pass the villa season with her, Caterina was more particular than ever as to her table. Those two were so delicate ; they needed strong *bouillon* and light dishes ; quite a different diet from Andrea's, which was also hers. She and Andrea ate underdone meat and refreshing salads ; and the fish question was a serious one at Caserta, an inland town, where the fish had to be sent from Naples and Gaeta, and was not always fresh. One day, in fact one evening, Caterina had sent Peppino, a labourer, to Naples, for soles ; her two guests often partook of this delicate, innocuous fish. And now, what with official entertainments, banquets, and hotels filled to overflowing, the market was cleared out in a moment.

Mouzu Giovanni, with whom she held a consultation every morning, shook his head doubtfully on the slightest provocation, saying sceptically : .

" If we can get any ! If there is any in the market ! If it isn't all gone."

This was the difficult question which Caterina was debating,

while the Princess Caracciolo requested the ladies to proceed
to the election of a vice-president, who in one report
would combine those of six divisions. Caterina was in continual fear of not having sufficiently mastered the study of
Lucia's tastes, poor nervous creature that she was, whose
digestion was completely destroyed. She had arranged a
pretty, fresh, airy room for her—hung with Pompadour
cretonne, a room full of pretty nicknacks, to please her. But
she believed that in secret Lucia hankered after her *prie-dieu*,
which she had taken away from her father's house to her own
in Via Bisignano. One afternoon, when Alberto and Andrea
had gone out riding, Caterina had entered the room and found
Lucia on her knees before a chair, just as she used to kneel
at school. If she could but arrange with Alberto to send
Peppino to Naples to fetch the *prie-dieu*, what a pleasant
surprise for Lucia! It could surely be managed without much
difficulty, and it would give her so much pleasure! Ah, she
must remember to write to Naples for good tea—Souchong;
for Lucia said that from September on she could only drink
tea in the evening : coffee was too exciting for her nerves.
The question was whether she should write to Caflish or to
Van Bol for Souchong; Andrea would know; he was always
well posted in such matters.

"Signora Lieti, will you come and vote?" broke in the
Princess Caracciolo, gently.

Caterina, scarcely realising what she was doing, wrote the
first name that occurred to her on her script, which she then
rolled up and dropped in the crystal bowl. Looking at her
little gold watch, she returned to her place. It was getting
late; they had been there, losing their time, for nearly three
hours.

Elsewhere, at home for instance, she could have employed
it usefully. The washerwoman had brought home an enormous pile of washing, and Caterina never allowed it to be
ironed until she had carefully examined it and ascertained
where a button or a tape was missing. The linen was new, but

she suspected the washerwoman of using potash, because of certain tiny holes she had discovered therein. She had taxed her with it, and the woman had replied that she was incapable of such deception, and that all she used was pure wood-ash and soap.

At last there was a stir in the meeting. The result of the voting was uncertain; it was even remarkable for divergence of opinion. Each lady appeared either to have given her vote to herself or to the person who happened to be sitting next her. The Princess read out each scrip with the same indulgent smile. She was a woman of unerring tact, who saw and noted all that befell in her presence. She requested the ladies to do their voting over again, and to make up their minds to one name, so that some result might be attained. They then formed into groups; the Colonel's wife went from one juror to the other, talking to each in an undertone.

"Signora Lieti, would you like to vote for the Member's wife? We ought to get an unanimous vote."

"I will vote for any one you please. Will the meeting last much longer?"

"Don't talk about it; it's torture. To-day I am supposed to be at home to the superior officers, and my husband is there waiting for me, and I shall find him furious. Shall we decide on that name?"

"I am quite of your opinion."

Andrea, Alberto, and Lucia were walking up and down the agricultural show. They had driven over to Caserta after luncheon, leaving Caterina in the Hall of the Didactic Jury, and promising to call for her soon. That day Alberto had declared that he felt perfectly well and strong, and he intended to see everything. Lucia, on the contrary, happened to be in a bad humour; still she had vouchsafed a smile of melancholy joy when the news was broken to her. Andrea was happy in his summer garments—a great relief to him after the evening attire which had sat so heavily on him the day befɔre. He felt at his ease, free and content, and frequently addressed himself to Alberto. Lucia, walking between them, listened in silence. They stopped before everything of interest—she longer than her companions—so that she did not always keep up with them.

"Are you in low spirits to-day?" queried Andrea at last.

"No, no," she replied, shaking her head.

"Do you feel ill?"

"Not worse than usual."

"Then what is it?"

"Nothing."

"Nothing . . . . is too little."

"It is nothing that spoils my life for me."

"Don't ask her questions," said Alberto to Andrea, as they went on in front; "it's one of her bad days."

"What do you do when she is in one of her bad days?"

"Nothing. If she doesn't care to speak, I ask her no questions; if she speaks, I don't contradict her. It's the least I can do for her. Do you realise the sacrifice she has made in marrying me?"

"What an idea!"

"No, no; I am right. She is an angel, Andrea, an angel! and a woman at the same time. If I could but tell you . . . . No lemons or oranges here, are there, Andrea?"

"No, Alberto. You must know that the soil is unfavourable to them. Besides, we are too far inland; they thrive well along the coast. Have you many at Scrrento?"

"Oh, a good many; and, *sai*, they yield six per cent. free of income-tax, while other produce only yields two and a half."

Lucia broke in with her faint, dragging intonation:

"Alberto, why don't we build a villa at Sorrento?"

"Eh! It wouldn't be a bad plan. I have thought of it sometimes myself; but building runs away with time and money . . . ."

"Not a palace; no big useless edifice. What would be the

good of it? But a microscopic villa, a nest for us two, with three or four rooms flooded with sun; a conservatory, and an underground kitchen that would not destroy the poetry of the house; no dining-room, but a porch hung with jasmin and passion-flowers; an aviary, where singing-birds would pipe and birds of Paradise hop from branch to branch—and go together, we two alone, into that fragrant land, washed by that divine sea, and stay there together, apart from the world : thou restored to health, I dedicating myself to thee . . . ."

She said all this to Alberto, looking the while at Andrea, who was rather embarrassed by such a demonstration of con-jugal affection. He pretended to be immersed in the study of onions, but not one of the slow, chiselled, seductive words escaped him.

"You are right; it would be delightful, Lucia. We will think about it when we get back to Naples. Oh! we really must build this nest. But where do you find these strange notions that would never occur to me? Who suggests them to you?"

"The heart, Alberto. Shall we sit down?"

"By no means; I am not a bit tired. I am flourishing—almost inclined for a ride. You are tired, perhaps?"

"I am never tired," was the grave, deliberate answer. "Sometimes, Signor Andrea, I ask myself what the people would do without bread."

"Eh!" he exclaimed.

"If the wheat were to fail! . . . . Who can have invented bread?"

They turned to her in amazement; Alberto attempted a joke.

"You should be able to tell us, Lucia. They must have taught you that at school, where you learnt so many things."

"No; there is nothing that I know. I am always thinking, but I know nothing."

She was looking singularly youthful, ·in her simple cotton frock, striped white and blue, confined at the waist by a leather band, from which hung a small bag; with a straw hat with a blue veil which the sun mottled with luminous spots; her chin was half buried in folds of the gauze that was tied under it.

They had halted before a large panel, a marvel of patience, whose frame consisted of dried beans strung together. Along it ran a design executed in split peas in relief; the ground of the tablet itself was in fine wheat, threaded grain by grain. On it, in letters formed of lentils, might be read: "A MAR-GHERITA DI SAVOIA: REGINA D'ITALIA."

" Whose work is it?" asked Lucia.

"Two young ladies, daughters of a landowner at San Leucio."

" How old are they?"

"I think . . . . about twenty eight or thirty."

" Are they beautiful?"

"Oh, no; but so good."

"That I am sure of. Do you know that in that tablet I can decipher a romance? Poor creatures! passing their lonely winter evenings imprisoned within their own walls, and finding their recreation in this lowly, provincial, inartistic work. And perhaps, labouring over it, they sighed for unrequited love . . . . an affection which their avaricious parents refused to sanction. Oh! they foresaw their own existence—an old maid's dull life. Poor picture! I should like to buy it."

"It's not for sale. Perhaps it will be sent to the Queen."

By degrees her melancholy was infecting her companions by the contact of her fascinating sadness. Andrea shrugged his shoulders in an effort to regain his good humour, but he had not the power to recall it—the spring was gone. Alberto, tugging at his scanty moustache, tried to shake off the impression of fatigue that had stolen upon him.

"Is there much more to be seen?" he inquired of Andrea.

"I," observed Lucia, "have no will of my own. Take me where you please. Do you know that I belong to the ladies' jury for flowers? Yesterday I received the appointment."

"These juries are an epidemic," exclaimed Alberto. "They take our wives away from us. The Signora Caterina has become invisible; now they want to sequestrate mine. I refuse my consent."

"Have your own way; I will do whatever you choose," said Lucia, with a smile. "Still the flower jury is a pretty idea . . . . To feel the delight of colour, perfume, exquisite form : to examine the most delicate, mysterious, extraordinary of flowers, and among them to seek the beautiful, the perfect one, the flower of flowers."

"After all, there would be no harm in your accepting . . . . Lucia," suggested Alberto.

"Very well, then; I will accept for your sake—to please you Signor Andrea, what do you think about it?"

"I am not a competent judge," said Andrea, drily.

Lucia, as if from fatigue, then slipped her arm through his, and leant on it. He started, smiled, and then quickened his step, as if he would run away with her . . . . They were about to enter the hemp-room : there it was, in the rough, in bundles, then combed, spun and made up in skeins; a complete exhibition of it in every stage.

"Look, look at this mass of hemp; it is like the tresses of a Scandinavian maiden looking down from her balcony on the Baltic, awaiting her unknown lover. And this, paler still, so finely spun; might it not be the hair of Hamlet, Prince of Denmark? Oh, how full of meaning are all these things for me!"

"She sees things that people like us never see," said Alberto, as if to himself. "Tell me, Signor Andrea, is it true that the lives of the hemp-spinners are as wretched as those of the unfortunate peasants who work in the rice plantations?"

"Not quite so bad, but nearly, Signora Lucia. Hemp-netting is done at midsummer, in the dog-days; a kind of heat that causes the exhalation of miasma. The water in which the hemp lies becomes putrid and poisons the atmosphere."

"But do you know that what you're telling me is odious? Do you know that our artificial life, that feeds on rural life, is

an anthropophagous one? Do you know that the daily homi-
cide . . . . Oh! let us go away, away from this place. This
exhibition represents to me a place of human butchery."

"There is a little exaggeration in this view of it," he replied,
not daring to contradict her flatly. "For the disease is
decreasing, and fatal cases are growing less frequent. Land-
owners supply quinine gratis to the women who fall ill.
Besides, if we think seriously on all things mundane, we shall
perceive that human life needs these obscure sacrifices.
Progress . . . ."

"You are as odious as you are wicked. I cannot bear you;
go away."

She dropped his arm, as if in horror. Alberto sniggered at
Andrea's sudden discomfiture.

"Oh! poor Andrea, didn't you know that Lucia was a
humanitarian?"

"I did not know it," he replied, gravely.

"Oh! my heart is full of love for the disinherited of life;
for the poor, down-trodden ones; for the pariahs of this cruel
world. I love them deeply, warmly; my heart burns with
love for them."

Andrea felt pained. He felt the weakness of Lucia's argument, but dared not prove it to her: he felt the predominance
she usurped in conversation and over those who approached
her, and shrank from it as from a danger. When she had leant
on his arm he had throbbed, in every vein, with a full and exquisite pleasure. When she had dropped it, he had experienced
a strange loneliness, he had felt himself shrink into something
poorer and weaker, and was almost tempted to feel his arm, so
that he might revive the sensation of the hand that had been
withdrawn. Now Alberto was laughing at him, and that
irritated him beyond measure . . . . That little Alberto, a
being as stupid as he appeared innocuous, was capable of
biting, when the spirit moved him. He could be poisonous,
when he chose, the consumptive insect! Why shouldn't he
crush his head against the wall? Andrea took off his light

grey hat and fanned his face to disperse the mist of blind rage that clouded his brain. All three pursued their walk in silence, as if isolated by their own thoughts. The embarrassing silence prolonged itself. Alberto had an idea.

" Make peace with Andrea, Lucia."

" No; he is a bad-hearted egotist."

" *Via*, make it up. Don't you see he is sorry ? "

" Are you sorry for what you said just now, Signor Andrea ? "

" *Mah !* . . . ."

" Repent at once, and we will be friends again, and you shall once more be my knight of the Exhibition. You do repent ? Here is my pledge of peace."

She separated a spray of lilies of the valley from the bunch at her waist and gave it to him. He placed it in his button-hole, and, taking her hand in his, tucked it under his arm . . . .

" And you, Alberto, who are the mediator between us, will you have some lilies ? ".

" What should I do with them ? I have no button-hole to this overcoat. You shall give me another pledge—a kiss . . . . when we get home."

Andrea squeezed the arm that rested on his, so hard that it was all she could do to suppress a cry.

" Yes, yes," she stammered, trembling.

" What is the average value of the Wine Show ? " inquired Alberto, who possessed vineyards in Puglia which produced the noted Lagarese. This he said with the air of a connoisseur . . . .

" Not much," replied Andrea, with forced composure. " For the vine-growers have not all sent exhibits. You see, there are the special viticultural expositions. But there's some good in that too."

" Is this your wine, that the Prime Minister praised you for ? "

" Yes ; and there is some more over there."

"Does this wine intoxicate, Signor Andrea?" inquired Lucia.

"That's according ; I have some of greater strength."

"Intoxicating?"

"Yes."

"Wine is an excellent and beneficent gift. It gives intoxication and forgetfulness," she said, slowly.

"Forgetfulness," murmured Alberto ; "and the Signora Caterina, whom we are forgetting."

The other two exchanged a rapid glance. They had indeed forgotten Caterina, who had been waiting for them for an hour in the Maria Carolina saloon, whence the other ladies had departed.

At table, between the roast and the salad, Lucia mentioned that she had been, and was, still in low spirits on account of poor Galimberti. The impending misfortune took her appetite away.

"What misfortune?" asked Caterina.

"His sister writes me that he begins to show signs of mental alienation."

"Oh ! poor, poor man !"

"Most unhappy being, victim of blind fate, of cruel destiny. The case is not hopeless, but he has never been quite *all there*. In addition to this, they are poor, and do not like to confess their poverty."

"Have you sent money?"

"They would be offended. I wrote to them."

A shiver ran through the circle. When they separated for the night, Andrea was pensive.

"What is the matter with you?" said Caterina, who was plaiting her hair.

"I am thinking of that unfortunate Galimberti. Let us send him something, anonymously."

"Yes, let us send !"

"All the more . . . . all the more because his misfortune

might befall any of us," he added, so low that she did not hear him. A sudden terror had blanched his face.

III.

" This morning I feel so well, that I shall go for a ride."

" It would be imprudent, Alberto," said his wife, from her sofa.

" No, no; it will do me good. I shall ride Tetillo, a quiet horse that Andrea is having saddled for me. A two hours' ride on the Naples road . . . ."

" It is too sunny, dear Alberto."

" The sun will warm my blood. I am recovering my health, Lucia *mia*. I am getting quite fat. What are your plans?"

" I don't care for anything. Perhaps I shan't go out. I am bored."

" Bad day," murmured Alberto, as, clanking the silver spurs on his polished boots, he took his departure.

Later on Caterina knocked at her door.

" What are you going to do? Are you going to the Exhibition?"

" No; it bores me."

" You will be more bored, all alone here. Alberto won't come home till late; Andrea and I are sure to be late. Come!"

" I won't go; the Exhibition bores me. I can never be with you for a moment there."

" We can't help that. I feel it too, but it's not my fault."

" And to-day, if I went, I should have to pace up and down those huge rooms alone."

" Andrea might stay with you," urged Caterina, timidly, ever conscious of their latent antipathy.

" We should quarrel."

" Still?" said the other, pained and surprised.

" That's how it is; we cannot agree."

Caterina was silent; after a pause, she said:

" But surely, to-day is the flower day ? "

" To-day? I think not . . . . True, it is to-day."

" Then you cannot avoid going."

" I can pretend to be ill."

" It's a bad pretext."

" Well, I see I must sacrifice myself, and come." There was irritation in her voice and manner as she hurriedly proceeded to dress. Caterina felt as humiliated, while she was waiting for her, as if she were to blame for the annoyance. During the drive from Centurano to Caserta, Lucia was silent, with a harsh expression on her face, keeping her eyes closed and her parasol down as if she neither wished to see nor hear.

Caterina congratulated herself on having sent Andrea on before, while Lucia's insufferable fit of ill temper lasted. They arrived at the Palace at half-past twelve. They separated, without exchanging many words, appointing to meet each other at four. Caterina mounted the stairs leading to the Didactic Exhibition, and Lucia passed through the garden to the flower-show. There were crowds of fashionably attired ladies and gentlemen in those regions. Lucia moved slowly along the gravelled path to the right, under the chestnut-trees, and those whom she met turned to gaze at her. She wore a dress of darkest green brocade, short, close-fitting, and well draped ; it showed her little black shoes and open-work, green silk stockings. On her head was an aërial bonnet of palest pink tulle—a cloud, a breath, without feathers or flowers, like a pink froth. Now Caterina had left her, she was smiling at her own thoughts. The smile became more accentuated when, on turning the palisades of the Floral Exhibition to enter the conservatory containing the exotics, she met Andrea.

" My dear Lieti, where are you going to ? "

" Nowhere," he replied, with embarrassment; " I was looking for a friend from Maddaloni."

" And have you found him ? " with an ironical smile.

" No ; he hasn't come. I shall wait for him. And you ? "

" Oh ! you know all about me. I have come to the flower jury."

"But it doesn't meet till two."

"Really? Oh! what a feather-head! and what shall I do till two? I may not go to the 'Didactics,' and the 'Agrarians' bore me."

"Stay with me," he entreated.

"Alone?"

"Here . . . ."

"Without doing anything? Every one will notice it."

"Who do you think is going to gape and watch?"

"Every one, my friend."

"They will look at you," he said, bitterly; although the words "my friend" delighted him.

"And if they do, we must provide against it; this is a scurrilous province. It hides its own *bourgeois* vices and slanders the innocent."

"Listen," murmured Andrea, taking her arm in his. "Why don't you come with me to the English Garden?"

"No . . . ."

"It is so beautiful. The great trees cast their shadows over it, the paths rise, fall, and lose themselves among the roses; under the water-lilies lies the still crystal water; under the reeds, the water murmurs as it flows; there is no one there, and it is so cool . . . ."

"Do not speak to me like that," she whispered, faintly.

"Come, Lucia, come. That is the frame for your beauty. You are like a rose to-day; come, and take your place among the roses."

"Do not talk to me like that, for pity's sake, or you will kill me . . . ." Her teeth chattered as if from ague.

He felt that she was losing consciousness, that she was going to faint. People were passing to and fro; he was seized with a fear of ridicule.

"Fear nothing; I will not say another word. Come to yourself, I beseech you. If you care for me at all, come to yourself. Shall we go to the cattle-show? It is crowded You will be safe there. Will you come?"

"Lead me where you please," she replied faintly, while her bosom heaved and her nostrils quivered in the struggle for breath.

They did not exchange a word on the way. They met several persons, who, seeing Andrea with a lady, bowed profoundly to him. Two young men made whispered remarks to each other.

" They take me for your wife."

" Do not say that to me, I entreat you."

" You are not brave, Signor Lieti; you are afraid to hear the truth."

" You have called me your friend . . . ."

" Do you wish to make me repent it?"

" Oh! don't torment me. Dialectics are your strong point; your thoughts are deep, weird, and often too cruel for me to fathom. I am at your mercy. You invest me, you capture me, and then you torture me. Remember that I am a child, an ignorant child—a child all muscle and no imagination. Spare me."

He raised his hand to his collar as if he were choking; while he spoke, the tears had gathered in his eyes and voice.

" Forgive me; I will spare you," she said, sweetly humbling herself in her triumph.

They passed under a great avenue of chestnut-trees where the sun cast little circles of golden light upon the ground. The heat was increasing. Some of the passers-by were fanning their flushed faces with their straw hats; ladies unfurled their fans as they moved languidly along, overcome by the weight of the atmosphere. They spoke but little to each other, looking down like two persons who were a prey to *ennui*. They turned and came to the first section. A walk led all round an immense rectangular meadow, which was enclosed by a stout palisade of medium height, divided into compartments for each animal. There was a little rack with a ring and a cord for each head of cattle ; the animals stood stolid and motionless, facing the spectators. The cows had good stupid heads,

benevolent eyes, and their ribs showed through their thin
flanks.

"Poor beasts," she whispered. "How ugly they are!"

"Ugly, but useful. They are hardy animals, and all the
better for being thin; the milk is all the better for it. They
are not so liable to disease, and they yield five hundred per
cent. of their value."

"You are fond of animals?"

"Very; they are strong, useful, and docile. We humans do
not always combine the same qualities."

"But we have intellect."

"You mean, egoism."

"Well; love is a species of egoism," affirmed Lucia, crossly.

They progressed slowly. From behind the palisade the oxen
gazed at them with serene eyes that were almost indicative
of thought. Some of them bending their necks, under the
sun that struck their hides, browsed bunches of grass. Now
and again the dull impatient thud of their hoofs struck the
scanty down-trodden grass of the meadow. The flies settled
on the hard rough hides with their many seams. Sometimes
an ox would strike his neck with his tongue and his flank with
his tail, to rid himself of them; but the flies returned insolentl
to the attack, buzzing in the stifling atmosphere. Lucia opened
a large Japanese fan, all gold-dust on a black ground, and
fanned herself rapidly.

"Do you feel the heat?"

"Very much. And how suffocating it is here!"

"Shall we sit down?"

"No; I am beginning to feel interested in the cattle. Besides,
I feel the sun broiling my shoulders. I would rather walk."

"Here are the buffaloes," explained Andrea. "You cannot
have seen any before. They are of a nobler breed than these
cows. Look at them; don't you see how wild they look? They
are shaking those heads with the twisted horns. They are of
a powerful, sanguine temperament; their blood is black and
smoking. Have you ever drunk blood?"

"No," she replied, in amazement, yet sucking her lips with a kind of longing. "What is it like?"

"A potent drink that puts strength into your veins. A drink for soldiers, sportsmen, and brave men trained to corporal exercises. A cup of blood expands one's life."

By degrees, while he spoke, Lucia's enthusiasm grew for the plenitude of strength expressed in Andrea's whole personality, for the vigour of his powerful frame and the plastic animalism that found in him its supreme and perfect development. A buffalo, in sudden rage, proceeded to bump its head against the wall. Lucia gazed in growing astonishment at the magnitude of these stalls built in the open air, and at the motley show of sturdy brutes.

"Are these buffaloes savage?" she inquired, timidly.

"Very: the blood goes to their heads, as it might to the brain of a strong man. They are subject to fits of sanguine madness. They loathe red, it sends incendiary fumes to their brain."

Lucia raised her perfumed handkerchief to her lips and stopped her nose with it. "This smell of cattle is not unhealthy," said Andrea, naïvely. "Indeed, it is good for the health. Doctors prescribe it for consumptive people. Your perfumes are far more injurious, they deprave the senses and shatter the nerves."

"Depravity is human."

"That is why I prefer the beasts, whose instincts are always healthy. We have come to the end of this section. Here is the finest of them all."

It was a bull, a black bull with a white mark on its forehead, between its superb horns; a sturdy, majestic creature, contemptuous of its rack, to whom had been given a long cord and a wide enclosure: he tramped up and down his habitation without taking any notice of the onlookers, who expressed their timid admiration by whispered eulogies.

"Oh! how beautiful, how splendid!" cried Lucia.

"He is magnificent. He belongs to Piccirilli, of Casapulla

we shall give him the prize. He is the pure exceptional type,
the perfection of the breed. A masterpiece, Lucia . . . .
What is the matter ? "

" I feel rather faint, take me down there to the water. The
sun is burning my arms, and my brain is on fire."

They went as far as the little fountain, under a tree, where
there was a wooden cup. He dipped a handkerchief in water
and applied it to her forehead.

"Thank you, I am better; I felt as though I were dying.
Let us return, or rather let us continue walking here, we are
too isolated."

They passed by the horse-boxes, a row of little wooden
houses that were closed that day. They could hear the
frequent neighings that came from under the semi-obscurity,
under the wooden roofs that were grilled by the midday sun,
and the restless impatient pawing of many hoofs.

" Those are the stallions, accustomed to free gallops across
their native plains. They cannot bear inaction. Some of
them can hear the mares neighing in the adjoining boxes.
And they answer them by neighing and beating their tails
against the walls."

She turned pale again while he spoke.

" Is it the sun again ? " he inquired.

" The heat, the heat . . . ."

Dark flushes dyed her cheeks, leaving them paler than before,
with a feverish pallor. She tried to moisten her lips with the
wet handkerchief; they were as dry as if the wind had cut
them. The arm that rested on Andrea's weighed heavily.

"Shall we enter that large building, Signor Andrea? At
least we shall be out of the sun there. Do you know what I
feel? Myriads of pricks under my skin, as close together
and as sharp as needle-points. I think the cool shade will
stop it."

They entered a sort of large ground-floor barn with a
slanting roof, where every species of domestic animal disported
itself in cages or little hutches. The grave white rabbit; with

their pink noses and comic, pendant ears, were rolled up like bundles of cotton-wool at the back of their hutches. You could not see them without stooping, and then they edged still farther back in terror at not being able to run away. The fowls had a long compartment to themselves, a large wired pen, divided into many smaller ones. Big, fat, and motionless, their round eyes, watchful, disappeared now and then under the yellowish, flabby membrane that covered them. They butted their heads against the wire and pecked languidly at bran and barley prepared in little troughs for them, pecking at each other under the wing and cackling loudly, as if that cry were the yawn of a much bored fowl. The turkeys wore a more serious aspect; they never stirred, maintaining their dignified composure.

"Look, Lucia; I always think that turkey-hens pipe for their chicks out in the world."

"I have never seen one before. Are there no doves here?"

"No, only animals for agricultural purposes. Doves are luxuries. Are you fond of them?"

"Yes. I had one, but it died when I was a little girl."

"I am sorry there are none here."

A cock awakening from his torpor, and perceiving a ray of sunlight that had filtered through one of the windows, began to crow lustily—cock-a-doodle-doo; then another answered in deeper tones, and a third broke in immediately. And the hens began to perform in high soprano, the turkey-hens in contralto, while the turkeys and their kin gobbled in deep bass. Crescendo, staccato, swelled the discordant symphony; and patient visitors stopped their ears, while nervous ones ran away. Lucia's grasp tightened on Andrea's arm; she leant her head against his shoulder to deaden the sound, stunned, coughing, laughing hysterically, struggling in vain for speech, while he smiled his good-tempered, phlegmatic smile at the animal chorus. Then by degrees came a decrescendo; some of the performers suddenly stopped, others waxed fainter; a few

solitary ones held on, and, as if run down, stopped all at once.
Lucia was still convulsed with laughter.

" Have you never heard this before ? "

A fat merino, of the height of a donkey, with abundant,
dirty wool, disported himself in solitary state in his pen.
Farther on, a greyish pig, with bright pink splotches that
looked as if he had scratched them that colour, stood forgotten
and unclassed, away from his fellows, like an exceptional and
monstrous being that eschews all social intercourse.

"Come away, come away," said Lucia, whose nerves had
been shaken, dragging her companion away ; " I won't look at
anything else." She was seized with cramps and violent
stitches, alternating with a stinging sensation which almost
paralysed her. All the fire which the sun had transfused into
her veins seemed to have concentrated itself at the nape and
set her nerves in combustion. Andrea, who knew nothing of
atmospheric effects, who could bask in the sun and walk
through two rows of animals without discomfort, was unconscious of these painful sensations ; he was as sane as Nature
herself. They passed out into the garden, past the horse-boxes,
where a ray of sun was beginning to broaden. Lucia hastened
along with bowed head ; now the pain was in the top of her
skull, the fluffy bonnet weighed like a leaden helmet; she
could scarcely resist a longing to loosen her plaits and throw
it off.

" I am burning, burning ! " she kept saying to Andrea.

" What's to be done about the jury ? "

" I'll go there. Oh ! this sun will kill me."

" What can I do for you ; dip the handkerchief in water
again ? "

" Yes, yes ; or rather let us hasten on."

They crossed the enclosure, where the bull was now resting
on his haunches, apparently infuriated by the sun, pawing the
ground with one of his forefeet. Then came the whole show
once more, with the buzzing flies, the glorious sun, and the
animals' sleepy heads bowed under it. Lucia stuffed her

handkerchief into her mouth and nostrils until she could hardly breathe. When she reached the cool anteroom next to the conservatory, her face was flushed, her lips blanched, and the brightness gone from her eyes.

"I thought I should have died," she said, after a while, to Andrea, who stood waiting in dismay and remorse. "Go away now, the ladies are coming."

The Duchess of San Celso had come to attend the flower jury from her villa. The veteran *mondaine* was, if that were possible, more painted than usual; her flabby charms draped in a youthful gown, and her dyed hair crowned by a small white bonnet; she passed to and fro with bent back, crooked neck, and a liberal display of feet that were presentable. Three or four ladies of the Neapolitan aristocracy had arrived: the Cantelmo, tall, fair and opulent of form; Fanny Aldemoresco, small, dark and zingaresque, with hooked nose, olive skin, and dazzling eyes, attired in deep crimson; the Della Mara, with her fair cadaverous face, dull, leaden eyes, and pale hair; there was besides a Capuan Countess, with a head like a viper; the fat, insignificant wife of the Prefect, addicted to low curtseys and ceremonious salutations; a general's widow; and Lucia Altimare-Sanna. These ladies had taken several turns round where the beds were planted, and were inspecting them through the tortoiseshell lorgnettes poised on their noses, with upturned chin and severe judicial eye, turning to discuss them with the young men who followed in their train, and chatting vivaciously with each other. A little expanse of many-hued verbena was admired; Fanny Aldemoresco pronounced it "mignon." The Altimare-Sanna, with whom she was acquainted, and to whom she addressed herself, replied that she hated verbena. She much preferred those musk-roses that grew so close and sweet-smelling, those large flesh-coloured ones with the curled petals. The Duchess of San Celso was of the same opinion; indeed, she took a rose and placed it in the V-shaped opening of her dress, against her skinny throat. That little animated group .

of ladies, with waving fans and parasols and floating laces, the bright-coloured group whence came the sound of silvery laughter and little cries like the bickerings of tomtits, was beginning to attract a court around it.

There was the oldest, perhaps the first, lover of the Duchess; he also had dyed hair, rouged cheeks, waxed moustachios of dubious flaxen hue, and flabby hanging cheeks ; and her young lover, handsome but very pale, with insolent black eyes, a sensual mouth, and the elegance of a poor young man enriched by her Grace's bounty. There was Mimi d'Allemagna, who had come for the Cantelmo, and Cicillo Filomarina, her unavowed adorer, who had also come for her sake, and many others, either to keep appointments or for the fête or for fun. The Prefect, in evening dress, was always by the Duchess's side. These people came and went, to and fro, forming into little groups, yet always keeping together; exhaling an odour of *veloutine* and a *mondain* murmur, from under the great horse-chestnut-trees. The judgment of the bedding-out plants was soon over. When questioned as to their votes, the ladies assumed a very serious air.

"We shall see . . . . we must consider . . . . we must decide . . . ." said the Aldemoresco, as serious as a politician who declines to be compromised.

They entered the great conservatory, in which cut flowers and bouquets and delicate exotics were exhibited. It had been provided by the Prefect with blue sun-blinds, and as the day wore on a gentle breeze cooled the air. In the centre, under a group of palms, a fountain had been erected for the occasion ; stools, wicker-chairs, and benches were hidden in the profusion of flowers that bloomed in every corner. The ladies, as they entered, uttered sighs of satisfaction and relief. Outside, the sun had scorched and the dust had choked them, and bedding-out flowers were of minor interest. Inside, the atmosphere was full of perfume and softened light. Pleasure beamed in their smiles; Lucia shivered and her nostrils dilated. Turning, the better to observe a great bush of heliotrope, she perceived Andrea in the doorway, where he was chatting with Enrico Cantelmo; she affected not to see him, but stooped to inhale a longer draught of its perfume. His eyes followed her absently, while he discussed horses with Cantelmo. Then he had a sudden inspiration: she turned round, and approaching a group of orchids, found herself in close proximity to the door; Andrea understood her. He left Cantelmo, advanced towards her, and held out his hand as if they met for the first time in the course of the day. They conversed with the coolness of ordinary acquaintances.

" How are you? "

" Better, thank you. Why have you returned? "

" . . . . I happened to pass this way. Besides, the place is full of people; there is no reason why I should not pass through it."

" Stay here, you must be fond of flowers."

" No; I don't care for them. This atmosphere is heavy with perfume."

" Do you think so? I don't notice it."

" Oh! it is overpowering. I don't know how so many ladies can endure it."

" I will exchange explanations with you, Signor Andrea. I adore these flowers and appreciate them. Look at this jasmin; it is a star-like Spanish flower of strong perfume—a creeper that will cling as tenaciously as humble, constant love."

" What do you know of love? " said Andrea, ironically.

" What is unknown to others, and what you do not know," she replied. " Look, look, how beautiful is that large sheaf of white and tea-roses, how light and delicate its colouring! "

" You wore the same flowers at the Casacalenda ball, and at the Inauguration the other day."

" You have a good memory. Does this inspection weary you? "

" No," he replied, with an effort, as if his mind had been wandering.

" Lamarra's exhibits are the best, Signora Sanna," said the

Cantelmo, stopping to talk to her. " We will award the prize to him. Just look at this flower-carpet."

She passed on. Andrea and Lucia crossed to the extreme end of the great conservatory, where the flower-carpet was. Stretched on the ground was a long rectangular rug, entirely composed of heartsease in varied but funereal shades of velvety violet and yellow, streaked with black ; some of them large, with luscious petals, and others no bigger than your nail : no leaves. This funereal carpet was divided down its centre by a large cross formed of snowy gardenias which stood out in bold relief.

" It looks like the covering of a tomb," she said. " I remember a picture of Morelli's : ' The Daughter of Jairus.' The carpet which is stretched on the ground and cuts the picture in two runs across the whole canvas."

" You take too much delight in sadness," said he, wearily.

" Because the world is sad. These Neapolitan Lamarras are uneducated people, yet they have a feeling for art ; they understand that a flower may express joy, but that it often expresses sorrow. Gardenias are refined flowers ; they remind me of double, or rather of glorified, jasmin. The gardenia might almost have a soul, it certainly is not devoid of individuality. Sometimes it is small and insignificant, with tightly curled petals ; at others as tall and delicate as an eighteen-year old maiden, and of transparent purity ; or it is full and nobly developed and of a passionate whiteness. And when it fades it turns yellow, and when it dies it looks as if it had been consumed by fire."

She was drawn to her full height before the mortuary carpet when she said this to him, absently and in an undertone, as if telling herself the story of the flowers. She was very pale, but her eyes were suffused with tenderness. A strong perfume rose from the gardenias so pungent that Andrea felt it prick his nostrils, mount to his brain and beat in his temples, where it seemed to him that the blood rushed heavily and swiftly.

"Here," he said, wishing to get away from the funereal carpet and the sight of the cross that stood out in such dazzling whiteness on its dark background of pansies ; " here is a beautiful bouquet."

" Yes, yes, it is pretty," said Lucia, approaching to examine it critically, and then moving away the better to observe its effect ; " really charming, with a discreet virginal charm of its own. Don't you think so ? It is composed of the most delicate and youthful-looking of exotics : the heart of the bouquet of minute fragrant mignonette ; then a broad band of heliotrope, contrasting the pale lilac of its lace-like blossoms with the green of the mignonette, and over all cloud-like sprays of heather which give an effect of distance to the whole. Heather is a northern flower, lacking perfume and brillancy, but reposeful and grateful . . . . Here at least is a group of pure and innocuous flowers."

Yet Andrea felt ill at ease while inhaling the delicate fragrance of mignonette and heliotrope. He felt as if his breath were failing him, with an unwonted oppression and a sensation of fatigue as if he had passed the night at a ball.

" What do you say to Kruepper, Signora Sanna ? " said the San Celso, who passed, leaning on the arm of her young adorer, like a ruin about to fall to pieces.

" I haven't yet seen it, Duchess."

" Pray look at it : that German has something in him, he is inspired ; don't you think so, Gargiulo ? "

" You always express yourself so well and artistically," replied the latter, with a tender inflexion in his voice, bending to kiss the bare skinny arm and hand which displayed the swollen veins of old age.

They passed on. The crowd increased. The murmur of voices waxed louder ; they smiled and jested more freely amid the luxuriant bloom ; some of them disappeared amid the shrubs and blossoming plants to chat with their friends, to reappear with flushed faces and laughing behind their fans. The atmosphere grew heavier and more than ever charged with ylang-ylang, opoponax, new-mown hay, and other pungent feminine odours, and the perfume exhaled by silken stuffs, silken tresses, and lace that had lain amid sachets of orris. Those women were so many artificial flowers, with lips and cheeks tinted like their petals, with eyes as dark as the velvet heartsease, and skins as white and fragrant as gardenias. And it seemed as if the vitiated atmosphere suited their morbid brains and lungs, refreshed their sickly blood, and revived their worn-out nerves. Lucia's face was tinted with pink in patches; her melancholy, leaden eyelids were raised, unveiling the lightning of her glance; pleasure acute as it was intense imprinted the smile on her lips.

Andrea began to see the spectacle as in a dream. He could no longer struggle against the torpor that was numbing his overtaxed brain. He made violent efforts to shake it off, but in vain, for he was mastered by a prostration that seemed to break his joints. As to his legs, they felt like cotton-wool, lifeless and powerless. He could only feel the leaden weight of his head, and he feared that it would fall upon his chest because the throat had ceased to support it. Unconsciously he wiped great beads of perspiration from his forehead, while his listless eyes still followed Lucia.

"Here is Kruepper, of Naples," said Lucia. "Oh! look, look, Andrea."

Kruepper, of Naples, exhibited many gradations of vases, wherein a monstrous tropical vegetation of cactus contorted itself with the twists and bends of a venomous green serpent: its pricks might have been fangs, its branches reared themselves or fell back as if their spine had been broken, or turned on one side as if overcome with sleep. These horror-inspiring branches supported a rich cup-like flower of transparent texture and yellow pistils, or a white blossom like a lily : superb flowers that lived with splendour and intensity for twenty-four hours, chalices wherein burned strong incense. Lucia bent over one of them to inspire its perfume, as if she would fain have drawn all its essence from it. When she raised her head, her lips were powdered with fine yellow dust.

"Smell them, Andrea, they are intoxicating."

"No, it would make me ill," he said, rubbing his eyes to clear them of the mist that veiled them. The truth was that he would have given anything to sit down and go to sleep, or rather to stretch his full length on a sofa, or throw himself prone on the ground. Sleep was gradually creeping on him while he strove with all his might, but in vain, to keep awake. He kept his eyes open by force and squeezed one hand in the other, trying to think of something to keep himself awake with. But he longed to lay his head somewhere, no matter where, against something, only to sleep for five minutes. Five minutes would have sufficed, he knew it; he was nodding already. The passers-by looked more than ever like phantoms gliding over the ground; there was no noise, only an ever increasing haze, in which the flowers dilated, expanded and contracted, assuming fantastic aspects, strange colours and perfumes. Oh! the perfume. Andrea felt it more acutely than anything else. It burned in his head like a flame, it filtered through the recesses and blended with the phosphorus of his brain. His nerves vibrated until exhaustion supervened, and then somnolence, and that all-compelling catalepsy from which his prisoned will struggled in vain to free itself.

All at once he turned: Lucia had disappeared. His pain at this discovery was so intense, that he would have uttered a loud cry but that his voice failed him. Then some of these female phantoms disappeared silently, as if the earth had swallowed them up. Could he get five minutes' sleep now, quietly? No ; a shade had approached him. Cantelmo was talking of flowers, of Kruepper again, and the warlike sound of the barbarous name annoyed him. What did he think of the hyacinths?

The hyacinths reared their stately heads in a jardinière of golden trellis-work. There were pink hyacinths, lilac ones and white, blending and uniting their voluptuous fragrance. Next to them, in a large Venetian amphora, stood a bunch of ten magnolias, exhaling the strongest perfume of them all.

In the lethargy that was upon him Andrea saw Lucia appear under the doorway. In her dark green dress, with her pink bonnet, she looked like a rose, a woman turned into a flower, a flower-made woman. To that flower Andrea felt all his being drawn—and he longed . . . . sole, supreme desire, to seize that flower, press it to his lips, and drink in its life with its perfume.

IV.

The fountain Michelangelo Viglia . . . .

> . . . . . SUL AUGUSTO ESEMPIO
> LO DO AD ALTRUIDA ME,

dripped tranquilly into its grey stone basin. The second part of the inscription :

> IL PELEGRINO, IL VILLICO,
> IL CITTADINO L'AVRA.
> VENITE, DISSETATEVI,
> FRESCA PER VOI QUI STA . . . .*

could not incite any one to accept its invitation. In the silent darkness of the night the solitary fountain repeated its purling cadence, for Centurano was asleep ; its grey, white, and yellow houses had all their shutters barred. The first lights to be extinguished had been those of the architect Maranca, who rose earlier than any one else to superintend the repairs of the dome of Caserta. Next to his, those of lawyer Marini, who had to plead a case on the morrow at the Court of Santa Maria ; and then those of Judge Scardanaglia, with whom they had been keeping rather late hours to play at *mediatore*, and

---

* Literal translation :—" Following an august example . . . I give it from myself to others . . . . The pilgrim, the peasant . . . The citizen may have it . . . . Come, quench your thirst . . . . Here is fresh water for you."

because on the following day there was no sitting for him in
the law courts. The friends of the Member for Santa Maria'
had driven off towards Caserta after an exchange of salutations
from the road to the balcony, in two sleepy carriage-loads—
lights, coachmen, and horses. The last lights to go out were
those of Casa Lieti, at the corner, overlooking the fountain.
The drawing-room had subsided into darkness; lights had
appeared in the two sleeping apartments, divided from each
other by an intermediate room, each having balconies that overlooked the street. Large and small shadows—tall, thin ones,
pigmies, and Colossi—had flitted across the window-panes,
defining themselves against the curtains. Then darkness.

   A dark night, dark with the profound density of meridional nights. A gleam of stars, a shining dust spread haphazard, hither and thither, with a beating motion, a palpitation
of the constellations. Under them, amid the black fields,
a whitish line was perceptible; the lane that led to the
high road towards Caserta. The lamps were out. Suddenly
the first balcony to the left opened; noiselessly, from the
narrow opening, a slight white form emerged, remaining
motionless on the balcony; it was unrecognisable. It stood
still, leaning again the balustrade. Was it gazing at the sky
or at the soil? Impossible to tell, nothing could be seen
of it except that every now and then the hem of the white
garment stirred as if an impatient foot had moved it. Behind
that form, which appeared elongated against the dark background of the night, the window remained ajar. It maintained its immobility and its attitude of contemplation. The
parish clock struck the quarter, and the calm sound rang out
gently on the silent air. Then, with a slight creaking of
hinges, the window to the right opened wide. A black mass,
that melted into the general darkness, appeared; but nothing
was defined. A luminous point glowed, the end of a lighted
cigar. At every breath drawn by the person smoking, the
lighted end glowed brighter, casting a little light on a heavy
moustache, and emitting a light cloud of smoke. Suddenly

the glowing ember sped like a star, from the balcony to the road, and the dark mass passed to the extreme end of the balcony to approach the one on the left. The white shadow fluctuated and trembled; it moved towards the right, standing at the corner motionless, then a breath traversed the space between them.

"Lucia."

The faintest breath made answer: "Andrea."

That was all, except that the fountain, ever fresh and young, continued singing its eternal song. Above shimmered the Milky Way that overhung Caserta. They, immersed in the profound darkness of the night, gazed at each other athwart its shade, straining their sight to see each other through it. Not a movement, not a word. And so the time passed, and again the parish clock struck the quarter—and they stood shrouded in darkness, without notion of space or time, losing themselves in the gloom, lost in the thought of searching each other's features. Once or twice the white figure leant over the balustrade, as if overcome by fatigue; once or twice the dark, massive one leant over it as if to measure its height from the ground. But they drew back and fell into their former attitudes. Once or twice the figures hanging over the sides of their respective balconies appeared to stretch out their arms towards each other, but they fell back again, as if discouraged; condemned to inaction, to the torture of unfulfilled desire; parts of that immovable, pitiless balcony, turned into statues of stone and iron. How long did it last, that torture of the minimum of distance, which in the night seemed immeasurable, the torture of not seeing, while knowing each other to be so near? At last a faint breath whispered: "Andrea." And a passionate one made answer: "Lucia."

Through the air projected by a trembling hand flew a white object, from one balcony to the other. He caught it on the edge of the balustrade, just as it was about to fall. From a neighbouring ruin, an owl screeched three times; a hoarse cry of terror answered from the left, and the white figure suddenly disappeared: the window closed. On the balcony to the right, the dark mass stood waiting and watching.

When Andrea re-entered his room, he found the lamp lighted and Caterina standing by the bed in slippers, fastening her wrapper.

"What ails you, Andrea?"

"Nothing; that's to say, I feel the heat."

"Are you feverish, like last night?"

"No, no; I was getting a little air on the balcony; go back to bed, Caterina."

"What is it?"

"Nothing; Nini, you have been dreaming."

"The cold air woke me. And when I felt for you, I found you missing."

"Were you frightened? Try to go to sleep again."

She threw the wrapper off; her mind was at rest.

"To-morrow—have you to rise early, Andrea?"

"Yes, early."

"At seven?"

"Yes."

"Good-night."

"Good-night."

Caterina put out the light, crossed herself, and immediately fell asleep, according to her wont. Andrea had waited, throbbing for that moment, to press to his heart the lace scarf, warm from the neck of Lucia, to kiss it, to put his teeth into it, to wind it round his hands and his throat, to cool his temples, and cover his eyes with it, during his long vigil.

Next morning Alberto alarmed the whole household by his sighs and groans. On rising he had coughed three times, and while washing his face he had coughed again. His throat was rough and relaxed, and he complained of an oppression on his chest.

"Where can I have caught cold? Where can I have caught it? I who am so cautious. I always wear a silk handkerchief round my neck, and a flannel shirt. A draught, I suppose."

He gave vent to his feelings in front of the glass, which reflected a pale face; putting out his tongue, trying to see down his throat, drawing long breaths to discover any possible obstruction. Lucia comforted him sweetly.

" Do you think I am ill? Do I look very seedy? "

" Why, no; don't indulge in fancies. You have your everyday face. Often, when I'm quite well, I cough on getting out of bed."

" Even when you wash your face ? "

" Oh! always."

" Oh! really? But I am so delicate . . . . "

" No, indeed, you are much stronger since we came here."

" True, but I must take care not to get ill. Listen, Lucia; I should like to go to Naples, to-day."

" What for? "

" For Carderelli to examine my chest thoroughly."

" And leave me alone? "

" For a shoit time, dear. *Sai,* just to reassure myself."

" I shall weary for you, Alberto *mio.* When do you return? "

" To-day, at half-past six, in time for dinner."

" Without fail, *caro mio ?* "

" Why, of course! When I arrive at the station, I shall breakfast; then go home for a moment; then to Carderelli, and back again."

" Return, Alberto *mio.* I shall not move from this room; I shall await thee here, counting the hours. Listen, my heart; don't you think you caught this cold riding the day before yesterday? "

" True, true; you are right, I am a fool; you tried to persuade me not to go. I never take your advice, my Lucia. You are my good angel. I will tell Carderelli of my carelessness."

" Ask him also if we are to stay on here."

" Why? I like being here. And you? "

" I am well wherever you are."

Lucia appeared at breakfast with red eyes, and hardly ate anything. Andrea was silent, and so was Caterina ; they exchanged looks of pity for the poor thing. Lucia recounted with much sadness the risk Alberto had run in insisting on riding, the cold he had caught by getting overheated, and her sorrow when she heard his harsh cough that morning.

"I felt knives in my own chest," she concluded, with a fresh fit of weeping.

Nobody ate another morsel. Caterina sat down beside her, trying to comfort her, holding her hands in hers, in memory of their school-days. Andrea stood by her side without finding a word to say to her. She regained her composure later.

Caterina had to go to that never-ending "jury"; luckily it was only to sit for two days longer. Lucia was so cast down that she did not even venture to propose that she should accompany her. Andrea, too, was obliged to go to Caserta, on business. Husband and wife took leave of her, Caterina kissed her cheek, Lucia sobbed and wept. This delayed their departure. Andrea was getting impatient, and Caterina feared that Lucia would perceive it. They bade her good-bye.

"Return soon, my friends; return soon," she said with intense languor. They turned to go. She called them back. They reappeared in the doorway.

"Whatever happens, you, my friends, will always love me?"

This question was addressed to both of them. They looked at each other : Caterina smiling, Andrea confused.

"Yes, yes, yes; I answer for him and for myself," cried Caterina.

"You, too, Andrea?"

"Yes," he replied, curtly.

"Lucia appears . . . . rather queer to you?" said Caterina, in the carriage, to her husband.

"To me? . . . . No."

"She is so unhappy."

"I know . . . ."

" How preoccupied you are ! "

"In the Faete vineyards—you know where they are—the vines have gone wrong."

" Oh, dear ! Tell me all about it."

The custodian of the English Garden bowed low to the pale lady in black, opened the gate for her, and inquired if she needed a guide. She refused, saying that she knew her way. Indeed, she trod the broad level path, whence branched many narrow ones, as deliberately as if she were accustomed to walk there. She had closed her black lace parasol, allowing the sun to warm her arms and shoulders under the slightly transparent gauze of her dress. Her black lace bonnet was fastened on with hammer-headed jet pins, like a veil. She hesitated when she reached the spot where the paths diverged. She turned and looked at the closed gate; through it she could catch a glimpse of the park, before her the enchanting incline of the walks, sloping under green boughs. She turned slowly into one that was bordered by a hedge of green myrtle, treading so lightly that her high heels hardly touched the cool ground. The trees formed a verdant arch, like the walls of a grotto, and far off, at the end of the walk, a hole let in the light. She wandered on through the grey twilight, suffering a stray leaf that dropped from overhead to rest on her garments, standing to watch the lizards at play. Then she resumed her rhythmic walk, while her dress brushed the myrtle hedge, and her gaze wandered through the murmuring solitude.

At the end of the slanting walk there was a little vale where other walks met and crossed; in its midst was a shady valley, shut in by dark hilly ground that was seamed in every direction by the yellow lines of the gravel. All round her stood horse-chestnuts, dwarf oaks, and tall, meagre, dusty eucalypti : complete solitude. She bent her steps towards the field, but all at once stopped midway, frightened and trembling, for Andrea had suddenly appeared before her. Without speaking, they looked into each other's eyes. He had come from below: she must have appeared to him like a Madonna, descending from the clouds.

They did not speak, but went on side by side, without looking at each other. They went down into the vale; Andrea, aggrieved because she was not hanging on his arm, yet not daring to ask her to do so.

"How is it that you are here?" she asked, suddenly and curtly.

"I can't tell you. Down there the heat and the boredom were enough to kill one."

"For no other reason?"

"I . . . . thought you would come here."

"And you were right; it is fate."

She looked tragic under her black veil, in her black gown, with the little silver dagger hanging from her waistband. The violet lines under her eyes gave them a voluptuous and sinister expression.

"If Caterina were to come . . . ." she said, grinding her teeth.

"She will not come . . . ."

"It would be better that she came; I could kill myself here."

"Oh, Lucia!"

"Do not call me by my name. I hate you."

Her tone was so passionate in its anger, her lips so livid, that he turned pale, and took off his hat to pass his hand across his forehead. Then suddenly two big tears burst from his frank, sorrowful eyes, ran down his honest, despairing face, and melted on his hands.

"Oh! Andrea, for pity's sake do not weep. Oh! I implore you, do not make me so unhappy, so unhappy!"

"*Che!* I am not weeping," he said, recovering himself and smiling. "It was a passing impression. It used to happen to me with my mother when I was a boy. Will you take my arm? I will take you all over this place."

"Where the shadow is deepest, where there is a sound of rushing water, where no one will think of coming," she murmured, in a melting mood. Leaning on his arm, in a narrow lane where the hedges were high, she gathered sheaves of wild anemones and stuck bunches of them in her waistband, in the lace round her throat, and the ribbons of her parasol.

Those hedges, blooming in the shade, pierced here and there by faint rays of sun, were full of wild anemones. She slipped some into the pockets of his coat and others in his button-hole. Andrea laughed silently, delightedly ; happy in the sensation of the touch of those light fingers on the cloth. They said nothing to each other, but because of the narrow path she kept very close to him. A little bird lightly grazed her brow. Lucia uttered a cry, started away from him, and ran on.

"Come, come, Andrea ; how enchanting !"

They had reached a platform, a sort of green terrace that looked down over another valley. High up, from the side of the rock, rushed a dancing, foaming torrent, falling straight down like a white, flaky cataract, and forming far below a wide, limpid, but shallow stream, that ran like a nameless river to an unknown sea, between two rows of poplars. From the terrace they could look down on the little northern landscape, the placid stream, and pale verdure : while the fine spray refreshed their faces, and they revelled in the grateful moisture and the soft breeze from the falling water.

"Oh ! how beautiful, how beautiful," said Lucia, absorbed.

"This is better than your drawing-rooms, where one cannot breathe," he said, with a long breath.

"It is beautiful . . . ." murmured Lucia. She rested her cheek against his shoulder, and he thrilled at the slight contact. Her hair was turned up high under the black lace, leaving the white nape bare ; her arm was bare under the silken gauze, and on the slightest pressure he could feel the rustle of the crisp diaphanous stuff.

"Let us try to get down to the stream, to see where it goes," said Lucia.

"There is no road down here."

"Let us find a way, an unknown way."

" We shall lose ourselves."

" Let us lose ourselves, for this is Paradise."

Soon they were making their way along an endless narrow path. They laughed as they hastened along. They came to an interminable avenue of exotic trees, ending in a square with a group of palms in its centre. They turned into a walk without knowing whither it led; she, who had relapsed into her melancholy languor, allowing herself to be dragged.

"You are tired; let us sit on the ground, instead of looking for the stream."

" Shall we die here?"

" Perhaps some one will pass."

" No, do not say that any one may pass; you frighten me— how you frighten me! Let us look for the stream."

At last they found it; shallower, narrower, slower than at its source, as if dying out under the trees. They stood by its edge, bending over it; Lucia leant down to gaze at its grey bed where green weeds waved mysteriously. A green light was reflected on her face. She cast her anemones into the water, watching them disappear and following them with her eyes; then she threw down others, interested and preoccupied in their destruction. When there were no more of her own, she took back those she had given to Andrea; he tried to oppose her.

"No, no; away with it all, all," said Lucia, harshly.

And she threw them away in bunches, closing her eyes. When her hands were empty, she made a gesture as if to let herself go after them.

" What are you doing?" he said, seizing her wrists. " Let us sit here, will you?"

" Not here. Let us find a secret place, that no one knows of; a beautiful green place that the sun cannot reach, where we cannot see the sky; I am afraid of all those things."

They began the search again eagerly, climbing steep ascents and descending little precipices; he supporting her by passing an arm round her waist. They crossed broad meadows, where

the damp grass wetted Lucia's little shoes; holding each other
by the hand, almost in each other's arms, with eyes averted,
subdued by the innocent intoxication of verdant Nature. They
came to a tiny stream; Andrea took Lucia in his arms and
placed her on the other side; when he put her down his light
pressure made her utter a cry.

"Have I hurt you?" he asked in contrition.

"No."

They had to stoop to pass under low-hanging boughs that
knitted into each other like those of a virgin forest. A hare
rushed by at full speed, to Lucia's great surprise.

"Ah!" cried Andrea, biting his forefinger, "if I had but a
gun."

"Wicked, cruel, how can you long for the death of an innocent animal?"

"Oh! it is rapture; you cannot understand the wild excitement of a man on the track of a hare. It is a combat of
animal cunning; the man does not always get the best of it.
But when he does hit his prey, and the animal falls in the
death struggle, and the hot blood rushes out in floods . . . ."

"It is horrible, horrible!"

"Why?" said the other, ingenuously.

"You have no heart, you have no feeling!"

"You are jesting?"

"*Che!* I am in earnest. Do not say these cruel, blood-
thirsty things to me. You can only realise hate, torture, re-
venge. You know nothing of love."

"But I neither hate nor love the hare. I kill it for the
pleasure of the thing."

"Pleasure! a great word; that which you sacrifice everything
to; it is brutality."

"I cannot argue with you," he said, humbly. "You always
conquer me by saying things that pain me."

"I wish you were good and tender-hearted," murmured
Lucia, vaguely. "You men have bursts of violent but short-
lived passion; but women have constant, enduring tenderness."

"'That is why love is so beautiful," he cried, triumphantly.

To save her from being scratched by a straggling briar, Andrea drew her towards him, murmuring close to her ear: "Love . . . . love."

She permitted him to do so at first, and tolerated his breath on her cheeks, but all at once freed herself in alarm, with eyes apparently fixed on a terrible vision.

"I want to go away, away from here," stamping her feet nervously, gasping from terror.

"Let us go," he said, bowing his head, subjugated, incapable of having any other will than Lucia's. He tried to find a way out, and went as far as the turning, where he disappeared amid the trees. Then he returned to Lucia, whom the thought of going away had already calmed.

"Over there," he said, "is the little lake I told you of, and the way out besides. We can get there by a short cut."

They wended their way in silence, he playing with the parasol, as if he meant to break it, while he tried to subdue his anger. They found themselves, by means of a descent so steep that it seemed as if it must lead underground, at the spot for which they had been seeking, but which they now no longer cared for.

It was a tiny, round lake; its clear water was of a transparent tint—deep-set in the wooded hills of the English Garden, which screened it from sight and made it difficult of approach; invisible, except to those who stood on its margin. This margin was planted with pale-leaved acacias, and tall, lean, dull-green poplars. Bending into its waters from the shore, a desolate, nymph-like weeping willow laved its pale-green hair. The ground was covered with short, close turf, studded here and there with bunches of shamrock. Flowerless, velvet-leaved aquatic plants floated on the surface of its still waters. In one spot, close to the shore, a Ninfea had risen from its depths to display the large white blossom that lures the male flowers, its lovers, to break from their roots and die. The landscape was steeped in a grey light, so soft that it appeared to fall through an awning ; a mere reflection of the sun, toned down and attenuated. No sound, complete forgetfulness; the cool, unknown, ideal spot where none came nor went. A hint of far-off, pale, blue distance, high up among the trees . . . . She stood in speechless contemplation on the shore.

"What is the name of this lake ?" she asked, without turning to Andrea.

"*Bagno di Venere.*"

"Why ?"

"Look there."

Behind the weeping willow there rose out of the waters of the lake a marble statue of the goddess. She was white and of life-size ; her head, like that of every other Venus, was too small and had the beauty of this imperfection. Her hair was partly bound to her nape, partly hanging on her neck. The water came up to her waist, hiding the lower part of her body; under the surface, reeds and other aquatic plants formed a pedestal for the white bust. The full-throated Venus leant forward to gaze placidly into the water, her still bosom inflated with delight, as if she had no cause of complaint against it, or the plants held her bound in their enchantments. When Lucia turned from the apparition to Andrea, her expression had undergone a change. Thought was on her brow, in her eyes, on her lips.

"And what is there over there, Andrea ?"

"Come and see."

It was something hidden in the trees. They went round the lake to it and found the ruin of a mock portico, with eight or ten columns, falling into utter decay, and a hole made in the roof through which the weeds grew in abundance. The cracked walls, after the antique, were peeling; the ivy was devouring the mock ruin in good earnest ; some of its stones had fallen. Under the damp shelter of the portico there was a musty smell that made one shudder, like the air of a vault.

"And this, Andrea ?"

" The ruin of a portico."

" There must have been a temple ? "

" Yes ; the temple of Venus."

"Venus, who at night descends from her altar to bathe in the lake," she said, dreamily. " One night, jealous Dian enchanted her and bound her in the waters. Never more did Venus return to the temple ; the temple, reft of the goddess, fell, and was no more. All that is left of it is the portico ; that will also fall. For all eternity, through the moon's spell, Venus is a prisoner amid the waters that gnaw her feet and the reeds that pierce her sides. One fatal day the rotten pedestal will give way, and fallen Venus will lie drowned at the bottom of the lake."

She was silent.

" Speak on, speak," whispered Andrea, taking her hand in his ; "your voice is music, and you say strange, harmonious things."

She left her gloved hand in his, but did not add another word, keeping her eyes fixed on the hole in the roof which let in the light. His fingers strayed idly to her wrist, and thence to where the glove joined the sleeve of her dress.

" Have you a pencil ? " she said.

Andrea took a gold pencil-case off his watch-chain and gave it to her. She sought the darkest corner of the portico, and thereon traced the outline of a heart. Inside she wrote :

A VENERE DEA
LUCIA,

and gave Andrea back the pencil. He stooped to read her inscription, and thus wrote his own name :

A VENERE DEA
LUCIA
ANDREA.

" Fate, fate," she cried, escaping from Andrea's outstretched arms.

She had seated herself on the ground, with her little feet almost in the water, so that the white lace of her petticoats peeped out from under the skirt of her dress. Her parasol lay on the ground, at some distance. She picked up little pellets of earth with her black-gloved hands and threw them into the lake, watching them dissolve in the water, and the concentric circles that widened around them like wrinkles. Beside her sat Andrea, noting the curves of her white throat, and the movements of the arm and fingers that played with the soil. He had cast aside his hat to let the cool, moist air play on his heated brow. Although she did not turn towards him, she appeared to feel the influence of that passionate gaze, for every now and then she swayed towards him as if to fall into his arms. He hardly dared to move, under the spell of a new and exquisite emotion, inspired by a woman as fragile as she was seductive. When she was tired of throwing grassy pellets into the water, she let her hand lie on the turf. Andrea took the hand and began gently to unbutton her glove, looking sideways at her, fearful of angering her. But no, Lucia closed her eyes as if she were going to sleep. When he had got one glove off, he thrilled with triumph ; then, reaching out a little further, he as gently took off the other. He threw them on the grass, near to his hat and the parasol. When he as gently stroked her arm through the transparent sleeve, Lucia drew it away, but without smile or anger ; she was looking at the Venus Anadyomene, through the green screen of the willow. Then she slowly unfastened the black lace scarf that fastened her bonnet under the chin and cast the ends behind her : she drew out the hammer-headed pins and stuck them in the turf, as if it were a pincushion, and, taking off her bonnet, sent it to join the gloves and parasol. Then she rose, bent over the water, and smiling took up some in the hollow of her hand and bathed her temples with it, her lips aflame, and her hair dripping. He lost his head, and, rising to his full height, clasped her in his arms and kissed her wildly on eyes, throat, and wrists . . . . She struggled in his embrace, but uttered no cry ;

her eyes were dilated, and her lips tightly drawn; with hair dishevelled, she screened her face.

"Leave me, leave me."

"No, love . . . . my love . . . ."

"Leave me, I implore you."

"Oh! my beautiful love, love of my life."

"Andrea, for the love I bear you, let me go."

He instantly loosed his hold on her. The lace round her neck was torn, and there were red marks on her throat and wrists; her breath came short and quick, yet she looked at him with the triumphant pride of a queen. Andrea, with nerves and senses calmed after the outburst, smiled in humble rapture. They resumed their places on the turf, she reclining, with one arm under her head, to keep it off the ground, looking up at the sky; he crosswise, so that his head scarcely reached her knee. Lucia still gazing at the sky, stroked his hair with a gesture that was almost maternal, while he rubbed his head against the hand that toyed with his curls, like a cat who is being petted. Then under the stillness of the great trees, a voice rang out, cool and clear:

"Andrea, what we are doing is infamous."

"Why, my sainted love?"

"If you do not realise our infamy, I cannot explain it to you. Remember two innocent beings who love us, who will suffer through us—Alberto and Caterina."

"They will never know."

"Maybe, but the infamy and the treachery will be ours. We are not meant to love each other."

"Why, if I love you? You are my heart, my sweetness, my perfume . . . ."

"Hold your peace. This love is a sin, Andrea."

"I know nothing about it. I love you, you are fond of me; you have said so."

"I adore you," she said, coldly. "I feel that this love is driving me mad; but it must cease. It is a sin before God, a crime in the eyes of man, a felony in the sight of the law."

"What care I for God, or man, or law? I love you . . . ."

"We are guilty sinners. Every tribunal, human and divine, condemns us . . . ."

"What matter? . . . . I love you!"

"We are full of deceit, bad faith, and iniquity.

"Love, cast these nightmares aside. Give me a kiss; no one sees us."

"No, it is a sacrilege. I belong to another man; you to another woman."

"Then what have we come here for?" he whined like a child. "Why did you give me your scarf last night? Why did you make me love you? What am I to do now? Must I die? I cannot live without you, without kissing you. I cannot live if you are not mine. You are beautiful, and I love you; it is not my fault."

"It is fate," she concluded, funereally crossing both hands under her head, and closing her eyes as if awaiting death.

"Lucia," broke in Andrea, in the tones of a melancholy child.

"Well?"

"Do you love me?"

"Yes."

"Say it: 'I love you.'"

"I love you," she repeated, monotonously.

"And how much do you love me, dear love?"

"I cannot measure it."

"Tell me, about how much," he persisted, childishly.

"Let me think," she said, crossly.

"What are you thinking of? Lucia *bella*, Lucia *mia*, tell me what you are thinking of?"

"Of you, rash boy," said Lucia, starting suddenly into an upright posture, and taking his head between her hands to look him straight in the eyes . . . . "Of you, unthinking creature, who are about to commit a terrible act, with nothing but love in your heart: neither fear nor remorse . . . ."

"Why remorse? I love you, I want but you, naught besides."

"Bravo! how straight to the goal! You will have your

M

way. Do you know what you leave behind you? Do you
gauge all that you lose or what the future holds in store for
you?"

"No, neither do I care; I only care to know that you love
me . . . ."

"Be a man, Andrea. Love is so serious a thing, passion is
so terrible. Beware; there is great danger for you, in loving,
in being loved, by me."

"I know it; that is what tempts me."

"I am not speaking for myself. I am an unhappy, suffering
being, a defenceless prey to human passion. I love you, and
I yield to this my love, even if it is to cost me my life. It is
for you that I speak. I am a fatal woman : I shall bring misfortune upon you."

"So be it. I love you."

"This love is madness, Andrea."

"So be it. I will have it so."

"You are binding yourself for life, Andrea."

"Oh! Lucia ; tell me that you love me."

She moved towards the shore, and spread her arms as if in
invocation :

"Oh! distant sky, oh! passing clouds, oh! trees that
crowd together to mirror yourselves in the lake, bear witness
that I have told him the truth. Oh! sorrowing willow, oh!
still waters, oh! reeds and lilies, you have heard my words.
Oh! Mother, Venus, Goddess, I have read the future for him.
Thou Nature, who liest not, bear witness that I have not lied.
'Tis he will have it so."

"How divine you are, joy of my life!"

She turned, and throwing her arms round his neck, gave
him kiss for kiss. Then, as if everything were irrevocably
settled, she calmly picked up her things.

"It is fate," she added. Then the tall, haughty, queen-like
figure moved slowly down the path, followed by her love-lorn
vassal.

PART IV.

I.

ONE rainy day, the Agrarian Exhibition closed, after a hurried ceremony, in which the prizes had been distributed in the presence of a scanty and discontented audience. Those who had not obtained prizes wrote incendiary articles to the local papers, and sent paid communications to the more important Neapolitan ones. The awards in the Didactic Exhibition had also been very unsatisfactory, for every teacher had expected the gold medal. The private school-teachers were wroth with parish school-teachers, and the latter with the "College" teachers. The ladies Sanna and Lieti had refrained from driving to Caserta on that occasion, on account of the bad weather, and because the fête had no attractions for them.

Caterina, freed from the necessity of wasting whole days in driving backwards and forwards between Centurano and Caserta, enjoyed being able to stay at home. She had so much to arrange, so many shortcomings to atone for, so many household projects to carry out. There were the preserves to make ; a great function in which Monzu succeeded admirably, although he needed a certain supervision, so that when the crystal jars were opened during the winter, at Naples, none of their contents turned out mouldy; that was what happened, last year, to two large jars of peaches : they had turned out quite green : such a pity ! Then there were the capers, gherkins, capsicums, and parsnips to pickle in strong four-year-old vinegar : they would need a great number of jars, for Andrea was fond of pickles and ate a great deal with *lesso* and

roast meat. Of course Caterina never touched these things
while they were being prepared, but her presence and advice
were necessary. Monzu had the greatest esteem for his own
culinary talents, but he always declared that *senza l'occhio della
Signora* [without the mistress's eye] he had no pleasure in his
work. Her rule was firm but gentle, she did not speak to her
servants more than was necessary, neither did she bestow
extraordinary *mance* [presents in money] on them. She preferred giving them left-off clothing; they had food and drink
without stint, and clean, comfortable sleeping apartments.
She inspired them with a certain affectionate respect, so that
they always boasted of their mistress to the servants of the
neighbouring villas. Oh! she had so much to think about.
There was more linen to be made up; the linen was a never-
ending affair. Andrea had declared that the collars of some of
his shirts were out of fashion, and that he wouldn't wear them
any more. He had ordered six of Tesorone, the first shirt-
maker in Naples, and after that she wished to have two winter
wrappers copied from a beautiful pattern of Lucia Sanna's,
although she feared that those flowing, voluminous garments
would not suit her little figure. And Lucia Sanna said that
she was glad to be able to stay at home with her dear husband.
Alberto continued to suffer from a cold, but he was getting
better; instead of coughing in the morning, he coughed at
night, an effect, he thought, of the coolness of the sheets.
Carderelli had told him that his lungs were delicate, but
healthy; that he must begin to take cod-liver oil, and continue
to take a few drops of Fowler's arsenic after dinner, and
occasionally a spoonful of *Eau de goudron* on rising. Diet—
he must be careful as to diet; milk food, eggs, no salted
viands, no pepper, nothing heating, no fries. This was a
matter that Alberto was fond of discussing with the Signora
Lieti, his good friend and under-nurse. He clung to her
skirts while she ordered breakfast and dinner, and Caterina's
patience in discussing the food was inexhaustible, in making
suggestions that he vetoed, and in eventually agreeing to

whatever he wanted. Alberto really felt very well; had he not ridden Tetillo that morning, and perspired and caught cold, by this time he would have been as strong as anybody. When he said this to Andrea and Lucia, those two exchanged a swift glance of commiseration.

Alberto was more than ever in love with his wife; for ever buzzing round her, glad of the closing of the Exhibition, which did away with so many walks and drives that were wearisome to him; for he took no interest in any thing or person. He liked staying at home, in his bedroom, to be present at Lucia's toilet, admiring her lithe figure and the undulations of her dark hair under the comb, her pink nails, and all the minute care she lavished on her person. Alberto had the vitiated tastes of a sick child who loves to lie among flounces and furbelows, the scents of toilet-vinegar and *veloutine*. He went to and fro among them, picking up a pair of stays, sitting on a petticoat, unstopping a bottle, dipping a finger into the dentifrice—languid, indolent, emasculated by physical weakness. He asked stupid questions, often conscious of their stupidity, but choosing to be idiotic with his wife, so that she might pity and protect him the more. Lucia answered him patiently, with a resigned smile on her face which was painful to behold, but which appeared to him the smile of love itself. When she rose, Alberto rose; when she entered the drawing-room, Alberto followed her; when she worked, he continued asking her stupid questions, to which she made answers of amazing eccentricity. More than ever Alberto admired his wife's singular ideas, wondered at the things she saw and that no one else saw, at her culture, her voice. Less reserved than he had been till now, he sometimes kissed her in the presence of others, hanging about her with singular tenacity. He even forgot his own health, for her. The acute egoism of the poor-blooded, fibreless creature was silenced by his love for Lucia.

Oh! Lucia, she too was delighted to stay at home. That Palazzo Reale had lost its charm, it was too huge, too heavy too architectural.

As to the park, it was a horror. Nature combed, flounced and powdered, with lakes full of trout and red fish for the delectation of the Philistines; with shaven turf, trimmed with scissors; and that eternal waterfall, an odious motionless white line.

"There is the English Garden," remarked Caterina one day.

" Have you seen it? " asked Lucia.

" No, never."

"Is it possible, four months of Centurano every year, and you have never seen the English Garden? "

"There has been no opportunity. I hardly ever enter the park. I will take you there, and we will see it together."

" I do not care to see it. I hate English gardens."

The subject dropped. Lucia was fond of staying indoors, but she spent many hours in dressing, continually changing her gowns. Her room was full of boxes and packing-cases ; she had written to Naples for new " half-season " dresses, fresh from the milliner's hands. She possessed every variety of tea-gown : white, ample, floating ones ; short, coquettish, bunched-up Pompadour ones ; lacy ethereal ones that you could blow away, and rich silken ones that opened over pleated satin skirts. They all became her as well as nearly everything suits a slight, lithe woman. When Caterina admired her, and told her that she was beautiful, and Andrea bowed ceremoniously before her, she would say with a placid smile :

" I dress for Alberto, not for myself."

" Of course," whispered Alberto to Caterina or Andrea, " poor Lucia sacrifices herself completely to me. She shall at least have the satisfaction of being beautiful for my sake."

After her toilet, Lucia breakfasted and then ensconced herself in her favourite corner in Caterina's drawing-room. She had begun a long fanciful piece of work on coarse, stout canvas, without any design. On it she embroidered the strangest things in loose stitches of wool and silk: a flower, a lobster, a white star, a cock, a crescent, a window grating, a serpent, a cart-wheel, haphazard from right to left. It was the last Paris fashion to have your drawing-room furniture covered with that coarse, quaintly embroidered canvas. It gave free scope to the imagination of the fair embroideress, and Lucia revelled in the strangest devices. Every one in the house was interested in the great undertaking and curious to know, from day to day, what Lucia would add to it.

" What shall you put in it to-day, Lucia ?"

" An onion, Alberto."

" An onion, an onion: oh ! how amusing ! yesterday a pansy and to-day an onion ! How shall you work it ?"

" In flame-coloured silk."

Next day : " Oh ! Lucia, tell me what you are going to put in it ?"

" An oaten pipe."

" *O Dio!* what an eccentricity ! What a mad drawing-room we shall have ! People will stand about, trying to find out the meaning of it, without thinking of sitting down."

They chatted a little when they worked. Caterina cut out at the large table, and Lucia, in whose taste she had the utmost confidence, advised her. Lucia had become more demonstrative in her intercourse with Caterina. She questioned her, and made her confessions that sometimes brought the quick blush to her cheek, but only when they were alone. When they remained indoors, Lucia retired to her room an hour before dinner.

" What can she be doing at this hour ? " inquired Andrea of his wife.

" I do not know. Probably she prays."

" Did she pray much at school ? "

" Very much ; indeed, too much for her health."

Lucia reappeared in the same dress for dinner, but with her hair differently arranged. She was always changing the style of her hair. Sometimes she wore it turned up high over a tortoiseshell comb, at others twisted round her head with a fresh rose on one side, or loosely plaited and studded with daisies, or bound, in Grecian fashion, by a thin gold fillet. The evenings on which she wore it like a Creole, with a red silk handkerchief, she was irresistible

" Wear your red foulard ; do wear it," entreated Alberto.

That was why she was fond of staying at home. But Alberto had confided to Caterina and Andrea that his Lucia was busy on another great work. No one was to know anything about it ; so silence, if you please. Lucia had begged him not to tell any one ; but they were dear, tried friends. It was no less than a great novel that Lucia was writing, a marvel of creative imagination, that was surely destined to surpass all other novels by Italian authors. Lucia worked at it after midnight. He, Alberto, went to bed ; Lucia placed the lamp so that it did not shine in his eyes—the dear soul was full of these delicate attentions—opened her desk, drew out a ream of paper, and sat with her head in her hand, buried in deepest thought. Then she would stoop over her writing, without pausing, for a long time. At times, under the influence of her inspiration, she rose, and paced up and down the room in great agitation, wringing her hands.

" Like a poet, who under the spell of his inspiration cannot light upon a rhyme. When I call her, she starts as if she were falling from the clouds. You see she is in the throes of composition. I have left off speaking to her in these moments, for I know that it disturbs her genius. I generally fall asleep, but Lucia, I believe, does not go to bed till two or three in the morning. They say that authors do not care to show their work before it is finished. I shall read it, when it is finished. I think she will dedicate it to me. It will be an amazing work."

Even Andrea was glad when the Exhibition closed; through it, he had neglected his own affairs for those of other people. He said that he had a world of care on his shoulders, which that condemned show had obliged him to put off. At last he was free to enjoy the peace of his own home, without the obligation of wasting the best part of the day in that solemn

Palazzo Reale, walking ten kilometres up and down the great
halls, on those polished red tiles, that are enough to tire the
most enduring legs. He rose earlier than usual, and drove
a pony down to Caserta, where he superintended the removal
of his own exhibits from the show. He returned in time for
luncheon and changed his clothes; he no longer wore the
white silk tie which used to serve as collar and necktie, but a
turned-down collar and black necktie, in honour of the ladies,
he said, laughing. At breakfast, he would speak vaguely of his
projects for the afternoon.

"Are you going out again?" asked Caterina.

"I don't know . . . . there are some things I ought to do.
Shall you ladies go out?"

"If Lucia cares to," said Caterina, timidly showing a wish
to stay at home.

"I don't care to," said she, raising her languid eyelids.
"Will you go out, Alberto?"

"I don't care to," repeated the latter.

"I don't know, perhaps I shan't go either," murmured
Andrea. But after breakfast, when they met in the drawing-
room, his impatience would get the better of him, and he
rose to go out. Sometimes he succeeded in dragging Alberto
with him in the phaeton; he drove him to Marcianise, to
Antifreda, or as far as Santa Maria. They drove up and down
the high-roads in the soft, mild autumn weather. Alberto,
meagre and undersized, in an overcoat buttoned up to his
eyes, with a silk muffler round his throat and a rug over his
knees, was a striking contrast to the vigorous young man with
the curled moustache at his side, attired in light clothes, and
wearing an eagle's feather in his grey huntsman's hat. Andrea
was a good whip, but he sometimes slackened the reins when
they were on the high-road, so that the horses started off at a
pace that alarmed Alberto.

One evening he said to his wife: "Andrea has homicidal
intentions towards me."

She looked fixedly at him, as if questioning his jesting tone,

When, during these drives, Alberto was inclined for conversation, he talked of his favourite subjects, his health and his wife . . . . he vaunted Lucia's beauty, the depth of her genius, the brightness of her repartee. He would sometimes smilingly add details that irritated Andrea, who had an aversion for the morbid confidences of his enamoured guest. Then he would whip up his horses violently, cracking his whip like a carrier, and indulging in a wild race along the high-road.

" You are as prudish as a vestal," sneered Alberto, more and more convinced that the muscles of these very robust men are developed to the detriment of their nerves. Strong men are cold, a reflection which consoled Alberto, who was a weak man.

They.returned to Centurano at a furious pace. Scarcely had they turned the corner, when they perceived a white handkerchief waving from the balcony; it was Lucia, tall, beautiful, and supremely elegant, saluting them, waiting for them. Sometimes Caterina's smiling face was visible, behind Lucia. She did not come forward, because she dreaded the remarks of her neighbours, who did not approve of public demonstrations of affection between husband and wife. Then Andrea cried, Hip, hip, to Pulcinella, and the fiery mare tore up the hill at full speed; he bowed rapidly to the balcony, and turning the corner in splendid style, achieved a triumphal entry into the courtyard. Lucia generally descended the stairs to meet them, to inquire how Alberto felt and shake hands with Andrea, whom she complimented on his charioteering. Caterina was never there, she was occupied with the last orders for dinner, for she knew how Andrea disliked waiting.

One of the reasons for which Andrea had longed for the closing of the Exhibition, was that he might have time for shooting. Of this his wife, who had passed five or six dreary days last year alone waiting for him, a prey to a melancholy alien to her well-balanced temperament, was well aware. So that this year she was afraid lest he should absent himself too

long and too often; an act her guests might deem discour-
teous. He had said nothing about it, but from one moment to
another she expected to hear him say, " I leave to-morrow."
Yet he said nothing, until, between two yawns, Alberto asked
him :

" About shooting, Andrea, shan't you get any ?"

He hesitated, then he replied with decision : " Not this
year."

" Why ?"

" I have made a vow."

" A vow ? To Saint Hubeit ?"

" To Our Lady of Sorrows."

Neither of the two women raised their eyes ; but, for different reasons, they both smiled. Caterina thought of Andrea's
kindness in not going away, out of courtesy to her friend
and that poor Alberto. She was always afraid that her guests
might bore themselves, and if Andrea had gone shooting, how
could she have managed, with her poor store of intellectual
resources ? Oh ! Andrea sacrificed himself without a murmur,
without any of those loud outbursts ; he never indulged in
those fits of anger that used to frighten her. Andrea even
attained the supreme politeness of not falling asleep during
the hour devoted to digestion.

II.

For a whole week after the scene in the English Garden,
their love had been so calm that it needed no expression ; it
was self-concentrated and subjective. They exchanged stolen
glances without any agitation, they neither blushed nor turned
pale, nor did they tremble at the touch of each other's hands.
Lucia had an absorbed air, as if she were immersed in the
contemplation of her own mind ; neither the outer world nor
her lover could distract her from their state of contemplation.
Andrea's demeanour was that of a man who is secure of
himself and of the future. When their eyes met for a moment

it was as much as to say: "I love you, you love me; all is
well."

The fact was that the day passed in the English Garden
had been too passionate not to have exhausted, at least for a
time, the savage impulse of their repressed love. To the acute
stage, a period of repose had succeeded—a sort of Eastern
dream in the certainty of their mutual love, a kind of annihila-
tion that to the sweets of memory unites those of hope.

It did not last long. Suddenly they awoke to passionate
misery. One morning Andrea arose troubled with a mad
longing to see Lucia. It was too early, she was sleeping. He
paced the drawing-room like a prisoner, looking at his watch
from time to time. Caterina, who had already risen, carried
his coffee into the drawing-room, and sat down beside him to
talk over household bills, and to remind him that he had to
drive to Caserta to pay the taxes. He listened while he
soaked his rusk in the coffee, without understanding what she
was saying to him. He was devoured by impatience. What
could Lucia be doing in her own room, at that hour? How
came it that she was not conscious of his longing to see her,
of his waiting for her? It must be the fault of that miserable
Alberto, who was never ready to get up—who clung, shivering
and grumbling, to the warm sheets; an odious, wretched
creature, who saddened poor Lucia's existence. The idea,
that Alberto kept her there and prevented her from coming,
was insufferable. He started to his feet, as if in protestation,
as if to go to her . . . .

"Will the tax-collector be there?" said Caterina, brushing
away the crumbs with one finger, with her instinctive love of
order.

"Where?"

"At Caserta?"

"Who knows?"

"We can inquire of lawyer Marini, who does the legal
part of the business; he is sure to know. Shall I send
Giulietta?"

" Send Giulietta."

She left the room, without noticing that anything was wrong. Andrea became calmer, knowing that Lucia must soon appear; it was unreasonable to expect her before half-past nine. He still longed for her presence, but with a gentler longing. He drummed a march on the window-pane, recalling the moment when she had entreated him not to embrace her "for her love's sake," and he, obedient as a child, had desisted. Lucia, his Lucia, should be loved in so many ways ; with passion, but with the utmost tenderness ; with youthful ardour, but with reverence. Oh ! all these things were in his heart. He would wait patiently for her coming, without any perilous, fiery outbursts. Lucia might be late, he who loved her would refrain from breaking in doors and damaging china or furniture.

Enter Caterina.

" Lawyer Marini says that the tax-collector will be there between nine and twelve to-day."

" What does that prove ?"

" You are in time to go there and back before breakfast. It will take you an hour to go there and back."

"No, I shan't go . . . ." said Andrea, after some hesitation.

Caterina was silent. She thought he was always right, and never contradicted him.

" I will go there after breakfast," he added, as if in explanation of his conduct.

" As you will," said Caterina, without remarking that after breakfast the tax-collector would be no longer there.

Andrea was becoming irritable again. Caterina standing like that before him, bored him. She seemed to be waiting for something, as if she meant to question him, to call him to account . . . .

" Listen, Caterina, do fetch me my writing-case from the bedroom ; I shall stay here and write some important letters."

Away she went, with her light, elastic step. Lucia's door

opened, and she entered; Andrea, pale with the pleasure of seeing her, ran to meet her. But a disappointment arrested him. She was followed by Alberto. Andrea's greeting was cool, his fine project of a prolonged contemplation of her melted away.

"Haven't you been out of doors this morning?" inquired Alberto, fatuously.

"No."

"Aren't you well?"

"I am always well. I am bored and worried."

Lucia looked at him as if to question him. She was so fascinating that morning, with the dark shadow under her eyes that lent them so much expression, her vivid lips that contrasted with the pallor of her face, and the air of delicious languor of a woman who loves and is beloved. In one sad, passionate glance behind Alberto's back, they spoke to and understood each other. He was sitting between them, sprawling in an armchair, with no intention of moving. When he realised this, a spirit of contradiction made Andrea long more ardently than ever to tell Lucia what she was to him. Only once to whisper it in her ear, as in the English Garden; once only, and he could have borne to go away. But say it to her he must; the words sprang to his lips, and it seemed as if Lucia read them there; her eyes dilated, and her expression became alternately rapt and troubled. Meanwhile Alberto yawned, stretched out his arms, drew a long breath to find out if there was any obstruction, and coughed slightly to try his breathing capacity. Now Andrea's only wish was that Alberto should go away for a moment, to the window or back to his room, so that he, Andrea, might tell Lucia that he loved her. *Ma che!* Her husband continued to sprawl at full length, staring at the ceiling—lolling, with one leg over the other; anything but move. Lucia pretended to read the paper that had come by post, but her hands trembled from nervousness.

"What is there in the newspaper?"

"Nothing."

"As usual: there never is anything. Does it amuse you?"

"Immensely;" her voice hissed between her teeth.

"Why don't you talk to us? Here is Andrea, who hasn't been out. The first day that he stays at home, you are absorbed in the *Pungolo.*"

"I have forgotten to bring your box of lozenges with me," she said, pensively.

"Here it is," said Alberto, drawing it from his pocket.

The commonplace but generally efficacious expedient had failed. The lovers were downcast, low-spirited, and discomfited. Meanwhile Caterina had returned with the writing-case.

"I have been a long time," she said, "but I could not find it. It was at the bottom of the drawer, under the stamped paper. It is so long since you have written."

She quietly prepared the necessary writing materials for her husband, and went to sit down by Lucia. Andrea, furious at the double surveillance, began rapidly to write senseless phrases. He wrote nouns and verbs and immensely long adverbs for the mere sake of writing, feeling that he could think of nothing, save that he wanted to tell his dear Lucia, his sweet Lucia, his dear love, that he loved her. Lucia, with her head thrown back, her face livid from irritation, her lips so puckered that they appeared to be drawn on an invisible thread, was looking at him from between half-closed lids, behind the paper. He might have risen to tell her that he loved her, but Alberto and Caterina were placidly chatting with her, saying that the rain had cooled the atmosphere, and that at last it was possible to walk, even when the sun was shining. Caterina had her look of serene repose, and Alberto continued to twirl his thumbs, like a worthy *bourgeois* immersed in the delightful consciousness of his own insignificance.

"There is nothing for it but to grin and bear it," muttered Andrea.

"What are you saying?" asked Caterina, whose ear was always on the alert.

"That we shall never get our breakfast. It is nearly half-past eleven. I am fit to die of hunger."

"I will run and hasten it," she said, perturbed by the savageness of his accent.

"I will come too, Signora Caterina," said Alberto.

The other two exchanged a rapid glance, so eager that it already seemed to bring them together. But on rising Alberto thought he felt a stitch in his chest; he began to prod himself all over, feeling for his ribs, in prompt alarm. Caterina had disappeared.

"I feel as if I had a pain here," he complained.

"I always have it," said she, gloomily, without looking at him.

"Do you speak seriously—at the base of the lungs?"

"Yes, and at the top of them too. I have pains all over."

"But why don't you say so? Why not see a doctor? Will you bring upon me the sorrow of seeing you fall ill? I, who love you so!"

The little table at which Andrea sat writing creaked as if his whole weight had fallen upon it. Alberto, on his knees before his wife, continued his inquiries as to her pains. Were they in the bones, or were they stitches? Forgetful of his own suffering, he entreated her, in adoration before that hard-set, sphinx-like face that allowed itself to be questioned, but vouchsafed no answer. Caterina found them in this attitude and smilingly designated them to her husband, who replied by an ironic laugh, quite at variance with his frank, good-natured face. But his wife's penetration did not permit her to distinguish between a simple smile and a sarcastic grin. Breakfast commenced in painful but short-lived silence. Lucia soon began to chatter with nervous volubility, playing with her knife and capriciously choosing to pour out Andrea's wine for him. She ate nothing, but drank great glasses of iced water, her favourite beverage. While Caterina watched the service, with her eye upon Giulietta, whom she addressed in an undertone, and her hand on the electric bell, Alberto cut all the fat and gristle away from his meat, reducing it to its smallest compass, and Andrea stared absently at a ray of light playing on a glass of water. Lucia continued to keep the conversation from flagging, by saying the most eccentric things, exciting herself, doubling up her fingers, as was her wont when her convulsive attacks were coming on. The usual question cropped up.

" Any one going out to-day ? " asked Andrea.

" Not I," said Alberto.

" Nor I," said Lucia.

" Nor I," added Caterina.

" And what do you intend to do at home ? " asked Andrea.

"I shall play at patience, with cards," said Alberto. " But perhaps I shan't, after all. As to me, when Lucia stays indoors . . . ."

"I shall work at my embroidery," said she, suddenly sobered.

" And I shall sew," said Caterina.

" How you will amuse yourselves ! " said Andrea, rising from his seat. " Come out driving, let's have the *daumont*."

" No," said Lucia. He understood her. What would be the good of that drive ? They would still be four people together. He would have no chance of telling Lucia that he loved her.

" I am half inclined to stay here to count your yawns," he growled, savagely.

" If you stay with me, then I'll say you're a good fellow," said Alberto.

He stayed with them : he hoped, he kept on hoping. But when he saw Alberto seated at the little table with his pack of cards, Caterina near the window with her basket of linen, Lucia on the sofa with the interminable canvas between her fingers, drawing her thread slowly, without raising her eyes, he thought it would never, never be ; and gloom and disappointment overwhelmed him. Those two obstacles, pacific, well-meaning and motionless, who smilingly let drop an occasional remark, were insurmountable. Never, no, never, would he be able to

N

speak to Lucia. He gave it up. He had neither the energy
to go, nor the patience to stay in that close room.

"I am going away to sleep," he said, as if he were about to
accomplish a meritorious action.

"What are you embroidering to-day?" inquired Alberto of
Lucia.

"A heart, pierced by a dagger."

Once in his room, Andrea closed the shutters and threw
himself on his bed, in a state of fatigue of which he had had no
experience till now. He had been mastered in the struggle with
circumstances. His impetuous nature, alien to compromise,
was incapable of endurance : he could neither wait nor calcu-
late. "Nevermore, nevermore," he kept repeating to himself,
with his face buried in the pillows.

Twice Caterina came in on tip-toe and leant over him,
holding her breath lest he should be sleeping. He feigned
sleep, repressing a shrug of annoyance. Was he not free to
shut himself up in his room, and vent his feelings by punching
a mattress? Need he submit to all this wearisome business?
But Lucia, dominant and imperious, once more occupied his
thoughts; Lucia, whose name, did he but murmur it, filled
him with tenderness ; Lucia, his dear love, a love as immense
and unfathomable as the sun. He turned over and over on
his bed, in a fever of nervousness, he who had never suffered
from nerves before; it seemed to him that he had lain for a
century, burning between those cool sheets. Two or three
times he fell into an uneasy slumber and dreamt that he saw
Lucia, with flaming wide-open eyes, tendering her lips to his
kisses. When with wild longing he approached her, some one
dragged her away from him, and he was bereft of the power of
moving from the spot to which he felt nailed : he tried to utter
a cry, but his voice failed him. Then, starting and quivering,
he awoke. "Lucia, Lucia," he kept repeating in his torpor,
trying to recall his dream, to see her again, to kiss her. And
in his dream he found her again, he on the balcony, she in the
street, whence she held out her arms to him ; and slowly he

threw himself off the balcony—slowly, slowly, never ceasing to fall, experiencing unutterable anguish. There was an incubus on his chest during that oppressed, restless slumber. When he really awoke his eyes were heavy, his body ached, and there was a bitter taste in his mouth. That eternal afternoon must be over, he thought. He opened the window, the sun was still high. It was five o'clock, two more hours till dinner-time. But in that pleasant light he awakened to fresh hope. *Ecco !* he would write to Lucia, on a scrap of paper, that he loved her. Not another word ; that was sufficient, and should suffice him.

Diamine ! couldn't he have given her that scrap of paper ? It was surely easy enough ; yes, yes, it was a splendid idea. He entered the drawing-room, pleased with his discovery. The first disillusion that befell him was to find no one there but Caterina and Alberto. Lucia was missing ; where was she ? He did not venture to ask. Alberto was smoking a medicated cigarette, recommended for delicate lungs, and attentively watching the smoke, with his right leg crossed over his left ; Caterina had put a band on a petticoat, and was running a tape in it. Lucia was missing ; whom could he ask about her ?

" Have you slept well ? "

" Yes, Caterina, very well ; have you worked the whole time ? "

" No ; the Signora Marini came to pay us a visit."

" I hope you had her shown into the drawing-room ? "

" Yes ; she stayed too long."

Not a word of Lucia. Whom could he ask ? Who would tell him what Lucia was doing ?

" . . . . And then Lucia, who is bored by stupid people," added Alberto, "felt ill and went to her room ; just now I went to see what she was doing . . . . Andrea, guess what she was doing ? "

" How can I tell ? "

" Guess, guess . . . ."

" You are like a child."

"As you cannot guess, I will tell you. She was kneeling on the cushion of the *prie-dieu*, and praying."

"Lucia stays too long on her knees, it will injure her health," observed Caterina.

"It can't be helped; on religious subjects she is not amenable. Indeed, she reproaches me for having forgotten the *Ave Maria* and the *Paternoster*. If I happen to cough, she prays for an hour longer," Alberto said.

Andrea had gone to the writing-table, and having cut a scrap of paper had written all over it, backwards and forwards, in every direction, in minute characters, "I love you," at least thirty times. This he did while Caterina and Alberto were still talking of her . . . . he felt as if he had done a deed of the greatest daring in writing those words under their very eyes. Before he had finished, Lucia re-entered the room. She was more nervous than usual; she went up to him and jested on his "middle-aged," provincial habit of "siesta." All he needed to make him perfect was a game of "tresette" in the evening, a snuff-box filled with "rape," and a red-and-black-checked cotton handkerchief. Would he play at "scopa" with her after dinner? And while her voice rang shrill and the others laughed, she put her hand in her pocket, as if to draw out her handkerchief; a scrap of paper peeped out. Then he, in great agitation, put a finger in his waistcoat-pocket and showed the corner of his note. Caterina or Alberto, or both, were always in the room. When one went away, the other returned; they were never alone for a moment. Andrea had folded his note in two, in four, in eight; he had rolled it into a microscopic ball, which he held in his hand to have it ready. Lucia dropped a ball of wool, Alberto picked it up. Andrea asked Lucia for her fan, but Caterina was the intermediary who handed it to him. It was impossible. Those two were frankly and ingenuously looking on, without a shade of suspicion ; therefore the more to be feared. Andrea trembled for Lucia, not for himself; he was ready to risk everything. From time to time a queer daring idea flitted

through his brain ; to say aloud to Lucia : " I have written
something for you on paper, but only you may read it." Who
could tell, perhaps Alberto and Caterina would not have
guessed anything, and his venture would be crowned with
success. But suppose that in jest they asked to see it?
Fear for Lucia conquered him; he ended by replacing the
little ball in his pocket. As for Lucia, her anger was so
nervous and concentrated, that it made her eyes dull and her
nose look as thin as if a hand had altered the lines of her face.
She moved to and fro without her customary rhythm, touching
everything in absence of mind, arranging her tie, lifting the
plaits from her neck, inspecting Caterina's work, taking a
puff from Alberto's cigarette, filling the room with movement,
chatter, and sound. It was impossible to exchange the notes.
Lucia put hers in her handkerchief, and dropped the handkerchief on the sofa ; but to reach the sofa, Andrea would
have had to pass Alberto's intervening body. After five
minutes, Lucia again took up her handkerchief and carried it
to her lips, as if she were biting it. Then they exposed themselves to a real danger. Andrea opened a volume of Balzac
that was lying on a bracket and replaced it, leaving his note
between its leaves.

" Hand me that book, Andrea."

"Nonsense," cried Alberto ; " would you begin to read now ?
It is dinner-time, *sai*."

" I shall just read one page."

" One page, indeed! I hate your wordy, doleful Balzac. I
confiscate the book." And he stretched out his hand for it.
Andrea drew it towards him, thinking, naturally enough, that
all was lost. · Lucia closed her eyes as if she were dying.
Nothing happened. Alberto did not insist on having the book.
After all, what did he care for *Eugénie Grandet*, so that his
wife chattered on instead of reading? Andrea drew a long
breath, and took his note back, no longer caring to give it to
her; his anxiety had been ineffable. Lucia, with her marvellous faculty of passing from one impression to another, soon

recovered her spirits. The note episode was over and done
for; they were very merry at dinner. Curiously enough, a
bright flush suffused Lucia's cheeks, ending in a red line like a
scratch, towards her chin. She felt the heat and fanned herself, joking with her husband and Caterina. She had never
been so animated before; now and then her mouth twitched
nervously, but that might have passed for a smile. Andrea
drank deep, in absence of mind. Lucia leant towards him,
smiling; she spoke very close to his ear, showing her teeth,
almost as if she were offering her clove-scented lips to him.
Then Andrea, what with the heat of the dining-room, its heavy
atmosphere, laden with the odours of viands, preserved fruits,
and the strong vinegar used in the preparation of the game,
the warm rays reflected from the crystal on to the tablecloth,
and Lucia's flushed face—the lace tie showing her white throat
—so near to his, Andrea was seized with a mad longing to
kiss her; one kiss, only one, on the lips. Every now and
then he drew nearer to her, hoping that the others would think
him drunk; anything might be forgiven to a drunken man.
He drew nearer to her to kiss her, tortured by his desire. He
shrank back in dismay, before his wife's pale, calm face, and
the bony, birdlike profile of Alberto. Suddenly Lucia saw
what was passing in his mind, and turned as pale as wax.
She saw that he was looking at her lips, and hid them with her
hand. But that made no difference; he could see them,
bright, moist, bleeding, with the savour of fresh blood, that had
gone to his head in the English Garden. He would taste them
for an infinitesimal fraction of time. And with fixed gaze and
a scowl that wrinkled his eyebrows, his clenched fist on the
tablecloth, he turned this resolution over in his mind, while
the others continued to talk of Naples and the approaching
winter festivities. They partook of coffee in the drawing-room.
He tried to lead Lucia behind the piano, so that he might
give her that kiss; which was absurd, because the piano was
too low. The candles were lighted, Caterina took her seat at
the piano, and played her usual pieces; easy ones, executed

with a certain taste ; some of Schubert's reveries, the Prelude to the fourth act of the *Traviata*, and Beethoven's March of the *Ruins of Athens.* Lucia was lying with her head far back in the American armchair, and her little feet hidden under the folds of her train, dreaming. Alberto, sitting opposite to her, was turning over the leaves of the Franco-Prussian war album, and discovering that Moltke was not in the least like Crispi, and that all Prussians have a certain family likeness. Andrea took several turns in the room, joining Caterina at the piano sometimes asking her to change her piece, or to alter her time. But he was haunted by Lucia's lips; he saw them everywhere, like an open pomegranate flower, a brightness of coral; he could see their curves and fluctuations; he followed, caught them, they disappeared. For a moment he would be free: then in a mirror, in a bronze candelabrum, in a wooden jardinière, he would fancy they appeared to him, at first pale, then glowing, as if they grew more living. Never to get to them! He went out on the balcony and exposed his burning head to the air, hoping that the evening dew would calm his delirium. Caterina begged Lucia to play, but she refused, alleging that she had no strength, she felt exhausted. Alberto drowsed. The two friends conversed in whispers for a long time, bending over the black and white keys, while Andrea watched from the window : now Lucia's lips played him the horrible trick of approaching Caterina's cheek. Oh ! if Caterina would but move away from the piano ; but no, there she sat, glued to her place, listening to what Lucia was murmuring.

Thus slowly passed the dreary hours, bringing no change to the aspect of that room. At midnight they all wished each other good-night ; Andrea worn out with a nervous tremor, she hardly able to drag herself along. Their good-night was spoken in the broken accents of those who have lost all hope. And, alone in the darkness, he lived over again the torment of that day in which he longed for a look and had not had it, for a word and had been unable to say or hear it, for a note that he had neither been able to read nor to deliver, for a kiss that he

had not given; his strength exhausted in that day of misery
that had been lost for love. Yes, it must be, it would be thus
for evermore. Death was surely preferable.

III.

Andrea, that overgrown child of nature, whose primitive
elasticity of temperament enabled him to pass with ease from
fury to tenderness, revolted against sorrow and rebelled against
anguish. Why would they not let him love Lucia? Who
dared to place themselves between him and the woman of his
love? When Caterina was in the way, he could have screamed
and stamped his foot, and sobbed like a child deprived of its
toy; his inward convulsions were like the terrible nervous
attacks of those obstinate infants who die in a fit of unsatisfied
caprice. Lucia saw his eyes swollen with tears, and his face
redden with the effort of repressing them; it made her turn
pale with emotion. When the unfortunate Alberto was the
obstacle, with his meagre little person, his hoarse voice, and his
little fits of coughing, Andrea could hardly resist the impulse
which prompted him to take him round the body and throw him
down; to walk over him and crush him underfoot. When Lucia
saw the breath of madness pass over Andrea's face, she rushed
forward at the first sign of it, to prevent a catastrophe. Then
he took up his hat and went out on foot, round the fields,
under the broiling sun, with hurried step, clenched teeth, and
quivering nerves, bowing mechanically to the people he met,
even smiling at them without seeing them. He returned home
limp, bathed in perspiration, and fatigued; he slept, the good
sleep of old times, for two hours, with clenched fists and head
sunk in the pillows. On awaking, he had an instant of supreme
felicity, a well-being derived from the rest he had enjoyed, the
restored balance of his powers. But suddenly the worm began
again to gnaw, and, like a whining child that awakes too early,
he thought: "Oh, God! how unhappy I am! Why did I
awake if I am to be so unhappy?"

He was in truth a very child in love, a child of no reasoning faculty, incapable of unhealthy sophistry or sensual melancholy. He loved Lucia, and desired her; that was his aim, clear, precise, and well-defined. He looked his own will in the face, straight as a sword-cut that finds its way to the heart. He knew that he did wrong, he knew that he was guilty of treachery; he looked his sin in the face without any mitigating sentimentalism. Not his were the terrors, the languors of an erring conscience, nor the mystifications of a depraved mind. He did wrong, not because he was impelled by faith or wrath divine, but because his imagination was wrought upon, and because he loved. He did not try to justify himself by the discovery of any imaginary defect in Caterina, nor wrongs nor shortcomings which would have made it excusable to bestow his love elsewhere. His conscience could not have endured the pretexts that might serve to lessen the conciousness of wrong-doing in a viler soul. They sinned and betrayed, because they loved elsewhere; that was all. Love is no fatality; love is itself, stronger than aught besides. So he suffered in not being free to love in the light of day, with the loyalty of a brave heart that has the courage of its errors. He could not understand obstacles; they were a physical irritation to him, as a cart across his path would have been. He would have liked to have pushed them aside, or ridden over them; he lamented the injustice of his fate, in that he could not surmount them. Sometimes, when they were all sitting together in the drawing-room, he felt tempted to take Lucia in his arms and carry her away. That was his right, the blind right of violence, suited to his temperament. Did she understand it? When he came too near to her, she shrank away with a slight gesture of repulsion. In proportion as his passion increased in intensity, so did the obstacles become more and more insurmountable. That consumptive creature never left his wife for a moment; drowsing, yawning, reading scraps by fits and starts, sucking tar lozenges, spitting in his handkerchief, grumbling, feeling his own pulse a hundred times a day, complaining of suffocation and cold sweats. Caterina, it is true, went to and fro on household avocations, and sometimes retired to write letters; but when her husband was at home she did her best to get her business done so that she could sit down to sew in the drawing-room. Alberto saw and inspected everything; and with the maudlin curiosity of a sick and indolent person, wanted to touch all that he saw. Caterina was more discreet, less curious, and of silent habit, yet she too saw everything. Impossible to speak to Lucia alone for a minute. Two or three times they had attempted this, almost oblivious of the others' presence; but having stopped in time, had found each other mute, pale from weariness, their faces drawn by suppressed yawns. Caterina and Alberto had nothing to say to each other. After five minutes they subsided into an inevitable silence. Alberto considered Caterina an excellent woman, a notable housekeeper, but rather stupid, and in every way inferior to his wife. Caterina judged no man, but all that Alberto inspired her with was quiet, unemotional compassion. There was no spiritual sympathy between them, rather a phy- sical repulsion. The impression produced by Caterina on Alberto was the negative one of absence of sex: she was neither beautiful nor ugly in his sight, nor a woman at all. In Caterina the instinct of health which recoils from disease, made him repellent to her. Then came the gloomy hours in which Lucia, in dumb despair, would betake herself to the sofa, where she would lie as rigid as the dead, her feet hidden under her skirts, her train hanging on the ground, with wreathed arms, and hands crossed behind her head, closed eyes and deathly pallor. She scarcely answered except in curt, harsh mono- syllables, passing hours in the same attitude, without opening her eyes. Alberto wasted his breath in questioning her, she never made him any reply. Caterina, who since their school- days was accustomed to these acute attacks of melancholy, signed to him to be silent, to wait for the fit to pass over: and they kept silence until the gloom fell upon them all. Andrea started to his feet and prepared to go out, without so much as looking towards the sofa. Caterina was troubled at his manner of absenting himself, for she knew that her husband could not abide these extraordinary scenes. She ran after him to the top of the stairs, calling him back, whispering to him.

" Have patience, Andrea," she said.

" But what is the matter with her?"

" I don't know; she has strange ideas that unsettle her brain. She says they are visions, and the doctor calls them hallucinations. She sees things that we do not see."

" What a singular creature !"

" Poor thing, she suffers a great deal, *sai*. If I could but tell you what she tells me, when neither of you are there. I fear we were to blame in advising her to marry Alberto . . . ."

" What does she say to you? Tell me."

" Are you going out?"

" Right you are : I am off. If any one wants me, say I am out on business. One can't breathe in the drawing-room ; it smells like a sick-room."

" They will soon be leaving us, and then . . . ."

" I don't mean that; you'll tell me the rest to-night. *Au revoir.*"

To make matters worse, sometimes in the evening, when Lucia chose to be most beautiful, she would gaze at him with a look of calm and persistent provocation that was torture to him. And he tortured himself, for he had neither the habit of patience nor the phlegmatic capacity for conquering obstacles. His was the haste of one who is accustomed to live well and quickly—who cares rather for a reality to enjoy day by day than for an ideal to live up to. What was this torment of having Lucia within reach—beautiful, desirable, desired—and yet not his? He would struggle on undaunted, clenching those fists that were ready to knock something down ; and then he would fall back, wearied to exhaustion, no longer caring for life, with the eternal refrain in his mind: " that it would always be the same; that there was no way out of it; that life was not worth having."

At night, it was no longer possible to pass an hour in the balcony. If the bed only creaked, Caterina awoke and inquired:

"Do you need anything?"

"No," was the curt reply. Sometimes he did not answer at all. Then she fell asleep again, but her sleep was light. He knew that had he gone out on the balcony Caterina would soon have followed him, in her white wrapper—a tiny, faithful, loving shadow, ready to watch with him if he could not sleep. Oh! he knew her well, Caterina. He had taken the measure of the calm, deep, provident, almost maternal affection that welled over in the little heart. At times, when her head rested trustfully against his broad chest, as if it had been a haven of rest, an immense pity, a despairing tenderness for the little woman whom he no longer loved, stole upon him. All that was over. Finis had been written and the volume closed. But from this very pity and tenderness arose more potent his love for Lucia, who slept or watched two rooms away from him. Some nights he could have run his head against the walls to knock them down. He felt a seething in his brain that made him capable of anything. At last he lighted on the desperate remedy of talking to his wife of Lucia whenever they were alone. Caterina, who was desirous of awakening her husband's interest in her friend, was fond of speaking of her. In a measure, Lucia's personality modified Caterina's temperament; her fantasy exercised a certain influence on her. Caterina proved this by her ingenuous employment of metaphor—she with whom it was unusual—when her talk ran on Lucia. .To tell the truth, Andrea was rather unskilled in interrogatory, and in veiling a too acute curiosity; but Caterina was no expert in such matters. She talked on, in her quiet way, a gentle, continuous flow of words. It was at night, before going to sleep, that these conversations took place. She told him of Lucia's mystico-religious mania; how she had turned the whole College topsy-turvy with her penances, her ecstasies, her tears during the sermons, her faintings at the Sacraments; she had even worn a hair-shift, but the Directress had taken it away from her because it made her ill. She told him of her strange answers, and of the fantastic compositions that excited the whole class; of the strange superstitions that tormented her. Sometimes, in the dead of the night, Lucia used to get out of bed and come and sit by hers (Caterina's), and weep, weep silently.

" Why did she weep ? " inquired Andrea, moved.

" Because she suffered. At school some considered her eccentric, some romantic, others fantastic. The doctor said she was ill, and ought to be taken away from there."

She continued talking of her curious fancies; how " she ate no fruit on Tuesday, for the sake of the souls in Purgatory; and drank no wine on Thursday, because of Christ's Passion. She ate many sweets and drank great glasses of water:"

" Even now she drinks them," remarked Andrea, profoundly interested.

By degrees the narrator's voice fell, the tale dragged, and he did not venture to rouse her. Caterina slept for a few moments, and then, in broken accents, began again. She ended by saying in her sleep, " Poor Lucia ! "

" Poor Lucia ! " repeated Andrea, mechanically.

Caterina reposed in sleep, but he remained awake, feverish from the tale he had heard, obliged to resist his longing to wake his wife and say to her, " Let us continue to talk of her."

He had unconsciously adopted the same method with Alberto. When he went out walking with him he ingeniously led up to the subject of his wife. No sooner said than done. Alberto did not care to hear another word. As with Caterina, Lucia was his one idea, his favourite topic. He had so much to tell that Andrea never needed to question him : he sometimes interrupted him by an exclamation to prove that he was an interested listener. Alberto had enough to talk about for a century : how he had fallen in love, how Lucia spoke, what she wrote, how she dressed when she was a girl. He remem-

bered certain phrases : The " Car of Juggernaut," the " Drama
of Life," the "Love of the Imagination," the "Silence of the
Heart," and he unconsciously repeated them, enjoying the
remembrance of them.   He recalled the minutest details—a
date, the flower she had worn in her hair on a certain day, the
gloves that came up to her elbow, the rustle of a silken shirt
under her fur wraps. Alberto had forgotten nothing. One
day he had found her in bed with the fever, with a white silk
handkerchief, that made her look. like a nun, bound round
her head.   Another day she had made the sign of the cross
on his chest—an ascetic gesture—to avert evil from him.
Another time she had told him that she was going to die,
that she had a presentiment about it, that she had already
made her will.   She wished to be embalmed, for she dreaded
the worms . . . . wrapped first in a batiste sheet and then
in a large piece of black satin, perfumed with musk, pearls
twisted in her hair, and a silver crucifix on her bosom.

"Enough to make one weep, Andrea *mio*," continued
Alberto. "I could not keep her silent. She would tell me
all, all. We ended by weeping together, in each other's arms,
as if we had been going to die on the spot."

When Alberto Sanna's confidences became too expansive,
and the unhealthy flush of excitement dyed his cheeks, Andrea
suffered the tortures of jealousy. Alberto grew enthusiastic
over the delicate beauty of his wife, the sweetness of her
kisses, and as he ran on his companion turned pale, bit his
cigar, and knew not how he resisted the temptation to throw
Alberto into a ditch. That invalid, whose breathing was
oppressed even on level, whose breath whistled through
his lungs on rising ground, that sickly homunculus dis-
coursed of the joys of love as if he knew anything about
them. Andrea looked him up and down, and decided that
he was a wooden marionette in that winter overcoat, with the
collar drawn up to his ears, and the hat drawn down over his
eyes ; so his anger was blended with contempt, and he threw
his cigar violently against the trunk of a tree. There were no

means of reducing Alberto to silence. His impudence was of the passionately shameless kind, so peculiar to those lovers who recount to the whole world how their mistress's shoulder is turned, and that her limbs are whiter than her face—a placid immodesty that made it possible for him to tell Andrea that Lucia wore blue silk garters embroidered with heartsease, with the motto, "*Honi soit qui mal y pense;*" and smilingly he inquired:

"What do you think of it?—pretty, eh!·"

The consolation turned to torture, the relief to anguish. Andrea grew grave and gloomy.

IV.

One day Lucia appeared in the drawing-room with a reso-lute and almost defiant look on her face. Her nostrils quivered as if they scented powder, and her whole being was ready for battle. Looking elsewhere, while Andrea handed her a cup of coffee, she calmly gave him a note. He trembled all over without losing his presence of mind. He found a pretext to leave the room, and ran down into the courtyard to read it. They were a few burning words of love written in pencil. "He was her Andrea, her own strong love; she loved him, loved him, loved him; her peace was gone, yet she was happy in that she loved, unhappy in not being permitted to love him. They must put a bold face on it . . . . Alberto and Caterina, poor, poor betrayed ones . . . . had no suspicions. He, Andrea, should study her, Lucia, so that he might under-stand what she said to him with her eyes; she was his *inamo-rata*, his mate, and she loved her handsome lord . . . ."

All the gloom had vanished. Andrea felt as if joy must choke him. He began to talk loudly to Matteo, the stable-man; called the hounds, Fox and Diana, who leapt upon him; seized Diana by the scruff of her neck; made Fox jump, tell-ing Matteo that he was in his dotage; that the dogs were worth two of him, but that, *vice versâ*, he was a good *bestia*. Two ladies' heads and the small head of a sort of scalded bird, looked down upon him from a window. He called out to the ladies that he proposed a good sharp drive : the ladies, like two princesses in disguise, in the victoria, he and Alberto in the phaeton.

"And how about luncheon?" grumbled the thin voice of Alberto, buried under a woollen scarf.

"Of course, we will lunch first," he thundered from the courtyard. And he mounted the stairs, four at a time, singing and shaking his leonine mane. When he got to the top, he took Alberto by the throat, and forced him to turn round the drawing-room, in the mazes of the polka.

Lucia watched this violent ebullition of joy, without stirring an eyelash.

"Since you are so gallant, to-day, Andrea," she said, coolly, "suppose you offered me your arm, to go into lunch. 'Tis a courtesy you are wanting in."

"I am a barbarian, Signora Sanna. Will you do me the honour to accept my arm?" he said, bowing profoundly.

The two others laughed, and followed, without imitating them. In the gloom of the corridor, Lucia nestled closer to Andrea; he pressed her arm until it hurt her. When they entered the dining-room, they were so rigidly composed that Alberto teased them. Caterina was happy, for her husband had gained his good temper. At table, Lucia's elbow came several times in contact with Andrea's sleeve, when she raised her glass to her lips, looking at him through the crystal. He kept his eyes open, casting oblique looks at Alberto and Caterina, but they neither saw nor suspected anything.

"To repay you for the arm that you did not offer me," said Lucia, with frigid audacity, "I offer a pear, peeled by myself."

And she handed it to him on the point of the knife. On one side the witch had bitten it with her small, strong teeth. He closed his eyes while he ate it.

"Is it good?" she inquired, gravely.

"Sorry to say so, for your sake; but it was very bad," he replied, with a grimace of regret. Alberto was fit to die of laughter. That rogue of a Lucia, who seriously offered a bad pear to Andrea, as if in gratitude, as if she were making him a handsome present! What wit! that Lucia! The ladies rose to dress for the drive. The first to return was Caterina, dressed in black, with a jet bonnet. Lucia was away some time, but, as Alberto afterwards remarked, she was worth waiting for. At last she appeared, looking charming, her height somewhat diminished by a dark plaid costume, with a thread of yellow and red running through it. She wore a blue, mannish, double-breasted jacket, with small gold buttons, a high white collar and a felt hat with a blue veil, covering it and her hair. A bewitching, mock traveller, with a little powder on her cheeks to cool their flush.

The victoria and the phaeton were waiting in the courtyard. The ladies entered their carriage and drew the tiger-skin over their knees: the men sprang into the phaeton and bowed to the ladies, who waved their handkerchiefs. Then the little vehicle, driven by Andrea, started at full speed, the other equipage following more slowly. This lasted some time; every now and then they turned back to look at their wives, who were smiling and chatting with each other. Andrea saluted them by cracking his whip. The wind blew fresh, and Alberto, who caught it in his face, doubled himself up for fear of taking cold.

"*Ma che!*" exclaimed Andrea, "don't you feel how warm it is? I wish I could take off my coat and drive in shirt-sleeves."

And he goaded on Tetillo until he broke into a canter.

"We are losing sight of the victoria, Andrea," pleaded Alberto, who thought that canter inopportune.

"Now we will stop and wait for them."

They were on the road to San Niccolo, between Caserta and Santa Maria. Andrea got down and stood awaiting the victoria, which arrived almost immediately. Francesco main-

o

tained all the gravity of a Neapolitan coachman, although he had whipped up his Mecklenburg trotters. Andrea and Alberto leant against the side of the little carriage, chatting with its occupants.

"Are you enjoying yourselves?"

"Oh! the speed intoxicates me," replied Lucia.

"It is a lovely day," added Caterina, simply.

"Yes, but windy," mumbled Alberto, stretching himself with the weariness of having sat doubled up.

"Well, shall we drive on?" inquired Andrea, impatiently.

"I want to make a proposal," said Alberto; "I submit it to the consideration of the ladies."

"Well, make haste about it then."

"Have pity on a poor invalid and take him into the victoria; it is sheltered from the wind, and this nice rug keeps one's legs warm."

"And leave Andrea alone, in the phaeton?" observed Caterina.

"True," he said, pondering; "how could we manage it? Take him in here, overload the carriage; and then who would drive the phaeton? Would one of you ladies take my place?"

They looked at each other interrogatively, and said, "Yes." Andrea took no part in the discussion, he listened patiently while he made a fresh knot in his whip.

"Would you, Signora Caterina?" continued Alberto, who had made up his mind to a seat in the victoria; "but no, that wouldn't do, we should be husband and wife and wife and husband. It would be absurd; people would take us for brides and bridegrooms! Lucia, are you too nervous to get into the phaeton?"

"I'm not afraid of anything," she said, absently.

"*Bè*, do me a favour; you go with Andrea. We will ask him to drive slowly, because of your nerves. Will you really do me this favour?"

"Certainly, Alberto *mio*. I was enjoying being with

Caterina, but sooner than you should be exposed to the wind . . . ."

Andrea assisted her to alight; she sprang out lightly, showing a glimpse of a bronze boot. She took leave of Caterina while Alberto ensconced himself well back in the victoria.

"Signora Caterina, you must pardon the exigencies of an invalid. You must fancy yourself a *garde-malade.*"

She turned her sweet patient smile on him. Andrea and Lucia silently made their way to the phaeton. He helped her up, and then got up himself; then, both turning towards the carriage, waved their hands once more. Then away like the wind.

"Oh! my love, my beautiful love," murmured Andrea, from whose hands the reins had nearly slipped.

"Run away with me, far away," she whispered, looking at him with languorous eyes.

"Do not look at me like that, witch," said Andrea, roughly.

"I love you."

"And I, and I—you cannot know how I love you."

"I do, though. Why don't you write to me?"

"I have written to you, over and over again, and torn the letters up. Oh! Lucia *mia*, how beautiful you are, and how dear!"

Close to him, in her trim tight-fitting dress, with little crossed feet, with the tender look on her face, shaded by the brim of her hat, she was fascinating. She looked like an enamoured child, with her pink chin, her delicate cheeks, and wind-blown hair.

"I shall drop the reins and kiss you."

"No; they are watching us."

"Then why are you so dear? Why is my brain on fire?"

The horse went on at full speed, arching its neck, almost dancing, the other equipage following at a distance of sixty paces.

"I have suffered the tortures of the damned, these past days."

"Do not tell it me. I thought I should have died of it. Do you love me?"

"Why do you ask me—you who know so much, you who know all?"

"I know not why," replied Lucia, in her caressing tones.

"Lucia, you will drive me mad, if you speak in that voice. Shall I run away with you here, on the high-road?"

"Yes, yes, run away with me. That is what I wish, that you should run away with me." Her eye, her lips, her little foot so close to him, all added to the provocation of her words.

"Have pity on me, my love; you see that I am dying for love of y ou.'

For a few minutes there was silence. He looked straight before him, biting his lips, for fear of yielding to the temptation. But it was too strong for him, he could not help looking at her. She was smiling at him with a feverish and caressing smile, her teeth gleaming between her lips.

"How dear you are! Why are you laughing?"

"I am not laughing, I am smiling."

"Sometimes, Lucia, I am afraid of you."

"Afraid of what?"

"I don't know. I do not know you well. And you, you are so completely mistress of yourself. I am entirely yours; so much your slave, that I tremble."

"Did not you say that you were ready for anything?"

"And I say it again."

"'Tis well, keep your courage in readiness."

She had grown serious again—a great furrow crossed her brow, her eyebrows were puckered, her eye sinister.

"Oh! do not say these things to me, do not be so austere; smile again, smile as before, I entreat you."

"I cannot smile," said Lucia, harshly.

" If you will not smile, I will drive this trap into that heap
of stones, and we shall be thrown out and killed," said
Andrea, in a rage. She smiled with a strange ferocity, saying
tenderly :

" I love you. You are mad and boyish, that is what
pleases me."

Andrea instinctively pulled at his reins ; the pace slackened.

" Oh ! Lucia, you are a witch."

" You will never recover, I shall be your disease, your fever,
your irreparable mischief."

" Oh ! be my health, my strength, my youth ! "

" Fire is better than snow, torture is more exquisite than
joy, disease is more poetic than health," said Lucia in ringing
tones, her head erect, her eyes flashing, dominating him.
Andrea bowed his head ; he was subjugated.

At Santa Maria, on the way home, the two equipages stopped,
the victoria had caught up the phaeton. They conversed from
one carriage to another. Alberto said he was very comfortable,
and that he had made the Signora Caterina explain to him how
to make mulberry syrup. It was so good for bronchial com-
plaints. He had described his journey to Paris to her.
Caterina nodded acquiescingly ; she was never bored. Then
they started again, the trap on before, the carriage following.
The sun was going down.

" *Oh, dio !* are we going back ? We are going back," moaned
Lucia ; " this lovely day is coming to an end. Who knows
when we shall have another ? "

" What dark thoughts ! Do not torment yourself with dreams,
Lucia. The reality is that I love you ; 'tis a fair reality."

" We are evil-doers."

" Lucia, you are striving to poison this hour of happiness."

" And what man are you, if you cannot bear sorrow ? What
cowardice is this ! Is all your strength in your muscles ? I
have loved you because I believed in your strength."

"I am weak in your hands. Your voice alone can either sadden or revive me. You can give me strength or deprive me of it. Do not abuse your power."

They were on the verge of a sentimental wrangle, whither she had been leading .him since the beginning of the drive.

. "Love is no merry prank, Andrea; remember, love is a tragedy."

"Do not look at me like that, Lucia. Smile on me as you did before; we were so happy, just now."

"We cannot always be happy. Happiness is sin, happiness is dearly bought . . . ." sententiously.

He turned his face away, profoundly saddened. He no longer goaded his horse, and Tetillo had subsided into a slow trot. Turning, Lucia beheld the victoria approaching. "On, on, Andrea," she said; "faster, faster!" The little trap flew like an arrow. She passed one arm through the arm of the driver, and with head erect, and hair blown about by the breeze, she gave herself up to the pleasure of the race.

"This is the *steppe*, the *steppe*," she murmured, with a sigh.

"Love, love, love!" repeated Andrea, in the excitement of their speed. The phaeton sped on; they no longer looked behind them, nor saw the double row of trees that flew past them, nor the people who met them, nor the cloud of dust from the road. The little carriage flew, assuming a fantastic aspect, like that of a winged car.

"Give me a kiss," said Andrea.

"No, they are behind us; they can see us."

"Give me a kiss."

Then she opened her white linen sunshade, lined with blue, and put it behind her; that dome screened them both and hid their two heads. Before them, no one, no one in the fields; and while the carriage sped along in the broad light of day, they kissed each other lingeringly on the lips.

V.

The audacity of their love increased day by day. Trusting in the quiescence of the other two, they dared all that lovers' imagination is capable of inventing. They chose seats beside each other, Andrea played with Lucia's fan or handkerchief, he counted her bangles: if they were apart they talked of their love in a special vocabulary that recalled every incident of the past—an open parasol, a lake, a green shade, a lace scarf, a phrase pronounced by one or the other, *then.* If Lucia saw Andrea preoccupied, she immediately led the conversation to the subject of the Exhibition, and placidly remarked that the day of the horticultural show had been one of the most delightful in her whole life; and Andrea would find means to drag the word *sorceress* into his discourse. They understood each other's every gesture and intonation, even to the movement of an eyelid or a finger. One day, Lucia called across the room to Andrea: "Listen, Andrea, I have something to tell you in your ear; no one else may hear it."

"Not even I?" said Alberto, in comic wrath.

"Neither you, nor Caterina, who is smiling over there. Come here, Andrea." He crossed the room and approached her: she laid her hand on his shoulder to draw him towards her, and whispered:

"Andrea *mio,* I love you."

He appeared to collect his thoughts for a moment, and then breathed in her ear:

"Love, my love, my witch—I love you !"

Then he returned to his place. But Alberto wanted to know absolutely; if he didn't, he should die of curiosity. Lucia, pretending to yield, confessed that she had said; " Alberto is as curious as a woman; let us tease him, poor fellow." This incident amused the lovers immensely, but they did not repeat the experiment. They had other devices : there was the proffer of the arm—indoors, on the terrace, on the stairs, and fugitive clasping and light touches in the corridor. Sometimes, for an instant, the two heads were so close that they might have kissed. When Caterina was not there and Alberto happened to turn his back to them, they exchanged glances as intense as if there had been pain in them. When they spent the evening in the drawing-room, Lucia chose her position with infinite art. She sat in the shade behind Alberto, so that she might gaze her fill on Andrea, without attracting any observation.

Sometimes she opened her fan before her eyes, looking through its sticks. Now and then, when Alberto was away and Caterina bent over her sewing, Lucia's great eyes flashed in Andrea's face: the lids dropped immediately. All the evening Lucia maintained her air of melancholy, her tired voice and weary intonation. If for a moment she found herself alone with Andrea, she would rise, quivering with life, and cry, close to his face:

" I love you."

She fell back exhausted, while he was like one dazed. Now they found a hundred ways of passing letters to each other, running the risk of discovery every time, but succeeding with amazing dexterity; hiding notes in balls of wool, handkerchiefs or books, in packs of cards, at the bottom of the box of dominoes, in a copy of music, under the drawing-room clock; in fact, wherever a scrap of paper could be hidden. Lucia's eye indicated the place; Andrea watched his opportunity, took a turn round the room; then, when he reached the spot, abstracted the letter with a masterly ease, acquired by habit, and substituted his own for it. Under an assumed hilarity and noisy joking manner, he concealed the most ardent anxiety and a continual uneasiness. Without looking at Lucia, he studied her every movement; he, great lion though he was, acquired the feline habit of certain tiger-like gestures; he, who was frankness personified, became accustomed to profound dissimulation; he grew sagacious, cunning and wily, oblique of glance and of crouching gait. During the night he meditated

the plan for the morrow, so that on the morrow he might give
Lucia a letter, or grasp her hand. He prepared all the mock
questions and departures, all the improvised returns, the
business pretexts and fictitious appointments. During the
night he rehearsed the lies that were to deceive Alberto and
Caterina on the morrow. Continual prevarication gradually
degraded his character and drowned the cries of his conscience,
to which perfidy and veiled evil were naturally repugnant. He
lent a new spirit to the letter of his doctrine, one steeped in
mental restrictions and jesuitical excuses.

But this same spiritual corruption that tainted every
characteristic of his frank, loyal nature, these hypocritical
concessions, this sentimental cowardice, bound him the more
firmly to Lucia. The more he gave himself up to her the more
he became penetrated by her influence, the more acutely did
he feel the delight of his slavery and the exquisite bitterness
of his subjugation. The sacrifice of his honesty, the greatness
of all his renunciations, strengthened the fetters that bound
him to her who inspired it. Although he was prepared for
anything, and ever on the look-out for any new, infernal,
love-inspired invention, that Lucia's brain might devise, she
always succeeded in amazing him. One morning they met
under a *portière*, on the threshold of the drawing-room; she
dropped the curtain, threw her arms round his neck, and flew
past him into the room. He thought he must be dreaming,
and could hardly restrain himself from running after her. One
evening, while Alberto was half asleep and Caterina playing
one of her eternal *rêveries*, she called him out to her on the
balcony, under the pretext of showing him a star, and there in
the corner had for a second fallen into his arms. Then she
said, imperiously:

" Go away."

In one of those moments he had murmured, with every feature
quivering:

" Take care : I shall strangle you."

Indeed, he often felt that he could have strangled the

woman who maddened him by her presence and her vagaries, and who always eluded him. Even her letters were so incoherent, so mad, so prone to pass from despair to joy, that they added to his perturbation. To-day she would write a sentimental divagation on pure love—she wished him to love her like a sister, like an ideal, impersonal being, for that was the highest, sublimest love; and Andrea, moved, lulled by these abstractions, by the tenderness with which they were expressed, replied that thus did he love her, as she would be loved, as an angel of Paradise. Next day her letter would be full of mysticism; she spoke of God and the Madonna, of a vision that had come to her in the night; she entreated him to have faith, she prayed him to pray—oh! to be saved together, what happiness, what ecstasy to meet in Paradise! And Andrea, who was indifferent in matters of religion, who lived in the utmost apathy, replied—yes, for her sake, he would believe and pray: he preferred to lie than to contradict her; her will was his, he had no other. But in another mood, Lucia would indulge in the most ardent phrases, filling a page with kisses, words of fire and yet more kisses, with languors and savage longing and kisses, kisses, kisses; ending with: "Do you not feel my lips dying on yours?" And Andrea did feel them, and those words, written in minute characters, were to him as kisses, and when his lips touched them a shiver ran through his burning veins: his reply was almost brutal in its violence. Then Lucia, in her alarm, would write that their love was infamy; that their treason would meet with the direst punishment; that she already felt miserable, unhappy, and stricken. Andrea, tortured by the inconstancy of her moods, by her continual blowing hot and cold, by the constant struggle, knowing not how to follow her, despairing of finding arguments that would convince her—replied, entreating her to cease from torturing him, to have pity on him. To which Lucia answered by return: "Thou dost not love me!" He suffered more acutely than ever, despite the daring, the letters, the stolen kisses and the embraces in doorways. Day by day Lucia grew

more strange; one morning her face was pale and her voice
hoarse and acrid. She neither gave her hand nor said good-
day: her elbows looked angular and her shoulders as if
they would pierce her gown; she even stooped as if suddenly
stricken with age, answering every one—her husband, Caterina,
and Andrea—disagreeably, especially Andrea. He held his
peace, wondering what he could have done to her. When he
could snatch an opportunity of speaking to her, he asked :

" What is the matter with thee ? "

" Nothing."

" What have I done ? "

" Nothing."

" Do you love me ? "

" No."

" Then I had better go away."

" Go."

In a moment like that, Andrea felt he could have beaten
her, so wicked did she seem to him. He went away to Caserta
to write her a furious letter from the post-office. When he
returned she was worse, absorbed in silence, no longer
deigning to answer any one. Those about her were so much
influenced by her bad temper that they did not speak either.
Every now and then, Alberto would ask :

" Lucia *mia*, is there anything you want ? "

" Yes."

" What ? "

" To die."

The newspaper shook in Andrea's hand; he was pretending
to read, while not a word was lost upon him.

" Lucia, shall we go to the wood to-morrow ? " ventured
Caterina, timidly, to give her something to talk about.

" No, I hate the wood, and the green, and the country . . . ."

" Yesterday you said that you loved them."

" To-day I hate what I loved yesterday," said Lucia, in her
sententious tone.

At last, one day, when she was shaking hands with Andrea,

who was going out, she fell down in the frightful convulsions
to which she had been subject from her childhood. Her
arms beat the air, and her head rebounded on the floor.
Neither Alberto nor Caterina could do much for her; Andrea
grasped her wrists, and felt them stiffen like iron in his hands;
her teeth chattered as if from ague, and the pupils of her eyes
disappeared under her lids. She stammered unintelligible
words, and Andrea, in dismay, almost thought he heard her
break into sentences that revealed their secret. Then the
convulsions appeared to abate, her muscles relaxed, and her
bosom heaved long sighs. She opened her eyes, gazed at the
persons round her, but closing them again, in a kind of horror,
uttered a piercing cry, and fell into fresh convulsions; struggling, and insensible to the vinegar, the water, and the perfumes
with which they drenched her face. Caterina called her, Alberto
called her; no answer. When Andrea called her, her face
became more livid, and the convulsions redoubled in intensity.
With her lace tie torn away from her throat, her dress torn at the
bosom, with dishevelled hair, and livid marks on her wrists,
she inspired love and terror. When she came to herself, she
cried as if her heart would break, as if some one had died.
They comforted her, but she kept repeating, " No, no, no,"
and continued her lamentations. Then, tired, worn out, with
aching bones and joints, incapable of moving away, she fell
asleep on the sofa, wrapped up in a shawl. Alberto stayed
there until, at midnight, Caterina persuaded him to go to bed,
and the two men retired. She sat up near a little table to
watch, starting up at the slightest sound. Towards two o'clock
Andrea stole in quietly; he was dressed, he had not gone to
bed, he had been smoking.

" How is she ? " he whispered to his wife.

" Better, I think ; she never woke up, she has only sighed
two or three times, as if she were oppressed."

" What horrible convulsions !"

" She used to have them at school, but not so badly."

" Why do you not go to bed ? "

" I cannot, Andrea ; I cannot leave the poor thing alone."

" I will sit up."

" That wouldn't do, *sai.*"

" You are right, but they haven't made my orangeade."

" The oranges and the sugar must be in the bedroom . . . . but I had better go and see . . . . Stay here a moment, I will soon return."

Then he knelt down by the sofa, laying his hand on Lucia's. She woke up gently and did not seem surprised, but hung on to his neck and kissed him.

" Take me away," she said.

" Come, love," he said, attempting to raise her.

" I cannot ; I am dying, Andrea." She again closed her eyes.

" To-morrow," he said vaguely, for fear the convulsions should come on again.

" Yes, to-morrow, you will take me away, far, far . . . ."

" Far, far away, my heart . . . ."

They were silent ; she must have heard an imperceptible sound, for she said :

" Here is Caterina."

Caterina entered on tiptoe, and found her husband sitting in his place.

" She hasn't moved ? "

" No."

" I have made you your orangeade."

" Have you made up your mind to sit up ? "

" Yes, I shall stay here ; you don't mind ? "

And as they were in the dark, but for the faint light of the lamp, she stood on tiptoe for him to kiss her. He went away as slowly as possible, and Caterina watched until dawn.

Henceforward, all the letters ended with, " Take me away ;" all of them were despairing.

Lucia wrote with such tragic concision, that he feared to open her letters. There was nothing in them but crime, malediction, suicide, death, eternal damnation, hellish remorse, teeth chattering, fever, burning fire. She was afraid of God, of man, of her husband, of Caterina, of Andrea himself; she felt degraded, lost, precipitated into a bottomless pit. "To die, only to die!" she exclaimed, in her letters. And she appeared so truly miserable, so really lost, that he accused himself of having ruined a woman's existence, and craved her forgiveness, as if she had been a victim and a martyr. " I am your assassin; I am your executioner; I am your torment," wrote Andrea, who had adopted the formulas of her emphatic style, with all its fantastic lyricism.

October was drawing to an end. One Sunday, at table, Lucia calmly announced that they would be leaving on the following Tuesday, despite the popular dictum.*

" I thought," said Caterina gently, " that you would have stayed till Martinmas."

" The fact is that Alberto's cough is a little more troublesome, owing to the damp of this rainy October. Our house in Via Bisignano is very dry, and it is quite ready for us."

" For the matter of that, I am better," volunteered Alberto; " I am sure that I have gained flesh. I have been obliged to lengthen my braces. I owe my recovery to this country air."

" I am sorry that Lucia has not been so well," said Caterina.

" What does it matter?" said the other with supreme indifference. " I am a sickly, unfortunate creature. Yet the time I have spent here at Centurano, Caterina *mia*, has been the brightest, most harmonious epoch of my life, the highest point in my parabola; after it, there can only come a rapid descent towards eternal silence, eternal darkness, eternal solitude."

Andrea did not open his lips, but in the evening he wrote, entreating her to stay a few days longer. He could not bear the thought of her departure. At Naples, she would no longer care for him. He would not let her go. She was his Lucia;

* "Nè di Venerdi, nè di Marte, nè si sposa, nè si parte."

why did she leave him? If she refused to stay, she must know that he would follow her at once.

It was of no avail. Lucia insisted on leaving. He clashed against an iron will, against a will with a steady aim. In one or two curt notes, Lucia replied so harshly as to fill him with dismay. She wished to leave, why should he detain her, why not let her go in peace? She wished to go, because her sufferings were intolerable, because she was so miserable. She wished to go, to weep elsewhere, to despair elsewhere. She wished to go, and he had no right to detain her, since he had made her so unhappy. She wished to go, so that she might not die at Centurano.

And she did leave; the farewell was heartrending. Lucia, whose departure had been fixed for midday, wept since early morning. Of everything that she looked upon, she said, "I look upon it for the last time." Of everything that she did she said, "I do this for the last time." Caterina was pale and with difficulty restrained her tears; Alberto was so much moved by Lucia's emotion, that he mumbled inaudible nothings. Andrea rambled about the house like a phantom, touching himself as if to make sure of his own existence. Lucia avoided him, and abstained from addressing him; she did but raise her tearful eyes to his. They lunched in silence; no one ate a mouthful. Afterwards Lucia drew Caterina into her room; there she threw her arms round her, and sobbed her thanks for all her goodness.

"Oh! angel, angel! Caterina *mia!* For what you have done to me, may happiness be yours! May God's hand be over your house! May love and joy abide within it! May Andrea ever love you more and more; may he adore thee as the Madonna is adored . . . ."

Caterina signed to her to be silent, for the strain was getting too much for her; they kissed each other over and over again. When they entered the drawing-room, Lucia's eyes were swollen.

"*Addio*, Andrea," she said.

"Let me take you to the station," he murmured.

"No, no, it would be worse. *Addio;* thank you. May the Lord bless . . . . "

She turned away sobbing, and was gone. The greetings from the balcony and waving of handkerchiefs lasted until the carriage had turned the corner to Caserta. Husband and wife were alone together. Suddenly the house seemed deserted, and the rooms immense. A chill fell upon it. Caterina stooped to pick up a white handkerchief; it was Lucia's, and Caterina wept over it, like a child who has lost its mother. Andrea sat down by her on the sofa, drew her head towards him, until it rested against his shoulder, and wept with her. Only two tears—burning, scalding, sacrilegious.

PART V.

I.

THE note was worded as follows

" I could not bear it without you. I gave out that I was going shooting ; have come to Naples instead. I implore you, let me see you for a moment ; just the time to tell you that I love you more than ever.   " ANDREA."

He had to wait for the answer, but it came :

"To-morrow, at ten. Let there be a closed carriage at the cloister of Santa Chiara, before the little door of the church. Blinds down and door open. I will come for a moment—to bid you farewell.   " LUCIA."

All night long he paced the room that he had taken at an hotel, reading that kind and cruel letter—inexplicable as she who had written it—over and over again. With all its rich store of vitality, Andrea's healthy temperament was impaired ; his nervous and muscular system degraded and unstrung. He missed the vigour of his iron muscles : he felt as weak as if his legs must refuse to carry him. His appetite, served by the wonderful digestive faculties upon which the harmony of the entire organism depended, had forsaken him. And he had acquired the tastes of Lucia for glasses of iced water, barely tinted with wine, spiced viands and sweets. Red meat disgusted him as it did her. He felt ill. Within him or out side him, he could see but one remedy for his evil—Lucia

P

She only could cure and redeem him, make the rich blood run its old course through his veins, restore to him physical equilibrium, with the exuberant gaiety and joy of life that he had lost. He was ill for want of her; it was an unjust privation. He felt that the first kiss, on the first day of happy love, would give him again health, strength and comeliness, and the power of defying sorrow and ill-luck. The bare vision of it made him shut his eyes as if the sun had blinded him.

"Lucia, Lucia," he kept repeating, with dishevelled hair and oppressed breathing. He could think of nothing but the appointment for the morrow, what Lucia would have to say to him, and how he would dissuade her from bidding him farewell. He was certain of dissuading her, for without Lucia he would die, and he did not mean to die. A thousand wild projects crowded his brain. He dreamt of kneeling before her and saying, "I have come to die by thy hand." He would take a dagger with him and offer it to her. He dreamt of not replying to her arguments except by, "I love you, you shall be mine." He dreamt of not saying a word, but of kissing her until his lips ached.

The livid November dawn found Andrea with parched lips and burning eyes, lost in fantastic hallucinations. He went out into the streets of Naples at seven, under a fine rain, without heeding the wet. At eight he was already driving up and down the Toledo, lolling on the cushions of a hired carriage, with his hat over his eyes and the curtains drawn down, consulting his watch every few minutes.

The heavy, iron-bound *portière* of padded leather fell behind a lady dressed in black, in deep mourning. There were few people in the church of Santa Chiara, which has but one nave, gay with gilding, large windows and bright painting; more of a drawing-room than a church. Lucia, crossing herself devoutly, took the holy water, and turned towards the principal entrance. Then she knelt before the altar of the *Padre Eterno*, a miraculous shrine hung with ex-voto offerings in wax and silver, in red or blue frames. She, kneeling on the marble steps, with her head against the balustrade, conversed with the Eternal Father, telling Him that He had thus ordained, for this was fate. Since bow she must to the decrees of Providence, she prayed Him to vouchsafe her counsel in that supreme hour. The Eternal Father had chosen to cast her into this tribulation, in which she had lost all peace and felicity: now she prayed Him to sustain her, to illumine her darkness so that she might find her way. Which was her way—the way of justice? To leave Andrea, so that he might do something desperate? Be his, in continual deceit? Be his, openly? She spoke humbly to the Eternal, awaiting the flash of the Holy Spirit that should illumine her terrible position.

"O Father, O Father, Thou wouldst have it so. Now help me."

After saying three final *Paternosters*, she rose. Grace had not come to her: the Eternal had not permitted her to hear His voice: she arose from prayer offered in vain: God the Father had not heard her. She crossed the whole length of the church and tottered up to the image of the Madonna, where she fell on her knees. She was an ancient *Madonna delle Grazie*, with a cadaverous face and large pitiful eyes that appeared to look at you, to appeal to you, to follow you as you departed. Lucia told the Madonna of her trouble, of her misery, and with her head resting on the balustrade, weeping and sobbing, she said to her:

"O! *Vergine Santissima*, as Thou hast suffered in Thy motherhood, so do I suffer in my womanhood. The anguish of these sorrows was not Thine, but from high Heaven. Thou seest and dost fathom them. O! *Vergine Santissima*, mine was not the will to do this thing. Before the Divine mercy, I am innocent and unhappy. I was led into evil and it overcame me, for my strength could not withstand it ; it was weakened by the misfortunes inflicted on me by Heaven. O! Holy Virgin, I may have sinned, but I am not a wicked woman. I am a tempest-tossed, tortured creature, a plaything of the fates. O! Holy Virgin, like unto Thee have they thrust seven

swords into my heart; like unto Thee, for fifteen years,
am I pursued by the sinister vision of martyrdom. I
am the most bitter tribulation that is upon the earth.
My heart bleeds, my brain is bound in leaden bands, my
nerves are knotted by an iron hand, my mouth is parched.
Madonna, do Thou help me, do Thou console me. O !
Madonna, who hast not known human love, mercy on her who
has learnt to know it, ardent, immense, devouring. O !
Madonna, Thou who knowest not desire, mercy on her who
has it within her, long, savage, insatiable. O ! Madonna, do
Thou tell me, shall I give myself to Andrea ? "

But Lucia's passionate eyes were turned in vain on the
Madonna : the Virgin continued to consider Lucia who was
praying earnestly, and a little woman who was reciting her
rosary and beating her bosom, with the same compassionate
gaze. Then Lucia recited half the rosary, on that lapis-lazuli
fragment of hers. She stopped at a *Paternoster*, and looked
at her watch. It was ten o'clock. Absent and indignant at
last that Divine grace had been withheld from her, she was
now only praying with her lips. They all left her to her fate,
even God and the Madonna—poor leaf that she was, fallen
from the bough and whirled in the vortex of destiny. It was
of no avail : they were all against her, they left her defenceless
and bereft of succour. In that dark hour, the ingratitude of
the world and the indifference of Heaven were revealed to her.
" Hyssop and vinegar, hyssop and vinegar, the drink they gave
to Christ," she kept repeating to herself, while she rearranged
the folds of her black dress, and drew her crape veil over her face.
Once more, when she passed the chief altar, she knelt and
said a *Gloria Patri*, crossing herself from sheer force of habit.
And it was with a gesture of decision that she sped through
the little door and dropped the curtain behind her.

The two-horsed hired landau was waiting in front of the
five steps. The wide quadrangle of the cloister was deserted.
Perhaps the noble Sisters were peeping from behind those
gratings. The fine close rain continued : the driver, indifferent
and motionless, sheltered himself under a big umbrella. The

carriage bore the letter M and the number 522. The door nearest the church was open. Lucia took in all these details. She walked down firmly, without looking behind her, and with one spring was inside the carriage. A voice cried: "*A Posilipo,*" to the driver, and the carriage-door closed with a snap ; then it started.

"O ! love, love, love," murmured Andrea, folding her in his embrace.

She tore herself away, and laughing ironically, said :

"Do you know that our position is to be found in *Madame Bovary ?* This is a novel by Flaubert ! "

"I have not read it. How can you be so cruel as to say these things to me ? "

"Because we are the performers in a bourgeois drama, or in a provincial one, which comes to the same thing."

"I don't know anything about it, I only know that I love you."

"Is this all that you have to say to me ?" she asked, with a sneer.

"Oh ! Lucia, be human. True, I have lost all sense, all dignity, but 'tis for love of you. Think how I have suffered in these three days ! Despair has nearly driven me to throw myself down from the *Ponte della Valle.*"

"They who talk of suicide are the last to commit it."

"But if I love thee, I do not mean to die. Oh ! cruel, not one kiss hast thou given me."

"There are no more kisses for our love," she replied, oracularly.

In her black attire, with her veil drawn over her face, under the green shade of the curtains, her feet hidden by her long skirt, and her hands by her gloves, without a thread of white on her person, her aspect was most tragic. Andrea shuddered with an acute sense of fear, he felt as if he were being irretrievably ruined by a malignant sorceress. But when she moved and the well-known perfume diffused itself in the circumscribed atmosphere, the painful sensation decreased and was soon gone.

"What is the matter with you?" he said   He had lost
heart, and seeing all his projects melt away, found nothing to
say to her.

"Nothing."

"Do you love me?"

"I love you," was Lucia's frigid reply.

"How much?"

"I do not know."

"Why did you say that there were no more kisses for our
love?"

"Because, like Siebel, you are accursed of Mephistopheles.
Siebel could not touch a flower without its fading and dying.
You have kissed me, and I am fading and dying.   There are
no more flowers for Margaret, no kisses for our love."

"I see," said Andrea, absorbed in a sorrowful dream.

"This is what I have to say to you, we must forget each other."

"No," cried Andrea, in a passion.

"Yes, the hard law of duty imposes this upon us."

"Duty is one thing, love is another."

"That is why.   Do you love Caterina?"

"I love you," he said, closing his eyes.

"Well, you are happier than I am ; I love Caterina, I love
Alberto ; to my mind, they are adorable beings."

"You love too many people," he said, bitterly.   He tried to
take her hand, she resisted.   Outside, the rain increased ; the
carriage rolled on noiselessly over the wet pavement of Santa
Lucia.

"Mine is a large heart, Andrea."

"You shall love me only."

"I cannot.   I love your wife and my husband, I cannot
sacrifice them to you.   Let us say good-bye."

"I cannot, Lucia.   I am doomed to love you, for ever.
You shall be mine."

"Never, never, never!"

"But are you not afraid of me?" he cried, red in the face,
furious.   "But do you think you can say all this to me with

impunity? Are you not afraid that I shall kill you? Couldn't
I do so, this instant?"

"Please yourself," she replied, calmly.

"Forgive me, Lucia; I am a fool and a savage. You are
my victim, I know it. I make you unhappy, and ill-treat you
into the bargain. All the wrong is on my side. Will you
forgive me? Tell me that you have forgiven me."

"I forgive you." She gave him her hand, which he kissed
humbly, through her glove. "Listen to me attentively, Andrea,"
she resumed; "when you have heard me, you will be convinced
that I am right. In sorrow, but of your own free will, you will
say good-bye for ever. Are you listening?"

"Say what you will. You cannot convince me, for I love you."

"I shall convince you, you'll see. I am not to blame for
what has happened in this dark, tumultuous drama. I did
not seek love, I did not seek you. I had married Alberto,
willingly sacrificing my whole life to him, in all affection. I
had already shunned you. Twice before you had crossed my
path with your conquering, all-compelling love. I would not,
I would not—you know that I would not. Do you confess to
this?"

"Yes, I confess it; you would not," repeated Andrea like
an echo.

"Do me this justice. Step by step have I fought against
your love, your tyrannic love. I have watched and prayed
and wept; deaf is Heaven, deaf the world, and fate, the implacable statue that has no entrails, that no human love can
move, is inexorable. Fate has willed it so."

"Fate, fate," repeated Andrea, in a tone of conviction.

"Now, although I know myself to be free from blame, my
sensitive conscience makes me decry myself, as if I were a
baneful creature. It is useless to struggle against fate; we
have bowed to its decrees and we have loved. Oh! Andrea,
I would not have said it to you—but at this supreme moment
the soul must reveal itself stripped of all artifice; I have sacrificed all to you."

" You are an angel . . . ."

" No, I am a miserable woman, who loves and is capable of sacrifice. Peace, tranquillity, conjugal duties, the ties of friendship, serenity of conscience, mystic love, of all these have you bereft me. What have you to offer me in exchange?"

" Alas! I can but love you," he cried, in despair at his own poverty.

" Love is not everything, Andrea."

" It is everything to me, Lucia."

" You would do anything for love?"

" Anything."

" Tell the truth, speak as if you were drawing your last breath, before passing into the presence of your Judge; would you do anything?" She had seized his hands, she was gazing fixedly, ardently into his eyes, as if she would have drawn his soul from him. Andrea, completely subjugated, simply said:

" Anything."

She permitted him to kiss both her hands. She was thinking. Then she raised the green curtain and looked out into the street. It was still raining—in fact the rain was heavier than ever, and fell in long, pointed drops, like needles. They had reached Mergellina. The sea under the rain was of a dirty grey colour, and a mist shrouded the green blot made in the landscape by the villa and the blurred blot made by the Fort. Neither boat nor sail on the sea.

" What desolation!" murmured Lucia, " on sea and land! Ours is an ill-starred love!"

" Lucia, Lucia, my beautiful Lucia, do not say these things. You have not yet given me one kiss."

" Kissing is your refrain; kiss me if you will."

She threw back her veil and let him kiss her cold, closed lips. He turned away from her, mortified.

" You are passionless; you do not care for me," he said.

" But do you not realise, unhappy man, that I can never be yours? Do you not realise that in being yours I should attain the utmost joy? but that I deny myself? Do you not

realise my renunciation of youth, passion, life? Oh ! unfortunate, who can torment me because you cannot realise . . . ."

" I admire you, Lucia, there is no other woman like you,
and I do not deserve you."

The driver stopped, they had arrived at Posilipo, on the road
that leads between the villas on the heights and those that
slope down to the sea.

" Via di Bagnoli," cried Andrea from the window.

" Whither are you taking me, Andrea ? "

" Far . . . ."

" No ; I must return to town. Alberto is awaiting me."

" Do not speak to me of Alberto."

" On the contrary, you must let me speak of him. He is
ill. I told him I was going to confession. You must drive
me quickly back to town."

" I will never take you back," he said emphatically.

Lucia looked at him, inquiringly, but a transient smile flitted
over her lips.

" You shall stay with me, you shall come with me. I will
not let you go, Lucia."

She looked as if she were too stupefied to reply . . . .

" You are going mad, Andrea."

" I am not going mad, I am speaking in all seriousness ; my
mind is made up."

The carriage had reached the Bagnoli shore.

" Let us get down here, it is rainy and deserted ; no one
will see us."

He obediently opened the carriage-door, helped her to get
down, and gave her his arm.

Leaving the carriage on the high-road, they walked down to
the sea under a fine rain, their feet sinking in the moist sand.
A damp mist hung over the deserted landscape. Nisida, the
convicts' isle, stood out before them, black on the pale horizon.
Round it, the sea was dark and turbid, as if all the livid horrors
from the bottom had floated to its surface : further on towards
Baia, it shone with frigid whiteness. The *Trattoria* of Bagnoli,

behind them, had all its windows closed ; the covered terrace was bare and empty, its yellow walls were stained by the damp. Further back still spread the grey plain of Bagnoli, where the soldiers go through their exercise, and Neapolitan duellists settle their disputes.

" It is like a northern landscape," she said, clinging to the arm of her companion. " It is not Brittany, for Brittany has bare rocks and terrible peaks. Neither is it Holland, for the Scheldt is white, and fair and placid, veiled in a milky mist. It is Denmark, with Hamlet gazing at the grey Baltic, with thoughtful eyes that betray his madness."

He listened to her, only conscious of the music of the voice that re-echoed in his innermost being. The fine, close rain poured down upon them until they were drenched, but neither of them perceived it.

" Have you ever been here, Andrea, when the landscape was blue ? "

" Oh, yes—look over there, behind those closed shutters. I once fought a duel in a big room in the inn."

" Oh ! my love, with whom ? "

" With Cicillo Cantelmo, a friend of mine."

" For whom ? "

" . . . . for a woman."

An embarrassing silence ensued.

" How little I know of your life, Andrea," she said gently, clinging ever closer to him. " I am a stranger to you."

" The past does not exist, love ; all that has been is dead."

" Oh ! love, I am dead, I am dead to happiness."

" Let me carry you away. Oh ! my heart, you shall be reborn."

" To-day you talk like a poet, Andrea, like a dreamer."

" You have taught me this language; I did not know it before. I had never dreamed. Come away, Lucia, come away with me."

" It's late, very late," she replied. " Come back to the carriage : let us return to Naples."

They regained the little green haven that cut them off from the rest of the world. They were both saddened. When they turned in to the Via di Fuorigrotta, Lucia shuddered, and turning to Andrea, said:

"And the future?"

"Do not think of it, let it come."

"You are a child, Andrea."

"No; you will find that I am a man. Will you trust me?"

"I am afraid, I am afraid;" and she clung to him.

"What are you afraid of?"

"I do not know . . . . I am afraid of losing myself. This love is ruin, Andrea. I can see the future. Shall I foretell it you? Shall I describe the fate that awaits us?"

"Tell, but give me your hands; tell, but smile."

"There are two ways before me. The first is the path of duty. After this gloomy, melancholy drive in the rain, in a carriage like a hearse, driven by a spectral coachman, we can coldly kiss and say good-bye, renouncing love. Ever to be apart, never to meet again, to betake ourselves, you to Caterina's side, I to . . . . Alberto, to a life as dry and arid as pumice-stone, to that humdrum existence that is the death of the soul. Forget our glorious dreams, our sweet realities: behold the future . . . ."

"No; I cannot."

"There is another future open to us. It is sin clothed in hypocrisy; it is hidden evil; it is fear-struck, trembling adultery, that degrades and deceives, that steals secret kisses, that is dependent on servants, porters, postmen, maids, and the tribe of them. It is what we have endured till now; it is odium, vulgarity, commonplace treason. To love as every one else loves! to imitate what a hundred thousand have done before us! It is unworthy of a woman like me, of a man like you!"

"Once you told me that deceit is merciful," he murmured. "You love Caterina and Alberto, in this way you could save . . . ."

She turned and looked at Andrea, her scholar who had

learnt her theories so well, whom she had taught to deny truth.

"Then," said Lucia, gloomily, "as I shall be never able to resign myself to hiding my love, since I can no longer practise deceit, we had better part."

"No; I cannot."

"We had better part."

. "I cannot; I shall die without you."

"What can I do? There is no other way out of it. Die! I, too, will die."

She turned up her eyes to the roof of the carriage and crossed her arms, as if she were waiting for death.

"I have let you speak," he said calmly, in a tone of decision, "because you would have your say. But I have a plan of my own, the best, the only one. Humdrum adultery, you will have none of it. Well, then, we will have brazen adultery, open scandal. We will leave Naples together . . . ."

"No," she cried, covering her face in horror.

" . . . . we will leave together, never to return. We will begin our life anew, in London, Paris, Nice or Brittany, wheresoever you will. Naples shall be wiped out of it. Since it is ordained that I love you, that you love me, we will pay our debt to fate."

"Fate, fate," she sobbed, convulsively, wringing her hands.

"Fate," repeated Andrea, bitterly. "We should never have loved each other. Now it is too late to draw back; you are mine."

"Oh, Caterina! oh, Alberto!" she exclaimed, weeping.

"It is fate, Lucia."

"My husband, my dearest friend!" Sobs rent her bosom

"I tell you again, your heart is too big. I love you and you only: you shall only love me."

"What torture, Andrea!"

"Have you not said, hundreds of times, 'take me away?' Now I am ready to take you away."

"You will take a corpse with you, pale with remorse."

"Then let us content ourselves with hypocrisy, with such love as suffices to others; yet that is what you cannot tolerate."

"Oh ! my God ! what torture is this ? I have not deserved it."

Suddenly it turned dark. She uttered a cry of dismay.

"It is nothing, we are passing through the Grotta. Fear nothing, I love you."

"This love is a misfortune, a tragedy."

"Have you not already told me this in the park ?"

"Yes . . . ."

"Well, Lucia, my life shall be passed in craving your pardon for having brought this misery upon you. I know that you are my victim. I know that I brought you to ruin. I demand of you an immense sacrifice. I know it, but are you not the personification of sacrifice? You are an example of noble abnegation, you are virtue and purity incarnate. You will see what my love for you is—how I shall adore you."

"And Caterina and Alberto?

"We will go away together, never to return," he persisted obstinately.

"We shall be accursed, Andrea."

"I shall take you away. Call me your executioner, I deserve it, but come with me."

"We shall be unhappy."

" *Che!* "

"Madonna *mia*, Madonna *mia*, why hast thou ordained my ruin ? "

"Will you come to-day or to-morrow ? "

"Neither to-day nor to-morrow. I am afraid ; let me think. You are pitiless ; no one has mercy on me."

"You are an angel, Lucia, you know how to forgive. To-day or to-morrow ? "

"Be merciful, give me time."

"I will wait for you, my love. I will wait, for I know that you will come."

A pale ray of light stole into the carriage through the blinds. Lucia was like one in a trance.

"You will leave me at the church *Della Vittoria.* I will pray there and walk home; it is only a few steps from home."

"And what am I to do? It is for you to decide what I am to do."

"Leave to-day for Caserta. In five or six days you will return to Naples, you and Caterina. By that time I . . . . shall have thought. But do not attempt to write to me or see me; do not ask me for appointments . . . ."

"You hate me, don't you?"

"I love you madly. But I must be left to myself for a time."

"You don't hate me for the harm I have done you?"

"Alas, no. We are all liable to do evil."

"Not you; I am evil, but I love you."

"Andrea, we have arrived; stop."

"Lucia, remember that there is no way out of it. We must go away, absolutely. Give me a kiss, oh, my bride!"

She stood up and allowed him to kiss her.

"Till that day, Andrea," said Lucia, with a gesture as tragic as if she were casting her life away.

"Till that day, Lucia."

The door of the carriage closed and it drove off in the direction of Chiatamone.

She found the church closed. That made an impression on her.

"Even God so wills it. O Lord, do Thou remember, on the day of judgment."

II.

Caterina was glad to return to Naples, to the house in Via Costantinopoli; for alone at Centurano, without the Sannas, and especially without Andrea (who had gone away shooting four times in a fortnight, to make up for lost time),

she had been very dull. In those two weeks she had busied
herself with putting the villa in order; the furniture had been
encased in holland covers and the curtains taken down, Lucia's
room left intact, in readiness for next year. Then the house
had been consigned to the care of Matteo, and when this was
accomplished she was glad to get away.

She intended making many innovations in her winter quarters. She discussed them at great length with Andrea, whose
advice was precious to her. For instance, the dining-room
wanted redecorating; she was thinking of having it panelled
half-way up with carved oak, an idea suggested by Giovanna
Gabrielli-Casacalenda, past mistress in the art of elegance.
Caterina had hesitated at first because of the expense, although
Andrea had given her permission to spend as much as she
chose. They were rich, and did not live up to their income;
their property was well managed and lucrative; but she was
economically-minded. As for altering the yellow drawing-room
which Andrea considered too showy and too provincial, that
would not be a serious expense, for the upholsterer was willing
to take back all its furniture and hangings, and to exchange
them for more modern, neutral-tinted ones. She often con-
sulted Andrea on these matters; he gave her rather absent
answers, being preoccupied with a lawsuit about a boundary-
wall on their property at Sedile di Porto.

His conferences with his legal advisers often obliged him to
be away from home. Indeed, that very morning he had been
out since eight o'clock, returning at eleven, apparently exhausted.

"Well, how goes the lawsuit?" inquired Caterina at luncheon.

"Badly."

"Why? Does our neighbour decline any compromise?"

"He does. He is obstinate; says the right is on his side."

"But what is the lawyer doing?"

"What can he do? He is moving heaven and earth, like
any other lawyer; or pretending to do so."

" Why don't you eat ? "

" I am not very hungry; out of sorts."

" After luncheon you ought to take a nap."

" What an idea !   I've got to go out again."

" To the Court ?   This lawsuit will make you ill."

" Then I shall have to get well again."

" Listen to me.   Suppose you let the neighbour have his own way ? "

" It's a question of self-respect; but perhaps you are right after all."

" This lawsuit is a nuisance.   This morning Alberto sent for you, and you were out."

" Who is Alberto?"

" Alberto Sanna."

" What did he want ? "

" The maid told me that he wanted to see you, to ask you to attend to some business for him because he was confined to the house.   She told me in confidence that Lucia wished me to know that Alberto spat blood last night in his sleep, but that he did not know it, and they were hiding it from him.   She also said that Lucia was crying."

" And Alberto is another nuisance," he rejoined, crossly and with a shrug of his shoulders.

" It is for Lucia that I am grieving.   How she must suffer ! "

No answer.

" I should like to go there to-day, for half an hour," she ventured to remark.

" What would be the good of it ?"

" Only to comfort Lucia . . . ."

" To-day I can't go there with you, and you know I don't care for you to go alone."

" You are right, I won't go ; we will go together this evening."

Luncheon was over, but they did not leave the table. Andrea was playing with his breadcrumbs.

" Besides our agent, Scognamiglio, will call to-day. He will bring some money for which you must give him a receipt. Tell him he can make a reduction for the third-floor tenants of No. 79 Via Speronzella. They are poor people."

" Am I to say anything else to him ? "

" Give him his monthly salary."

" A hundred and sixty lire ? "

" Yes ; but let him give you a receipt."

" All right ; another cup of coffee ? "

" Yes ; give me another cup, it is weak to-day."

" Because of your nerves. I wanted to ask you, are we going to the ball of the *Unione ?* "

" . . . . Yes."

" Shall I order a dress of cream brocade for that ball ? "

" Will the colour suit you ? "

" The dressmaker says so."

" They always say so. But order it, anyhow."

" I will wear my pearls."

He did not answer. He was gazing abstractedly into the bottom of his cup. Then he looked at her so long and so fixedly that Caterina wondered.

" Well," he said at last, looking at his watch, " I must be going."

He rose, and as usual she followed him. He went right through the house ; stopping before his writing-table to take a bulky parcel out of it, which he put into his pocket.

" It makes you look fat," she said, laughing.

" Never mind."

He dawdled in his bedroom, as if he were looking for something that he had forgotten. Then he took up his hat and gloves.

" You should take your overcoat with you, the air is biting."

" You are right ; I will take it."

He finished buttoning his gloves. She was standing, looking at him with her serene eyes. He stooped and gave her an absent kiss. Then he turned to go, followed by his wife.

"*A/rivederci*, Andrea."

" . . . . *A/rivederci*."

He began to descend the stairs ; she called out to him from the landing :

"Shall you return late ? "

" No. Good-bye, Caterina."

Lucia had risen late. She told Alberto that she had passed a feverish night. Indeed, her lips were dry and discoloured, her heavy eyelids had livid circles round them. At eleven, she languidly dragged herself, in a black satin dressing-gown, to be present at her husband's breakfast—two eggs beaten in a cup of *café-au-lait*—capital stuff for the chest. She sat with her head in her hands. Every now and then dark flushes dyed her face, and she pushed her hair off her temples with a vague gesture that indicated suffering.

"What is the matter with you? You are sadder than usual ! "

" I wish I could see you well, Alberto *mio*. I wish I could give you my heart's blood."

" What is it all about ? Am I so ill, then ? "

"No, Alberto, no. The season is trying to delicate lungs."

" Well, then, what of it ? But I see that you are so good as to be anxious about me. Thank you, dear. But for you I should have been dead by this time."

" Do not say that—do not say it."

" Now she is in tears, my poor little thing ! I was joking. What a fool I am ! My stupid chaff makes you cry. I entreat you not to cry any more."

" I am not crying, Alberto *mio*."

" Have a sip of my coffee."

" No, thank you, I don't care for any."

" Have some ; do have some."

"I am going to take the Sacrament to-day, about one."

" Ah ! beg pardon. I never remember anything. What church are you going to ? "

" The same church, Santa Chiara."

" But your religion makes you suffer, dear."

" Everything makes me suffer, Alberto *mio*. It is my destiny. But it is well to suffer for God's sake ! "

" Let us both take holy vows, Lucia."

" You are joking, but I did seriously intend to be a nun. It was my father who prevented me from doing so. God grant that he may not repent of it."

" Why, Lucia ? Think, if you had become a nun, we should not have met and loved each other, and you would never have been my dear wife."

" What is the good of love and marriage ? All is corruption, everything in this world is putrid."

" Lucia, you are lugubrious."

" Forgive me, Alberto *mio*, the gloom that overshadows my soul leaks out and saddens my beloved one. I will smile sooner than you should be sad."

" Poor dear, I know what I cost you. But you'll see how soon I shall get strong, and how we shall amuse ourselves this winter. There will be fêtes, balls, races."

" I shall never be gay again."

" Lucia, I shall have to scold you."

" No, no ; let us talk of something else."

" If you are going to church, you are but just in time."

" Do you send me away, Alberto ? "

" It is midday ; you have to go as far as Santa Chiara . . . and the sooner you go the sooner you will be back."

" True, the sooner back . . . . I must go, mustn't I ? "

" Of course, the air will do you good. Go on foot, the walk will be good for you."

" What will you do, meanwhile ? "

" I shall wait for your return."

" . . . . You will wait."

" Yes ; perhaps I shall go to sleep in this chair."

" Are your hands hot, Alberto ? "

"No; feel them."

"Pain in your chest?"

"Nothing of the sort, only slight stitches in the sides, automatic stitches, as the doctor calls them. What are you thinking of? Don't you see that I am better? Yesterday, I coughed eighteen times; this morning, seventeen; I'm improving."

"Alberto *mio,* may health be yours!"

"Yes, yes, I shall get as strong as Andrea! I sent for him this morning, but he never came. He is out in all sorts of weather. Lucky dog!"

She stood listening, with hanging arms and downcast eyes.

"Go and dress, dear; go."

She moved away slowly, turning to look at him. In half an hour she returned, dressed in black, enveloped in a fur cloak, in which she hid her hands. She came and sat down by him, as if she were already tired.

"You are not fit to walk, Lucia; call a *fiacchere.*"

"I will . . . ." she said in a faint voice.

"What have you got under your cloak?"

"The prayer-book, a veil, a rosary."

"All the pious baggage of my little nun. Be a saint to thy heart's content, my beauty. Thanks to you, we shall all get into Paradise."

"Do not laugh at religion, Alberto."

"I never laugh at the objects of your faith. Time's up, my heart; go, and come back soon."

Lucia threw her arms round his neck, kissed his thin face, and whispered:

"Forgive . . . ."

"Am I to forgive you for taking the Sacrament? Hasn't your confessor told you that I . . . . absolve you?"

She bowed low. Then she drew herself up and looked round, wildly. She went away, bent and tottering, but returned almost immediately.

"I had forgotten to bid you good-bye, Alberto."

She squeezed his hand.

"Think of me in church, my saint."

"I will pray for you, Alberto."

And she went away—tall, black, and stately.

III.

Night was closing in; in the December twilight the air had grown more chill. Under the lighted lamp Caterina sat writing to her cousin Giuditta at school, to invite her to spend next Sunday with her. The clock struck six. "Andrea is late," thought Caterina; "I am glad I made him take his overcoat, the days are getting so cold." She finished her letter and laid her hand on the bell. Giulietta appeared.

"Have this letter posted, with a halfpenny stamp."

"Shall I order dinner to be served?"

"Yes; your master will be home in a few minutes."

But the master kept them waiting till half-past seven. Caterina waited patiently, yet she felt a certain inward spite towards the business that took up so much of Andrea's time. It struck her that the house in Via Constantinopoli was rather cold, and it needed fireplaces. How long would it take to put in a grate? It would please Andrea.

The bell rang. That must be Andrea . . . . but it was only Giulietta.

"A letter from Casa Sanna, and one by post."

"All right; you can go. See that dinner is kept hot."

Although she was disappointed by Andrea's non-arrival—it was nearly eight o'clock—Caterina eagerly opened the letter from Casa Sanna.

"Signora Caterina, for pity's sake, come to me.

"ALBERTO."

The handwriting was shaky and blurred, as if the pen

had trembled in the writer's hand. The address was in a different hand. Caterina was alarmed. What could have happened? Nothing to Alberto; no, for then Lucia would have written. Then something must surely be the matter with Lucia. What dreadful accident, what awful trouble, could it mean? She must go at once. She rang.

"The carriage, Giulietta."

The maid looked at her in astonishment and left the room. All at once Caterina, who was proceeding to put on her bonnet and wrap, stood still. Andrea! Had she forgotten Andrea? If Andrea did not find her at home when he returned he would be angry. What was to be done? She sat down a moment to collect her thoughts; she was not accustomed to rely on herself in any difficulty—she had no will of her own. She decided on writing a line to Andrea, apologising for going out for half an hour, and enclosing Alberto's note. She would return immediately; he was not to wait dinner for her. She placed the letter, with the letter-weight over it, in full view, on the writing-table. Then she saw the letter that had come by post. "From Giuditta," she thought.

She opened it, still preoccupied with the thought of what could have happened to Lucia, and read:

"Oh! Caterina, mercy, Caterina; have pity upon me; mercy, mercy, mercy! I am unfortunate. I am leaving with Andrea. I am a miserable creature; you will never see me again. I suffer. I am leaving. I am dying. Have pity!"

"Lucia."

She read it over again, re-read it, and read it for the fourth time. She sat down by the writing-table, with the letter in her hands. She was stupefied.

"The carriage is at the door," said Giulietta. Caterina's head moved as if in reply. Then she rose to her feet, but she felt the floor give way beneath them. "If I move I shall fall," she thought.

She stood still; her giddiness increased; the furniture turned round her; there was buzzing in her ears and a bright light in her eyes.

"Surely, I am dying," she thought. But the giddiness began to decrease, the whirl became wider and slower, and then stopped. Then she read the letter over again, replaced it in the envelope, put it in her pocket and kept her hand over it. She passed into her room, took her bonnet and wrap out of the darkness, but did not put them on. She crossed the anteroom with them in her hands.

"Shall you return early, Signora?" said Giulietta.

She looked at her, dazed.

". . . . Yes, I think so."

"What shall I say to the master?"

"There is . . . . yes, there is a note for him."

She descended the stairs and entered the carriage. The coachman must have had his orders from Giulietta, for without waiting for further instructions he drove off through Via Sebastiano. Caterina, sitting on the edge of the cushion, without leaning back, had placed her bonnet and shawl opposite to her, and still kept her hand on the letter in her pocket. She felt the discomfort of the chill air that came in through the open window. She could not resist the impulse that led her, by the fugitive light of the street-lamps, to read Lucia's letter over again for the sixth time. What with the movement of the carriage and the sudden shadows that succeeded the flashes of light, the written words jumped up and down; and Caterina felt them jumping in her brain, knocking against her brow and at the back of her head, beating in either temple. It was a tempest of little blows, a beating of the drum under her skull. Every now and then she bent her head, as if to escape it. She folded the paper; the sensation became less intense, died away, and stupefaction once more dulled her brain.

She mounted the stairs slowly, keeping a firm, mechanical hold on her shawl. She found the door wide open. In the

anteroom the maid was talking with animation to the man-
servant, emphasising her discourse by expressive gestures.
When they saw her enter noiselessly, in indoor attire, without
either bonnet or gloves, they became silent. Then she forgot
where she was, halting in indecision. She no longer knew
what she had come for, when the maid whispered to her
that:

"The Signore was awaiting her."

Of whom was she talking? Caterina looked fixedly at the
maid, without the quiver of an eyelash.

"The poor Signore had again spat blood at about three
o'clock. He noticed it this time. This evening, when he
received the Signora's letter, he turned red and screamed; he
got very excited and coughed—and again spat blood, saving
your presence."

"La Signora, blood! what were they talking of?"

"Now I will show you in, Signorina. But bear up, both of
you, it was inevitable."

At these words Caterina trembled all over; a change came
over her face. Glued to the spot, she gazed at the maid with
eyes full of sorrow.

"What is done, can't be undone, Signora *mia*! Let us go to
the poor Signore."

Preceded by the maid, she followed submissively. Lucia's
boudoir was in great disorder. The little armchairs were
turned upside down; the music on the piano was torn and
dispersed, the empty work-basket was topsy-turvy, the reels
rolling about the carpet, the wools entangled, and the coarse
canvas at which Lucia used to work was lying like a rag on
the ground; the writing-case was opened on the little writing-
table, the drawers were empty, the letters littered the ground:
a battlefield.

"The Signore made this havoc, he was like a madman,"
explained the maid.

Leaving the darkened drawing-room to the right, they
entered the bedroom. Within was sufficient light to make

darkness visible; a night-lamp under an opaque shade so placed that the bed lay in shadow. Profound silence: solitude. A pungent odour of drugs and the smell peculiar to sick-rooms filled the atmosphere. Instinctively, Caterina strained her eyes and advanced towards the bed. Alberto was lying there, supine, his head and shoulders resting upon a pile of graduated cushions. He was dressed, but his shirt was crushed and torn, and his legs were wrapped in a woman's shawl. On a night-table by his side stood bottles, phials, glasses, wafers, red pill-boxes and packets of powders. A white handkerchief peeped out from under the pillow. On the side where Lucia slept, between the bed and the wall, the *prie dieu* had been turned upside down. Caterina stooped over the bed. His eyes were closed and his lips half open, the breath that escaped them was short and faint, his chest scarcely heaved. He opened his eyes, and when he saw her they filled with tears. The tears coursed down his spare cheeks and fell on his neck; the maid took a handkerchief out of the pocket of her apron and wiped them away. He signed to her with his hand to thank and dismiss her.

" Will you have another bit of snow ? "

" Yes," in a faint whisper.

The maid took a little from a basin and put it in his mouth.

" The powder ; is it not time ? "

" No ; go away."

She took a turn round the room and went away as quietly as possible. Caterina, hugging her shawl, had remained standing. Now she realised all that she saw and heard; indeed, sensation had become so acute that the noise of the words hurt her, the light dazzled her, the sick man's hectic features became visible; she saw the knife-like profile, the thin protruding chin, the skeleton chest, the miserable legs. She saw, felt, and understood too much.

" Come nearer and be seated. I can neither turn nor raise my voice. It might bring on hæmorrhage again."

She took a chair and sat down, facing the bed, so that she

could see Alberto's face, crossed her hands on her lap, and waited. He made an effort to swallow the bit of snow, then with all the despair of which a hoarse, low voice is capable said to her:

" You've heard, eh ? "

Her eyelids quivered two or three times, but she found nothing to say to him.

Alberto, who was lying sunk in his pillows, with half-closed eyes and upturned chin, gazed vaguely at the white curtains instead of at her.

" I should never have suspected such treason. Would you have suspected it ? No ; of course not."

Her gesture signified, " No." Her inert will had no power over her nerves, so that she had absolutely no strength wherewith to articulate.

" Lucia appeared to be so fond of me. She was so good, she thought of nothing but me. You saw, you must have seen, how fond she was of me. How could she do this to me ? "

Husbanding his breath, he continued his complaint in an undertone, never turning to Caterina, but addressing his lamentations to the bed, the room, the curtains.

" Even this morning she kissed me three times. I ought to have known that she was going away. I ought not to have let her go out."

A short, harsh cough interrupted him.

" Give me . . . . give me a little snow."

She handed the saucer to him ; he put a little in his mouth and was silent until he recovered his breath.

" Has she written to you ? "

Caterina drew the letter from her pocket and handed it to him. Alberto raised it eagerly to the level of his eyes.

" Not a word as to where they are going, nor at what time they left. But I have found out the hour. They left at half-past two, by the Paris-Turin express. They posted the letters at the station. What has Andrea written to you ? What does he say ? Why has he done this to me ? What does he write ? "

"Nothing,' said Caterina, whose head had fallen on her bosom.

"Nothing! But what infamous creatures they both are! They are a couple of assassins. Listen, listen; I tell you, they will certainly be the death of me."

He had almost risen to a sitting posture, choked by impotent rage, clenching his diminutive fists, opening his mouth to breathe, to utter a cry. She gazed at him with wide-open eyes, struck once more with the stupor that from time to time paralysed her brain.

" Then you have not received anything but that letter; you know nothing of their doings? You know only that they have gone? That is why you are so cool! If you only knew . . . . only knew . . . . what infamy . . . . what infamy . . . .!"

She exerted her will and succeeded in raising her head, drew nearer to him, and questioned him with her eyes.

" I will whisper it to you. The doctor advises me not to waste my breath. When you see me getting excited, stop me. Horrible treason! It has gone on for some time, you know, since our stay at Centurano . . . ."

A wild look passed over the face of his listener, but he did not observe it.

" . . . . but in reality, those infamous assassins were betraying us. Centurano indeed! It began before my marriage. One day that they were alone, in your house, Andrea kissed Lucia, on the neck . . . ."

Caterina wrung the helpless hands that were lying in her lap.

" . . . . afterwards they made love to each other under our very eyes; writing, speaking to each other, making appointments with an impudence . . . . We never noticed anything. All through that accursed Exhibition! How could I tell that they would have served me like this? Do you know that they kissed . . . ."

He ground his teeth as he told these things, casting savage glances around him, revelling in the ecstasy, the intoxication of his rage when he recalled the voluptuous details of the love-story. On Caterina's face, which was turned towards him, there was still the same look of grieved surprise.

" . . . . they kissed again, the accursed assassins. He has tasted the ripe red lips of my Lucia, those lips that were mine, and mine only ; he took them from me, and scorched and faded them with coarse, brutal kisses. I wish that in those kisses thou hadst sucked arsenic and strychnine, and that their sweetness had poisoned thee, vile thief, deceitful villain ! Ah ! they were sweet, were they, the kisses of my Lucia ? Ah ! they pleased you, and so you've taken them for yourself and gone off with them, vile thievish clod—brigand ! "

A fit of coughing that lasted a long time choked him, his head rebounded on the pillow, and his chest heaved with a hoarse rasping sound. Trembling all over he grasped his handkerchief and expectorated, examining the handkerchief carefully with a hurried, frightened gesture.

" It is white," he said, with a voice as thin as a thread. He fell back, paler than ever from fright, in his pillows, his chest heaving painfully. After this vehement attack, he was obliged to rest a little. She waited, watching his every move-ment : when he expectorated, a sense of nausea caused her to turn her head aside.

"Give me the blue bottle, with the spoon by it. It's codeine."

Caterina's hand wandered over the table for some time before she could find what she looked for . . . . When she gave it him, he swallowed it, thanked her, and looked at her fixedly, perhaps because her trembling silence and her immo-bility began to strike him . . . .

" It must have made a great impression upon you," he muttered. " I was already upset, half dead, in fact, for I spat a little blood. I sent for the doctor and for Lucia, at the church of Santa Chiara, at once. The doctor came ; Lucia didn't come. They hadn't found her at Santa Chiara. I was getting desperate ; I went all over the house and turned it

upside down. When, lo, and behold, a letter, brought by hand.
I opened it, screamed, and fell down. I bit my hand and broke
a pane of glass. I knocked the furniture about, all that had
belonged to Lucia. If I could have got at her for a minute,
ill and weak as I am, I should have strangled her. Then a fit
of coughing came on, but I didn't expectorate. Then a little
scraping; it was red, red as flame. They have killed me,
they have killed me . . . ."

The fever of his complaint had left him in a stupor until the
arrival of Caterina, now it was passing into the acute stage, as
the temperature increased and the fever mounted from his
chest to his brain. His ideas were becoming incoherent.
"What happened afterwards, I don't know. I sent for you,
and the doctor came again. You see I threw the *prie-dieu*
down; I wanted to kick it to pieces, but I couldn't. She took
away the Byzantine Madonna. She was pious, she was
religious, she went to confession, she took the Sacrament;
how could I tell that with all that she would commit this
horrible crime! But . . . . you know . . . . they were a
couple of lovers awaiting their honeymoon, like bride and
bridegroom . . . . infamous wretches, assassins . . . . and
to-night, to-morrow; while I lie here, dying alone, like a
dog . . . ." She shuddered, in terror at sight of the little
mannikin wrapped up in a woman's shawl.

" . . . . I had always loved her," he said after a pause,
speaking in a lower tone. " I married her for love, because she
was good and beautiful and clever, and spoke poetically;
. . . . because she was unhappy in her father's house. I
didn't mind her marriage portion being small. Some of my
friends remarked at the time that women always marry from
interested motives. I didn't believe it. She wrote me such
beautiful letters! Oh! she was a famous hand at letter-
writing. She wrote to Galimberti, who went mad; to me, to
you; and she wrote some to Andrea. She gave them to him
in books, she put them under the clock, everywhere. I
ought to have known that she married me for money. Do

you know what she has taken with her besides the Madonna? Her diamonds, the diamonds that I gave her." And a sneer of irony distorted the invalid's lips.

"The diamonds, you know! My mother's . . . . who was an honest woman . . . . that I had given her. She will wear them in her ears for him, and he will kiss her throat; she will wear them in her hair, and he will kiss her hair; she will wear them on her bosom, and he will sleep on that bosom. O God! if you exist—cruel God, vile God!—make me die an hour before the time."

A gloomy silence reigned in the room after that imprecation. She shrank away with outstretched hands, in dread of the delirious sufferer in whose thoughts fever of blood and brain had wrought such terrible havoc, while it lent him a fictitious vigour equal to the strength of a person in rude health.

" . . . . Wherever they were, they betrayed us. At home, at the Exhibition, in the carriage—everywhere, everywhere they made fools of us. In the wood, in the English Garden they were together . . . . They snatched each other's hands on the stairs, on the landing; they kissed each other, while we went on before. On the terrace, in the corner, they kissed over again. It's a horrible, crying shame! I think the servants must have noticed it at Centurano. They must have laughed at us, that *canaille* must have laughed its fill behind our backs . . . ."

There were two bright red spots on his cheekbones, and he was gasping.

" . . . . And do you know why I call them assassins, why I say that they have killed me? And by God, I am right! The most odious, the most cruel part of it all is, that through their damned love affair I have caught this illness, that might have been spared me. On a chilly night, Lucia stood out on the balcony, the whole night through, and so did Andrea. I slept all night with the window open, with the cold air penetrating my lungs and inflaming them, making me cough for two months, making me so ill! They gazed at each

other, called to each other and blew kisses: I caught the
cough that has lasted two months, and made me spit this
blood to-day." He looked at her. In her horror, she hid her
face in her hands. "You wonder how I know all this? You
remember the novel that Lucia was writing? Another lie.
It wasn't a novel, it was a journal. Every day she wrote
down all that happened to her, all her thoughts and fancies.
The whole love affair is in it, from beginning to end—every
look, every kiss, every act. Oh! there are splendid bits of
description, beautiful things are narrated therein. It is
instructive and interesting reading. You can profit by it, if
you like. Read it, it will amuse you."

Then grinning, like a consumptive Mephistopheles, he drew
a bulky manuscript from under the pillow. He threw it into
Caterina's lap; she left it there, sooner than touch it, as if she
were afraid of its burning her fingers.

"Yes," he said, having reached the lowest depth of bitterness,
"Lucia wished me to know how it all happened. She took
the Madonna, she took the diamonds, but she has had the
goodness to forget the journal! Do read it! It is a charming
novel, a fine drama."

He was exhausted, with the fever came a return of the
stupor. His eyes were half closed, his feeble hands, with the
violet veins standing out in relief, were like yellow wax. In
the gloom, Caterina kept turning the pages of the journal, at
first without reading, then glancing at a page here and there,
grasping an idea, or discovering a fact amid the fantastic divagations in which its pages abounded. At certain parts she
shuddered and fell back in her chair. He coughed weakly in
his torpor, without unclosing his eyes. Suddenly a violent
attack tore his chest, the cough began low, grew louder, died
away, seemed to be over, and began again, cruelly, persistently.
In the short intervals he groaned feebly, clutching at his ribs,
as if he could bear it no louger. Then he expectorated
again, and once more made that hurried gesture of examination. He fell back with a faint cry. He had spat blood.

She had watched this scene; when she saw the blood, she shuddered and closed her eyes, as if she were about to faint.

"So these medicines are no good to me? The doctor is telling me a parcel of old woman's tales. Why doesn't he stop the hæmorrhage? I have swallowed such a lot of snow, I have taken such a lot of syrup of codeine and gallic acid, to stop the blood! Am I to spit all my blood away? Why haven't they given me something stronger to-night, instead of to-morrow, if it is to do me any good?"

His lamentations, persistent, hoarse, torturing to his listener, filled the room. His voice had the aggrieved intonation that is peculiar to invalids who feel the injustice of not being cured. He continued to grumble at the doctor, the medicines, the syrup that failed to relieve his cough; the snow was useless, for it did not stop the hæmorrhage. Still complaining, he turned to Caterina:

"I beg your pardon; do you mind giving me that little paper of gallic acid, and a wafer?"

With the patience of one to whom these things are habitual, he made a pill and swallowed it, with an air of resignation. She had closed the journal.

"Had enough of it, eh? I have read every word of it, and shall read it again, to learn how these frightful crimes are committed. Well, I couldn't have done such a thing to Lucia. To me she was the dearest and most beautiful of women. I was in love with her; *via*, to tell the truth, I was idiotically in love with her. She ought not to have behaved as she has done to me; she knew how ill I am, she might have spared me. She knew that I was alone, how could she abandon me . . . . !"

He considered the deserted room, the *prie-dieu* lying upside down, the empty space where the Madonna had been, the open drawers, and fresh tears coursed down his cheeks. They were scant tears, that reddened the tight-drawn skin as they fell.

"What do you intend to do, Signora Caterina?"

She started and looked at him, questioningly, surprised.

" I asked you what you were going to do ? "

" Nothing," she said, gravely.

The despairing word rang through the room, accentuating its void.

"Nothing; true. What is there to be done? Those two love each other, have gone off together . . . . and good-night to them who remain behind. Follow them ? It would be useless; useless to catch them. Besides, who is to go ? They have killed me. Well, I am so weak, so mean, so vilely ridiculous, that, despite *all*, I feel that I still care for Lucia . . . . I care for her still—it's no use denying it, for all her wickedness, her betrayal, and her perpetual deceit—I care for her, because I love her, *ecco !* I am so tied to her, so bound up in her, that the loss of her will kill me, if this hæmorrhage doesn't. Oh ! what a woman, what a woman it is ! How she takes possession of you, and carries you away, and never loosens her hold on you . . . . ! "

His eyelids were wide open, as if he beheld the seductive vision of her ; he held up his lips, and stretched out his arms to her, calling on her, in a transport of love, that was part of his delirium.

" Oh ! if she could but return, for a moment ! If she could but return, even if she went away again ! Oh ! return, that I might forgive her . . . . return, return, to see me die ! Not to let me die alone, in this icy bed, that my fever does not warm ; in this great room, where I am afraid to be alone ! "

He was wandering. Presently he felt under the pillow, and drew out a letter and a small packet.

" . . . . listen, she sent me this, with the letter. They are the wedding rings. Here is the one I gave her, here is the one you gave Andrea. Do you think she will ever return ? "

" No," said Caterina, rising to her feet, "they will never return." She took her own ring and went away, leaving Alberto still wandering.

" If she had but lied a little longer ; she might have waited

R

for my death! She would not have had long to wait, miserable . . . ."

IV.

In the night, in her dark room, seated beside her bed, Caterina pondered. She had returned home without speaking to any one; no one had said anything to her, for they all knew what had happened. The house was in order, composed, cold, and silent; on the table was the note she had written to her husband, to apologise for having gone out alone. She tore it up, and threw the pieces into the waste-paper basket. Giulietta, who had crept in after her, to try and proffer a word of consolation, was dismissed as usual with a gentle good-night. The maid told the coachman that the Signora had not shed a tear, but that the expression of her face was "dreadful." They all pitied her, but they had long foreseen what would happen; they knew of it at Centurano: you'd have to be blind not to have seen it.

Then the conventicle dispersed, and the house was wrapped in profound silence. Caterina had extinguished the light in her own room, but had not undressed. Instinctively she craved for darkness, wherein to hang her head and think. She could distinguish the whiteness of the bed in the gloom, and it frightened her. She sat with one hand over the other, pressing the point of her nails against the third finger of the hand that bore the two marriage rings. Now and again, when she became aware of the contact of that second ring, she started and moaned. Her life, quiet and uniform as it had been, came before her with such distinctness of detail that it seemed as if she lived it over again. She had had a mother until she was seven; a father, until she was nine; and lived with her aunt until she was eleven. A peaceful childhood, except for the formless, shadowy sorrow of those two deaths, a sorrow bereft of cries or tears. She had always been ashamed to cry in the presence of other people; she had wept for her dead at night, in her little bed, with the sheet drawn

over her face. Later, at her aunt's, she had been seriously ill,
a very dangerous illness—a combination of every disease that
is incidental to childhood. She remembered that the Sacrament had been administered to her in great haste, in the
fear that she would die. She had not understood its meaning,
and had not been very strongly impressed ; since then she had
retained a calm religious piety, devoid of mystic enthusiasm,
but characterised by the rigorous strictness of observance with
which she fulfilled all her duties.

When she recovered, her aunt had put her to school, the
best school in Naples, and had undertaken the management of
her fortune. She was a cold, trustworthy, childless aunt, who
did not incline to demonstrations of affection, but who visited
her punctually on Thursdays in the parlour, and drove her
out on Sundays, and took her to the theatre. Caterina
recalled the first year at school, where she had been happier
than at home, where she had given herself to the simple
pleasure of being with other children ; not playing, but watching
them play; not speaking, but hearing them speak. Study she
found rather hard ; she had been obliged to apply herself to
succeed in learning anything ; the teachers had always given
her the maximum marks for good conduct, but not so many
for study. She had never been punished nor reproached that
first year, and at the final examination she came out fifteen,
among twenty-eight : she had gained a silver medal for good
conduct.

The duality of her school-life began with the appearance of
Lucia, whom she had met with in the second class. A wonderful pupil, who surpassed all her fellows ; a slight, thin girl,
whose long black plaits hung down her back, who spent three
days in school and three in the infirmary, who was an object
of charity to the teachers, the assistants, and her companions.
She was a sickly, pensive child, whose great eyes swallowed
up her whole face, and who could master anything without
opening a book. Many girls desired her friendship, but one
day she said to Caterina, in her weak voice :

"They tell me that you have neither mother nor father; my mother is dead too, and that is why I wear a black band round my arm, for mourning. Will you be my friend?" All at once, Caterina remembered that she had begun to love the lithe, melancholy creature with her whole heart, the girl who was as slender as a reed, who never played, and who talked like a maiden of fifteen when she was but a child of eleven. She remembered how this childish love was strengthened by their living together under one roof. In the hours of recreation they had walked up and down the corridors like the others, they had held each other by the hand, but without speaking. During school-hours they sat on the same bench, lending each other a pen, a scrap of paper, or a pencil: at table they sat opposite, looking at each other, and Caterina passed her share of pudding to Lucia, who could eat nothing else. In chapel they prayed together, and in the dormitory they were not far apart. In talent, in beauty, and in stature Lucia had always surpassed Caterina, a fact that Caterina had tacitly acknowledged, and the whole College recognised. In the College the two friends were always designated as, "the one who loved, and the one who submitted to be loved." The one who permitted ✓ herself to be loved was the beauty, the *bellezza ;* the one who loved was the *capezza,* the ass's bridle, a patient, humble, devoted, servile thing. The *bellezza* was entitled to everything, the *capezza* had no rights, but all the duties. She was permitted to love, that was all. In the Altimare and Spaccapietra bond, Lucia was the *bellezza,* and Caterina the *capezza.*

She could remember having been punished several times in her stead, for having been bewitched into following her in an escapade, for having taken her part against the *maestra,* for having done the sums that were too dry for Lucia's poetic mind. Lucia wept, was in despair, fainted, when Caterina was punished for a fault of hers; and Caterina ended by consoling her, telling her that it was nothing, praying her to stop crying, because she rather liked punishment. Lucia was a profoundly affectionate creature, expansive to enthusiasm, ever ready to sacrifice herself for the sake of friendship; Caterina, who could never find words to express herself, whose affection was calm and silent, who could never behave enthusiastically, and who had never fainted, was sometimes ashamed of loving so little. In everything Lucia surpassed her. So they passed from class to class. Caterina was always a mediocre scholar, obtaining a bronze medal or honourable mention at the examinations, on which occasions she never came to the fore—an insipid pupil, who was neither appreciated nor bullied by the professors. There was nothing interesting in her character—like, for instance, Artemisia Minichini, who was insolent and sceptical; or Giovanna Casacalenda, who was provoking and coquettish. The Directress did not give herself the trouble of watching her. Her greatest charm, her only distinguishing quality, was her friendship for Lucia—"Where is Altimare?" "Spaccapietra, tell us where Altimare is." "How is Altimare?" "Spaccapietra, surely thou knowest how Altimare is to-day!"

Lucia, on the contrary, passed a brilliant yearly examination, took the gold medal for composition, and wrote congratulatory addresses on the Directress's birthday. Her compositions were notable productions: one of them had been read in the presence of three assembled classes. But more remarkable than anything else was the strange disposition which aroused the curiosity of the entire College. Her fits of mysticism, her fits of deep despondency, the tears she shed in shady nooks, about the College; her passion for flowers, her nausea in the refectory, her convulsive nervous attacks, claimed universal attention. When she passed, tall, lithe, with dreamy, pensive eyes, the other scholars turned and pointed her out to each other, and whispered about her.

The Directress watched her. Cherubina Friscia had special instructions with regard to Lucia Altimare; the professors kept their eye on her. In the parlour, the little girls described her to their mothers in undertones as, "Un tipo strano," an extraordinary type. She knew it, and cast languid glances round her, and indulged in pretty, pathetic movements of the head. She was the incarnate expression of suffering—

slow, continual, persistent suffering, that weighed her down
for weeks together, and ended in a heartbreaking crisis.
Oh! Caterina had always felt a profound compassion for her,
which she had never been able to express, but was none the
less as intense as it was sincere. The last year at school had
been a tumultuous one, it was a wonder that Caterina had
maintained her placid serenity in the midst of all those girls,
who were yearning for freedom, panting for life; who already
boasted adorers, affianced husbands and lovers; who hated the
College, and treated the *maestre* with impertinence. Her aunt
had informed her that Andrea Licti was to be her husband; she
had no anxiety for her own future. But she was very anxious
about Lucia, who during this last year had been unusually
delicate, who had turned Galimberti's head, who had made up
her mind to be a nun, and attempted to commit suicide.
Caterina had saved her life. And last, like a dream, the last
night at school, when they had entered the chapel, had knelt
down and sworn, before the Madonna, to love each other for
ever, reproduced itself in her memory . . . .

Lucia vanished, Andrea entered upon the scene. Andrea
had been kind and amiable to Caterina during their courtship.
At first, it had been a marriage of convenience; the young man
wanted a wife, her fortune suited him, and the orphan girl
had to be married. Andrea was a very good match for
her; the engaged pair got on capitally together. Andrea's
vigorous, often violent temperament, was well balanced by
Caterina's calm and gentle nature. He neither wrote letters
nor offered flowers, nor paid more than two or three visits
during the week, while they were engaged, but Caterina had
not missed these demonstrations of love. Love she read in
Andrea's honest, merry eyes, when they met hers. She had
admired him from the first, for the herculean comeliness
of his fine physique, and the grace of a gentlemanlike athlete,
with which he wore either morning or evening attire. And
immediately she had begun to love him, because she had

found him good and honest and just. The strong man, who could be a very child, in whom she divined a feminine delicacy, won her heart. As usual, from timidity and the habit of reserve, her emotion was self-contained. Later on, in her married life, she had always been shy and retiring with her husband, neither expressing her love for him by well-turned phrases or poetic imagery. But perhaps he knew it, for from morning till night she busied herself in the house, and with the food, forestalling his wishes, preparing a cool sitting-room for him in the summer, and a warm bedroom in winter. The viands he preferred his wife carefully dressed, ever placid and smiling. No, she had never found words to tell him the happiness that flooded her heart when he raised her in his strong arms, kissed her throat, and called her "Nini"; but every day her gratitude proved it to him, and her constant thought and care for him. She did not tell him that when he went shooting and left her alone for days, she wearied after him, and longed for his return . . . . On his return, he was so happy and so pleasantly tired, that she had never spoken of those solitary hours to him. If they separated for eight or ten days, she wrote to him every day, just a line about household matters, or the people who had called . . . . There was no flourish about her letters; they began with *Caro Andrea*, and ended with *la tua affetzionatissima moglie, Caterina.* She murmured inwardly against her own timidity, and often felt that she was very stupid. That poor Galimberti had once said to her: "Spaccapietra, you are entirely wanting in imagination." Then she had taken heart when it occurred to her that Andrea must know how well she loved him; if she said nothing, her every act spoke for her. Luckily Andrea was of a frank, open disposition; he did not like affected grimaces, he did not make melting speeches; his was a well-conditioned love that could exist without his perpetually asking her during the honeymoon, "Do you love me?" Besides, she knew of no other answer than "Yes." Again Lucia appeared on the scene; Lucia, more beautiful than herself,

nervous, suffering, fantastic. Lucia and Andrea stood together
in the foreground of her life. Oh! how she could recall her
trouble, through their disputes and their reciprocal dislike.
Her heart had been torn between love for Andrea, to whom
Lucia was odious, and love for Lucia, who held Andrea in
contempt. She could neither venture to coerce them, nor
could she divide herself in two. She loved them both, each
in a different fashion. When they had begun to know each
other, and their antipathy had turned to a more cordial
sentiment, then there had been thanksgiving in her heart, that
the miracle she prayed for with all her might had come to
pass. She had not told either of them how much her love
for them had grown since they had deigned to be friends;
but during the whole year she had tried to prove her gratitude
to them. She passed her life between them, for them, ever
devising a way to make their life pleasant; tending and caring
for them, body and soul, thinking of naught but the two
persons in whom her life was centred. Thus had Caterina
Licti lived and had her being, thus it was that her whole
existence appeared to her like a series of events, of which she
was a spectator on that winter night. Her memory was as
clear and definite as the facts it recalled. With calm patience,
staring into the darkness the better to discern them, she
searched for other memories; if perchance she had overlooked
any incident of a different nature, anything singular, exceptional, like all that she had already recalled. Was there
nothing, really nothing? Twice she repeated this question to
herself, but she found nothing. Her conscience had been
calm, equal, unvaried; it had known two constant and active
loves—Andrea, Lucia.

Well, now all was clear to her. The science of life had
come to her in a flash, sweeping faith and innocence from
her heart. Her intellect opened wide to the cruel lesson,
applied as by a blow from a hammer. She felt like another
woman, one suddenly aged and become more capable, a woman

of cool, clear judgment, searching eye, and an implacable conscience. She no longer discovered in herself either indulgence, pity, kindness, nor illusions; in their stead she found the inflexible justice that could weigh men and things.

Now she understood it all. Lucia's personality encroached on the life around her; Lucia the Protagonist, Lucia the Sovereign. The personality rose, clearly defined against her horizon, as if in harsh relief, without any softening or veiling of the contours, without any optical illusion, cruel in its truth. In vain Caterina closed her dazzled eyes not to see this truth, it filtered through her lids, like the sun. The gigantic figure attracted all the others, fascinated them, bewitched them, seized them, absorbed them, and down below there only remained certain pitiful, shrunken shades, that vaguely struggled and despaired within a grey mist. Lucia reigned, beautiful and cruel, not bending her eyes on those who wrung their hands, nor hearing their groans, her eyes half closed so that she might not see, her ears unheeding; contemplating herself, adoring herself, making an idol of herself.

Surely this was a monstrous creature, a spirit ruined in infancy, an ever-swelling egoism that assumed the fair cruel features of fantasy. At bottom, the heart was cold, arid, and incapable of enthusiasm; its surface was coated with a prodigious imagination that magnified at will every sensation and impression. Within, a total absence of sentiment; without, every form of sentimentalism. Within, indifference to every human being; without, the delirium of noble Utopian theories, fluctuating aspirations round a vague ideal. Within, a harsh spongy pumice-stone, that nothing can soften, that is never moved; without, the sweetness of a voice and the tenderness of words. And artifice, so deeply rooted in the soul as to mock nature, artifice so complete, so perfect that by night, alone with herself, she could persuade herself that she was really unhappy and really in love; artifice that had become one with disposition, temperament, blood and nerves, until she had acquired the profound conviction of her own goodness, her own virtue, and her own excellence.

The vision became more and more distinct, cynically revealing the falseness of its character, and the lie that was incrusted in its every line. To have the fantasy of error, the fantasy of sentiment, the fantasy of love, the fantasy of friendship, the fantasy of sorrow ; never anything but blinding, corroding fantasy, put forward in the guise of all that is sweet and wholesome. To weave fancies on God, the Madonna, the affections, on everything ; to barter the realities of life for the unreality of a dream ; to be master of the fantasy that endows the eye with seductive charm, the voice with voluptuous melody, the smile with fascination that makes the kiss irresistible ; to feed one's nerves on the torments of others, bringing about the enacting of the drama that is artificial for oneself, and terribly earnest for everybody else. That was Lucia.

That smiling and weeping monster, with the moving tears, the enchanting voice, the bewitching flexibility and poetry of diction, that profound and feminine egoism, had absorbed all that surrounded her . . . . Caterina had pitied and loved her, Galimberti had loved and pitied her, Alberto had loved her, Andrea had loved her. She had stood in their midst and had drawn all the love out of them. At the languor of her countenance, all had languished ; in her mystic prostration, all had suffered ; her mock passion had burned deep into their flesh. Her egoism had battened on sacrifice and abnegation : yet they who loved her, loved her more and more. Whoever had approached her had been taken. Those whom she took never regained their freedom. Their souls blended with her soul, they thought her thoughts, dreamed her dreams, shuddered with her thrills ; their bodies clung to her irrevocably, without hope of deliverance, receiving from her their health and their disease. And for the aggrandisement of this potent egoism, its glory and its triumph, Caterina beheld the misery of those who had surrounded Lucia : the fate of Galimberti, who was dying in a madhouse ; the misery of his starving, despairing mother and sister ; the lugubrious and dishonoured agony of

Alberto, the husband she had abandoned; the dishonour of her father and her name; the ruin of Andrea, who left home, wife, and country to live a life of despair with Lucia; and the last most innocent victim, Caterina herself, bereft by Lucia of her all.

All these wrongs were irreparable. Horrible was the agony of the dying, who cried for Lucia and loved her; horrible the life of the survivors, who hated, cursed, and loved her. Irreparable the past, irreparable the present. Lucia towered above the ruins, enthroned, audacious, triumphant, formidable, casting on the earth the shadow of her inhuman egoism, obscuring the sky with it.

The dawn rose livid and frozen. Caterina was still there, stiffened in her chair, pressing the wedding ring that had been returned to her between her icy fingers. She uttered a cry of terror when, in the grey morning light, she saw the white bed, so smooth and cold; a cry so terrible that it did not sound human. She opened her arms and threw herself down on the spot where Andrea had slept—and wept upon that tomb.

V.

"You had better go to bed, Signora," said Giulietta, pityingly; "you haven't even undressed."

"I was not sleepy," replied Caterina, simply.

"Will you breakfast?"

"No."

"At least, I may bring you your coffee?"

"Bring me the coffee."

The tears had ceased to flow, but her eyes burned painfully. She passed into her dressing-room and began to bathe them with cold water. She dipped her whole head into the basin, and felt refreshed. When Giulietta entered with the coffee she found her still bathing her head.

"The maid has come from Casa Sana. The poor gentleman wandered all night; this morning, saving your presence, he spat blood again. The maid says it is a heartrending sight. Madonna *mia,* how did this dreadful thing happen ? "

Caterina raised her cold, severe eyes, and looked at her. Giulietta, who was intimidated, held her peace.

In the kitchen, she announced to the man-servant, the coachman, and the cook that " the Signora was a woman in a thousand. You will see with what courage she will bear her misfortune."

" What can she do ? " quoth the man-servant. " If Signor Sana were well, she could have gone to stay with him . . . ."

" Sst ! " the cook silenced him. " The Signora is not a woman of that kind. I know her well, for I have seen a great deal of her. She wouldn't do it."

" I say there is no chance of the master's returning," added the cook later. " My ! that Donna Lucia is a clever woman."

Caterina busied herself in her room, putting away the few things that were lying about, such as her bonnet and shawl; opening and shutting the wardrobes, reviewing the linen shelves, counting their contents, as if she thought of cataloguing them. She stopped to think every now and then, as if she were verifying the numbers. This long and minute examination took some time. All her husband's things were there, and in one corner stood his gun and cartridge-box. The room was in order. She passed into the morning-room, where on the previous evening she had read that letter. The drawers of her husband's bureau were open, and the key was in one of them; she inspected them, paper on paper, letter on letter. They were business papers, contracts, donations, leases, bills, letters from friends, letters that she, Caterina, had written to him during his absence: all the Exhibition documents were there, reports and communications. She patiently turned all these pages, and read them all, holding the drawer on her knee, leaning her elbow against the bureau, with her forehead resting on her hand. She was conscious of feeling stunned, of a void in her head and a buzzing in her ears. But that passed, and she soon recovered the lucidity of her mind. When she had finished reading, she tied up all the letters with string, made separate packets of the business papers, and wrote the date and name on each in her round, legible hand. It did not tremble while she wrote, and when she had finished her arduous task she wiped the pen on the pen-wiper and shut down the cover of the inkstand. At the bottom of the big drawer she found another bundle, containing ten pages of stamped paper, forming her marriage contract. She read them all, but replaced them without writing on them. She closed the drawers, and added the key to the bunch that she kept in her pocket.

"It is midday," said Giulietta. "Will you breakfast, or will you wear yourself to rags?"

She ventured on the brusque, affectionate familiarity that is peculiar to Neapolitan servants when there is trouble in a house.

"Bring me another cup of coffee."

"At least dip a rusk in it; you mustn't starve."

Caterina seated herself in the armchair, waiting for Giulietta to bring her the cup of coffee. She sat without thinking, counting the roses on the carpet, and observing that one turned to the left and the other to the right. She drank her coffee and then went over to her little writing-table, where she kept her own letters. They were already classified, with the order which was characteristic of her. There were letters from her aunt, from Giuditta, from her teachers, and from Andrea. The bulkiest packet was the one labelled "Lucia." This packed smelled of musk; she untied and with calm attentiveness read those transparent, crossed, and closely written pages, one by one. They took her so long to read that her face began to show signs of fatigue. She locked the writing-table and added the key to the others in her pocket. Lucia's letters had remained in her lap; she lifted up her dress like an apron, knelt down before the fireplace, and there burned the letters, page by page. The thin paper made a quick, short-lived flame, that left behind it a white evanescent ash, and a

more pungent odour of musk, blended with that of burnt
sealing-wax. She watched the pyre, still kneeling. When it
was consumed, she rose to her feet, mechanically flicking the
dust off her dress at the knees. The iron safe stood next to the
mantelpiece. Andrea had left it and his bureau unlocked, with
the keys in them. She opened it and inspected its contents.
Andrea had taken with him a hundred thousand francs in
coupons payable to bearer, and in shares of the National Bank.
He had left the settlements of his inheritance, Caterina's
marriage contract, and a bundle of other bonds. In one
corner were the cases containing Caterina's jewels. She
counted the money, classified the gems, and wrote a list of
both on a scrap of paper, which she left in the bureau, took
some small change and a ten-franc-note, and locked the safe.
A new impulse caused her to spring to her feet again. She
passed into an adjoining room, and from thence into the drawing-room, whose windows she threw wide open. The splendid
December day broke in with its deep blue sky, its glare of
light and its soft air. Caterina had nothing to do in the drawing-room, but in passing she stopped near a window to grace-
fully arrange the folds of a curtain, moved the Murano glasses
from one table to another, and went a few steps away from
them to judge of the effect. When she had inspected everything, in the bright light that lit up pearl-grey brocaded hangings into which were woven coral-coloured flowers, the crystals,
the statues, the bric-à-brac, she closed the windows, fastened
the shutters, and left the drawing-room and the yellow room
behind her in darkness.

When she reached the dining-room, Giulietta hastened to
meet her, thinking that her mistress would eat something. But
Caterina was only looking at the high sideboards, making
mental calculations.

"How many glasses are missing from the *Baccarat* service,
Giulietta?"

"One large tumbler and a wineglass."

"That's right; and this set of Bohemian glass?"

" Only one; Monzu knocked it down with his elbow."

" I see. I think there is a fork with a crooked prong."

" Yes, Signorina."

" Well, you can go; I know you have some ironing to do to-day."

Giulietta went away quite comforted. If the Signora had time and inclination to take such minute interest in the house, it was a sign that she had made up her mind to bear her trouble. And if men were such wretches, what was the good of taking it to heart? The master used to be good, but he had quite changed of late. Giulietta, standing before a table heaped up with rough-dried linen, sprinkled it with the water she took up out of a basin in the hollow of her hand. Caterina passing slowly by her, stopped for a moment.

" Be careful of the shirts, Giulietta; last week there were two scorched."

" That was because I overheated the irons; I will be careful to-day."

Caterina entered the kitchen. Monzu, who was carrying on an animated conversation with the man-servant, became suddenly silent. She cast a cool glance of inspection round her, the look of the mistress, severe and just.

" Monzu, tell your kitchen-boy to scour the corners well. It is no good cleaning just in the middle of the floor."

" I have told that boy about it so often, but Signora *mia*, he's good for nothing. I'll give him a scolding when he comes to-day."

" Are your accounts made up, Monzu?"

" We were to settle on Monday, the day after to-morrow."

" Let us settle to-day instead."

He drew out the large account-book in its red leather binding, and placed it on the corner of the table, where his mistress added it up. He had sufficient money in hand for another week.

" Am I to provide for the Signora only?"

" Do not provide for me; I shall not be dining at home. Think of the servants."

The cook cast a triumphant glance after her, as turning quickly she went away; he knew that the Signora was a woman of spirit, and was not going to give way . . . .

Caterina went back to her room and looked at her watch. It was about three, she had barely time to dress. She chose her black cashmere gown and her fur. Slowly, bestowing on her toilet the utmost care, she changed from head to foot. She had already wound her hair in a great knot, and fastened it with a light tortoiseshell comb. She looked at herself in the glass: she was rather pale, with two red lines under her eyes; but for that she looked much as usual. She put her handkerchief and purse in her pocket, and while she was drawing on her black gloves she called Giulietta.

" Order the carriage," she said.

She waited in her room for the carriage to be announced. Had she forgotten anything? No, nothing. The house was in order from top to bottom; there was nothing lying about, nothing out of place; everything was locked up and the keys were on the ring. She had not overlooked anything. She felt in her pocket for an object that she needed, and found it there; nothing had been omitted. She waited without impatience; she had plenty of time, having, as usual, dressed early. When Giulietta returned, she rose and let her put her wraps on her. Passing before her she said:

" Giulietta, I am going to Centurano on business."

" But there is no one at Centurano, except Matteo!"

" He will do. You can keep house here."

" May I not come?"

" I shall only stay one night at Centurano."

" Then you will return to-morrow?"

" Of course. *A rivederci*, Giulietta."

" The Madonna be with you, Signorina; never fear, all will be right here."

She accompanied her as far as the stairs. Caterina went away without looking back, with rhythmic step, and veil drawn down over her eyes.

" The Madonna be with you, and give you a good journey and a speedy return."

" Good-bye, Giulietta."

The latter went, however, to look after her mistress from the window of the anteroom that overlooked the courtyard. Caterina entered her carriage without turning to look behind her, and said to the coachman :

" To the station."

In the Via di Foria she met Giovanna Casacalenda, in a *daumont*, with her husband. Giovanna sat, upright and beautiful, with the black brim of her Rubens hat shading her proud, voluptuous eyes : the Commendatore Gabrielli wore the look of composure that became his age, his beard correctly trimmed to a fringe, his oblique glance from behind the gold-rimmed spectacles, and the twitch of the lips that denoted a tendency to apoplexy. Husband and wife neither spoke to nor looked at each other. Behind them followed a smart, high equipage, with spider-like wheels, driven by Roberto Gentile, in his showy, cavalry uniform. He drove close to the *daumont*, while Giovanna assumed unconsciousness, and her husband maintained his grave, assured demeanour. Giovanna smiled and waved her hand to Caterina, the husband raised his hat. It was evident that her friends had not yet heard anything.

There was only a pair of German fellow-travellers in the first-class carriage, occupied by the solitary little lady who was so neatly gloved and wrapped in furs. Whether they were husband and wife, brother and sister, uncle and niece, or father and daughter, it was impossible to decide, so red were they of face, light of hair, indefinite as to age, and alike in all respects. They were laden with shawls, rugs, bags, and Baedekers ; they gabbled continually, glancing furtively betimes at the little lady, who, seated in a corner, gazed at the Neapolitan twilight landscape. When they arrived at Caserta, the youthful lady crossed the carriage, and bending

S

in salutation, descended: the two travellers uttered a sigh of relief.

"Raise the hood, and drive to Centurano," she said to the driver of a fly. Only once, in passing the Palazzo Reale, solemn, silent, and closed, pale with the solitude that had once more fallen upon it, she leant forward to contemplate it, a stretch of park, and far, far away a white line that was the waterfall, through the arch of the great gate. But she drew herself back immediately, and did not look out again through the rest of the drive. The short winter twilight deepened; a fresh breeze blew over the ploughed fields and the bare trees.

The villas of Centurano were nearly all closed, except two or three that were inhabited by their owners all the year round. Little lights shone in the dwellings of the tenantry. Matteo, who was leaning against the portico quietly smoking his pipe, did not at first recognise his mistress until she had paid the driver. After the latter had wished her "una santa notte" (a holy good-night), he turned and drove away.

"O Signorina . . . . O Signorina . . . ." stammered Matteo, in confusion, hiding his pipe behind his back.

"Good evening, Matteo; is it open up there?"

"I have the key here, Signora."

"Can one pass a night here?"

"Certainly, Signora; it is always ready—beds made, floors swept."

Taking an oil-lamp from his room on the ground-floor, he led the way upstairs, jingling his keys as he went.

"And the Signore, will he be here soon?"

"No, the Signore is not coming. I can manage without him."

"I wanted to show him how fit Fox and Diana are. They are getting so fat, from having nothing to do."

"I will tell him to-morrow."

"Shall you stay here to-night, Signorina?"

"Just for one night. I must find some important documents, and I had no one I could send."

"But about dinner, Signorina? If you don't mind it, Carmela can toss you up an omelette and a handful of vermicelli with tomato sauce. Of course, it's no food for you, but for once . . . ."

"I have dined at Naples; I don't want anything."

Despite Matteo's care, the upstairs department looked cold, dreary, and unhabited. She shivered when she entered the drawing-room, where she had passed so much of her country life.

"No; we'll soon have a fire burning in the grate."

While he knelt down and blew the lighted wood she drew off her gloves, stretched them, and placed them on the table.

"Beg pardon, Signorina, but how is the Signora Donna Lucia?"

"She's well."

"All the better, poor young thing; she was always so sickly. And that husband of hers, who hadn't a ha'porth of health, the Signor Don Alberto, how is he?"

"He's ill."

"The severe weather, eh? But when the Lord calls we must obey."

"True, Matteo; so the house is in order."

"From top to bottom, Signorina *mia*. What you have told me to do, that I have done. The Signora Donna Lucia's room is just as she left it. Would you like to see it?"

"Let's see it."

She followed Matteo, who carried a light, into the room. On the threshold she was arrested by the same shivering sensation.

"Every morning I air the room and let in the sun. Carmela sweeps, I dust. Look, look, Signorina, there is no dust. Tell the Signore . . . ."

"Yes, I will tell him. Shut the door, Matteo; we will go to mine."

They went there. When they got inside her teeth began to chatter.

"Shall I light the fire in here, too, Signorina?"

"Yes, light it, and bring me another lamp."

She took off her furs and threw them on the bed. The room was full of shadows, which the faint light of the wick of the lamp he held, of the kind in use among the peasantry, did not dispel. Matteo returned with a larger lamp. She took her place on the sofa. Matteo remained standing before her, as if he were ready to make his report.

"Well, what news?" inquired Caterina, seeing that Matteo wished to be questioned.

"It happened a week ago that the wind was very high, and through the forgetfulness of Carmela, who had left the windows open, four panes were broken in the dining-room."

"Have you had them replaced?"

"Certainly."

"You will put them on the bill?"

"Don Claudio, the parish priest, called. They want a new roof to the church, and count on the charity of the faithful. He says that he hopes that the Signorina, who gives so much away in alms, won't forget the church."

"What did you say?"

"That he must write to you at Naples."

"That was right. And what else?"

"And then the Mariagrazia's boy died."

"That fine child?"

"*Gnorsi:* Mariagrazia has been at death's door herself, saving your presence."

"You will tell Mariagrazia how sorry I am for her. What is she going to do?"

"She is going to service in Naples, poor woman. Did Pepe Guardino go to Naples?"

"Yes, he came."

"Then he must have given you the message about the millstone that split. Have I told you all? Yes, it seems to me that I have. No; I was forgetting the best. One day that

* *Gnorsi*, corruption of *Signora si.*

she was dusting, Carmela found a paper, with writing, under the
clock. She always meant to put it in an envelope and send it
you, Signorina. Then, as I had to go to Naples, I said, ' I
will take it to the Signora myself.' Shall I go and fetch it?"

"Go," she said.

A slight expression of fatigue came over her face, the heavy
lids dropped for want of rest. The warmth from the grate
had overcome the sensation of cold. She tried to shake off
the torpor. Matteo returned, carrying a sheet of foreign letter-
paper, folded into microscopic compass.

"As neither Carmela nor I can read, your fate might have
been written here, and we should have been none the wiser."

She opened the sheet and read it. Its perusal made no
visible impression on her. She put it in her pocket.

"It is a list of certain things that I had forgotten. You can
go to bed, Matteo."

"There is nothing I can do for you?"

"Nothing else."

"Don't be afraid of anything, Signorina. I shall be here below.
The bell rings in my room ; if you want anything, ring."

"I will, if I want anything. But I shall not want anything."

"What time will you have your coffee in the morning?
Carmela knows how to make coffee."

"At nine. I shall leave by the twelve o'clock train."

"The gig at the door at eleven, then?"

"Yes."

"Do you want anything else, Signorina?"

"No."

"Do you want to write?"

"I have nothing to write to any one."

"I am going to supper; a leaf or two of salad and a scrap
of cheese, and then to bed; but always ready for your Excellency's service. Perhaps you'd like your bed warmed?"

"No."

"It would be no trouble to light a bit of fire in the kitchen.

"No."

"Good-night, Signorina; sleep well."

"Good-night, Matteo."

He went away with his lamp, closing the door behind him. She heard the steps dying away in the distance, and the last door close. At that moment the clock struck half-past eight. She fell back on the sofa, as pale as though she had fainted.

She waited for two hours without rising from the sofa, in a species of stupor that made her limbs ache. She heard the quarters ring while she counted them. The fire in the grate had gradually turned to ashes, leaving a tepid warmth in the room. She turned her back on the moon. When the clock struck twelve she rose to her feet. The two hours' rest had restored her strength. She went to the window, but could not distinguish anything. Then, without moving the light, she entered the drawing-room, one window of which overlooked the courtyard. There was no light in Matteo's room; he must have been asleep, for two hours profound silence reigned in the house.

Then she thought the hour had come. She returned to her room, and with infinite precaution passed out of it again through the drawing-room, the billiard-room, the dining-room, and the ante-chamber. She shaded the light with her hand, and as she passed through the room her little black shadow grew, as it was projected on the wall, to giant stature. She passed a landing, descended two steps, and entered the kitchen. She rested the light on a marble table, crossed the kitchen on tiptoe, placed a chair against the panelling, and unhooked from the wall, where it hung amid shining saucepans and moulds, a copper brazier, with brass feet fashioned like cat's claws. It was heavy, and the weight of it nearly threw her down. She placed it on the ground near the hearth; then, stooping over the arched angle where coals were kept, she noiselessly took up some pieces of coke with the tongs and filled the brazier with them one by one. She blew the coal off her fingers, but when she came to raise the brazier she found that it needed the support of her two hands, and that it was not possible to carry the light at the same time. She put it down, and carried the light back to her room. Then, in the dark, she crept back to the kitchen and took the brazier, setting it down before every door, which she closed behind her. She crossed the entire length of the house, carrying the burden that bore her down. She had seen an old newspaper lying in the drawing-room, picked it up, entered her room, and locked the door. When she saw her hands in the lamplight she perceived that the coke had soiled them, and proceeded to wash and dry them carefully. She crossed to the window with the intention of closing the shutters; the stars shone high and bright in the night, and the fountain in the street sang its fresh, eternal melody. She preferred to leave the shutters open, returned to the fireplace, and burned the letter in which Lucia had craved her pity— and the love-letter to Andrea that Matteo had found. She mixed the ashes, as she had done at Naples, so that no trace was left of anything. She took the fur wrap off the bed and laid it on the sofa. Was there anything else to be done? Yes; the keys. She took them out of her pocket and laid them on the mantelshelf, well in sight. That was all she had to do.

Then she placed a chair under the image of the Madonna by the bedside, and, kneeling on the carpet, prayed as she used to pray in her school-days. Her face was buried in her hands; she prayed without looking at the Madonna. She neither wept nor sobbed, nor even sighed. It did not transpire whether she repeated her usual prayers or only told the Virgin her thoughts. It was a long, calm, mute prayer, unbroken by thrill, start, or shiver. Twice she made the sign of the cross, glanced for an instant at the Madonna, and rose. Then she put the chair back in its place. She tore a strip off the news-paper, and folded it in four. This she placed under the door, thereby effectually shutting out the draught. With a small roll of paper she closed the keyhole, from which she had pre-viously withdrawn the key. She tore another strip and placed it under the window. She stopped up a tiny hole that let in the rain-water. She placed her head against the window fastening to feel if there were any draught : no, the two sides closed so accurately that there was none. She looked round, wondering if the air could get in anywhere. No. She drew the brazier into the middle of the room, and, with a strip of paper lighted at the lamp, set fire to two small pieces of coal. She blew the fire to spread it. Then she carried the light to the bedside and unlooped the white curtains, standing a moment absorbed in thought. She turned to look at the brazier ; one coal caught fire from another, and the whole mass was gradually becoming incandescent. She felt an increasing weight in her head. Without hesitation she blew out the light, and, drawing the curtains, lay down on the bed, on the place where she had been accustomed to sleep.

The bright winter sun shed its light on a room flooded with a light haze. Behind the white curtains lay a little dead woman. She was dressed in black, her feet outstretched and close together, her head resting on the pillows. She looked like a child, smaller than in life. Her face was of leaden hue. The hair was unruffled, the mouth open as if in the effort to breathe, the lips violet, the chest slightly elevated, and the rest of the body sunken in the bed. The glazed eyes of the little dead woman were wide open, as if in stupefaction at an incredible spectacle ; and round the violet fingers of the leaden-hued hands there was twisted part of a broken rosary of lapis-lazuli. .

PRINTED BY BALLANTYNE, HANSON AND CO.
LONDON AND EDINBURGH

EDITOR'S NOTE.

—•••—

THERE is nothing in which the Anglo-Saxon world differs more from the world of the Continent of Europe than in its fiction. English readers are accustomed to satisfy their curiosity with English novels, and it is rarely indeed that we turn aside to learn something of the interior life of those other countries the exterior scenery of which is often so familiar to us. We climb the Alps, but are content to know nothing of the pastoral romances of Switzerland. We steam in and out of the picturesque fjords of Norway, but never guess what deep speculation into life and morals is made by the novelists of that sparsely peopled but richly endowed nation. We stroll across the courts of the Alhambra, we are listlessly rowed upon Venetian canals and Lombard lakes, we hasten by night through the roaring factories of Belgium; but we never pause to inquire whether there is now flourishing a Spanish,

T

an Italian, a Flemish school of fiction. Of Russian novels we have látely been taught to become partly aware, but we do not ask ourselves whèther Poland may not possess a Dostoieffsky and Portugal a Tolstoï.

Yet, as a matter of fact, there is no European country that has not, within the last half-century, felt the dew of revival on the threshing-floor of its worn-out schools of romance. Everywhere there has been shown by young men, endowed with a talent for narrative, a vigorous determination to devote themselves to a vivid and sympathetic interpretation of nature and of man. In almost every language, too, this movement has tended to display itself more and more in the direction of what is reported and less of what is created. Fancy has seemed to these young novelists a poorer thing than observation; the world of dreams fainter than the world of men. They have not been occupied mainly with what might be or what should be, but with what is, and, in spite of all their shortcomings, they have combined to produce a series of pictures of existing society in each of their several countries such as cannot fail to form an archive of documents invaluable to futurity.

But to us they should be still more valuable. To travel in a foreign country is but to touch its surface. Under the guidance of a novelist of genius we penetrate to the secrets of a nation, and talk the very language of its citizens. We may go to Normandy summer after summer and know less of the manner of life that proceeds under those gnarled orchards of apple-blossom than we learn from one tale of Guy de Maupassant's. The present series is intended to be a guide to the inner geography of Europe. It offers to our readers a series of spiritual Baedekers and Murrays. It will endeavour to keep pace with every truly characteristic and vigorous expression of the novelist's art in each of the principal European countries, presenting what is quite new if it is also good, side by side with what is old, if it has not hitherto been presented to our public. That will be selected which gives with most freshness and variety the different aspects of continental feeling, the only limits of selection being that a book shall be, on the one hand, amusing, and, on the other, wholesome.

One difficulty which must be frankly faced is that of subject. Life is now treated in fiction by every race but our own with singular candour. The novelists of the Lutheran North are not more fully emancipated from prejudice in this respect than the novelists of the Catholic South. Everywhere in Europe a novel is looked upon now as an impersonal work, from which the writer, as a mere observer, stands aloof, neither blaming nor applauding. Continental fiction has learned to exclude, in the main, from among the subjects of its attention, all but those facts which are of common experience, and thus the novelists have determined to disdain nothing and to repudiate nothing which is common to humanity; much is freely discussed, even in the novels of Holland and of Denmark, which our race is apt to treat with a much more gingerly discretion. It is not difficult, however, we believe—it is certainly not impossible—to discard all which may justly give offence, and yet to offer to an English public as many of the masterpieces of European fiction as we can ever hope to see included in this library. It will be the endeavour of the editor to search on all hands and in all languages for such books as combine the greatest literary value with the most curious and amusing qualities of manner and matter.

EDMUND GOSSE.

HEINEMANN'S
Scientific Handbooks.

A KNOWLEDGE of the practical Sciences has now
become a necessity to every educated man. The de-
mands of life are so manifold, however, that of many
things one can acquire but a general and superficial
knowledge. Ahn and Ollendorff have been an easy
road to languages for many a struggling student;
Hume and Green have taught us history; but little
has been done, thus far, to explain to the uninitiated
the most important discoveries and practical inventions
of the present day. Is it not important that we
should know how the precious metals can be tested as
to their value; how the burning powers of fuel can be
ascertained; what wonderful physical properties the
various gases possess; and to what curious and powerful purposes heat can be adapted? Ought we not to
know more of the practical application and the working of that almost unfathomable mystery—electricity?
Should we not know how the relations of the Poles to
the magnet-needle are tested; how we can ascertain
by special analysis what produce will grow in particular
soils, and what will not, and what artificial means can
be used to improve the produce?

In this Series of "Scientific Handbooks" these and kindred subjects will be dealt with, and so dealt with as to be intelligible to all who seek knowledge—to all who take an interest in the scientific problems and discoveries of the day, and are desirous of following their course. It is intended to give in a compact form, and in an attractive style, the progress made in the various departments of Science, to explain novel processes and methods, and to show how so many wonderful results have been obtained. The treatment of each subject by thoroughly competent writers will ensure perfect scientific accuracy; at the same time, it is not intended for technical students *alone*. Being written in a popular style, it is hoped that the volumes will also appeal to that large class of readers who, not being professional men, are yet in sympathy with the progress of science generally, and take an interest in it.

The Series will therefore aim to be of general interest, thoroughly accurate, and quite abreast of current scientific literature, and, wherever necessary, well illustrated. Anyone who masters the details of each subject treated will possess no mean knowledge of that subject; and the student who has gone through one of these volumes will be able to pursue his studies with greater facility and clearer comprehension in larger manuals and special treatises.

The first volume will be a Manual on the Art of Assaying Precious Metals, and will be found valuable not only to the amateur, but to the assayer, metallurgist, chemist, and miner. The work will be a desirable addition to the libraries of Mining Companies, engineers, bankers, and bullion brokers, as well as to experts in the Art of Assaying.

The second volume of the Series is written by Professor Kimball, and deals with the physical properties of Gases. He has taken into account all the most recent works on "the third state of matter," including Crooke's recent researches on "radiant matter." There is a chapter also on Avogadro's law and the Kinetic theory, which chemical as well as physical students will read with interest.

In the third volume Dr. Thurston treats, in a popular way, on "Heat as a Form of Energy"; and his book will be found a capital introduction to the more exhaustive works of Maxwell, Carnot, Tyndall, and others.

On account of the requirements of the subject, a large number of wood-cuts have been made for the first volume, and the following volumes will also be fully illustrated wherever the subject is susceptible of it.

The first three volumes are now ready. Others will follow, written, like these, by thoroughly competent writers in their own departments; and each volume will be complete in itself.

Heinemann's Scientific Handbooks.

I.

MANUAL of ASSAYING GOLD, SILVER,

COPPER, AND LEAD ORES. By WALTER LEE
BROWN, B.Sc. Revised, corrected, and considerably enlarged, with a chapter on THE ASSAYING OF FUEL,
&c., by A. B. GRIFFITHS, Ph.D., F.R.S. (Edin.), F.C.S.
In One Volume, small crown 8vo. Illustrated, 7s. 6d.

Colliery Guardian.—"A delightful and fascinating book."

Financial World.—"The most complete and practical manual on everything which concerns assaying of all which have come before us."

North British Economist.—"With this book the amateur may become
an expert. Bankers and Bullion Brokers are equally likely to find it useful."

II.

THE PHYSICAL PROPERTIES OF

GASES. By ARTHUR L. KIMBALL, of the Johns
Hopkins University. In One Volume, small crown 8vo.
Illustrated, 5s.

CONTENTS.

Introduction.	Thermodynamics of Gases.
Pressure and Buoyancy.	Avogadro's Law and the Kinetic
Elasticity and Expansion with heat.	Theory.
Gases an l Vapours.	Geissler Tubes and Radiant Matter.
Air-Pumps and High Vacua.	Conclusion.
Diffusion and Occlusion.	

Chemical News.—"The man of culture who wishes for a general and
accurate acquaintance with the physical properties of gases, will find in
Mr. Kimball's work just what he requires."

Iron.—"We can highly recommend this little book."

Manchester Guardian.—"Mr. Kimball has the too rare merit of describing first the facts, and then the hypotheses invented to limn them
together."

III.

HEAT AS A FORM OF ENERGY. By

Professor R. H. THURSTON, of Cornell University. In
One Volume, small crown 8vo. Illustrated, 5s.

CONTENTS.

The Philosophers' Ideas of Heat.	Air and Gas Engines, thei Work and
The Science of Thermodynamics.	their Promise.
Heat Transfer and the World's	The Development of the St am
Industries.	Engine.
	Summary and Conclusion.

OTHER VOLUMES IN PREPARATION.

LONDON: WM. HEINEMANN, 21, BEDFORD STREET, W.C.

TELEGRAPHIC ADDRESS—
SUNLOCKS, LONDON.

DECEMBER 1890.

MR. WILLIAM HEINEMANN'S

ANNOUNCEMENTS

AND

NEW PUBLICATIONS.

THREE NEW PLAYS.

Now ready.

In One Volume, Small 4to,

HEDDA GABLER:

A DRAMA IN FOUR ACTS.

By HENRIK IBSEN.

Translated by EDMUND GOSSE.

In One Volume, Small 4to,

THE

FRUITS OF ENLIGHTENMENT:

A COMEDY IN FOUR ACTS.

By Count LYOF TOLSTOI.

Translated by E. J. DILLON.

In Preparation.

In One Volume, Small 4to,

MAHOMET:

A DRAMA.

By HALL CAINE.

In the Press.

In 8vo,

THE SALON OF
MARIE BASHKIRTSEFF.

LETTERS AND JOURNALS.

With Drawings and Studies by the youthful Artist.

---

21 BEDFORD STREET, LONDON, W.C.   3

In the Press.

In Two Volumes, Demy 8vo,

DE QUINCEY MEMORIALS.

*IN LETTERS AND OTHER RECORDS HERE FIRST PUBLISHED,
WITH COMMUNICATIONS FROM COLERIDGE, THE WORDS-
WORTHS, MRS. HANNAH MORE, PROFESSOR WILSON, AND
OTHERS OF NOTE.*

Edited, with Introduction, Notes, and Narrative,

By ALEXANDER H. JAPP, LL.D., F.R.S.E.

THESE volumes include letters to De Quincey from his mother whilst he was still at school, from his sisters Jane and Mary, his brothers Henry and Richard, and his guardian, the Rev. Samuel Hall. Letters also from the Marquis of Sligo, Professor Wilson, Sir W. Hamilton, "Cyril Thornton," Hannah More, the Brontës, Coleridge, Professor T. P. Nichol, the Wordsworths, and many others, add to the value of the book, and with De Quincey's own letters, throw new light on many points in his career, and present confirmation by documentary evidence of the truth of some of his statements regarding the most extraordinary incidents in his early career, some of which have been doubted at various times.

The work will be handsomely printed, in two volumes, and will be illustrated by various portraits of De Quincey and members of the De Quincey family.

Early in 1891.

In Volumes, Crown 8vo,

THE

POSTHUMOUS WORKS OF
THOMAS DE QUINCEY.

VOLUME I.

ADDITIONAL SUSPIRIA DE PROFUNDIS.

WITH ESSAYS,
CRITICAL, HISTORICAL, BIOGRAPHICAL, PHILOSOPHICAL,
IMAGINATIVE, AND HUMOROUS.

VOLUME II.

CONVERSATION AND COLERIDGE.

WITH OTHER ESSAYS.

Recovered from the Author's Original MSS., and Edited by

ALEXANDER H. JAPP, LL.D., F.R.S.E., &c.

In announcing a collection of unpublished writings of De Quincey, the publisher believes he is presenting to the public an essential addition to every library, as without these volumes the editions of De Quincey's works now before the public will be incomplete. The additional *Suspiria* alone would justify this claim for it, some of them being absolutely necessary to complete the significance of the *Suspiria* already published. In addition to this there are other essays, on history, speculation, criticism, and theology, which will attract and appeal to a varied class of readers. A collection of notes under the heading *Brevia* are added, which will give the reader closer access to De Quincey in his private life and thoughts than anything that has hitherto been published. By means of these notes the reader is, as it were, introduced to the opium-eater when he was communing with himself by means of his pen.

In the Press.

THE

COMPLETE WORKS OF
HEINRICH HEINE.

I.

PICTURES OF TRAVEL.

TRANSLATED BY

CHARLES GODFREY LELAND, M.A., F.R.L.S.,

President of the Gypsy Lore Society, &c. &c.

A WANT has long been felt and often expressed by different writers for a complete English edition of Heine's works. That this has never been done is the more remarkable, because HEINE is, next to GOETHE, the most universally popular author in Germany, and one who, although he termed himself an unlicked Teutonic savage, wrote in a style and manner which have made him a leading favourite in all countries.

The first volume will be the REISEBILDER, or PICTURES OF TRAVEL, probably the most brilliant and entertaining, while at the same time the most instructive or thought-inspiring work of its kind ever written; to be followed by II., FLORENTINE NIGHTS, SCHNABELEWOPSKI, and THE RABBI OF BACHARACH; and III., THE BOOK OF SONGS. Other volumes will be announced later.

‐ Dr. Garnett is preparing a "Life of Heine," which will be uniform with this edition of Heine's works.

** *A Large Paper Edition will be printed, limited to one hundred and fifty copies, numbered, and signed by the translator.*

MR. WILLIAM HEINEMANN'S LIST.

Now Ready.

In Two Volumes 8vo, £3, 1:8. 6d.

THE

GENESIS OF THE UNITED STATES.

A NARRATIVE OF THE MOVEMENT IN ENGLAND, 1605–1616, WHICH
RESULTED IN THE PLANTATION OF NORTH AMERICA BY ENGLISH-
MEN, DISCLOSING THE CONTEST BETWEEN ENGLAND AND SPAIN
FOR THE POSSESSION OF THE SOIL NOW OCCUPIED BY THE UNITED
STATES OF AMERICA; SET FORTH THROUGH A SERIES OF HIS-
TORICAL MANUSCRIPTS NOW FIRST PRINTED, TOGETHER WITH A
RE-ISSUE OF RARE CONTEMPORANEOUS TRACTS, ACCOMPANIED
BY BIBLIOGRAPHICAL MEMORANDA, NOTES, AND BRIEF BIO-
GRAPHIES.

COLLECTED, ARRANGED, AND EDITED

By ALEXANDER BROWN,

Member of the Virginia Historical Society and of the American Historical Association, Fellow of the Royal Historical Society.

With 100 Portraits, Maps, and Plans.

THE crucial period of English occupancy of North America was
that included between the return of Weymouth to England in July
1605, and closing with the return of Dale to England in July 1616.
This period has hitherto been most imperfectly understood, partly
because of the misrepresentations made by early authorities who have
been followed too implicitly, but chiefly because of the ignorance by
later historians, and even by early writers, of the part played by
Spain in attempting to thwart the movements of England.

No historical work for many years has attracted such attention as
is sure to be given to this. Its peculiar significance consists in the
fact that it contains so much important matter never before printed
in any language. Mr. Brown's researches, pursued through many
years and at large expense, were rewarded by the discovery, in the
secret archives of Spain, of numerous documents throwing light on
the contest in Europe for the possession of the American Continent.
These documents, with rare tracts of that period (in all 365 papers,
of which 294 are now for the first time made public), accompanied by
Bibliographical Memoranda, Notes, Maps and Plans, Portraits and
Autographs, and a Comprehensive Biographical Index, lend special
value and importance to this work.

A prospectus, with specimen pages and full description, will be sent
on application. Orders may be sent to Booksellers, or direct to the
Publisher.

HEINEMANN'S SCIENTIFIC HANDBOOKS.

Now Ready.

In One Volume, Crown 8vo, Illustrated, 7s. 6d.

MANUAL OF ASSAYING GOLD, SILVER, COPPER, AND LEAD ORES.

By WALTER LEE BROWN, B.Sc.

REVISED, CORRECTED, AND CONSIDERABLY ENLARGED,

WITH A CHAPTER ON THE ASSAYING OF FUEL, ETC.

By A. B. GRIFFITHS, Ph.D., F.R.S. (Edin.), F.C.S.,

This work gives full details of the assaying and valuation of ores containing gold, silver, copper, and lead. The assaying of gold and silver bullion, fuels, &c., and full descriptions are given of the necessary apparatus, appliances, and re-agents, the whole being fully illustrated by eighty-seven figures in the text.

In One Volume, Crown 8vo, Illustrated, 5s.

THE PHYSICAL PROPERTIES OF GASES.

By ARTHUR L. KIMBALL,

OF THE JOHNS HOPKINS UNIVERSITY.

CONTENTS.

Introduction.	Diffusion and Occlusion.
Pressure and Buoyancy.	Thermodynamics of Gases.
Elasticity and Expansion with heat.	Avogadro's Land and the Kinetic Theory.
Gases and Vapours.	Geissler Tubes and Radiant Matter.
Air-Pumps and High Vacua.	Conclusion.

In One Volume, Crown 8vo, Illustrated, 5s.

HEAT AS A FORM OF ENERGY.

By PROFESSOR R. H. THURSTON,

OF CORNELL UNIVERSITY.

CONTENTS.

The Philosophers' Ideas of Heat.	Air and Gas Engines, their Work and their Promise.
The Science of Thermodynamics.	The Development of the Steam Engine.
Heat Transfer and the World's Industries.	Summary and Conclusion.

In preparation.

In One Volume, Demy 8vo,

DENMARK:

ITS HISTORY, TOPOGRAPHY, LANGUAGE, LITERATURE, FINE ARTS, SOCIAL LIFE, AND FINANCE.

Edited by H. WEITEMEYER.

With a Coloured Map.

*** *Dedicated, by Permission, to H.R.H. The Princess of Wales.*

In One Volume, 8vo.

THE COMING TERROR.

ESSAYS.

By ROBERT BUCHANAN.

In One Volume, Crown 8vo.

GIRLS AND WOMEN.

By E. CHESTER.

A NEW NOVEL

By OUIDA.

A NEW NOVEL

By FLORENCE WARDEN.

A NEW NOVEL

By HANNAH LYNCH.

HEINEMANN'S INTERNATIONAL LIBRARY.

THE CHIEF JUSTICE. By KARL EMIL FRANZOS.
Author of "For the Right," &c. Translated from the German by MILES CORBET.

Manchester Guardian.—"Simple, forcible, and intensely tragic. It is a very powerful study, singularly grand in its simplicity."

Sunday Times.—"A series of dramatic scenes welded together with a never-failing interest and skill."

IN GOD'S WAY. By BJÖRNSTJERNE BJÖRNSON.
Translated from the Norwegian by ELIZABETH CAR-MICHAEL. With Introduction by EDMUND GOSSE. In One Volume, crown 8vo, 3s. 6d. ; or Paper Covers, 2s. 6d.

Athenæum.—"Without doubt the most important, and the most interesting work published during the twelve months. . . . There are descriptions which certainly belong to the best and cleverest things our literature has ever produced. Amongst the many characters, the doctor's wife is unquestionably the first. It would be difficult to find anything more tender, soft, and refined than this charming personage."

Saturday Review.—"The English reader could desire no better introduction to contemporary foreign fiction than· this notable novel."

Speaker.—"'In God's Way' is really a notable book, showing the author's deep insight into character, giving evidence that his hand has lost none of its cunning in the delineation of Scandinavian character, and proving, too, how the widespread spirit of criticism is affecting Northern Europe as elsewhere.

PIERRE AND JEAN. By GUY DE MAUPASSANT.
Translated from the French by CLARA BELL. With Introduction by EDMUND GOSSE. In One Volume, crown 8vo, 3s. 6d. ; or Paper Covers, 2s. 6d.

Pall Mall Gazette.—"So fine and faultless, so perfectly balanced, so steadily progressive, so clear and simple and satisfying. It is admirable from beginning to end."

Athenæum.—"Ranks amongst the best gems of modern French fiction."

₊ *The Books of which the titles follow*
this have been published during
the present year.

THE GENTLE ART OF MAKING ENEMIES

As pleasingly exemplified in many instances, wherein
the serious ones of this earth, carefully exasperated, have
been prettily spurred on to indiscretions and unseemli-
ness, while overcome by an undue sense of right. By J.
M'NEIL WHISTLER. In One Volume, pott 4to, 10s. 6d.

Punch, *June* 21.—"The book in itself, in its binding, print, and
arrangement, is a work of art."

Punch, *June* 28.—"A work of rare humour, a thing of beauty and
a joy for now and ever."

THE PASSION PLAY AT OBERAMMERGAU,

1890. By F. W. FARRAR, D.D., F.R.S., Archdeacon and
Canon of Westminster, &c. &c. In One Volume, small
4to, 2s. 6d.

Spectator.—"Among the many accounts that have been written
this year of 'The Passion Play,' one of the most picturesque, the most
interesting, and the most reasonable, is this sketch of Archdeacon
Farrar's. . . . This little book will be read with delight by those who
have, and by those who have not, visited Oberammergau."

THE GARDEN'S STORY; or, Pleasures and

Trials of an Amateur Gardener. By G. H. ELL-
WANGER. With an Introduction by the Rev. C. WOLLEY
DOD. In One Volume, 12mo, with Illustrations, 5s.

Scotsman.—"Deserves every recommendation that a pleasant-
looking page can give it; for it deals with a charming subject in a
charming manner. Mr. Ellwanger talks delightfully, with instruction but without pedantry, of the flowers, the insects, and the birds.
. . . It will give pleasure to every reader who takes the smallest
interest in flowers, and ought to find many readers."

New Works of Fiction.

THE BONDMAN. A New Saga. By Hall
Caine. Fourth Edition (Twelfth Thousand). In One Volume. Crown 8vo, 3s. 6d.

Mr. Gladstone.—"The 'Bondman' is a work of which I recognise the freshness, vigour, and sustained interest no less than its integrity of aim."

Count Tolstoi.—"A book I have read with deep interest."

Standard.—"Its argument is grand, and it is sustained with a power that is almost marvellous."

IN THE VALLEY. A Novel. By Harold
Frederic, Author of "The Lawton Girl," "Seth's Brother's Wife," &c. &c. In Three Volumes. Crown 8vo, with Illustrations.

Athenæum.—"A romantic story book, graphic and exciting, not merely in the central picture itself, but also in its weird surroundings. This is a novel deserving to be read."

Manchester Examiner.—"Certain to win the reader's admiration. 'In the Valley' is a novel that deserves to live."

Scotsman.—"A work of real ability; it stands apart from the common crowd of three-volume novels."

A MARKED MAN: Some Episodes in his
Life. By Ada Cambridge, Author of "Two Years' Time," "A Mere Chance," &c. &c. In Three Volumes, crown 8vo.

Morning Post.—"A depth of feeling, a knowledge of the human heart, and an amount of tact that one rarely finds. Should take a prominent place among the novels of the season."

Illustrated London News.—"The moral tone of this story, rightly considered, is pure and noble, though it deals with the problem of an unhappy marriage."

Pall Mall Gazette.—"Contains one of the best written stories of a *mésalliance* that is to be found in modern fiction."

New Works of Fiction.

THE MOMENT AFTER: A Tale of the Unseen.
By ROBERT BUCHANAN. In One Volume, crown 8vo, 10s. 6d.

Athenæum.—" Should be read—in daylight."
Observer.—" A clever *tour de force.*"
Guardian.—" Particularly impressive, graphic, and powerful."
Bristol Mercury.—" Written with the same poetic feeling and power which have given a rare charm to Mr. Buchanan's previous prose writings."

COME FORTH!
By ELIZABETH STUART PHELPS and HERBERT D. WARD. In One Volume, imperial 16mo, 7s. 6d.

Scotsman.—"'Come Forth!' is the story of the raising of Lazarus, amplified into a dramatic love-story. . . . It has a simple, forthright dramatic interest such as is seldom attained except in purely imaginative fiction."

THE MASTER OF THE MAGICIANS.
By ELIZABETH STUART PHELPS and HERBERT D. WARD. In One Volume, imperial 16mo, 7s. 6d.

The Athenæum.—"A success in Biblical fiction."

THE DOMINANT SEVENTH: A Musical Story.
By KATE ELIZABETH CLARK. In One Volume, crown 8vo, 5s.

Speaker.—" A very romantic story."

A VERY STRANGE FAMILY: A Novel.
By F. W. ROBINSON, Author of "Grandmother's Money," "Lazarus in London," &c. &c. In One Volume, crown 8vo, 3s. 6d.

Glasgow Herald.—"An ingeniously-devised plot, of which the interest is kept up to the very last page. A judicious blending of humour and pathos further helps to make the book delightful reading from start to finish."

𝔑ew 𝔚orks of 𝔣iction.

HAUNTINGS : Fantastic Stories. By VERNON
LEE, Author of "Baldwin," "Miss Brown," &c. &c. In
One Volume, crown 8vo, 6s.

Pall Mall Gazette.—"Well imagined, cleverly constructed, powerfully executed. 'Dionea' is a fine and impressive idea, and 'Oke of
Okehurst' a masterly story."

PASSION THE PLAYTHING. A Novel. By
R. MURRAY GILCHRIST. In One Volume, crown 8vo, 6s.

Athenæum.—"This well-written story must be read to be appreciated."

Yorkshire Post.—"A book to lay hold of the reader."

THE LABOUR MOVEMENT IN AMERICA.
By RICHARD T. ELY, Ph.D., Associate in Political
Economy, Johns Hopkins University. In One Volume,
crown 8vo, 5s.

Weekly Despatch.—"There is much to interest and instruct."

Saturday Review.—"Both interesting and valuable."

England.—"Full of information and thought."

National Reformer.—"Chapter iii. deals with the growth and
present condition of labour organisations in America . . . this forms
a most valuable page of history."

ARABIC AUTHORS: A Manual of Arabian
History and Literature. By F. F. ARBUTHNOT, M.R.A.S.,
Author of "Early Ideas," "Persian Portraits," &c. In
One Volume 8vo, 10s.

Manchester Examiner.—"The whole work has been carefully
indexed, and will prove a handbook of the highest value to the
student who wishes to gain a better acquaintance with Arabian
letters."

IDLE MUSINGS: Essays in Social Mosaic.

By E. CONDER GRAY, Author of "Wise Words and Loving Deeds," &c. &c. In One Volume, crown 8vo, 6s.

Saturday Review.—"Light, brief, and bright are the 'essays in social mosaic.' Mr. Gray ranges like a butterfly from high themes to trivial with a good deal of dexterity and a profusion of illustrations."

Graphic.—"Pleasantly written, will serve admirably to wile away an idle half-hour or two."

IVY AND PASSION FLOWER: Poems. By

GERARD BENDALL, Author of "Estelle," &c. &c. 12mo, 3s. 6d.

Scotsman.—"Will be read with pleasure."

Woman.—"There is a delicacy of touch and simplicity about the poems which is very attractive."

Musical World.—"The poems are delicate specimens of art, graceful and polished."

VERSES. By GERTRUDE HALL. 12mo, 3s. 6d.

Musical World.—"Interesting volume of verse."

Woman.—"Very sweet and musical."

Manchester Guardian.—"Will be welcome to every lover of poetry who takes it up."

21 BEDFORD STREET, LONDON, W.C.

1500/26/12/90.